When Love Walks In

"Well, you cook about the best meal I've ever had."

She smiled. "Why do I have the feeling you could eat a rubber tire and think it was good?"

She heard his soft chuckle near her ear. "I'm an easy keeper, Jolie," he said in his velvety baritone voice. "I want you to know that."

A tiny panicky joy burst through her. She turned to look at him, saw his green eyes even more intense than usual and before she knew it was coming, his head lowered and his mouth brushed hers. When she didn't flinch or pull away, his mouth brushed again, then squarely covered hers. His lips were warm and soft, unthreatening. The room seemed to be spinning around them and as much as her head believed this could be a bad idea, she had no intention of stopping him or herself. She kissed him back.

He broke the kiss and his hand tenderly cupped her jaw. When an unfamiliar heat began to course through her and her insides began to shake, she pulled back, looking wide-eyed into his face. "Jake, I—"

"Jolie," he murmured, stroking a tendril of her hair back from her face. "Pretty, gentle Jolie."

"I've never . . ." She stopped. "I'm not an experienced woman," she blurted.

"I know that."

"How—how do you know?"

"Darlin', I've spent a good part of twenty years knowing more about people than they know about themselves."

Also by Sadie Callahan

Lone Star Woman

Man of the West

SADIE CALLAHAN

A SIGNET ECLIPSE BOOK

SIGNET ECLIPSE
Published by New American Library, a division of
Penguin Group (USA) Inc., 375 Hudson Street,
New York, New York 10014, USA
Penguin Group (Canada), 90 Eglinton Avenue East, Suite 700, Toronto,
Ontario M4P 2Y3, Canada (a division of Pearson Penguin Canada Inc.)
Penguin Books Ltd., 80 Strand, London WC2R 0RL, England
Penguin Ireland, 25 St. Stephen's Green, Dublin 2,
Ireland (a division of Penguin Books Ltd.)
Penguin Group (Australia), 250 Camberwell Road, Camberwell, Victoria 3124,
Australia (a division of Pearson Australia Group Pty. Ltd.)
Penguin Books India Pvt. Ltd., 11 Community Centre, Panchsheel Park,
New Delhi - 110 017, India
Penguin Group (NZ), 67 Apollo Drive, Rosedale, North Shore 0632,
New Zealand (a division of Pearson New Zealand Ltd.)
Penguin Books (South Africa) (Pty.) Ltd., 24 Sturdee Avenue,
Rosebank, Johannesburg 2196, South Africa

Penguin Books Ltd., Registered Offices:
80 Strand, London WC2R 0RL, England

978-1-61664-117-7

Copyright © Jeffery McClanahan, 2010
Excerpt from *Lone Star Woman* copyright © Jeffery McClanahan, 2009
All rights reserved

SIGNET ECLIPSE and logo are trademarks of Penguin Group (USA) Inc.

Printed in the United States of America

PUBLISHER'S NOTE
This is a work of fiction. Names, characters, places, and incidents either are the product
of the author's imagination or are used fictitiously, and any resemblance to actual per-
sons, living or dead, business establishments, events, or locales is entirely coincidental.

The publisher does not have any control over and does not assume any responsibility for author or third-party Web sites or their content.

For my husband, George, and my daughter, Adrienne,
still my biggest fans and relentless supporters.

1

Working in the dim glow from a handheld flashlight, Jolie Jensen shoved the last of her ten-year-old daughter Danni's clothing into a black plastic bag. She had packed most of her things earlier and loaded them into the car. Tension squeezed her chest as tightly as a steel band. Her body was on alert, every nerve taut and close to the surface. She threw a glance at the plastic clock on top of a narrow bookcase. Two a.m.

Outside, a torrential rain pounded the thin walls and roof of the single-wide mobile home where she lived. Like the flash of a giant camera, lightning brightened the room for an instant.

Ka-boom!

The earth-shaking thunderclap startled Jolie so, a shot of adrenaline burst through her and she almost dropped her armful of clothing. A wind gust slammed the walls of the trailer, rocking and rattling the whole flimsy structure. "Oh, God," she mumbled, and planted her feet firmly, overcoming the sensation she was losing her balance.

She held her breath, listening for signs the racket had awakened her husband sleeping in the next room. *No*, she corrected herself. Her *ex*-husband. She had divorced him during his last six-month stay in jail.

She eased back up the hallway to the larger bedroom she had shared with Billy Dean Jensen for ten years and peeked inside. He was sprawled all over their double bed on his back, broadcasting loud snorts and rumbles from his nose and throat. After coming home at midnight from no telling where, drunk or drugged up or both, he had staggered to the bed and fallen onto it fully clothed. So that he would be comfortable enough not to wake up, Jolie had removed his boots, during which his rhythmic snore—loud enough to be heard above the roaring storm—faltered not a beat.

Out cold. Thank God for small favors.

Jolie returned to her packing, her mind scrambling, her hands moving in frantic jerks, stuffing the clothing into the bag. If Billy awoke for some reason and caught her, only God knew what would result. Jolie couldn't let herself think of that. She couldn't allow any thought that might prevent what she knew she had to do.

"Do we have tornado warnings, Mama?" Danni whispered.

Of course there were tornado warnings. There were always tornado warnings in East Texas in April. The day had been heavily humid and hotter than blazes for this time of year, bringing on the evening's storm. TV news had earlier reported golf-ball-size hail up in Greenville to the north and six inches of rain. "I don't think so," she whispered back. "Be quiet now."

"Can I take this?" Danni whispered. She held a faded stuffed dog in the flashlight's spotlight. The toy had once been pink. Now it was natty and gray from years of being petted by Danni's hands.

Jolie hesitated. She had already told Danni they could take nothing they didn't need, but she knew her daughter had sneaked some things into her book bag.

"Please, Mama." Danni's whispery voice quivered.

The tattered toy had been with Danni for longer than Jolie could remember. It was one of the few things in their lives that had always been there. In an ill-afforded sentimental moment, Jolie relented and spread the gaping mouth of the bag. "Hurry. Throw it in here."

She tamped the toy down on top of the clothing, then drew the bag's plastic cord tight and tied it.

Ready.

She fanned the flashlight around the cramped room one last time, scanning for some irreplaceable item she or her daughter might later wish for. For an instant, her emotions stumbled into her task. For so many years she had lamented the size and dreariness of this tiny room. When Danni was a baby, it had been barely large enough for a crib and a small chest of drawers. Now it was barely large enough for Danni's twin-size bed, the same chest of drawers painted a different color and a narrow bookcase. Tonight Jolie was glad it was too small to hold much, glad they owned so few material items that were worth keeping.

Picking up the bag, she motioned with her hand toward the laundry room, then switched off the flashlight. In the dark, carrying the bag and moving ahead of Danni, she eased up the short, narrow hallway to the space housing an ancient washing machine and dryer. It could hardly be called a "room." It was so small she could cross it in two strides and be out the back door.

Two strides.

Two strides between this moment and the rest of their lives.

She hesitated an instant, thinking through her plan one last time. For the past two days, at opportune moments, she had been secreting pillowcases filled with necessities in the trunk. Today, after coming home from work, she had parked their old Ford Taurus so that no more than six steps from the back door would take them to it. She had removed the lightbulb from the car's overhead light and left the key in the ignition.

She had put a laundry basket full of her and Danni's clothing in the backseat. If Billy noticed the plastic basket, he wouldn't have been suspicious. He knew that when she had the money, she sometimes did their laundry at the coin-op in town where the washing machines and dryers were newer and cleaner and she could finish the chore faster using multiple machines all at one time.

Another thunderclap and a wind gust shook them and the pounding rain escalated. Jolie shuddered and clenched her jaw. After so much rain, some creek between her and freedom was bound to be out of its banks. Bad weather or flash floods were horrors her escape plan hadn't included.

She placed the bag at the back door, then returned to the hallway, making room for Danni to enter the laundry room. This was it. The moment of truth.

For a few seconds she stood in the doorway, staring back at the exit door as if it were the entrance to a cave where a monster lived. In the windowless room, she could see only faint outlines of the washing machine and dryer and Danni's form, but she could hear her daughter's breathing. Danni was so scared. For the first time Jolie noticed her own heart hammering.

Well, whatever demon might lie in wait on the other side of that back door, it couldn't be much worse than the one passed out in the bedroom.

She had already schooled Danni on what she had to do: run to the passenger side and climb into the car. Period. She was not to hesitate, not to slam the car door. It could be closed securely later. She bent, placing her mouth close to her daughter's ear. "Okay, now. Everything's okay. Don't be scared."

Jolie carefully opened the trailer's door, being cautious to avoid the metallic clack that accompanied the opening and closing of the mobile home's metal doors. She gripped the edge of it tightly to keep a wind gust from catching it and slamming it back against the side of the trailer. Outside, the night was black as pitch. Rain sluiced off the trailer roof in wide sheets. Even before she left the protection of the trailer's doorway, a horizontal rain stabbed at her arm and face with cold, needlelike pricks.

Jolie held the mobile home's door with one hand and the flashlight with the other while Danni sprinted through the mud of the so-called yard, around the rear end of the car. As soon as the ten-year-old reached the passenger door and scooted in, Jolie herself grabbed the overstuffed plastic bag and made the short dash. She yanked open the car's back door, threw the bag and the flashlight into the backseat and only half closed the door. Then she climbed behind the wheel and fired the ignition. The Ford started with no more than a cough. *Yes!*

Then, without headlights, she herded the sedan through the raging storm and the dark pine growth that hid their mobile home from the county road, up the two-mile-long dirt driveway that had now turned into a tire-grabbing soup.

Like water dumped from buckets, rain poured over the windshield, blinding her.

Whap-screek! Whap-screek!

The windshield wipers, even set to the max, couldn't keep the windshield clear. When she'd had the car serviced earlier in the week, it hadn't occurred to her to have the windshield wipers checked.

At the end of their driveway, almost by instinct, she turned onto the paved county road and switched on the headlights. They were almost useless, but they struggled to make a dim impression on the overpowering wall of rain that showed like silver shards in the headlight's golden deltas. Jolie clenched the steering wheel at ten and two and crawled along, her neck craned, her eyes squinted and straining to see.

Five miles later, she reached Bob's, a convenience store that closed at midnight every night. She stopped in the dark parking lot, got out and shut all the car doors tightly, then scooted back into the driver's seat, drenched and shivering.

She glanced across to the passenger seat and saw Danni's hands tucked between her knees, her narrow shoulders huddled and shaking. Jolie wiped her own soaked hair off her damp face, turned the heater to full blast and without looking back, pulled back onto the county highway.

"It's dark, Mama," Danni murmured in her quivery little-girl voice.

"It's the rain, honey. Don't be scared. You must be tired. Can you go to sleep?"

"I don't know. Maybe."

"You could try. The heater's getting warm now. I know you're tired. Just close your eyes and you'll be asleep before you know it."

Jolie returned her attention to the road and the weather. She no longer knew exactly where they were. She could see nothing to the sides of the car, could see nothing ahead of her but black night and the pathetic weak fan of the headlights against the downpour.

She rued that she had been so fearful of driving the shorter route straight through Dallas where there were at least streetlights. But she hadn't wanted to risk a breakdown on one of the freeways in her eleven-year-old car.

More than that, she hadn't wanted to chance an encounter with the Dallas police in case Billy awoke and reported the car missing. That possibility was why she had replaced the Ford's license plates with a set she had stolen. With stolen license plates, being stopped for even a minor traffic violation might result in a trip to jail. She believed this because that very thing had happened to Billy.

Until the last few weeks, she had never imagined herself doing something like stealing license plates, but yesterday she had exchanged the license plates from her Ford with those on a car parked in an out-of-the-way space in the parking lot of the restaurant where twenty-four hours ago she had been employed. The car belonged to another restaurant employee who Jolie was sure had no warrants or history that would cause police to stop her. The extra miles added to her trip by arcing Dallas and Fort Worth didn't matter anyway, she told herself now. She had filled the gas tank after work and she would get well past Abilene before she would need to stop for gas again.

Cocooned inside the car by the deafening storm and lulled by the hum of the engine, Jolie felt her nerves starting to calm. A weird out-of-body sensation had overtaken her. She attributed it to swallowing some No-Doz and now having been awake almost twenty-four hours.

She had worked a full shift as a waitress at the Cactus Café today, or actually, yesterday now. She had held that job for several years. She felt guilty abandoning the café owners without giving notice. Donna and Mike Harmon had treated her with fairness and compassion, helping her during the various times she had left Billy in the past. But she couldn't have risked telling them her plans. Once her husband sobered up and figured out she had fled, the Cactus Café would be the first place he would go for information.

The next place would be her mother's trailer in Terrell, but her mother knew nothing of Jolie's escape plan. The fewer people who had information, the better, Jolie had figured. She wasn't worried about her mother being confronted by Billy. As the manager of a blue-collar bar, Evelyn Kramer was as tough as Billy was mean.

Almost an hour later, in spite of the blinding rain, Jolie recognized the deserted streets of the small town of Ennis, a bedroom community southeast of Dallas. Just ahead, the red of a traffic light at a state highway intersection shone like a lighthouse beacon.

She stopped and waited for a green light, then made a right turn and headed west.

An hour and a half later, the rain began to dissipate and signs became readable in the black night. She soon spotted one that directed traffic to I-20. Despite being exhausted, despite her nerves being frazzled, a feeling of freedom filled her heart. She could think of nothing that would make her turn back.

2

Sunrise broke the horizon on a dripping world, but the storm had moved east, leaving a deep lavender sky spotted with gray scud. Jolie turned off the highway into a rest stop, thinking to grab a quick nap. She parallel-parked near the restrooms, in front of an eighteen-wheeler. She felt safe near most truck drivers. They had been her customers for years. The truck's cab was dark and silent, so her arrival must not have awakened the driver.

Danni, still sleeping, stirred in the passenger seat. Her naturally curly brown hair, now dry, frizzed like an aura around her head. Jolie studied her for a minute, touched a ringlet on her cheek. She couldn't deny that Danni looked like her father. Jolie had thought him handsome back before drug and alcohol abuse took its toll on his appearance. Now he looked ten years older than his thirty-one years. He even had graying hair.

Her mind spun back to two weeks ago when she had made the absolute decision she had thought about for years, but had found excuse after excuse to put off. At that moment, she had called Amanda Mason, her cousin in Lockett, Texas, and said, "I'm ready. Help me get out of here."

Amanda had been only too happy to assist in the getaway. She had always considered Billy a worthless bastard. Two days after Jolie called her, the cousin had found Jolie a job as a cook and kitchen manager on a big cattle ranch. "It's twenty-eight miles from nowhere in any direction,"

Amanda had said. Jolie had had a brief phone conversation with the ranch's owner, Mrs. Fallon. The ranch would pay her a small salary and found and she would receive the same benefits as the other ranch employees. When Jolie had asked what "found" meant, Mrs. Fallon had told her it meant room and board. For the house cook and kitchen manager at the Circle C Ranch, "found" amounted to a furnished two-bedroom house and all she and Danni could eat. Jolie couldn't believe it. A *house*. She had spent her entire life in a single-wide aluminum box.

Otherwise, all Jolie knew about this arrangement was what Amanda had told her.

The pay in dollars and cents was lousy, but the opportunity sounded like the best one Jolie had heard in a very long time. Now all she had to do was get there. She had never been to West Texas, never been out of Grandee, really, except to go to Terrell sometimes and Dallas a couple of times, but as of this moment, the Circle C Ranch in Willard County, Texas, population 1,632, was home.

A wave of true panic threatened Jolie for the first time since the escape from the trailer just a few hours earlier. She knew almost nothing about where they were going, much less what life would be like when they got there. Working as a cook and kitchen manager for a family? She had never done such a thing. Still, waiting tables for years and sometimes helping in the kitchen in the Cactus Café had taught her a little about food and cooking. Managing to continue to eat, pay a few bills and keep Danni in school while dealing with a raging alcoholic and drug user with an unpredictable temper might have taught her a little about managing, but she wasn't sure of that.

She closed her eyes and pressed her fingertips into her forehead, as if she could physically push those negative thoughts out of her mind. Didn't her favorite pep talk to Danni tell her she could do anything she set her mind to? Jolie opened her eyes and heaved a great sigh. Today was a new day in her and Danni's lives.

"Where are we?" Danni asked, interrupting Jolie's inner journey. The ten-year-old rubbed her eyes with delicate fingers beringed with junk jewelry, which always brought a smile to Jolie. She had always been a girly girl herself, loved makeup and nail polish and jewelry. In that way, Danni was like her.

"Just outside of Abilene," Jolie answered.

"How much longer?"

"An hour, maybe two. Are you hungry?"

"A little."

"I brought some food." She reached for the small foam cooler she had stashed behind the passenger's seat. When she left the restaurant yesterday afternoon, she had taken several bottles of juice, two bottles of milk, two ham and cheese foot-long hoagies and four brownies. She figured that was enough food for two days.

"How about a sandwich?" She unwrapped the large sandwich, which she had already cut in fours, and handed a piece to Danni. Then she opened a bottle of the milk for her.

"Are we really going to have a house?" Danni asked, chewing on a bite of her sandwich.

"That's what Amanda said. A house. Not a trailer."

"I've never lived in a real house."

"I know, Danni. Neither have I."

After they ate, Jolie reached into the backseat for the small duffel in which she had stashed some of their personal belongings and they went into the ladies' room. With the early hour, they were the only ones in the restroom. Jolie had already splashed cold water on her face before seeing there were no paper towels. She used her shirttail to dry her face, then stared into the mirror. Her eyes looked hollow and sunken from lack of sleep. Her hair was still damp and straggly. She had been wearing it blond lately and it looked like straw. She was so exhausted she could hardly stand, so she gave up the idea of putting on makeup.

Still jittery, probably from the No-Doz and the tension, she waited as Danni brushed her long, thick brown hair. She stepped behind her and braided it for her, glancing often at her mirror image. She was often overwhelmed by how pretty and smart her daughter was. Sometimes she couldn't believe such a perfect human being had come from the likes of herself and Billy Jensen. And it was at those times that pure gratitude gripped her, shook her like a powerful hand and reminded her that it was her duty to give Danni the best life possible. She had failed in that charge up to this point, but from this moment forward, Jolie intended to do everything possible to see that her daughter was blessed with chances Jolie herself had never had.

Before driving away from the rest stop, she called Amanda and told her they were only a couple of hours away. Then they were on the road again.

Sheriff Jake Strayhorn of Willard County, Texas, was always out of bed no later than sunrise. He had become accustomed to being an early riser while doing an eight-year hitch in the army. He had never lost the habit, though eleven years had passed since his military days.

As always, his first thought was of the jail, for which he had total responsibility. No prisoners resided behind bars this morning. In fact, Willard County's two-cell jail hadn't had a prisoner since Jimmy Hayes stayed two days after getting drunk and giving his wife a black eye. That had happened more than a week ago. Having zero tolerance for wife beaters, Jake had kept the bullying little shit behind bars as long as the law allowed.

He put coffee on to brew, then went about his morning routine. With the showerhead plugged by mineral buildup from the hard water, he bathed under what amounted to only slightly more than a trickle. He'd had a plumber come up several times from Abilene and install new showerheads, but they never lasted long. West Texas water was so corrosive, mere ordinary plumbing didn't stand a chance. He was forced to acknowledge again that his living quarters were far from luxurious. In that way, he was no different from most Willard

County residents. But then, with no one but himself to consider, Jake didn't require luxury.

Shaved and dressed, he poured a cup of coffee and made his way to his office located between his living quarters and the jail. He found a note on his desk from his deputy, Chuck Jones, saying one of Hart's cows had gotten out of the fence, onto the highway. Chuck had gone out early and herded it back home.

A few faxes awaited him—hot sheets from Austin, some from the FBI. Other than that, all was quiet.

He locked the office door and sauntered over to Maisie's Café, Lockett's only eatery besides the Dairy Queen. If he ate breakfast out, Maisie's was his choice. If going for lunch out, he usually ate at the Dairy Queen. Since the county picked up the tab, he tried to be fair about where he spent the taxpayers' money.

The usual breakfast gathering hummed and buzzed in Maisie's. Some were dressed for church, some for work. At the lunch counter, he spotted Pat Garner, a local rancher and horse trainer. Pat had arrived in Willard County nearly at the same time Jake had. He had come from Terry County a hundred miles away. These days, if he was in the café, he usually had Suzanne Breedlove with him. Suzanne was Jake's cousin's best friend. This morning Pat sat alone.

Jake crossed the dining room, headed for the lunch counter. Everyone spoke as he passed. He touched his hat to them and called most of them by name. Straddling the padded vinyl stool next to Pat, he set his hat on the empty stool to his right. He wore his .45 on his belt on the right side. If he sat down in public armed, he always chose a spot with an empty seat on his right. "Mornin', Pat."

Pat looked up at him. "'Lo, Jake." He switched his mug to his left hand and sipped his coffee.

"You had breakfast?"

"Yep."

Jake appreciated that Pat Garner, like himself, was a man of few words. In Jake's mind, actions spoke louder than words and Pat had proved himself with his actions many times. Jake turned over the thick mug in front of him.

Before either he or Pat could say more, Nola Jean Hart appeared with the coffeepot and poured Jake's mug full. "Mornin', Sheriff. Listen, I 'preciate Chuck comin' out and getting our ol' cow back into our pasture. We didn't even know she was out 'til he come told us."

"I saw Chuck's note about that," Jake said. "It's no problem, Nola Jean. Glad we could help out." He picked up his mug and blew across the top of the steaming dark liquid, then savored his first sip. The coffee he made in his kitchen didn't compare to the coffee at Maisie's.

The waitress set the coffee carafe on the counter and pulled a small order pad from her apron pocket. "Eatin' breakfast, Sheriff?"

"Yeah."

"Same thing?" She began to write. "Two sausage patties, two eggs over easy, two biscuits with gravy. Anything else?"

Jake was a methodical man. What he ate for breakfast rarely varied. "Nope," he said to Nola Jean.

"It would've been a big loss to us if somebody had run over that cow," she said as she wrote. "She's our best one. Brings a good healthy calf ever' year." Nola Jean tucked her pad back into her apron pocket, picked up the coffeepot and turned toward Pat. "Want me to top you off, Pat?"

"Sure." Pat slid his mug toward her.

Jake waited until the waitress moved out of earshot. "Where's Suzanne this morning?"

"Truett came in off the road yesterday, so she stayed home last night." Pat sipped again.

Suzanne's father was a long-haul trucker, away from home most of the time. Jake smiled. "If you made an honest woman out of her, you wouldn't be sleeping alone."

"She likes the sleeping arrangements the way they are. You're one to be talking to me about sleeping alone. I haven't seen you with a woman in a coon's age."

And if Jake had his way, Pat wouldn't see him soon,

either. Jake kept his social life out of town. Lockett was a gossip mill. The county sheriff shouldn't be the center of a soap opera. "Women are a lot of trouble."

"Suzanne ain't." Pat sipped his coffee again.

Jake looked at Pat's profile for a few beats. The man had changed since he took up with Suzanne. He seemed happier, more easy-going. A few years ago, Pat's wife had left him for "life in the city." The City of Lubbock to be precise. Jake considered Lubbock an overgrown small town, compared to, say, Dallas or Houston. Pat had been so overwrought when she left, Jake figured he wouldn't take up with a woman again. His now hanging out with Suzanne just went to show how being lonesome and finding somebody pretty who filled up the void could change a man's attitude.

"Got anybody I know in jail this morning?" Pat asked.

The Willard County Jail was more likely to see a prisoner on a Sunday morning than any other day of the week. Jake chuckled and shook his head. "Guess the natives weren't that restless last night. Truth is, Willard County's a peaceful place most of the time."

Pat nodded. "Heard you're running for sheriff again."

"Might as well. I'm not qualified to do anything else."

"Lucky for Willard County. Damn few little places like Lockett got a man with your whiskers to do that job. You're the reason we don't have some of the problems some of the other counties around here have."

To some degree, Pat was right. He referred to Latino gangs that had steadily moved into West Texas, along with meth labs. Jake had made the consequences clear on both those issues soon after taking office years back. On one occasion, he and one Texas Ranger had settled a drug manufacturing matter in a shoot-out that had resulted in three dead gang members, the destruction of a large meth lab and the arrest of a whole nest of international criminals who had been operating without interference for years. He shrugged. "Just doing what I'm supposed to. That shit's poison. It's not right for honest people to have to live alongside it."

Jake listened to Pat talk horses, bitch about the politicians and bemoan the price of beef, the price of feed and the price of fuel. They passed harmless gossip about Willard County's citizens, most of whom Jake knew. The population was declining, though. With virtually no employment except cowboying at the Circle C Ranch or working at a low-paying job in town, most young people left the county. Since the price of a barrel of oil had jumped, some new oil field activity had erupted, but every West Texas native knew the continuation of that boon to the economy depended on who got elected to Congress. These days, most of the oil companies' workers were temporary and from out of town.

Jake was one of the few people who had actually returned to Lockett to live. He hadn't once regretted the decision. He had led an unrooted life and Lockett was as close to a hometown as he had. He had lived here longer than he had lived in any other place, had gone to school through ninth grade here. One of the happiest parts of his life had been spent here as well as one of the most tragic. But he refused to dwell on the tragic, believing his contentment outweighed it.

He had to admit, though, that the sameness of every day was starting to grate on him. He was lonesome and he didn't know why. He wondered if it was because he was looking uphill at forty and his chances of finding a companion with whom to share the rest of his life were shrinking. That had never been important to him before. He didn't understand why it should be now, but he couldn't deny thinking about it.

Flanked by treeless pastures, barbed-wire fences and grazing cattle, Jolie drove behind her cousin, Amanda Mason, for what seemed like forever before coming to a pair of stanchions made of some kind of rust-colored stone. They made a right turn, rumbled across a steel cattle guard and were now driving on a crooked caliche road.

"Where're we going, Mama?" Danni asked.

"This is where we're going to live, Danni."

"Oh, no. There's nothing here." Danni began to sniffle.

"Don't cry, Danni. It's a big ranch. It'll be a good job. I'm going to be in charge of the kitchen all by myself. Don't cry, now, okay?" Danni wiped her eyes. "Let's give it a chance, okay?" Jolie said. "Things are going to be a lot better for us. I just know it. Amanda says these are really nice people."

Out of nervousness and fatigue, Jolie was talking ninety miles an hour. But she stopped herself from saying to Danni that she believed they would be safe from Billy. For the first time since leaving Grandee, Jolie thought about the family who was willing to hire her and wondered what Amanda had told them about her and Danni's circumstances.

They reached a split wrought-iron gate, each of its halves adorned with a big circle with a C inside it. "See?" Jolie said to her daughter, pointing at the circles. Even as little as Jolie knew about ranches, she knew the symbol had to be a brand. "It's the Circle C Ranch."

Danni said nothing, only stared out the window.

Seeing that she couldn't be easily persuaded, Jolie heaved a great sigh.

Amanda stopped ahead of them and spoke into a box on a steel post and the gate slowly opened. They drove on a narrow paved road lined with big trees, the canopies spreading across the road. Amanda came to a stop on a circular driveway in front of a massive three-story house that seemed to go on forever in all directions and was made entirely of rust-colored stone. The single-wide trailer she and Danni had left behind in Grandee wouldn't fill a wing of it. Huge barns and outbuildings too numerous to quickly count sprawled all over the landscape, all painted dark red. Pristine white pole corrals were attached to almost every outbuilding.

"Oh, my Lord," Jolie mumbled. It was one thing to see a mansion in a fancy neighborhood in the city, but this one was all by itself in the middle of nowhere. She was so awestruck, she nearly ran into Amanda's back bumper.

Danni stared at the house, big-eyed, evidently stunned out of her disappointment. "Is *this* where we're gonna live?"

Two men and a woman—dwarfed by the sheer size of the house—stood on the long front porch. A wave of anxiety washed over Jolie as she glimpsed her still-damp hair in the mirror.

She glanced at Danni. Their clothes looked as if they had slept in them, which, in Danni's case, she had. "Come on, let's get out," Jolie said. "And don't forget, be polite."

Amanda waited for them to exit the Ford, then walked with them toward the front porch.

"You're gonna really like these people, Jolie," Amanda said. "This is gonna turn out just fine."

The three strangers met them in the middle of the grassy yard and Amanda made the introductions. The woman named Jude Fallon was just as pretty as Jolie had imagined she would be when they had talked on the phone. The two men were Mrs. Fallon's husband and father. Mrs. Fallon bent forward, her long reddish brown hair falling across her shoulder, and put her right hand out to Danni. "Hi, Danni. How old are you?"

Jolie held her breath as Danni took her hand. "Ten," Danni said in her little-girl voice, obviously cowed by all around her.

"I have a stepson just a year older. He'll be coming to stay with us for the summer when school's out."

"Oh, that's great," Jolie said, mustering a smile. She had worried about how Danni would spend the idle summer hours, and now that she had seen how far from everything this ranch was, she worried even more. She looped an arm around Danni's narrow shoulders and gave a squeeze. "Isn't that great, Danni? A friend your age?"

"I guess so," Danni mumbled.

"She's a little tired," Jolie said to Mrs. Fallon. "Please don't think anything of the way we look. We've been on the road all night."

"Then you both must be tired," Mrs. Fallon said.

The men talked about the weather, then excused themselves and walked toward the barns.

"Let's go inside," Mrs. Fallon said, gesturing toward the front door. "Have y'all had breakfast?"

"We ate something," Jolie said.

"Well, I haven't eaten," Amanda said, appearing to be perfectly at ease with Mrs. Fallon. "You don't think I'm going to pass up a chance to eat in the Circle C's kitchen, do you?"

Mrs. Fallon, who looked to be about the same age as Amanda, laughed. "You're such a character, Amanda." They trooped through the wide front entrance onto to a rusty red tile floor, then toward an aroma of spicy food and fresh coffee.

"Believe me, we're glad to see you," Mrs. Fallon said to Jolie. "Since our former cook passed away, Irene and I and my husband have been trying to do the cooking. Brady's fair at it as long as it's something simple. But I'm awful and Irene only knows how to make Mexican dishes with lots and lots of jalapeños."

They entered a huge high-ceilinged kitchen with white-tiled walls. "Irene's our kitchen helper and her husband is our maintenance guy and groundskeeper." Mrs. Fallon said, her voice almost echoing off the hard kitchen surfaces. "They go to early church in town on Sunday mornings."

Mrs. Fallon directed Amanda to the stove where a plate of something rolled in tortillas sat. "Brady made burritos for breakfast. They're good, too. They've got scrambled eggs and chorizo and just a few jalapeños. Irene made the chorizo from scratch."

"Lemme at 'em," Amanda said.

Laughing, Mrs. Fallon dragged a plate out of the cupboard and handed it to Amanda.

Amanda took it and helped herself to two burritos.

"Y'all sit down in the breakfast room." Mrs. Fallon pointed them toward a sunlit space just off the kitchen. "Jolie? Danni? Would you like a burrito?"

"We've already—"

"I guess so," Danni said.

"They have jalapeños," Jolie said to her daughter. "You don't like jalapeños, remember?"

"How about a bowl of cereal?" Mrs. Fallon asked. "I have cereal for breakfast most of the time. We've got half a dozen kinds. Do you like Cheerios?"

"Okay," Danni said.

"Amanda and I've known each other forever," Mrs. Fallon said to Jolie as she poured Cheerios into a bowl. "We were in the same grade in school." She turned to Amanda. "Do you want coffee?"

"Sure."

Mrs. Fallon brought the cereal and a jug of milk to the table and set them in front of Danni. She went back to the kitchen and returned with a small dish of salsa, two thick mugs and the coffeepot and poured the mugs full. "Do you want some orange juice or some milk?" she asked Danni.

"Orange juice," Danni answered, still speaking in a tiny voice.

While Jude went for orange juice, Amanda took a seat at the round, glass-topped table, so Jolie did, too, and told Danni to sit beside her. She looked around the room that would now be part of her domain. The walls were stucco, painted a light tan. A wall of windows looked out onto a huge red stone patio, where Jolie saw a large rock barbecue pit. She relaxed for the first time since yesterday afternoon. In fact, if she wasn't careful, she could drop off to sleep.

"You aren't having coffee?" Amanda asked Mrs. Fallon.

Mrs. Fallon was pouring a tall glass full of orange juice. "I've never been a big fan of coffee. And since I've been pregnant, it upsets my stomach."

"Oh, my gosh," Amanda said, her eyes popping wide. "You're pregnant?" She slathered her burritos with salsa from the dish Mrs. Fallon pushed toward her.

"I am. Six weeks as of today." She set the orange juice in front of Danni.

"Oh, my gosh," Amanda said again. "When are you due?"

"October."

A baby, Jolie thought, and glanced at Danni. Her daughter had never been around a baby or seen a newborn.

"Does everybody know?" Amanda asked.

"I doubt it. I haven't told anyone but family and Suzanne."

"Can I tell everybody?" Amanda asked, obviously excited.

Mrs. Fallon shrugged. "If you want to. It isn't a secret."

While Amanda returned to her meal, they went on to discuss how thrilled Mrs. Fallon's father was at her pregnancy, and how it was too bad her grandfather had passed away before the event and how it was definitely going to change life at the Circle C. Jolie listened in silence, immediately liking Mrs. Fallon. She didn't behave like a rich person. She seemed down-to-earth and kind.

Soon Amanda rose and announced she had to get to work. "Tell Brady I thought his burritos were great," she said.

After Amanda left, Mrs. Fallon said, "You must be ready to drop. Let me show you the house where you'll live."

Jolie forced herself to her feet and followed the energetic Mrs. Fallon. At the back door, Mrs. Fallon pointed toward a small square brick cottage the length of a football field away. It had an attached carport.

"Look, Mama," Danni said. "Our car's never had a place to park."

"Just follow the driveway that goes around the garage," Mrs. Fallon said. "I'll meet you there and give you the keys."

3

After breakfast, Jake returned to his office. His deputy, Chuck Jones, had arrived. Laughing, he told about herding Hart's cow with his truck. Jake laughed with him. Jake had worked in law enforcement in the highest crime locales in the world and had confronted his share of danger. He relished the idea that the only escapee he had to worry about in Lockett was somebody's cow.

A few minutes later, his assistant/receptionist/dispatcher/9-1-1 operator and last, but not least, deputy, Amanda Mason, bustled through the front door. "Sorry I'm late," she said, sinking into her chair behind her desk. "I had to meet my cousin. She got here early this morning. I went ahead and took her out to the Circle C. Got there in time for breakfast burritos. Brady Fallon made them, if you can believe that."

"Brady's a versatile guy," Jake replied.

"They're sure missing Windy out there."

Windy Arbuckle, the Circle C's chuck wagon cook for years, then the ranch's kitchen cook in later years, had died from a sudden heart attack a month ago.

"What's going on out at the Circle C?" Chuck asked.

Jake had no desire to discuss the Circle C Ranch with his two employees. He left the discussion to them and walked into his office, sat down behind his desk with a report from Homeland Security and INS about drug and people smuggling across the Mexican border. Unable to clearly read the title page, he sighed and pulled a pair of glasses out of his shirt pocket. He had finally broken down and gone to Lucky's Grocery, Lockett's only grocery store besides the Circle C supply house, and bought a pair of "readers." Suzanne Breedlove, who worked there, had helped pick them out—little gold-framed half-glasses that perched on the end of his nose. He hated wearing glasses. Worse than that, he hated admitting he needed them. Until now, it had never occurred to him that thirty-eight years old was old enough to need glasses.

In the tiny sheriff's office, he couldn't keep from overhearing Chuck and Amanda's conversation.

"You ain't gonna believe this, either," Amanda was saying.

"What?"

"Jude Strayhorn's pregnant."

Jake glanced up from his reading, his attention diverted to the local gossip.

"She ain't Jude Strayhorn anymore," Chuck said.

"She'll always be Strayhorn in Willard County," Amanda retorted. "Maybe in the whole state of Texas."

Jake didn't disagree. Strayhorn roots went deep and far. Just a little more than a year ago, Jude had married one of Jake's childhood friends, Brady Fallon. He was glad she hadn't done one of those pretentious hyphenated things like calling herself Jude Strayhorn-Fallon. She had been satisfied to become just "Jude Fallon." Jake was sure Brady hadn't asked her to abandon her maiden name. And he knew Jude well enough to know she had done it by choice.

Jake had stood up with Brady when the wedding took place in the church that had been built by Jake and Jude's great-great-grandfather, Roslyn Shaffer Campbell. Just looking at her and Brady together on that day, Jake had known it was only a matter of time before she got pregnant. He had never seen two people more into each other. In some ways Jake envied Brady.

Jake had never had such intense feelings for a woman, had never found one to whom he had been willing to give so much of himself.

"She just found out," Amanda said. "Says she's due this fall. October."

"Hunh," Chuck said. "Hope they get that boy they've been wanting. To be the Strayhorn heir, I mean."

A hundred mixed emotions stirred within Jake. There had been a time years ago when he himself had been a male heir to the Circle C empire. Now he was an outsider just as surely as if he hadn't been born with the name or spent the first fourteen years of his life on the ranch that sprawled over more than half of Willard County. Still, he felt no jealousy of Jude. She was one of his favorite relatives.

Besides, his grandfather, Jeff Strayhorn, had taken care of him and Jude and their cousin, Cable, equally. The patriarch of the family had set up trusts for his three grandchildren and set aside additional funds to send them each to college. As established by the old man, Jake had taken ownership of his trust fund when he was thirty and he assumed Jude and Cable had, too. Employed as a cop for Dallas PD, Jake had left the fund in the charge of the banker in Abilene and told him to build it for his retirement. Now he was well off. He dipped into the trust fund proceeds occasionally, because no man could get along very well on what Willard County paid its sheriff.

Even if Jake were not content with his lot, in a litigious society, had he been interested after the old man's death last year, he could easily have found some lawyer willing to take on the challenge of suing Strayhorn Corp for a piece of their vast holdings. But doing it would have been a foolish endeavor, Jake believed. Knowing the thoroughness and ruthlessness of his grandfather, Jake was pretty sure the man had wrapped up any inheritance issues and tied them with a tight knot. The Strayhorns had enough power and influence to keep something like a lawsuit that might destroy the family enterprise tied up in court for a hundred years. Jake also believed that the biggest beneficiaries from suing an empire were the lawyers.

In spite of those benign feelings toward his paternal

family, in his secret heart, Jake sometimes wondered what might have been if his father Ike Strayhorn had been a man of honor instead of an alcoholic, philandering sonofabitch. He hated being saddled with guilt for what the father he barely remembered had done.

Amanda came into his office and plopped into the chair on the other side of his desk. "Listen, Jake, I want to thank you again for speaking to Jude for Jolie. That's my cousin's name, by the way. Jolie Jensen. Jude might not have hired her if you hadn't said something."

Jake knew only a smattering of Amanda's cousin's problems—spousal abuse and the accompanying ills. As a career cop, he had heard it and seen it many times. All such cases were fundamentally the same. "I was glad to do it, Amanda."

"Well, thanks anyway. She's thrilled to death to be here."

"That's good, that's good," Jake said.

When Amanda had asked him to talk to Jude about the kitchen job at the Circle C, she had said her cousin was honest and trustworthy and had a child to support. Jake had the utmost faith in Amanda's judgment and in her word. If he didn't, he wouldn't have hired her in the first place. He had done nothing more than mention to Jude that Amanda had a cousin who had years of restaurant experience and needed work. Jude had been more than glad to give her first consideration simply because Jake had asked. Now that the Circle C had hired the woman and furnished her a house, Jake only hoped he didn't come to regret his role in the hiring.

Jude shrugged into a jacket and started the trek back to the cottage that had always been known as the "cook's house." The brisk walk would be good for her. But as she walked, an uneasy feeling nudged her. She had never had a moment's worry about who lived in the cook's house before because for the past fifteen years the resident had been Windy Arbuckle, one of her dad's oldest and best friends. Now a stranger would be moving in and it was a stranger who was nervous as a cat. Jude suspected she was hiding out. Anyone could see it. But why? And from whom? And why here? There had to be plenty of places closer to Dallas where Jolie could have gone to work.

Amanda had said Jolie and her husband had split up and Jolie needed a job, but not much more than that. Jude trusted Amanda. Beneath Jolie's obvious nervousness, Jude thought she saw sincerity and she also trusted her own instincts about people. She saw something else, too, that she hadn't quite identified yet, but she would eventually.

Jude unlocked the door and showed Jolie and Danni into the two-bedroom cottage. "I hope Amanda told you it isn't necessary for you to live here unless you want to. A furnished house has always been part of the pay for the kitchen manager, but if you—"

"No," Jolie said quickly. "Living here is fine."

"Good, then. I hope you'll be comfortable. It isn't a real big house, but it has big rooms."

As they stepped into the living room, Jude couldn't keep from thinking of Windy and sadness passed through her. She missed Windy gimping around the kitchen with his crippled leg, missed his corny cowboy talk. He had been a presence in her life for as long as she could remember. At times she had regarded him as an old windbag who tattled on her. She had sometimes been angry at him, but that didn't mean she didn't care about him. He was like family.

"We've never lived in a house," the little girl said. "We've only just lived in a trailer."

"Danni, shh," Jolie said.

"Of course you should treat the place like your own," Jude said, ignoring the scolding. "You're far enough away from the ranch house to have your privacy. We don't want to interfere with your life."

Jude led them into the bedroom behind the living room. The bedrooms were arranged at either end of a hallway, with the bathroom between them. A brand-new queen-size mattress still enveloped in clear plastic lay on a bed frame. It had been delivered from a furniture store in Abilene just this week. "We've bought new mattresses for both beds," Jude said.

Jolie made a little gasp. "Oh, my gosh. That's wonderful."

"Windy lived here a long time. It was just time for new mattresses."

"That's just . . . wonderful," Jolie said again.

They moved on to the bathroom and stepped inside. "The plumbing's been replaced, too. It was plugged with mineral. That happens pretty often around here. We have very hard water and it devours plumbing. You probably didn't have that problem in East Texas."

"No, we didn't," Jolie said.

"In the ranch house, we get our drinking water from cisterns. Feel free to bring water back to the cottage for your own use if you want to. There's a water softener here, but the softened water just doesn't taste as good as rainwater."

"What's cisterns?" Danni asked.

Jude smiled at the little girl's curiosity. She liked this kid already. Being a teacher, Jude could see she had an agile mind. "Big concrete holding tanks where we catch rainwater."

They moved on and peeked into the back bedroom, where a smaller bed was located and another brand-new mattress. Then they walked back toward the kitchen, where several plastic jugs of water sat on the counter. "This is water from the cisterns," Jude said, placing her hand on one of the jugs. "I asked Reuben to put it here in case you want to use it to wash your hair. I wash mine in the softened water in the house, but sometimes I use the cistern water just because it feels so good."

"Thank you," Jolie said, and Jude saw a puzzled expression on her face. She would learn to live here soon enough, Jude thought.

"Do you speak Spanish?" Jude asked.

"I'm sorry. I'm afraid I don't. Do I need to?"

"Not really. Irene speaks broken English and she's learning more all the time. Windy was teaching her and she takes some classes from the Catholic church in town. Reuben— that's her husband's name—speaks hardly any English at all. They came from a village in Mexico. They're good help and very loyal. I don't speak Spanish, either, except for a few words. So sometimes communication is a challenge."

"I could learn, too," Jolie said, interested in the idea of learning another language. "I do know a little bit already. If you live in Texas, I think you just do."

Jude chuckled. "Right. I'm the same way."

"I'm sure I won't have any trouble getting along with them," Jolie said. "We'll figure out how to talk to each other. What does Irene's husband do?"

"He does the outside maintenance around the ranch house and takes care of the yard and orchard. He worked on a farm in Mexico. He says he's a good gardener, so he wants to start a garden this year. The ranch used to always have a garden, but in his later years, Windy didn't want to fool with it. He went to the farmers' market in Abilene and bought fresh vegetables and fruit."

"I'm afraid I'm not much of a gardener, either," Jolie said, "but I'm willing to learn to do that, too."

"Okay, but don't feel that you have to. Even if Reuben's garden turns out, I doubt he'll be able to grow enough to supply the house and the cookhouse. You'll still have to shop at the farmers' market or somewhere. Abilene has several of the large chain grocery stores, including Walmart. We also have an account at Lucky's grocery store in town and you can shop there, too. But basically, we try to buy everything wholesale and a lot of what we need gets delivered. You can coordinate with the cookhouse cook when he places orders."

"Cookhouse?" Jolie asked.

"It's attached to the bunkhouse. We feed two hearty meals a day to at least forty hands. Even the hands who don't live in the bunkhouse come to eat breakfast and dinner if they want to. And sometimes we have special meals for their families. By the way, you and Danni are free to have all of your meals in the ranch house or you can bring food from the ranch house here to your place. One thing we never have is a shortage of food."

Jolie gave a faint smile.

"Daddy takes care of the kitchen budget," Jude went on. "You'll have to work with him, too. He's the moneyman since Grandpa passed away."

"You aren't in charge of the kitchen?"

Jude huffed out a laugh at the thought of herself fumbling around in the kitchen. "Oh, Lord, no. I can barely boil water without a disaster. I mostly manage the bull herd and work with Doc Barrett and with the horses. *You'll* be in charge of the kitchen."

Danni's voice broke into the conversation. "Can I have a horse?"

"Danni!" Jolie said. She shot a quick glance at Jude, then back at her daughter. "The horses belong to Mrs. Fallon and the ranch. They're for work."

"That's okay," Jude said, smiling at Danni. "We've got horses you can ride. We've got a couple of gentle ones my stepson and his half brother ride when they come to visit." She turned to Jolie. "And you don't have to call me Mrs. Fallon, Jolie. Everyone calls me Jude. It's short for Judith Ann."

"Okay," Jolie said.

Jude started for the front door. "Well, I'll leave and let you get settled. Do you need some help bringing your things in? I can find—"

"No, that's okay," Jolie answered too quickly again. "We don't have that much to unpack."

"Okay, then," Jude said. But for some reason, she was reluctant to leave. She could see the fatigue in Jolie. "Tell you what. I'll help you myself."

Unloading Jolie and Danni's belongings took less than half an hour. Most of what they carried into the house were pillowcases stuffed tightly with something and a couple of laundry baskets. Jude could tell the woman had left from somewhere in a hurry, but told herself Jolie's problems were none of her business. All the Circle C expected was for her to be honest with the money she would be in charge of and to do what was expected in the kitchen. Reminded of laundry by the stuffed pillowcases and laundry baskets, Jude said, "There isn't a washer and dryer in this house. You can use the utility room in the ranch house to do your laundry."

"That'll be fine. With just Danni and me, we won't have that much washing to do."

Jude started to leave again. "Oh, I should tell you, you'll also have to get with Daddy on some payroll information. He'll get you enrolled in our insurance plan. We provide our employees with group insurance and a small life insurance policy. Daddy can fill you in on all those details." With a big smile, she handed the house keys to Jolie. "As I said before, we're glad you're here."

Before finally leaving, she stopped one more time. "Jolie, I don't know what you left behind, but you're safe here. You don't have to worry. We take care of our people."

Jolie's eyes took on a sudden glister and Jude wondered if she might cry. "Thanks, Mrs. . . . uh, Jude. I—I know we'll be happy here. And I'll do the best job I can."

Jude smiled. "Amanda told me you would and I believe her." She started to leave again, but thought of yet another thing. "I'm a teacher at the high school here. I can probably help you get your daughter enrolled. We don't have that many students. The whole school's in one building."

As soon as Mrs. Fallon—or Jude—left, Jolie returned to the Ford for the laundry basket on the backseat. She stood a few minutes, studying the license plate on the back bumper. At some point she would have to renew the registration. She had just done that a couple of months back, but she didn't know the expiration date on the stolen plates.

If Billy was somehow able to trace her to Lockett, even if he didn't see her or Danni in person, if he saw the Ford, he would recognize it no matter what license plates it had. On the other hand, if he turned her in to the cops for taking the car, they would be looking for the original plate number. Given Billy's history with the police, he might not contact them for any reason. She wondered if she should tell Amanda about the stolen plates, but decided against it. Amanda had helped her get this job. No way would she want to make her an unknowing participant in a crime. And last of all, Amanda worked for the county sheriff and she might be obligated to report a stolen license plate.

With her mind foggy from stress and exhaustion, she couldn't think clearly. In a split second she decided to leave the stolen license plates right where they were and to keep her mouth shut. She might be functioning on pure adrenaline, but at least the sun was shining, the sky was clear and it was as blue as Danni's eyes.

Carrying one last laundry basket into the cottage's living room, Jolie found her daughter slumped in the corner of the sofa and scowling. Jolie fought not to break into tears. She had planned so carefully, taken a huge risk by uprooting their lives, and what if Danni, in the end, was unhappy?

She took a few minutes, slowly turning in a circle and taking in her surroundings. The house was old, but she could already tell it would be comfortable. She had never had so much space, had never lived with a floor so solid. The furniture, though obviously old and used, was far better than what she had left behind.

Her survey stopped with a natural stone fireplace in the corner of the living room. She had never had a fireplace, hadn't even been in many buildings that had one. "Did you see the fireplace, Danni?"

"Yes," her daughter said in a small voice. "But where will we get some wood to burn?"

Jolie wondered the same thing, because so far, she hadn't seen an abundance of trees growing naturally. She was sure the huge old trees around the ranch house had been planted a long time ago. "I don't know, but we'll get some. I think the winter is colder here than in Grandee. A fireplace will be nice. We really don't need it for now. It's spring. We'll worry about burning a fire in the fall."

If we're still here, she thought. Jolie had no idea where she and Danni would be come fall. Once Billy knew she had pulled out, they might be on the run.

Danni got to her feet and went to the fireplace, ran her small beringed fingers along the highly varnished wooden mantel. Jolie set down the basket of clothing and joined her, looped her arm around her shoulder. "Just think, Danni. We can put up Christmas stockings. Can't you see our stockings hanging here and a big fire?"

"I guess so," Danni said with little enthusiasm.

She wrapped Danni in her arms in a tight hug, rested her cheek on her daughter's hair. "Listen, we're going to be okay. We'll take a day to get straightened out and rest. Then tomorrow we'll see about getting you into school."

"But why do I have to, Mama? School's almost out and I've already learned everything."

Jolie squeezed her eyes tightly shut, pushing back tears. This behavior wasn't like Danni. She loved school, was a good student, but the last twenty-four hours had surely scared her. Jolie couldn't blame her if she just couldn't stand the thought of one more big change.

Jolie would love nothing more than to grant her daughter's wish about not enrolling in school. Having her attending public school could be a way Billy might find them. But she couldn't allow Danni to not finish the school year. "Because you have to get a good education. You need to pass fifth grade so you can be in sixth."

She set her daughter away and brushed tendrils of her long brown hair off her face. "Did you decide which bedroom you want?"

Danni answered with a scowl and a nod of her head.

"Which is it?"

"The last one."

"Good. The sheets are in the hall closet. Go ahead and

get them and start on the bed. I'll come help you as soon as I put these clothes away." Jolie picked up the laundry basket and carried it to her bedroom.

There, she paused and heaved a great breath, her gaze landing on the queen-size bed and its new mattress. The Jensens had never slept on brand-new mattresses.

As she set the laundry basket on the bed and began to sort through the folded clothing, she looked around the room. The walls were painted beige and the floors were made of some kind of wood. There were two tall windows side by side, with white blinds and white crocheted curtains. Besides the bed, she had a bedside table and a lamp, a dresser and a matching chest of drawers and a wooden rocking chair. She walked over to a closet with sliding doors and peeked inside. The closet was huge, far more than enough room for her wardrobe.

A sliver of happiness began to peek through Jolie's fatigue and gloom as she thought of what Jude had said: *"Jolie, I don't know what you left behind, but you're safe here. . . . We take care of our people."*

Already she felt it. Safety. Working as a waitress for so many years had afforded her an uncommon ability to read people, and she sensed that Mr. and Mrs. Fallon were what Amanda had said they were—good, fair people. On the way back to her daughter's room, she stopped off in the bathroom. She found a corner in the bathroom closet and left the laundry basket there to collect dirty clothing, remembering that Jude had told her to feel free to use the washing machine and dryer inside the ranch house.

She tried not to think of that ranch house. Not yet. She couldn't even guess how many rooms it must have. Going to it every day and going inside, having free run of that fancy kitchen, she would feel like a princess. She already felt as if she had entered a fictional world.

Robotically, she walked to Danni's room and began to help her with the sheets. On the wall opposite the regular-size bed was a blank wall painted a soft yellow, which was probably why Danni had chosen this room. "I was thinking, Danni, after I get a paycheck, maybe we could get a little bookcase where you could put all of your books. Wouldn't that be neat?"

"I could put my stuffed animals in it if I had some."

Jolie felt a stab of guilt over her daughter's collection of stuffed animals they had left behind, including the brand-new stuffed bunny Jolie had bought her for Easter. But she couldn't let little things affect her shaky resolve. Stuffed toys were easily replaced. She thought about a desk for Danni. A place for her to work on her lessons would be a luxury. Maybe someday, once Jolie established some order in their new lives, she could even think about a computer. "Maybe soon we could get you a desk and put it right over there." She pointed toward the corner.

For the first time, Danni's eyes sparked with interest in what they were doing. "Could I get a bulletin board?"

"We could do that. There's plenty of room for it. Soon as we get organized and I start making some money, we can work on it."

4

Jude glanced away from her monitor toward the outside and the barns and corrals. From her office in the back of the ranch house, she had a clear view of the big red horse barn with a huge encircled C painted on the second story. She could see Clary Harper, the horse wrangler, working a colt in the round corral attached to the barn. This was unusual, as most Sundays only a few hands worked at chores that were absolutely necessary.

Jude's husband and her father, their backs to her, had their arms hooked over the corral's top rail, watching Clary and the colt. The two men were about the same height. Both had a right boot braced on the bottom rail. Both had on Wranglers and long-sleeve light-colored shirts, both wore gray hats. Jude couldn't keep from grinning. Brady and Daddy were such total cowboys. Other than herself, that was probably the most profound connection they had. In the year and a half that had passed since she had married Brady, he and her father had grown close. Since her father had always wanted a son, she was happy to see him bond with her husband.

She left her desk and ambled out to the corral to see what was going on. She walked up between them. "Hey," Brady said, and hooked an arm around her shoulders. "How you feeling?"

She'd had a few bouts of morning sickness, but that phase of her new pregnancy seemed to have settled down. "Great."

"You ate something, right?"

"Bowl of cereal, just like every morning."

He gave her his white-toothed grin and a smack on the lips. God, she loved him.

"What do you think of the cook?" her father asked.

Jolie was the first ranch employee Daddy hadn't had a direct hand in hiring. He had left it entirely up to her. Jude still hadn't told him Jake had recommended Jolie, but her father was so happy these days, he probably wouldn't care that Jake's two bits had gone into the hiring of the kitchen help.

"She seems okay. I told her not to worry about the kitchen until Tuesday. She has to enroll her daughter in school tomorrow. Y'all want a sandwich for dinner? I could probably manage that without doing too much damage."

"Sure," Daddy said. "When did you learn to cook?"

She gave him a flat look and he chuckled.

"Sounds good," Brady said. "I'll help you. As you should recall, I'm pretty good at sandwiches."

The very first meal Jude had shared with Brady had been a bologna and cheese sandwich he had made in his antiquated kitchen at the old 6-0 ranch that had been left to him by his aunt. And for the rest of Jude's days, "baloney and cheese sandwiches" would hold a special place in her heart. Brady grinned and Jude grinned back.

Her father's face took on a blank expression. He didn't get the private joke and Jude made no effort to explain.

The three of them sauntered toward the ranch house, with Jude walking between them, Brady resting his big hand at the base of her neck. She slid her arm around his waist. "Whose colt is Clary working with?" she asked.

"Betsy's," her father answered. "Remember, we bred her to Sandy Dandy a couple of years ago?"

Betsy was one of the ranch's best broodmares and Sandy

Dandy was a prizewinning stud. "Oh, wow. I do remember. That should be a good horse."

"Clary thinks so, too. That's why he's working him on Sunday. He doesn't want to miss a single day."

In the kitchen, with Brady's help, Jude made three ham, cheese, lettuce and tomato sandwiches, sliced them into halves and laid them on plates. Then she found tortilla chips in the pantry. They took seats at the glass-topped breakfast table and discussed branding the spring calves while they ate. The branding would occur in June as it had every year for generations. Soon Brady and the hands would start to tally how many calves would be branded and Daddy would determine if they needed to hire extra temporary help.

At the end of the meal, Jude offered to make a tuna casserole for supper. Suzanne had given her the recipe.

"Don't mean to hurt your feelings, punkin," her father said, "but I think I'll just go to town later and eat supper at Maisie's." He left the table for his office on the other end of the house. Soon after Grandpa's death, Daddy had taken over Grandpa's office.

Brady hung behind. As she rinsed their dishes in the sink, he came up behind her and wrapped his arms around her waist. "Ride to Abilene with me?"

She turned in his embrace, placing her palms on his chest. "What're you doing in Abilene on a Sunday?"

"I was thinking if I had a hot date, I might take her to a nice dinner somewhere, then to a movie."

She smiled up at him. She had never been as happy as she was now. "Dinner and a movie. Hmm."

"Yep," he said.

They kissed, thoroughly enjoying each other. When it ended, she said, "Lord, I can't remember the last time someone wasn't here to eat supper. This old house won't know what to think if all of us are gone at suppertime."

"I'll bet it'll still be here when we get back."

"I'll bet so, too," Jude said, still smiling.

Abilene was an hour-and-a-half drive from Lockett. As

they turned onto the highway, Brady said, "I heard what you told your dad, but what did you *really* think of the cook?"

"I don't know yet. She's a woman with a past, I think. But obviously, I didn't want to mention that to Daddy."

"Couldn't have much of a past. She can't be thirty years old."

"Amanda said she's twenty-seven. She seems older than that. I sense that she's very responsible and Amanda says she can cook. I'm just going to keep an eye on things for a while. Not with the cooking but with the management of the kitchen and the budget. I know she's Amanda's cousin, but we don't know her. And Amanda might not know her as well as she thinks she does."

Jolie removed the remainder of the food she had brought from the Cactus Café from the cooler and spread it on the table in the dining area off the kitchen. She opened bottles of milk for Danni and herself and they sat at the table to eat. "Tomorrow we'll start eating in the ranch house," she said.

"Do you think there's some kids here?" Danni asked, mincing at her sandwich.

"You heard Mrs. Fallon, er, Jude. She has a stepson near your age."

Danni finally took a bite of her sandwich, then said, "But he doesn't live here. And she doesn't have any girls."

"Your aunt Amanda said the ranch has around fifty employees and most of them live here on the ranch. Surely some of them have girls."

They ate the rest of the sandwiches in silence. "Are you tired?" Jolie asked.

Danni nodded.

"Me, too. I'm worn out. We could watch TV and maybe take a nap on the sofa. This might be the last day we aren't busy. It might take all day tomorrow to get you enrolled in school."

Danni grimaced.

"It'll be fine, Danni. You'll see. Just try, okay?"

"Will I have to ride the school bus?"

"You rode the school bus in Grandee."

"But I knew everyone."

"You'll know everyone again. You're a sweet, friendly person and all the kids at school will want to be your friend."

"No, they won't."

"I'll drive you for a few days, just until you get used to things. And I was just thinking. I wonder if we could figure out a way to enroll you using a different last name."

Jolie didn't know if this was even possible or legal, but she intended to try it. Dealing with Danni in a new school had been a worry from the moment Jolie had begun to formulate her escape plan. When she had removed her from school in Grandee, she had told the principal they were moving west for work and the principal's office had given her all of Danni's records. Unfortunately, they had her last name as "Jensen."

"Why?"

"So Billy won't be able to find you. I was thinking maybe we could get the school to let you enroll as Danni Kramer. That used to be my name before I married Billy. You wouldn't mind, would you?"

Danni answered with a shake of her head. "Will Billy hurt us?"

Danni had never called her father "Dad" or "Daddy" or anything other than Billy. Most of the time, he hadn't given her the time of day. They had lived almost as if Danni were just Jolie's child and Billy had had nothing to do with her existence.

Who knew if Billy would hurt them? Not Jolie, even after living with him for more than ten years. She believed he was capable and she did know that he would be really mad that she had left and even madder that she had taken their only dependable vehicle. His old pickup ran only half the time. "We just won't let him find us."

* * *

Pat Garner dismounted the blue roan stallion he was training for a calf roper in Abilene and headed for the end of the arena. An engine noise caught his ear. He recognized Suzanne Breedlove's daddy's pickup truck and felt a lift in his chest. Just seeing that woman could turn a dark day bright. He led Blue Streak outside and waited for Suzanne to come to a stop.

She scooted from behind the steering wheel looking beautiful. Her long blond hair had that messy look like some of the movie stars wore. She had a big smile on her full, kissable lips. Lord, he loved just the sight of her. He couldn't help it.

Without a moment's hesitation she walked straight to him, slid her arms around his middle, rose to her tiptoes and kissed him. Still hanging on to Blue Streak's reins with one hand, he kissed her back in a long, languid joining, not even trying to hide his hunger. He'd had that hunger almost from the beginning of their relationship and it had never waned. When they stopped for air, he was hard as a rock and Blue Streak snorted in his ear. "Even this horse knows how you tear me up."

She grinned up at him and rubbed his fly where his erection pushed against his zipper. "Did you miss me last night?"

He huffed a grunt. "What do you think?"

"I missed you, too. I've gotten so used to sleeping with your long hairy legs and big strong arms, I have insomnia when I'm not in your bed."

He smiled. She had a way of making him feel ten feet tall. "Yeah? Well, you're welcome to stay over any time."

"Hmm. I can see that." She kissed him again, pressing her belly against his erection.

Blue Streak snorted and stamped and Pat broke their kiss. "Did your daddy get home okay?"

"Sure did. I had the house all clean and shining and supper on the table when he got here. His favorite. Fried pork chops and mashed potatoes and gravy."

Pat knew Suzanne felt an obligation to provide a haven

for her father to come home to. He spent his days driving an eighteen-wheeler on the highways and his nights in his sleeper cab parked in some grocery store parking lot. She believed he had been an unhappy man when her mother was alive and she wanted him to have something to look forward to now.

"Damn," Pat said. "Wish you would've invited me. I had a frozen pizza."

"You're invited tonight. Daddy spent last night in the Walmart parking lot west of Fort Worth. Before he started home he went inside and got some great T-bones."

They kissed again and she rubbed him more. Dammit, if she didn't quit it, he might just go off in his shorts. "I was just going to the house for a sandwich," he said huskily. "But I could be arm-twisted into having dessert first."

She gave him a wicked grin. She knew what she had done to him. "You know that old saying. Life's uncertain; eat dessert first." Then she drew back and looked up at him with an earnest expression. "I came to talk to you about something."

Uh-oh. What's gone wrong? Things with her were just going too well to not have something happen. The enthusiasm in his jeans softened. "Okay. But I need to put this horse away."

She helped him unsaddle Blue Streak. As they brushed him down, Pat on one side and her on the other, she said, "Guess what?"

"Don't know."

"Jude's pregnant."

He stopped and looked at her across Blue Streak's back. Jude Strayhorn was Suzanne's best friend. They had known each other since they were kids. Jude's family was richer than all get-out and owned most of Willard County. Pat had lived here only a few years, but it was common knowledge Jude's dad and granddad had been waiting for her to get married and have kids. Sons, preferably. "No kidding. That ought to make all of them happy. A new Strayhorn heir."

"Jude's an heir."

Pat laughed and returned to brushing Blue Streak. "But she's the wrong sex. You know how they are."

After they turned the horse loose in the pasture, they walked toward the house hand in hand. Pat had a nice house. Three bedrooms and two baths. He had gutted the old house that was here originally and started over. It wasn't a mansion, but after the major remodel, it was the newest house in the county and he was proud of it. He had more or less redesigned it himself, then gone into hock to pay for it, all for his ex-wife, Becky. He felt he owed his bride a decent place to live. She had walked out of it as if it were a shack and had never looked back.

Inside the house, they headed straight for his bedroom. In record time they were washed up, undressed and under the covers and they were kissing and exploring each other as if they had been apart for weeks instead of only a day. Just touching her voluptuous body anywhere he wanted, filling his hands and mouth with her breasts, making her scream with pleasure would thrill him forever. He still couldn't believe that she wanted him as much as he wanted her.

"I'm so hot," she breathed, urging him on top of her.

He was, too. Thoughts of her and the time they spent together constantly circled in his mind no matter what he was doing. He crawled between her thighs, trailed kisses over her face, down her neck, licked her nipples and suckled in the way she had told him she liked. She moaned in the way *he* liked.

"You said you wanted dessert first," she said huskily. Her hands pushed on his shoulders, urging him down.

On a deep hum he moved his open mouth down her middle, stopped and licked her right hipbone, felt her belly quiver. "Feel good?"

"Yesss." She arched to him.

He trailed his tongue over her soft fragrant skin, flicked it along the edge of her crisp pubic hair until he reached the other hipbone. He pushed her left knee high and wide, inhaling her woman's scent. He would go to his grave with her female smell branded on his brain. He kissed the inside of her thigh, licked his way up to her knee and back, stopped between her legs and buried his face in her nest of curls and licked the seam of her sex.

On a big sigh, she raised her opposite knee, opening herself completely, and he pushed his tongue into her warm, salty slickness. "Oh," she murmured, and he felt her fingers in his hair. Pushing her knees high and hooking them over his shoulders, he began thrusting his tongue in a sexual rhythm and at the same time suckling her sweetness into his mouth. She squirmed within his grasp and little gasping noises came from her throat.

Soon she was moving against his mouth. Her fingers clawed at his head, yanking a fistful of his hair, almost to the point of pain. "Now, Pat . . . now."

Oh, yeah, he was ready, too. His balls were on fire, his dick throbbed and blood pounded in his head, but he gripped her ass and held her still and kept teasing her. He intended to make this last as long as possible.

She was breathless and panting. "Dammit, Pat . . . hurry."

"Say please," he mumbled against her sweet, wet flesh.

"Please, dammit."

He leisurely slid his tongue up to her clit, sucked the firm little button of flesh into his mouth and she went crazy. She sobbed and panted and came and came. He was ready to burst into flames himself. His cock couldn't get any harder without exploding, but he fought against his own orgasm.

After she finished, she tugged him up by the hair. "Get up here," she said. "Put it in. Please, Pat. . . . I wanna come with you inside me."

He crawled up, kneeling between her thighs, hovering over her, his penis hot and eager.

She reached between them and frantically guided his member to the right spot. Though it was torture, he teased her some more by giving her just the head.

"Pat," she whined, arching herself up to him.

He pushed into her, shuddering from the powerful sensation of his hard flesh gliding along the soft, hot walls of her tight sheath.

Her legs came around his waist and her heels dug into his ass cheeks. He pushed one more time and seated himself deeply inside her. Her vaginal muscles clamped down on him and he almost lost control. She did that on purpose, he knew. He gave a grunt. Too close to climaxing for her tormenting, he pressed his face against her neck. "Goddamn, you're killing me. . . ."

"Please don't die. You feel too good."

He braced himself on his hands, looking down at her glistening parted lips and closed eyes, and began to rock in a steady rhythm.

"Yesss," she hissed, moving with him. "I love your big cock inside me."

He kissed her, quick and fierce, sought a sweet spot. "Feel good when I do this?"

"Yes, yes. . . . Like that. . . . It feels like it's up in my stomach."

They moved in perfect practiced rhythm, her fingers digging into his biceps. He sensed her restlessness. She was as hot as he had ever seen her. He picked up the pace, striving to make every stroke count before he lost it. Their breathing became labored pants. She cupped the back of his neck and pulled his face against her cheek, her mouth against his ear. "Harder. Fuck me harder."

She was the only woman he had ever known who talked like that during sex. It turned him on big-time. He had no trouble giving her what she wanted. He pumped hard and fast, making her pant and cry out and making the headboard bang the wall. Moments later when her sweet pussy clutched him and milked him with powerful contractions, he couldn't last through it. Orgasm burned through him like a raging fire and he jetted his seed into her over and over until he was empty.

Still heaving for breath, she wrapped her arms around

his back and held him close. When the storm began to calm, she whispered in his ear, "That was stupendous, you big brute. Fantastic. You're *always* fantastic."

Lord God, sex with a woman who liked it was amazing. He sure as hell knew the difference. He had been married to one who barely endured it. "You make me that way. I never was before." Getting his breath back, he covered her mouth with his for a long, lush kiss.

They lay with legs entwined for a long while, drifting in hazy satisfaction. The smell of sex filled the air around them and they both had slick bellies. They fucked without rubbers. She took the pill. There was almost no chance she would get knocked up and zero chance she would catch an STD from him. And he wasn't worried about catching anything from her, either. They had already crossed that bridge.

He hated to move, but finally he said, "Guess I oughtta get a towel." He left the bed and washed himself in the bathroom. He returned carrying a towel, which he used to wipe her stomach and between her legs. He dropped it on the floor and crawled under the covers again and they snuggled belly to belly.

After a while she said, "We should clean up, huh? So we can have lunch."

"Yeah, I'm starved." He freed himself and started to sit up, but recalled her earlier statement at the arena and the serious look on her face. He turned on his side, propped himself on his elbow and placed a hand on her silky hip. "What do you want to talk to me about?"

"It could be a long conversation. You sure you want to get into it now?"

He stretched alongside her. "You've got my curiosity aroused. And my undivided attention."

She gave him a tentative smile. "Okay, here goes." She turned onto her stomach, braced on her elbows and looked down at him, her tousled hair a messy aura around her head and shoulders. Her lips were pink and swollen from their kissing. He loved seeing her like this, the way no one else ever saw her. He touched the corner of her mouth for no reason other than he just liked touching her.

She caught his finger and kissed it. "How long have we been, you know, doing the nasty?"

He couldn't put his finger on exactly when things began to change between him and Suzanne. Of course he clearly remembered the first time they'd had sex. She informed him one day that she had been taking birth control pills for a month preparing for the day they would do it and she was tired of waiting for him to make a move. What had followed was one of the most embarrassing sexual experiences he'd had in his life. That first time, he had been so nervous, nothing worked the way it was supposed to. The second time, though, he had settled down and gotten it right and experienced the most mind-blowing sex he'd had up to that moment. Thinking about it now, he chuckled and tucked a sheaf of yellow hair behind her ear. "I don't know. Since before Jude got married. Over a year."

"And how many fights have we had?"

"None. I always give up and let you have your way." That wasn't entirely true, but teasing her was part of their relationship.

"You do not." She leaned over and placed a quick kiss on his shoulder. "My point is we get along, right?"

He gave her an even wider grin and gently tugged at her hair. "We sure do."

"So what would you think if I got off the pill?"

His grin fled and words failed him. He looked at her, only able to blink. He thought he knew what she meant, but just to be sure, he finally asked, "Why? Are they causing you problems?"

"No, no. It's just that . . ." She turned away from him and stared at her interlocked fingers.

Now he was concerned. "What is it, Suzanne?"

"Well . . . they're keeping us from making a baby, Pat."

More than words failed him. His ability to think and breathe flew right out the window. "God, Suzanne—"

An expression of hurt fleetingly passed through her eyes. "I was hoping you wouldn't tell me not to."

He had never seen that look on her face. She was the last person in the world he wanted to hurt, but he couldn't be cavalier about what she had said. "But why all of a sudden do you want to have a baby?"

"I don't know. You know how you sometimes just feel like it's time for something?" She turned her head away from him and focused her attention on her fingers again. She began rubbing her two thumbs together. "Maybe it's because my best friend's pregnant and she and Brady are so happy. Even Jude's dad is happier than I've ever seen him. He came all the way into town just to tell Lucky and Carlene about being a grandpa."

Lucky and Carlene Henson owned Lucky's Grocery, where Suzanne worked. Pat knew Lucky and Jude's dad, J. D. Strayhorn, had been friends their whole lives. While Pat thought about how the wealthy Strayhorns interacted with the community they practically owned, he didn't reply to what Suzanne had said.

"Maybe I'm envious of all that," she continued. "My dad would be happy to be a grandpa, too. . . . Or maybe it's because I'm thirty-two years old and not getting any younger." She looked at him pointedly. "You aren't getting any younger, either."

She was right about that. He would be thirty-five his next birthday. Both of his sisters were married with families. They and his parents nagged him all the time about being single and childless at thirty-five. He had never been opposed to having kids. When he was younger, he had even thought that was what he would do someday. His far-from-perfect marriage had reversed that attitude for a while, but he still believed a man should have kids with the right woman.

But was Suzanne the right woman? His mind spun backward to when his relationship with her began, when she had first returned to Lockett carrying a flaming torch for Pro-Rodeo and PBR bull rider Mitch McCutcheon. With a plan to return to barrel racing, she had hired Pat to help her get her old horse Buck into shape. While they had worked at that, Pat commiserated with her about her former lover. On some days, she would be so distraught she would break down in tears and have to leave their workout. But she would show up the next day and doggedly try again. There had been times when they had spent more time discussing McCutcheon and her failures as a woman than working with poor old Buck. Back then, Pat hadn't had the heart to tell her Buck was simply too old to ever make it as a winning barrel-racing horse.

As much as she had talked about that good-for-nothing fucker McCutcheon, who had abused her emotionally and physically, Pat still didn't know if she and he had been married or if they had just hung out together for a long time.

Pat wasn't a man to shrink from reality. Even with as well as he and Suzanne had gotten along from the first, even as close as the two of them had grown, even with the sex as good as it was, he still didn't know if she still secretly carried that torch for Mitch McCutcheon. Pat might not mind the idea of having kids, but he had to ask himself if he wanted that with any woman who had settled for him while in her heart of hearts she loved another man.

"Hey," she said softly, running her finger along his biceps, "you're not talking to me."

He pulled the woman he loved more than he had ever loved the one he married into his arms, their faces only inches apart. He looked into her sky blue eyes intently. "By now you know me," he said gently, treading lightly, fearing revealing all that was tumbling through his mind. "You know I'm a dull turd. I own a house, a few acres and an arena. Not much to offer. I don't know why you'd want to have a baby with me."

Her head shook slowly and he thought he saw love glowing in her eyes. "God, Pat, you don't even know all that you have to offer. You're good and kind and honest and funny. You're not dull. You're smarter than anyone I know." Her palm cupped his jaw and her eyes locked on his. "Maybe I think a little kid would be lucky to have you for a daddy. I can see you teaching him or her to ride, to know about horses, to know about the cattle. I can see you teaching a son what it means to take responsibility and be a man."

Those words hit home, overwhelming his negative musings. A lump swelled in his throat. An image of her big with his child charged into his mind. How many times had he seen pregnant cows, mares, dogs, cats? How many times had he helped them give birth? The process had always humbled him and made him feel closer to God. What would it do to him to watch a woman he loved go through pregnancy and pain bearing a child he had sired? "But you'd have to put up with a lot. You'd be in pain. I don't know if I could stand that."

She kissed him tenderly. "Pat. You raise cattle and horses. You know the females are supposed to have babies. It's the scheme of things."

He placed his hand on her flat stomach. "But you'd get fat."

"Shh." She planted a fierce kiss on his lips.

"You've thought about this," he said, stalling, struggling to get a grip on his emotions. "This isn't just a whim. Like you said, Jude is—"

"Jude doesn't have anything to do with it. I was thinking about it a long time before I heard about Jude. I guess her news brought it to the front of my mind."

"You know I'm a traditional guy, Suzanne. We've never talked about it, but you must have figured out I'm not the kind who'd believe in all this free love and single parent stuff. As it is, I sometimes worry that what you and I are doing is wrong. I couldn't take it, you being pregnant and me not being there for every minute of it. And I wouldn't want a kid of mine to be a bastard."

She gave him a grin he could only call sly. "I know."

Damn her orneriness. He grinned back at her. "Are you

trying to tell me something I don't know? Did you already stop—"

"I'm not pregnant, if that's what you mean. I'd never stop those pills without talking to you about it."

"Okay, I'm dense. You're gonna have to clue me in."

"Pat. I know you wouldn't want to be a single parent, okay?"

"So are you asking me to marry you?"

"I'm just saying that if you said it was all right if I stopped the pill, I would. And if you don't want to be a single parent, I'd probably say yes."

He had never told her he loved her, had been afraid she would think he was hanging on too tightly and would run away. He loved her more at this moment than he would ever have dreamed possible, but so much emotion had filled his chest, the word wouldn't come out. "You know how I feel about you. You know I can't refuse you anything."

Her beautiful blue eyes grew misty and she sniffled. "I love you, too, Pat. And I want a little boy with wavy brown hair and big brown eyes who'll remind me of you every time I look at him."

"Yeah?" Now he was grinning like a damn fool, latching on to the idea of fatherhood and spending the rest of his life with Suzanne. "And what if I want a pretty little blue-eyed blonde who'd remind me of you?"

She laughed. "Oh, my Lord. We might have to have two." Her face grew solemn. "Pat, please don't ever think what we've been doing is wrong. You saved my life. After Mitch, I thought I could never care about any man."

"And what about Mitch?"

"There is no Mitch. He's gone. Forever."

But Pat wondered. Sometimes when they were in bed making love and she closed her eyes, he wondered if she fantasized that Pat Garner was Mitch McCutcheon. And here and there, she had said some things that made him question if one day the sonofabitch might show up.

5

Pain woke Billy Jensen. It shot from temple to temple behind his eyes. His mouth was drier than bar popcorn and tasted the way cat shit smelled. He blinked himself fully awake and sat up, but fell backward when his head spun. He tried to remember what the day was. Sunday? Hell, yes, it was Sunday. He knew, because he thought he had spent yesterday afternoon where he spent many Saturdays—in the Starlight Club, a titty bar in Dallas. He put one foot on the floor and tried sitting up again more slowly. "Jolie?" he yelled. "Bring me some goddamn coffee!"

He heard no sound. Jolie should be home. She usually didn't work on Sundays. Danni should be home, too. "Jolie?" he yelled again, but no answer came.

Where the fuck are they?

Frowning, he creaked to his feet and staggered to the bathroom. He relieved himself, then bent over the sink to splash water on his face and nearly fell forward. At last he managed to wash his face and capture his balance, straightened and stared at his reflection. What he saw was a gaunt man who looked older than his thirty-one years. His face was drawn. His eyes were bloodshot. His teeth were bad. He needed a haircut and a shave. His filthy clothes needed changing. He had lost count of how many days he had been wearing them and they stunk of stale sweat and body odor.

He stumbled out of the closet-size bathroom. Hell, the

shitter in the goddamn bar was bigger than the bathroom in this fuckin' trailer house. He had always been pissed off at Jolie's mother for not buying them something bigger to live in.

He couldn't remember the last time he had eaten, but he suspected it had been days back. He staggered to the kitchen and yanked open the refrigerator door. The fridge in his house always had food. Jolie cooked stuff for herself and the kid and she was a good cook. She also brought stuff home from the Cactus Café, a joint he couldn't afford to eat in. He found a full liter of Dr Pepper and chug-a-lugged nearly half the bottle, then pulled out a plastic bowl and opened it. Macaroni and cheese. He dragged out a beer, took it, the bowl and a spoon over to the ratty recliner that huddled in front of the TV. Duct tape covered several tears in the vinyl upholstery. He plopped down, picked up the remote and turned on the set, then stuffed mac and cheese into his mouth while he channel-surfed.

After ten minutes, he gave up. He had cleaned the bowl and daytime TV sucked anyway. He left the recliner and ambled to the front door, carrying his beer. He swung the door wide and looked outside, stretching his stiff muscles and wondering again where Jolie was. The part of the front yard that wasn't a mud hole was slick with wet grass and washed dirt. It must have rained like a sonofabitch through the night.

He stared toward where the Ford was usually parked and it dawned on him that he saw no tire tracks. His brow tugged into a frown as he thought about that. Did that mean the car had been driven away before daylight? Even bald tires would have made some tracks in the mud. So she had to have left before the storm. *What the fuck?* A tiny panic began to creep through him, along with intuition that before now, he hadn't known he had.

He strode up the narrow hall, straight to Danni's room, his temples pounding with each heavy step. He yanked open the closet door and peered into the hole in the wall that passed for a closet. It was damn near empty. He looked around the room, but everything seemed neat and in place, the way Jolie and Danni kept it. Stuffed toys clustered in the center of the neatly made bed; a kid poster was stuck on the wall. He marched a few more steps up the hall, to the bedroom he and Jolie shared, and slid back a bifold closet door. Jolie's clothes were hanging there all right, but there seemed to be fewer of them. *What the fuck?*

Or maybe she just didn't have as many clothes as he thought she had.

He dug for his cell phone that usually stayed in his pants pocket, but didn't find it. He searched the floor around the bed, saw it lying just under the edge. He picked it up and speed-dialed the Cactus Café.

"I need to speak to Jolie," he blurted when the owner, Donna Harmon, answered.

"Sunday's Jolie's day off."

"I know that. But she ain't home. I figured she was working."

"Nope. Not here."

He disconnected in the café owner's ear. He didn't give a shit. Donna and Mike Harmon had never liked him anyway.

Feeling off balance and more insecure than he had felt in years, he keyed in the number of the woman he knew hated his guts and who just might be tough enough to whip his ass—his mother-in-law. The fact that he was calling her just showed how off-kilter he felt.

Evelyn Kramer answered the phone with a heavy smoker's gravelly voice.

"Evelyn, this is Billy. Is Jolie there?"

"Why would she be here?"

"'Cause she ain't at home." To Jolie's mother, he didn't add *where she oughtta be*, but he thought it.

"Well, she ain't here, either. I ain't even talked to her on the phone in a couple of months."

Billy chewed on his lower lip, trying to decide the best question to ask next, one that would get him some information. But his mind was fuzzy and he gave up. "Look, if you see her, tell her I need the car for something. My old pickup ain't been running good for a couple of weeks. I need her to get on home soon as she can."

A snort came from his mother-in-law. "Like she should care. I'll be sure to tell her." The phone disconnected in his ear.

"Bitch!"

Stuffing the phone into his pants pocket, he sauntered back to the living room, the trailer suddenly seeming silent even with the TV blaring. He sank onto the recliner seat and punched in another number on the cell phone. A growling hello came on the other end of the line.

"Randy, this is Billy. Listen, I need a ride."

"Where are you?"

"Home, dammit. Where the hell you think?"

"Where's your ol' lady?"

"She ain't here. I need to get to town. I gotta work on my truck and I need some parts."

Cussing and grousing rumbled through the phone. And from somebody who was supposed to be a friend, too.

"Look, goddammit, I think she pulled out," Billy said. Unexpectedly, a lump sprang in his throat, but he swallowed it back. Hell, he couldn't let his partying buddy think he was upset. "I think she took the car and the kid and split. I got to get the truck fixed so I can get around."

"What makes you think she left?"

"I dunno. Just something I feel."

"Where you think she went?"

"I dunno. But when I find her, I'm gonna kick the livin' shit out of her for stealing that goddamn car."

April in the Texas Panhandle was chilly. J. D. Strayhorn snuggled deeper into the pink ruffled covers of Maiselle Thornton's queen-size bed, enjoying the warmth of her pleasingly plump body. He felt at ease with Maisie, felt free to let his guard down. He couldn't say that about many women. God knew, no man had made worse choices when it came to the fairer sex than he had.

When his affair with Maisie began years back, they'd had a passionate relationship and he had known as much lust as any man. But after twenty-something years, the fever of lust wasn't as important as the fact that he and Maisie just liked being with each other. He didn't know why. They couldn't have more opposite personalities. She was outgoing and good-looking, smart and free-spirited, while he was reserved, withdrawn and scared shitless of feelings of any kind.

Propped on her elbow, her legs entangled with his, she used her fingertip to trace the deep indention left at his temple by the earpiece of his glasses. "This looks like a bad scar, J.D., like somebody hit you upside the head with something. You should get some new glasses that fit you."

He didn't open his eyes, enjoying her touch that was as delicate as a butterfly's wing. He hadn't known a lot of softness in his life. "It doesn't bother me."

"Oh, don't be such a hardhead. It isn't like you can't afford to go get new glasses. If you got some that fit better, pretty soon this mark would probably go away." She traced the deep indentation again, then leaned down and kissed his temple.

Women. The things that were important to them had always puzzled him. He couldn't keep from smiling. "Would you like me better if I didn't have it?"

She giggled and ran her instep up the outside of his calf. "I couldn't possibly like you better, you old cuss."

He turned to his back, pulling her closer and guiding her head to his shoulder. "That's all that's important." Totally relaxed, his eyes closed, he stroked her dyed-blond hair.

Her small hand lay on his chest. "Lord, J.D., I can't believe I'm soon gonna be calling you Grandpa. I was beginning to wonder if Jude would ever even get married, much less have kids."

He covered her hand with his own. "Me, too."

"And that Brady. He's such a good man. He's a good-looking devil, too. It nearly killed every single woman in Lockett when he picked Jude."

"Salt of the earth, Brady is. He's like my own son. And he adores my daughter. I can see it in his face. He's no slouch in the job of general manager, either." Then J.D. added on a chuckle, "In fact, he's so good, I'm having a hard time finding things to do."

"Poor J.D. All of a sudden after forty years, he's got free time on his hands."

He rubbed the back of her hand with his fingertips. "Hard to believe, isn't it? Over the years, I've gotten used to those fourteen-hour days."

"Are Jude and Brady doing all the work now?"

"Almost. I'm still the investment man, but she and Brady have taken on almost everything else. Brady knows how to delegate tasks better than I ever did and he's got the patience to get people to do what he wants them to. I was never very good at that. I sometimes got so frustrated, I'd just throw up my hands and do everything myself."

"And that's why you worked fourteen-hour days, my love. You're a true Type-A personality. It's a wonder you haven't had a heart attack."

"I'm working on being a different type. I've been thinking, Maisie. Since the Circle C's in such good hands, maybe you and I should go somewhere. I've got that jet airplane that sits unused in Abilene most of the time. We should just get in it and fly somewhere. Anywhere. Where would you like to go? Pick a place."

She made a little gasp and propped herself on her elbow again. "J.D., you and I cannot fly off together. Why, Lockett would never recover from the scandal. They'd be praying for us in church. In fact, they'd already be praying for us if they knew all the years we've slept together."

He opened his eyes and gave her a grin. "You think they don't know?"

"I do think that. We've kept our secret, J.D. Believe me, I'd hear about in the café if we hadn't. As plainspoken as your daughter is, if she knew, don't you think she would've said something?"

J.D. and Maisie had become lovers a couple of years after her second husband had died in a farming accident. The man had turned a tractor over on himself and died an agonizing death before he could be rescued. But J.D. and Maisie had *known* each other most of their lives, had gone to school together in Lockett. Their friendship had ebbed during his college years and their two marriages to other people, but had reburgeoned in between those events. He had been a friend to her through her divorce from her first husband, had stood by her side when she buried the second. Now that Windy was gone, she might be the best friend he had.

He, too, propped himself on his elbow and faced her. "I was figuring it out the other day. It's been twenty-one years we've been together."

"Twenty-two, J.D. And that's a long time for a woman to be loyal to a man she's not married to. And keep it a secret, too."

"I'm serious about us spending more time together. Things have changed. With Dad gone, I don't care what people say. We're wasting time. I'm sixty-two years old and you aren't far behind me. Who knows what tomorrow will bring?"

"I know what you mean," she said softly. "I've buried both my parents, too. And I seem to be going to more funerals lately."

"Dad's death made an impression on me. That day he died, he and I ate dinner, had a good conversation about the remuda and before suppertime, he was gone. He was a lonely old man, Maisie. In that way, I don't want to be like him. Besides, you're barely eking out a living in the café, so why—"

"Don't remind me. If you didn't help me out, I'd probably go under. Probably *would've* gone under a long time ago. Either that or just left town."

Years back, Maisie had talked about leaving Lockett to

make a decent living somewhere, J.D. had subsidized her café here and there in those days to help her out. Soon, the extra money had become a habit. Maisie never left town and over twenty years, he figured he had fed enough cash into Maisie's Café to own the place. He chuckled. "No way would I have let you leave town. Even if I'd had to buy that café outright."

"I'll have you know, J. D. Strayhorn, if I had *wanted* to leave Lockett, you couldn't have stopped me."

"Then I'm glad you didn't really want to."

A laugh burst from her chest. She had a rich deep laugh with a raucous ring to it. For forty years he had thought it was sexy. "You know me too well, Jasper. But just for the sake of argument, let's say I forgive you for never owning up to us as a couple and never standing up for us with your family and let's—"

"Come on now. Don't start that. You know all my reasons. They go back a long way."

"And if we *outed* ourselves, how do you think Jude would react to me being her daddy's mistress?"

"I don't believe she'd be upset. She's so happy right now. I can't imagine that she wouldn't want me to be happy, too."

"You know what a stodgy old stick-in-the-mud I am. I'm too old for dramatic changes. Why can't we just leave well enough alone and keep on like we are?"

"I was sort of hoping you might like to spend more days with me. . . . And nights. In all the years we've been to-gether, we've rarely spent a night together."

Maisie shook her head. "I don't know, J.D. It's so ironic we would start talking about this now. I have to tell you I'll never stop resenting that we didn't make a connection when we were younger."

J.D. had no one to blame but himself for that. He and Maisie had dated off and on through high school, had ex-plored sex together after a homecoming football game one night. Nineteen sixty-six, his high school senior year. It seemed like only yesterday. He had always been too busy to dwell on the past, but he thought about it now. After graduation that year, with no commitment between him and Maisie, he went off to college in Bryan, maintaining only minimal contact with her or anyone from Lockett except his family. "I know, darlin'. But I can't undo it."

"Would you? If you could?"

He couldn't answer. He didn't know.

She sat up and got to her feet with an exaggerated sigh, slipped on a lacy pink robe.

Damn. Now she was mad. "What do you want me to say?" he asked. "What's the point in talking about something I can't change? I'm trying to plan the future."

"That's part of the problem, J.D. From your perspective, there's no point in talking about most things. And as for the future, I guess I should feel grateful you've finally gotten around to me."

6

On Monday, after sleeping like a rock on her brand-new bed, in the safety and silence of her new little cottage home, Jolie awoke early and showered and stumbled through washing her hair and rinsing it with rainwater from plastic jugs. It was unbelievably awkward and inconvenient, but she would learn to do this, she was certain.

Putting extra effort into her appearance this morning, she dressed in newer jeans and a red sweater, then fluffed her medium-length blond hair and applied her makeup carefully. Today was a new beginning in a new place with new people. She wanted to meet it looking her best. She took a turn in front of the vanity mirror for one last look, drew in a breath and exhaled. Time to wake up Danni.

But first, she called Amanda and made an arrangement to meet her in town at the Dairy Queen for a burger at lunchtime. This could be her last day off for some unknown period. Jude had failed to mention what the family expected in regard to time off.

She got Danni up. Having gone through the bathing and hair washing ritual with her daughter last night, Jolie helped her get ready for school. Danni had no dresses, so Jolie helped her into her best jeans, the ones with pink flowers embroidered on the legs. She slid a bright pink top with long sleeves over her daughter's head. The weather was definitely cooler than what they had left behind in East Texas.

"What if they don't like me?" Danni asked.

"They'll love you, Danni." Jolie sat down on the bed, guided her daughter onto her lap, wrapped her in a hug and began to pull socks onto her feet. Danni could put on her own socks, but Jolie just wanted to hug her. "You just be yourself and you'll get along just fine."

"Can I wear my jewelry?" Danni asked.

Danni had a cheap little ring for every finger and tiny gold studs for her pierced ears. Jolie had bought her the junk jewelry, but the tiny earrings she had gotten when her ears were pierced were made of real gold. Jolie tweaked her nose. "Sure you can." Grateful her daughter no longer resisted enrolling in school, Jolie said, "Now. Put your shoes on while I find your sweater. We'll go to the ranch house for breakfast; then we'll go to the school."

At the ranch house, Jolie found nowhere to park except in the big barn's parking lot. Since it was full of pickup trucks, she assumed it was where the hands parked. The only other option was in front of the ranch house's four-car garage or on the circular driveway in front of the house. She chose parking in front of the garage, which caused her to have to walk around the building to the back of the house. She knocked on the back door and was met by the aroma of pungent spices and a Mexican woman who introduced herself as Senora Irene Asaro.

Irene had to be one of the jolliest, friendliest people Jolie had ever met. While she fussed around the kitchen warming tortillas, frying some kind of sausage, scrambling eggs with peppers and cheese, Danni and she began speaking to each other in Spanish. Jolie was surprised. She knew Danni had learned some Spanish in school, but until this moment, she hadn't known how much.

Knowing Jolie couldn't interpret what they were saying, Danni turned to her. "Senora Asaro says she doesn't have any kids and I can be her little girl. She's going to teach me to make chorizo."

Acceptance. Jolie laughed, feeling welcomed. In her mind's eye she could see herself and Danni fitting in just fine. So far, this was turning into a very good day. "I'm the one she needs to teach to make chorizo."

Irene nodded and said, "*Sí, sí.*"

The three of them were still laughing together when Jude came in, dressed in tan slacks and a green polo shirt. "Good morning," she said. "Hope you had a restful night."

Her long hair was pulled back and held at her nape with a barrette and she wore large gold hoop earrings. Jolie thought she looked very classy. "Yes, we slept good. It was wonderful. It's so quiet."

"Sure is," Jude said. "About the only thing we hear around here at night are coyotes."

"Will they come and get us?" Danni asked.

Jude smiled at Danni as she pulled a box of cereal from the cupboard. "They keep their distance. They're afraid of people." She poured cereal into a bowl, her attention still directed at Danni. "Want me to meet you at the school and help you enroll?"

"We don't want to put you to any trouble," Jolie said.

"No trouble. I'll be there anyway."

Irene handed Jolie and Danni plates of eggs and sausage and said something to her in Spanish. "She wants me to eat a good breakfast," Danni interpreted for Jolie and Jude.

A laugh burst from Jude. "Your daughter speaks Spanish?"

"Why, I guess so," Jolie said in amazement. "She must know more about it than I thought."

Jude gestured for them to sit down at the glass-topped table in the breakfast room. Jude brought her cereal to the table and Irene served them milk and juice.

"Your father and Mr. Fallon have already eaten breakfast?" Jolie asked Jude.

"They eat with the hands at four forty-five. It's something Daddy's done his whole life. I can't imagine him ever changing. And now Brady's gotten into the habit, too. I might as well forget seeing him early in the morning unless I wake up at four a.m."

While they ate, Jude told Danni about school. The fifth grade had ten students. Sixth grade had roughly an equal number. The same teacher taught both grades. Since the teacher taught the entire class at the sixth grade level, most of the fifth graders learned as much as the sixth graders. So if the fifth grade students could pass the tests at the end of the year, they could skip sixth grade and move right into seventh.

Danni's eyes grew wide with interest. "Really?"

Jolie could see that the idea of skipping a grade had hit a hot spot in her daughter. Some of her typical little girl enthusiasm was coming back and Jolie had Irene and her new employer to thank.

She felt encouraged about registering Danni under a different name. Surely a school that had so few students that two grades were taught as one would be more amenable to bending the rules a little.

After breakfast, as they left the house, Jolie sent Danni to the car so she could speak to Jude privately. "I'm wondering if it's possible I could enroll Danni with a different last name."

Jude didn't reply at once and she had a skeptical look on her face. "I don't know," she finally said. "I'm sure there are a lot of rules about that. It would be up to the principal. Do you mind if I ask why you want to?"

Jolie saw she had to tell her new boss some smattering of the truth. "Amanda must have told you my husband has alcohol and drug problems. If he found Danni at school, he might . . . well, I don't know what he might do. I don't want her life to be disrupted any more than it already has been."

"If you're worried about him harming her or taking her, Jolie, you should be talking to the sheriff. In this county, we're lucky. Our sheriff isn't just a country sheriff. He's been a hard-nosed cop his whole life. He's very capable of protecting you and your daughter. He's my cousin. If you like, I can speak to him for you."

Jolie felt a pinch in her stomach as she thought of her stolen license plates. The last thing she wanted was a hard-nosed cop snooping into her life for any reason. What she wanted was to fade into the woodwork and be left alone. She shook her head. "No, no, I don't want to call attention. It seems like things never turn out very well when cops get involved. There might be no reason to go that far."

But she knew Billy. If he was drunk or stoned, he was irrational. His temper was volatile and even sober, he might be out for revenge. "Look, I don't want to make waves. If I can just get Danni into school with a different name, that's all I want."

Jolie could tell by the expression in Jude's eyes she was reluctant to be an accomplice. But after a few seconds' pause, she said, "Okay, I'll see what I can do to help you."

Jolie gave a mental sigh of relief. Her positive opinion of her new boss rose a few more notches. Having help from someone who was rich and who owned this big ranch had to be a benefit.

It was close to noon by the time she was able to get away from the school. She left Danni in good spirits and already melding into the environment and chatting with other girls her age. She had seen the Dairy Queen when she arrived in town yesterday, knew it was on the main street, which was a highway passing through town. The highway appeared to be the only paved street in the whole town.

The DQ building was one of those round structures painted red and white, with windows all around it. From the looks of it, Jolie figured it had probably been built thirty years before her birth. It reminded her of drive-in restaurants she had seen in old movies. As she parked the Taurus nose-in in the parking lot, she recognized her cousin's pickup truck parked a few slots away. She could hardly wait to tell Amanda how well the morning had gone and that, with Jude's support, she had succeeded in enrolling Danni as "Danni Kramer."

To Jake, a cold ham sandwich for lunch in his kitchen held little appeal. He headed to the Dairy Queen. He parked in the DQ parking lot and immediately noticed an unfamiliar car. The older Ford Taurus in need of a paint job—faded brown color with one gray-primer-coated back door—was not an entirely unnoticeable vehicle. He spent a few seconds studying it.

Something about the car bothered him, but if someone asked him what, he couldn't explain. The concern came from that intuition that a thing wasn't always as it appeared, the arcane instinct that most good cops had. He knew most of the cars that belonged to residents of Willard County. In a population of fewer than two thousand souls, such knowledge was easy for a man with his training and experience. Beyond that, when some Lockett citizen was fortunate enough to acquire a new or different car or truck, it was the subject of gossip for days.

He ran through a mental list of people to whom such a car as the faded brown Taurus might belong, but no one came to mind. A few newcomers were in Willard County temporarily. An uptick in the oil and gas business had brought some new jobs, thus new citizens. Most were following the work and would move on. Not even one would stay in a place like Lockett. He pulled a small spiral notebook from his pocket and, just for the hell of it, jotted down the license plate number.

"Look," Amanda said, her face brightening as she looked out into the parking lot. "There's my boss. He eats lunch here sometimes."

Where else would he eat? Jolie wondered. She had always thought of Grandee as a tiny town, but compared to Lockett, Grandee was a metropolis. But that was fine. She had no complaint about the town. She glanced up and out the windows, just as a tall, lanky man emerged from a white SUV with a bar of red and blue lights perched on top and a black and gold WILLARD COUNTY SHERIFF logo on the door. He looked like many of the rural Texas sheriffs and deputies she had sometimes seen on TV news—pressed and creased jeans, long-sleeve dress shirt no matter the temperature, boots and a cowboy hat. He had a big gun strapped onto his belt.

"He looks like a movie star, doesn't he?" Amanda said, a dreamy glow in her eyes. "If I wasn't a happily married woman . . ." She sighed and let the sentence go unfinished.

Good grief, does Amanda have something going on with her boss? Surely he must have a wife. "Isn't he married, too?"

"No. He doesn't even go out with anybody in this town. Of course, I don't blame him there. Most of the single girls in Lockett are losers. He dated a schoolteacher who was here for a while. Everybody thought they were serious, but nothing came of it. She moved to Amarillo. I've heard he's dated some women in Abilene."

Jolie couldn't imagine the man she was watching "dating." It seemed like a silly word when applied to him. He paused in his step and gave her car a long look. Jude's words flew into her mind. *Our sheriff isn't just a country sheriff. He's been a hard-nosed cop his whole life.* Jolie felt a sudden surge of weakness and was glad she was sitting down.

A minute later, he sauntered toward the Dairy Queen's front door. Then before Jolie could get her breath, he was standing just inside the doorway, his hands resting on his hips as he perused the room.

He spotted them and touched the brim of his hat, then walked over to the order counter. After placing an order, he made a beeline for Jolie and Amanda's table. Jolie's eyes homed in on the gold badge on his shirt pocket and she thought her heart might leap out of her chest. But something less easily defined than alarm slithered through her system. Up close, he was even better-looking than he had been walking across the parking lot. What was wrong with her? She must still be suffering from the stress of leaving Grandee.

Amanda looked up at him with a look Jolie had never seen on her cousin's face. Jolie was nervous herself, but Amanda was behaving like a cheerleader with a crush on the quarter-back. "Hey, you didn't say you were coming here for lunch today," she said to him.

Dragging a chair back from the table, he flashed a grin that showed bright white against his tanned and slightly freck-led face. As he sat down, Amanda tossed back her long hair as if she were a schoolgirl. He set his hat on an adjacent empty chair, revealing reddish brown hair. Like Jude's, Jolie thought, but the sheriff's was shot with a few gray strands at his temples. He rested his crossed forearms on the table-top, the long sleeves of his shirt failing to hide muscled arms. Jolie didn't know if her own case of nerves came from be-ing at the same table with a cop or because he was one of the best-looking men she had ever seen in person.

"Wasn't in the mood for my own cooking," he said to Amanda. He had a low voice that seemed to rumble up from somewhere deep in his wide chest. "I assume you've or-dered."

"Yeah," Amanda said. "Diet food. Bacon cheeseburger with fries. We might top it off with a soft-serve cone for dessert."

He chuckled, the corners of his eyes crinkling. "Me, too."

"You'd better be careful, boss man. You'll have to run ten miles tomorrow morning instead of your usual five."

"You're right about that," he said.

Run five miles? Jolie couldn't imagine someone running five miles, much less ten. She doubted Billy could *walk* five miles. Of course she knew she couldn't judge most other men by Billy.

"Slow day today," Amanda said to him.

"Yep. But that's okay. In our business, slow's the best kind of day."

"Oh, Jolie," Amanda said, as if she had just noticed Jolie's presence. "This is Jake Strayhorn, my boss. Jake, this is my cousin, Jolie Jensen."

The sheriff did a half stand and offered his right hand. "Ma'am."

In Jolie's ordinary world, men had no manners. Even in the blue-collar world of the Cactus Café, she had encountered only a few men who offered courtesy. Thrown off balance by the show of chivalry on top of everything else, Jolie put out her own hand and stammered, "Uh, how do you do?"

As he took her hand, his eyes caught her. They were green—not partially, not sometimes-green-and-sometimes-brown, but a true pale sage green color outlined by a dark blue circle. And they seemed to be looking into her. She couldn't keep from looking back at him, even as she fought the urge to fidget in her chair. Her mind scrambled everywhere and landed on the fact that the sheriff and Jude were related. So why wasn't he working at the ranch?

Just then the counter clerk brought them their burgers in red plastic baskets lined with parchment, along with three red plastic glasses of Coke.

"This place makes the best burgers in Texas," Amanda said around a huge bite, but Jolie was almost too nervous to eat.

"You're the new cook out at the Circle C?" the sheriff asked, laying his cheeseburger in its basket and dabbing at his mouth with a paper napkin.

"Yessir, I am. Starting tomorrow." Jolie took a tiny bite and chewed self-consciously.

"Amanda said you came from over by Dallas?"

"Yessir—" She stopped herself. Calling him "sir" made her sound silly and childish. "I mean, yes, I did. A little town called Grandee."

He nodded. "I've heard of it. I lived in Dallas for a time."

Jolie's heart took off on another crazy tangent at the possibility, however remote, that he might have run into Billy. "It's a small town."

He nodded again. Now his attention was back on his cheeseburger. "Get your daughter enrolled in school okay?"

"Yes, she seemed to be having a good time when I left her."

He stopped eating and gave her a direct look. "That's good. If you or she have any problems, you let me know."

Jolie held a french fry suspended and swallowed a gulp. From a man like him, that simple statement was surely a promise.

And she wondered just how much he already knew about her.

7

The next morning, as Jolie made the twenty-eight-mile drive from the school in Lockett back to the Circle C ranch, she thought about all that was happening, including yesterday's encounter with the local sheriff and the obvious fact that Amanda, who had a husband and teenage kids, was nuts over him.

The sheriff was a good-looking guy and Jolie had to admit he had some kind of magnetism about him because he had stayed in her mind most of the night. She had awakened a few times and his green eyes and ruggedly handsome face had popped into her consciousness and made it hard for her to go back to sleep. She didn't understand it. She couldn't remember the last time any man had caught her eye.

This kind of thinking was ridiculous. Her and Danni's circumstances being so tenuous, attraction to a man was the last thing she needed. She had too many problems. And that grim reminder took her to contemplation of her future, which was just as uncertain now as it had been last week. The only thing she knew for sure was she could think of no reason to ever return to Grandee, Texas, or a life with Billy Jensen, even if he made a complete reformation. Where he was concerned, her heart was an empty well.

Looking back, she wondered if she had ever really loved him, but she didn't have to ponder why she had married him.

She had been sixteen and pregnant and he had promised to take care of her and their baby forever. He had betrayed her in so many ways.

The system had sent Billy to counselors, to rehab programs, to jail. None of it had ever worked. Billy had no discipline, no ability to stick to anything. He had never held a job for very long, never given up partying with his friends and blowing money they couldn't afford. He had been known to spend their last dime on booze or drugs. Jolie had learned more than she had ever wanted to know about alcoholism and drug use. With meth use came other women—sleazy, pathetic girls who were also meth users. Meth had been the last straw, a one-way trip to hell. At about the time she learned about it was when she mentally accepted that her life with Billy was over. Escaping physically had taken a little more time.

She forced her thoughts to Danni, who had come home from school yesterday afternoon excited about her new friends and her teacher and about fraternizing with sixth graders. She had jabbered all of last evening about her busy day, had even wanted to call her grandmother and tell her about it. With Billy having grown up in the Dallas foster system, no grandmothers existed on his side of the family. Jolie's mother was the only person Danni knew who carried the title "grandmother." And she was the only family member Jolie had stayed in touch with over the years.

Mom had known she was leaving Billy, but Jolie had shared no details with her. If the woman knew nothing, she could tell nothing. Thus, last night, Jolie had kept Danni from calling her. Jolie's cell phone's voice mail box wasn't overflowing with messages from her mother, either, a reminder, as if Jolie needed one, that she and her mother were not best friends. They got together at Christmas for Danni's sake, but in the interim between seasons, they had rarely chatted on the phone, hadn't often visited each other. Jolie had never taken her problems to her for a mother-daughter heart-to-heart. Always, she had solved her own problems as well as those of her younger sisters.

Still, Jolie sensed that the last few years, her mother had recognized the distance she had put between herself and her children and reached out. But in Jolie's mind, it was too late. Mom had been absent in spirit and body for too long. She had worked most of her life at odd hours juggling drunks and managing blue-collar bars in various locations around Dallas. She was a hard, self-centered woman who had been married four times, given birth to three children for whom she had little time, empathy or affection. She had missed every school event, no matter what it was, that Jolie and her sisters had participated in. In Jolie's mind, a stray cat was a better mother than Evelyn Kramer had been.

Now, Jolie supposed, her frayed relationship with her mother had ended as completely as her connection to Billy. She doubted Mom would ever make a trip to West Texas to visit and she couldn't imagine herself ever going back to Grandee. At some point—she didn't know exactly when—she had relegated her mother to a place in her heart only a few notches higher than Billy. *Hell.* She didn't even know what last name her mother was using now.

As she spotted the entrance to the ranch ahead, she forced her thoughts away from the past. She was knee-deep in the future and her day had started off too well to have it derailed. She felt safer than she had in years. The tension that had hovered in the background of everything she did was already starting to fade. She was determined to show the Strayhorn family they hadn't made a mistake by hiring her.

In the Circle C kitchen, she plunged into learning her job. The work didn't frighten her. She suffered no lack of confidence when it came to cooking, though she wasn't a trained cook. She had no doubt she could manage the kitchen, though she had never had a restaurant manager's job. She had worked with food and food service for all of her work-

ing life. First as a teenager in fast-food joints, then as a dishwasher and waitress and sometimes cook in busy cafes. The
Cactus Café, for instance, located at an intersection that was
an interstate exit, was a large, busy place, with customers
ranging from truckers to travelers in luxury RVs. Beyond
that, being the oldest of three sisters and with her mother
working long hours for as long as Jolie could remember, at
a young age, out of necessity, Jolie had taught herself to cook
and manage their small household. The Circle C Ranch's
kitchen couldn't be much different.

Jude had told her no one would be eating breakfast or
dinner through this week, but she, her husband, Brady, and
her father would all be present for supper every evening at
seven and Jolie should not be surprised if unexpected guests
showed up. By now, Jolie had figured out that in this household, "dinner" was lunch and "supper" was dinner and they
expected a full meal every evening.

The respite from having to prepare lunch for the coming
few days would give Jolie the time and opportunity to get
acquainted with her environment. She started with being shown
the formal dining room by Irene. Jolie had never seen anything like the old long, massive oak table with its twelve
leather chairs that were surely antiques. She was awed by a
massive mahogany sideboard, which must be an antique as
well. It stood on one wall. Columns of carved curlicues and
leaves flanked its gold-veined mirror. The huge iron chan-
delier that hung over the table looked like something she
might see in a fancy restaurant and cast an amber light over
the table. Beautiful western paintings hung on the walls.
Jolie believed they must be originals because each one of
them had those little rectangular lights hanging over them.

On the wall behind one end of the table hung a large
grainy black-and-white photograph of a tall man in a suit
and vest and wearing a big hat, standing alongside an American Indian with a braid and a blanket folded over his shoulder. Irene didn't know who the people in the picture were,
but Jolie sensed that both images were men of importance.

Being in any part of the Circle C ranch house was like being in another world, but in the dining room, that feeling was especially prevalent.

Midmorning another Mexican woman appeared. She introduced herself as the housekeeper, Lola Mendez, and made a point to say in English only slightly less broken than Irene's that she ran the household outside the kitchen.

They moved from the dining room into the kitchen and Irene showed her where to find all of the dishes and cooking utensils in the cabinets. Jolie had never seen such a well-equipped kitchen. It had almost every tool a cook might ever need. The basic food stores were kept in a hall-like pantry off the kitchen. Behind that, she found another huge room large enough to be a bedroom. She stood in the doorway, staring in amazement, realizing that this huge room had been a pantry, and it made her wonder how many people had lived here back in the old days.

The walls were lined floor to ceiling with shelves that held a little bit of everything. Irene pointed out an oversize freezer in the back corner of the room. Jolie wound her way through various pieces of furniture, boxes and piles and opened the freezer. It was filled with packages wrapped in white butcher paper, which Jolie assumed was meat. There was also an abundance of other frozen food.

Among the miscellaneous items, she found a package of frozen puff pastry dough and immediately thought of the delicious individual chicken pot pies Donna Harmon sometimes served in the Cactus Café as a lunch special. Jolie had helped make the pies herself many times when the kitchen had been shorthanded. If she had been able to produce a product fit to sell in the demanding Cactus Café, she could do it now. She pulled out the puff pastry and a chicken, telling Irene she would thaw it and cook it for supper.

Back in the kitchen, Irene dragged a brown paper sack out of the refrigerator and began lifting out foil-wrapped packets. "You like tamales?" She opened a foil packet.

"Are those homemade?" Jolie asked.

"*Sí.* I make. At my home. Senor Strayhorn, he love. You want?"

"For lunch? Of course. I love homemade tamales."

Irene heated the tamales in the microwave. Her husband, Reuben, came in and the three of them sat down at the breakfast table for lunch, struggling to communicate with each other in languages none of them fully understood.

After lunch, Irene took her to the cookhouse to meet the chuck wagon cook, Buster.

The cookhouse was a long walk from the ranch house. Jolie was no judge of distance, but she decided it must be a good half mile. Through a storm door, they entered a long building made of wood painted white and attached to one end of a bunkhouse. The aroma of sweet cooking fruit met them. They stepped into a huge dining room with windows all along two sides and various ranching artifacts hanging on walls made of boards also painted white. The space was furnished with several long tables with benches, sort of like extra-long picnic tables Jolie thought, except that the tables and benches were highly varnished. A potbellied woodstove stood in one corner of the room. Overall the room had a welcoming old-fashioned atmosphere.

"Buster?" Irene called out.

"I'm in here," a raspy male voice answered from an adjoining room. They found the owner of the voice in the kitchen at an island counter doing something with dough. On seeing him, Jolie instantly thought of a character out of the movies. He had a white handlebar mustache and white wavy hair sticking out in spikes from under a ragged cowboy hat. He wore a Western shirt, jeans and boots and a white butcher's apron. All that was missing from his costume was a pair of spurs.

Irene introduced her in Spanish, so obviously Buster spoke Spanish.

Buster wiped his hands on his apron and came toward them. He was so bowlegged he almost waddled. He put out his right hand. "Buster Wardlow, ma'am. I know the family's glad you're here."

"I'm glad to be here," Jolie said, smiling and shaking his hand. "Something sure smells good."

"Oh, you must mean that peach smell." He turned toward where a Mexican woman was stirring something in a big pot on the stove. "Juanita and me's making a few empanadas outta some fresh peaches I got down in Abilene a couple of days ago."

"Oh, that sounds so good," Jolie said. She had never made the small pies herself, but she was familiar with them. "It's early for fresh peaches, isn't it?"

"Come up from South America. Guess it ain't too early down there. Juanita does a fine job. We add a few pecans just to dress 'em up a little."

"Hmm. Peaches and pecans. That does sound good."

"Yep. The hands all like 'em."

"I'll bet," Jolie said, looking around. All of the equipment was commercial-type, she noticed, made of stainless steel. "Maybe you can teach me someday."

"I heard Miz Jude had hired somebody," Buster said. "This yer first day?"

"Yes. I'm getting acquainted with everything. I'm starting out by cooking just suppers this week. Jude said her father and her husband eat breakfast out here in the cookhouse."

"Yes, ma'am, they do. J.D.'s been eatin' breakfast with me for as long as I been the cook here. We all like havin' him eat with us. The old man never would come out 'cept ever' once in a while. Sometimes J.D.'d bring him out and he'd eat dinner with us."

Jude nodded, having no clue who he meant.

"Grandpa. He die," Irene said, as if she sensed Jolie's confusion.

"Oh, pardon my manners," Buster said. "Old man Strayhorn, I meant. Jeff. He passed on a year or so ago. Next,

poor old Windy followed 'im. Hard thing, Windy dropping
dead like he did. Him and me knowed each other a long
time. Cowboyed together when we was kids."

Jolie nodded again. She hadn't heard much about the
former cook.

"How can I help you?" Buster asked.

"I don't know right this minute, but Jude told me to call
on you if I needed to. She said you feed forty people every
day."

"Yes, ma'am, we do. Breakfast and dinner. For supper,
the hands have to make do for theirselves. Right now we
got about forty-five who come and eat with us. The Strayhorns are real generous. They believe a belly full of good
food makes a good cowhand."

He showed her around the large kitchen, a butcher room
and a cold room where sides of beef and pork hung. "Oh,
my gosh, you do your own butchering?"

"Yes, ma'am, we do. We feed Strayhorn beef, but we buy
pork from a pig farmer down by Abilene. Chickens, we get
from Lucky's. Feedin' two meals a day to forty-five hungry
cowboys takes a lot of grub. This is where you'll come get
yer meat if it ain't already in the freezer in the big house. You
want a roast, some good steaks, maybe some pork loin and
you can't find it, just tell me and I'll cut it for you."

"Oh, my gosh," Jolie said again. "That's really something. I'd like to know how to butcher."

"Well, then. Next time I cut, I'll let you know. If you got
the time, you can come out and I'll give you a lesson or two.
Ain't nothin' to it. Just takes a few sharp knives."

After they finished the tour of the cookhouse, Buster
said, "Hon, I don't know what yer experience is, but just do
the best you can and don't be nervous. Strayhorns are real
long on toleratin'. You couldn't be workin' in a better place."

And at the moment, Jolie didn't disagree.

Back in the ranch house, now that she knew what food
items she had on hand, she sat down at the glass-topped breakfast table to plan the week's suppers from what was already

available. Irene told her the family liked dessert after supper, so Jolie added desserts to her meal plans. Following that, she baked a chocolate cream pie for the coming evening meal. A long time ago, one of the cooks at the café had taught her how to make cream pies from scratch and everyone loved her pies. When she started to clean up, Irene shooed her away from the sink, communicating that it was her job to clean. Jolie felt like a real chef.

While Irene cleaned up after the pie-making and before starting on the chicken pot pies, Jolie set out to explore the huge pantry off the kitchen. On the back wall next to the freezer, she spotted three shelves of old cookbooks. Besides the books in print, she found journals containing recipes handwritten in old-fashioned writing with fading ink on yellowed paper.

One in particular caught her eye. It was fancy, with a deep burgundy tooled leather cover and ornate silver corner protectors. A handwritten label on front said PENELOPE ANN'S FAVORITES and she wondered who Penelope Ann was. Probably not the hired help, Jolie determined, considering the quality of the book. Thumbing through it, she found page after page of recipes written in nearly perfect calligraphy-like script. Some of the pages had grease spots, some had smeared ink. The recipes had obviously been used. At some point, this Penelope Ann must have enjoyed cooking.

A sense of history settled around Jolie. For the first time, she started to realize just how old this ranch and the family that employed her were. She couldn't imagine what it must be like to live with such deep roots. The oldest thing she possessed was her car. And she couldn't put her hands on her birth certificate if she had to.

By the end of the week, Danni actually wanted to ride the school bus to be with the new friends she had made. Jude and Brady and Mr. Strayhorn had heaped profuse compliments on the meals Jolie had created and requested more pie. She had heard not one word from anyone in Grandee. Common sense told her this was only the lull before the storm, but she intended to make the most of it. Her spirits had never been higher.

On Saturday morning, having decided to make a pie from a recipe she found in "Penelope Ann's Favorites," she realized the pantry was lacking a few ingredients. She made her way to the cookhouse to see if Buster's pantry held what she needed. When she and Buster concluded that he couldn't help her and he wouldn't be placing a wholesale order for another ten days, he told her to just make a list and go shopping in town at Lucky's. Jolie felt confident enough to do this. Mr. Strayhorn told her that though the ranch had an account at Lucky's, he preferred she shop with a credit card. He gave her one with the ranch's name on it and the keys to one of the ranch's pickups and away she went. Inside, she glowed at the idea that after only a week, Jude and her father put so much trust in her.

After perusing the small grocery store's limited inventory and shopping for an hour, she had filled her cart. Since she was shopping, besides picking up the items she needed, she filled in some miscellaneous things she liked using as well as boxes of Jude's favorite cereals. She rolled her full basket to the checkout, where a blond cashier awaited her.

When she handed over the credit card, the blonde said, "Holy cow, you're the new cook." She came around the end of the counter and stuck out her hand. "I'm Suzanne Breedlove." Jolie offered her hand and the blonde pumped it heartily. "Jude Strayhorn, well, Fallon now, is my best friend. I'm telling you, you couldn't be working for a better bunch of people than the Strayhorns."

"I feel really lucky," Jolie said.

"Jude told me you're not married."

Jolie hesitated. Why, she didn't know. It would be normal for Jude, or anyone, to discuss a new hire with her best friend. "Well—"

"Separated, huh? Listen, I know how that goes. Half my girlfriends are separated or divorced. There's a few single women in Lockett, but only a few. And even fewer single men. This isn't a very big place, you know. But I could introduce you."

In the course of planning her escape, Jolie had given zero thought to a future social life.

Caution surged within her. For now, she would be better off to just stay at the ranch and leave socializing for another day. "That's nice of you, but I don't think I'm going to have much free time. I have a ten-year-old daughter, too, and I always help her with her homework."

Suzanne flopped her hand at her. "Oh, I know you're busy. But everyone needs friends. Just let me know when you're ready." Suzanne returned to the cash register, yanked off the receipt and handed it to her. "Want me to get someone to help you load all this stuff?"

"Okay," Jolie said. "I'd appreciate that."

Suzanne spoke into an intercom. "Eddie, come up front. A good-looking blonde needs help loading her groceries."

Jolie couldn't keep from laughing.

"He's a teenager," Suzanne said. "We don't see that many good-looking blondes around here."

8

Jake strolled up the sidewalk toward Maisie's Café, intending to enjoy a cup of good coffee. He hadn't run his five miles this morning and he felt a need to get his butt off his chair and move around. Preoccupied as he was with planning the rest of his day and paying little attention to his surroundings, a second too late he became aware of the grocery store's plate-glass door swinging open. He jumped backward, but couldn't avoid colliding with an exiting grocery cart filled with plastic sacks. He caught himself on the edge of the door to keep from falling.

In the confusion, the grocery cart escaped and rolled up the sidewalk with Eddie Moore, Lucky's stock boy and all-around helper, chasing after it. It bumped off the sidewalk, teetered a few seconds, then turned on its side on the pavement. Its entire contents spilled onto the street.

Jake started toward the cart to help, but a blond woman rushed to his side, looking up at him and clasping his forearm. He recognized her as the new cook at the Circle C. Julie? Joey? He couldn't remember her name exactly. She was a head shorter than he. And she did have the deepest brown eyes. But her hair was the color of straw.

"I'm so sorry," she said. "Are you hurt?"

"No, ma'am," he answered, too embarrassed at his exhibition of outright clumsiness to look directly at her.

Suzanne Breedlove appeared in the grocery store's doorway. "Are you all right, Sheriff? What happened?"

He felt like a fool. "I'm okay," he answered, raising a palm.

Up the sidewalk, Eddie had righted the cart and was now picking up the sacks. Jake strode toward him, leaving the two women at Lucky's door. "Let me give you a hand," he said to Eddie as he squatted and began to help him.

"Oh, God, Sheriff, I'm sorry," the teenager said in a rush. "I didn't look before I went through the door."

"Not your fault, Eddie," Jake told him. "I should've been watching where I was going."

Now the blond woman and Suzanne were beside him helping put the last of the sacks back inside the cart. After the task was done, all of them straightened and he looked down at the woman. "You okay?" he asked her, not certain if he had crashed into her, too.

She laughed. "I'm totally okay. You and the grocery basket came out the worst."

He managed to laugh, too, still feeling sheepish. "Yeah," he said, and thumbed back his hat. Eddie had wheeled the cart over to the bed of the white pickup truck. With its brown Circle C logo on the door, Jake recognized it as the one Windy Arbuckle had always driven. "Let me help Eddie load those groceries into your truck." He walked over and helped Eddie lift the sacks out of the cart and into the bed. Eddie repeated that he was sorry.

"It's no problem, Eddie," Jake told him.

"Yessir," Eddie replied, backing away. He was almost shaking.

Jake watched as the kid grabbed the cart and pushed it away from the truck bed. Eddie was obviously afraid of him. He had never meant for law-abiding people to be afraid of him, but he seemed to have that effect on teenagers. He didn't know if that was a good thing or a bad thing.

"Back to work," Suzanne said to Eddie, grabbing him by the shirtsleeve.

"Thanks, y'all," Jake said.

"You're welcome," Suzanne replied with a wicked grin. "I wouldn't have missed that dido you did with the front door for anything." She and Eddie and the empty grocery cart disappeared back into the grocery store, leaving him alone on the sidewalk with the woman. He felt unsettled and uncertain, as if he had to say something. "Shopping day at the Circle C, eh?"

Shit. That was on a par with *Nice weather we're having.* But he was the first to admit he had never been an artful conversationalist with women, especially those he didn't know.

"This is my first shopping trip for the ranch," she said, smiling.

She had a pretty smile, but she still seemed nervous, just as nervous as the first day he met her, which continued to puzzle him. He was the one who should be nervous. And she still aroused the same curiosity he'd had about her the first day he saw her. He couldn't quite put his finger on why. Maybe he just needed to get to know her better. If she was employed by the Circle C, she was now a Lockett citizen. "Before the crash, I was headed to the café to get a cup of coffee. Want to join me?"

She glanced at the truck bed and the pile of grocery sacks. "Well, I—"

"Oh, you've probably got groceries in there that'll spoil."

"No," she said too quickly. "Actually, no, I don't. It's mostly stuff for the pantry."

"You don't have to worry about anyone in Lockett stealing the sacks," he said. When she didn't agree to accompany him right away, he added, "Maisie's got awful good coffee."

Jolie hesitated a few more beats. How could she say no? He was the law. If she turned down the offer, he might think she had done something illegal. She drew a great breath to quell her stress, and the scent that filled her nostrils was his aftershave. It smelled clean and woodsy and only made her more nervous. She had come in close contact with only a few men who smelled good. "Okay, sure. A cup of coffee sounds good."

Maisie's was only three doors away from the grocery store, so in a matter of five minute they were seated and had ordered coffee from a plump woman with frizzy hair. The lunch crowd hadn't started to congregate. Except for a couple of men at the counter, they had the place to themselves.

"So, how's it going for you out there at the ranch?" he asked her, setting his hat on the chair seat to his right. He crossed his forearms on the tabletop, which made him seem even closer to her.

"So far, so good," she answered, hoping she appeared normal but wringing her hands in her lap under the table. "I haven't had any mishaps and the family seems pleased."

He nodded. "You'd hear about it if they weren't. They aren't usually ambiguous in expressing their feelings."

Uh-oh. Ambiguous. She didn't know the meaning of that word. She couldn't remember ever hearing anyone say it.

The waitress reappeared with a coffee carafe, turned over the mugs sitting upside down in front of them and poured them full of coffee. "Anything else I can getcha?" she asked.

A questioning look came at Jolie from the sheriff. Jolie looked up at the waitress. "No, thank you. I'm fine."

"We're all right, Nola Jean," the sheriff said.

As soon as the waitress left, Jolie glanced across the table at the sheriff, who was already sipping his coffee. Of course he drank it black. That fit the impression she had of most cops because that was what the DPS guys patrolling the interstate did when they had come into the Cactus Café. "Uh . . . what does that mean exactly?"

He set down his mug. "What does what mean?"

"I . . . I don't know that word you said."

His eyes narrowed, and then he cocked his head and said, "Ambiguous?" He sat back. "I should've used a different word. I should've said they're straightforward. They don't play games. If they don't like something, they'll tell you."

"Oh." Jolie smiled, then added both cream and sugar to her coffee. "I like that." She sipped and said, "This really is good coffee."

She reached for the purse she had set on the floor beside her chair, dug into it and came out with a pen and a notepad. He watched her. His gaze was unnerving, but she always looked straight at people when she talked to them. Tilting her head to the side, she said, "What's the word again?"

"Word? . . . Oh, the word. Ambiguous." He picked up his cup and sipped again.

"I try to write down new words I hear so I can look them up later." Then she realized she didn't know how to spell it. Holding her pen poised over the notepad, she said, "Can you spell it?"

The sheriff chuckled. "Mind you, I haven't spelled it in years, but here goes." He spelled the word and she wrote it on a blank page in the notebook.

"There's a study in the ranch house that has a whole wall of books," she told him. "Jude said for me to feel free to use them. There must be a dictionary." She looked up at him, feeling embarrassed by having to ask him the meaning of a word, but she still managed to smile. "I want my daughter to be smart, so I need to set an example."

The sheriff nodded. "I see. Is your daughter a good student?"

"She is. She's in fifth grade. She's really excited about maybe skipping ahead. I don't know for sure, but I'll bet she can do the work. But next year, she'll only be eleven. That seems to be too young to be in seventh grade."

Jake smiled back at her. He had good teeth, even and very white, and his eyes crinkled at the corners. "Well, it isn't quite that simple. The kids have to be able to pass a test. And to be honest, few of them do."

"Oh," Jolie said, a part of her relieved. In her mind, seventh grade was a huge step for Danni. "Since she hasn't gone to school here all year, she might not pass, then."

One of his shoulders lifted in a shrug. "But if it's any

consolation, believe it or not, Lockett has a good school. I went to it myself until about ninth grade. Most of the young people who leave here fare pretty well against students from bigger and richer schools. Somehow, this little place has gotten ahold of good teachers. Your boss has a lot to do with that, I suspect."

That bit of information was no surprise. It appeared that the Strayhorn family influenced everything in the county, maybe in the whole state of Texas.

A tiny regret stabbed Jolie. She hated to think of Danni leaving to go to college or work somewhere away from her. But she could see there was zero opportunity for young people in Lockett. "And the kids do have to leave, don't they? I can see that. But that's a long way off for Danni. I'm just trying to get her through one day at a time. I don't know what the future holds for us."

He pushed his mug aside and again folded his forearms on the tabletop. His eyes locked on her face. "So, tell me about that. You've come here running away from something? Or somebody?"

Her heartbeat kicked up. Was this some kind of interrogation? Her fingers tightened on her mug handle. "Not really, no." He still seemed to be studying her, as if he were looking inside her head and heart. Did he not believe her? As smart as he was, even if he didn't think she was lying now, he would probably figure it out soon. "Or at least I don't call it running away," she added. "A lot of people might say I ran away from Grandee. But I—I call it leaving something I can't fix and moving on." Her hand dropped to her lap again and she felt herself clasping her hands in a tight knot.

"It's true enough that some things in life can't be fixed," he said. "And some things are out of your control. Sometimes the best plan is to do what you're doing. Moving on."

Suddenly this conversation sounded more personal than two strangers merely having a cup of coffee. Now her curiosity outweighed her nervousness. "Have you ever had something in your life that couldn't be fixed?"

"Indirectly. Most people have. In my case it was a long time ago and I, too, moved on. Look, I want you to feel at ease. I want you to feel free to talk to me."

"Has, uh, Amanda told you about me?"

"No details. Just said you're changing your life."

Jolie heard the front door open behind her and the sheriff glanced toward it. She resisted the urge to turn around, telling herself it couldn't possibly be Billy. The sheriff lifted two fingers in greeting to whoever came in and she felt her shoulders sag with relief.

"Local rancher," he said, and smiled, as if he sensed her anxiety. "Small operator. Nothing like the Circle C."

She smiled, too, and let out the breath she had suppressed. "I know it's a big ranch. And they have so many animals. No one's told me much about it. Amanda just said it's huge. How big is huge?"

"Big. More than three hundred thousand acres. More than half this county. Last I heard they had 469 sections under fence."

"Sections?"

"In big ranching country, people talk about land by sections. A section is a square mile."

Jolie felt her eyes widen as perspective dawned on her. Never had she known anyone who owned so much. "Oh, my gosh. You mean they have fences around 469 miles? That's a lot of fence wire, isn't it?"

Jake chuckled. "It sure is. And when I was a boy, my cousins and I rode horses over a good part of it. So, where did you grow up, Grandee?"

She didn't want to tell him she had grown up in several little towns outside Dallas, that her mother had dragged her and her sisters from one to the other, depending on whom she happened to be dating or married to. "I was born in Terrell," she said, in lieu of going into detail.

The sheriff signaled the waitress to bring more coffee. For a reason Jolie didn't understand, she decided to just tell him more about herself. "My mom worked—actually, still works—as a bartender and bar manager. We sort of moved around to wherever she could find a job that paid better than the last one."

"Amanda did tell me your husband was abusive."

Damn Amanda. Why would she tell him, or anyone, about her problems with Billy? Then she remembered she had never told Amanda she had divorced Billy. She swallowed. "Is, uh . . . is this an official conversation?"

"No. I'm trying to be your friend."

She turned her head and stared at the floor. "Well . . . he didn't beat me up if that's what you're getting at." She thought of the last fight she and Billy had had. He had been so drunk or stoned, or both. He had grabbed her arm and flung her against the refrigerator. She returned her gaze to the contents of her mug. "He just . . . sort of pushed me around a little sometimes. . . . But I was afraid it was coming to something worse." She looked up again and into his penetrating eyes. "And that's part of why I left."

He sipped, then carefully placed his mug back on the table. "No matter what the feminist movement and the movies would like for us to believe, in physical strength, most women are no match for a man. Is your husband a drinker? Involved with drugs?"

What should she tell him? She looked away again and nodded.

"Did you participate?"

She shook her head. Thank God she could say that honestly. Looking back on it, she couldn't say how she had avoided it. "Danni was born when I was seventeen. I always had her to take care of. And I always had to hold down a job."

He continued to look at her and she felt a need to somehow defend Billy, not wanting Jake Strayhorn to think she had chosen a loser for a husband. "Billy wasn't so bad in the beginning."

The sheriff took a notebook from his shirt pocket. "Tell you what. Give me your husband's full name."

She felt as if a stone had dropped in her stomach, felt her eyes bulge. "Why? I don't want him to—"

The sheriff stopped her with a lifted palm. "I won't do anything that'll lead him to you. I just want to know who he is, in case he shows up."

She gave him Billy's full name, his birth date and a physical description. The sheriff wrote in his notebook and slid it back into his shirt pocket, giving her a smile. "Everything's going to be okay," he said.

She believed him. Even if she didn't necessarily feel it herself, she believed that the tall, taciturn man across the table from her could make it so.

"We can talk about something else if you want to," he said.

"Oh. Well . . . uh, I don't know what to say." As a flood of relief washed over her, she managed to smile. "You said you left here in ninth grade," she said. "Why did you leave?"

"Family blow-up. A long story. Not worth repeating."

"But you came back?"

"I've traveled over half the world since then. I consider Lockett my hometown. I lived here longer than I ever lived anywhere else. You can never forget home. I believe everybody's got a yen to go back home, and I'm no different."

"Oh, my gosh," she said. "If somebody asks me where my hometown is, I make up something. I wish I could feel like some place is home."

He smiled. "If you stay around long enough, maybe you'll feel that way about Lockett."

9

Billy Jensen hadn't expected to run into Ginger O'Neil when he went to Pop's Pizza & Burgers for a pizza, but here she was, sitting at a table with two little kids. They were eating hamburgers.

He had always thought Ginger was kind of good-looking, even if she was a little on the chunky side. He knew she was several years younger than Jolie. She had brown deer eyes and long straight brown hair. Today she was wearing it in a ponytail that was starting to come loose and had fallen to one side and her skin looked sweaty and shiny. His eyes traveled to her breasts. Man, one of those big bazooms would fill up both of his hands.

He didn't know Ginger that good, but he knew that like Jolie, she was a waitress at the Cactus Café. And somebody at that café had to know where Jolie had gone. So far, all he had gotten from the owners was a cold shoulder. And he hadn't dared call Jolie's mother again.

He ordered a small pizza with pepperoni, took his number and paid. It was cool that the State of Texas let him buy pizza with his Lone Star card, which was just like having a free credit card. That was the good thing about Jolie divorcing him. When they had been married, she had made too much money for them to get food stamps. Now, since he didn't have to pay for food, he could use his money to buy other stuff.

He sauntered over to Ginger's table. She had on one of those tight-fitting tops with skinny little straps that looked like they were straining to hold everything up. Standing in front of her, he looked right down the front of it and he could see that one of those soft-looking titties had a big red rose on it. The edge of it stuck out of the neck of her top. Sexy tattoos turned him on big-time. He felt a quirk in his shorts. "Care if I sit down?"

"Oh, hi, Billy. Sure. Take a load off."

He sank to the one empty chair at the table for four. She was unwrapping a straw for one of the kids seated with her. One was dark haired and dark eyed and the other was blond and fair. "You babysitting today?" he asked her.

She huffed a laugh and her cleavage jiggled. "Not hardly," she said, stuffing the unwrapped straw into a cup of something and handing it to the little blond girl. The kid's face was dotted with grease and mustard. "These are my kids. That's all the babysitting I need."

"Oh," Billy said.

He must have been looking more closely at the two kids than he realized because she said, "I know what you're thinking. Yeah, they got different daddies." She pointed to the dark one. "Rosie here belongs to Alonzo Flores. You know him, don't you?"

"Naw," Billy answered.

She moved her finger to the blond. "That one's Emily. She's Jason Wilson's."

"Oh, yeah, I know Jason. I didn't know he had any kids."

"He don't admit it. He thinks she ain't his 'cause we only did it once and I got knocked up." She grinned. "Well, we did it more than once but it was just one night. I could prove she's his if I had the money to get one of those tests."

The thought of sex took Billy's gaze to her nipples that showed like little peas on the front of the bright green top. What had been a quirk in his pants became a stir. Shit, he had lost track of the last time he had gotten a little. Jolie had cut him off a long time ago. This chance meeting had suddenly taken on rewarding possibilities. "Yeah, well, that can happen, I guess."

The counter clerk called his number. He shifted, left his seat and picked up his pizza.

"What do you hear from Jolie?" Ginger asked when he sat back down.

He wasn't about to admit to somebody Jolie had worked with that he hadn't heard from her since she left nearly two weeks back. "Oh, she's havin' a good time, her and the kid."

"I knew she would. She talked about her cousin in West Texas sometimes and how much she liked her."

Bingo! Jolie's cousin Amanda. He knew she lived in some hick Podunk town in West Texas, but he couldn't remember the name of it. He leveled a look at Ginger. Where there was one bit of information, there was bound to be another. "She did? What else did she say?"

"Not much. She didn't talk that much about her life."

He opened the box and offered Ginger and the two kids some pizza.

"We've had enough," Ginger said.

He dug into the pizza. Hell, he hadn't eaten all day. "So, Ginger," he said around a greasy bite, "where you goin' from here?"

"Nowhere. I'm off for two days. I'm just hanging out."

"Me, too," he said, scarfing down another big bite of pizza. Feeling grease on his chin, he grabbed a napkin and wiped it off. The little dark-haired girl stared at him big-eyed and he again offered her and her sister some pizza. Tentatively, the little girl reached for a piece, then tore it in half and gave some to the blonde.

"You ain't working?" Ginger asked.

"Not right now. I was cleaning up on construction jobs for a few days, but that petered out. House-building's gone to hell around here. None of the builders are hirin'."

"Yeah, I know. Practically everybody I know's out of work."

"My ol' truck's been broke down, so I been workin' on it." And he had spent damn near his last dime on it, too.

"Get it fixed?"

"Looks like it. 'Til it breaks down again." He laughed and she did, too. "Listen, since you're just hangin' out, want me to hang with you?"

One corner of her mouth tipped into a half smile. "Sure. Why not? Jolie's gone, right?"

"Aw, to hell with her. She's nothin' but a narrow-minded bitch."

"But no drugs. I could lose my kids."

He shook his head, lifting another slice of pizza. "I'm clean." And he had been for more than a week.

"Okay. But I should drop my kids off at my sister's. I don't want them around while . . . well, you know."

"Okay." He gulped down more pizza, unable to believe his good luck. "I don't know where you live. Guess I can follow you."

"Okay."

He wiped his hands on another napkin, now more interested in Ginger than food. He leaned across the table and spoke in a low voice. "Want me to, uh, get some rubbers?"

He had a lot of faults and he knew it, but he had always been careful of both disease and unwanted pregnancies. Back in the day when he and Jolie still got it on, she would have kllled him if he had brought her either.

Ginger shrugged. "I ain't got any. And I sure don't need any more kids."

He nodded, knowing a Walgreens was located in the shopping center. "Don't go anywhere. I'll be right back." He pushed the remaining pizza toward the two kids and left the table.

"You're getting married?" Jude said on a gasp as she came out of the bathroom, her cell phone pressed against her ear. Yet, while her best friend's news was stunning when presented suddenly, it wasn't really a surprise. For at least a year, Suzanne had spent almost all of her free time with Pat

Garner. Pat had been head over heels since he first started working with Suzanne's horse Buck. She and Pat had come to the Circle C together for supper several times and even Daddy had called them "lovebirds."

"When?" Jude asked.

"We're thinking summer. Sometime after Pat's mom and dad get through with branding."

Pat's parents were small ranchers in a neighboring county. July popped into Jude's head. "I can't believe it. Good grief, you'll have to change Buck's name to Cupid."

Suzanne laughed. "I should, shouldn't I? Cupid the Horse. I wonder if he'd like that."

"So now I don't have to worry if Mitch is still lurking in the dark shadows of your mind?"

Jude followed the remark with a laugh, though it was only half a joke. Ever since Suzanne had returned from wherever she had been during the years she had been away from Lockett, she had made cryptic remarks about her former relationship with a ProRodeo bull rider named Mitchell McCutcheon. To this day, no one, including Jude, knew if Suzanne and he had been married or had been just lovers. Whatever they were, they'd had a stormy relationship that had left Suzanne bruised physically, devastated emotionally and giving up on men. Jude felt positive Pat Garner would never treat her so badly.

"I'll never hear from Mitch again," Suzanne said. "If he was interested in me, he could've found me easily enough."

Another answer that avoided the question about her true feelings for the mysterious Mitch.

Jude didn't want to believe she had heard a rueful note in Suzanne's reply, but she was sure it had been there. And this made her wonder if Mitch showed up tomorrow whether Suzanne would change her mind about Pat. "What prompted Pat to pop the question? He's so shy, I'm surprised he found the nerve."

"Maybe *I* prompted him a little. I told him I want kids and he said the only way he'd agree is if we make it legal."

"Kids? You?"

"Yep. And soon. You're not the only one with a biological clock, you know. We want a boy and a girl. The boy's gonna have wavy brown hair and brown eyes like Pat and the girl's gonna be blond and blue-eyed like me. That's what we both want. We even want to get married in church."

"I'm so excited, Suzanne. That's such great news. If it's going to be a summer wedding, we could have the reception here at the ranch, out on the patio. I could ask Buster to barbecue."

"Hmm. You might need to rethink that." A somber tone had sneaked into Suzanne's voice. "Pat's asked Jake to stand up with him. Of course he'd want his best man to be at the reception."

Uh-oh. "Do you think Jake wouldn't come to the ranch?"

"Hell, he's *your* cousin. And it's *your* family scandal his dad was involved in. What do you think?"

"I don't know. I honestly don't know. I do know he hasn't been to the ranch since he came back to Lockett. He didn't even come when Grandpa died, even though Cable was here. Cable wouldn't have seen him at all if he hadn't gone to his office in town."

"Has Jake ever been invited to the ranch?" Suzanne asked. "Since he came back, I mean."

"I don't think so. I'm fairly sure Daddy has never invited him, and if Grandpa did, nothing was ever said. You know how Grandpa was. No one was ever more closemouthed than he was."

Suzanne sighed. "That river runs deep, girlfriend. I don't suppose anyone will ever know that whole story."

"I know what you mean. Except for Daddy and Jake's mother, the people who do know it are all dead or dying."

"I'll see if Pat will ask him if he would be willing to go to a reception at the Circle C. Listen, Jude, I appreciate your volunteering to do that. A backyard barbecue would be great, especially in a backyard like yours."

"Well, if I'm going to be matron of honor, hint, hint, the least I can do is have the reception. It'll be part of my gift."

"Oh, my gosh. I completely forgot to ask you about the matron of honor thing. I guess I just took it for granted that you'd know you'd be it. You'll have to overlook me. I haven't planned that many weddings."

They talked a few more minutes and disconnected, laughing.

"Was that Suzanne?" Brady asked, glancing up from his book. He read in bed every night.

Plugging her cell phone into the charger, Jude smiled at her husband. "Suzanne and Pat are getting married."

"The hell."

"This summer. After branding."

Brady closed his book. "Wow."

Jude crawled between the covers and he laid his book aside. She snuggled close to his warm body. His arms came around her and pulled her closer still. "I just told her I'd do the reception here, but there's a small problem."

"Which is?"

"Pat's going to ask Jake to be his best man."

Brady's low chuckle coming from his wide chest vibrated against her ear. "Jake's seeing a lot of action as best man. He might decide he'd rather be a groom."

"I can't imagine. But you know Jake better than I do. Has he said something to you? Is he interested in someone?"

Brady's fingers stroked her arm. He was a big man, but his touch was soft as lamb's wool. One thing she had learned about him was that he was a "toucher." If they were near each other, he was touching her somewhere. She loved that about him. "No, but he's got a lonesomeness about him these days. Sometimes I think he might be tired of living alone. He bought that old Petry place out on the canyon rim."

"He did? When?"

"Closed on it a couple of weeks ago."

"I've been to that place," Jude said. "It's got a decent house and barns."

"If the right woman came along, ol' Jake might fall."

"Not Jake. He's probably thinking about somewhere to retire after he no longer wants to be sheriff. If he were asked to be best man at a friend's wedding, do you think he'd relent and come to a reception at the Circle C?"

"I don't know, but I doubt it."

She flopped to her back and stared at the ceiling fan, lifting and opening her palms for emphasis. "But why? I know all that stuff about the Campbell Curse and the family scandal, but no one here's ever been mean to him. We're his family."

"He might see *you* as family, but it stops there."

"What if I talked Daddy into asking him?"

Brady turned to his side and propped himself on his elbow. His free hand slid under her flimsy short gown and began to stroke her body.

"Now, can you see that happening?" he said. The backs of his fingers trailed down her stomach. "I haven't known your dad long, but I spend some part of just about every day with him. I've never heard him mention Jake's name. And I've never had the nerve to mention Jake to him, either."

Now his fingers were tracing her hipbone and she was having a hard time concentrating on this conversation. "I just wish someone would tell me what happened. It seems ridiculous for a member of the family not to be able or willing to come and visit at another member's house."

"It's Jake's choice, sweetheart. And your dad's. Whatever happened all those years ago is a mountain that neither one of them can see over and neither is willing to climb. Leave it alone. If it's meant to be, things will work out." His large hand came to her stomach. "How's our boy tonight?"

Jude smiled and turned to face him, belly to belly, wriggling against his erection. "She's just fine. I really can't tell she's there."

"Did I hear you say she?"

She looked into his eyes and kissed him and they became lost in a long, languorous kiss. When their lips parted, she said, "Suzanne says they want to have kids."

"She's jealous?"

"It would be fun, the two of us having kids the same age."

Brady began to trail kisses down her neck to her breasts. "Let's talk about it later."

Two days later, Billy Jensen left Ginger O'Neil's house. If he hadn't run into her, he would never have thought of Jolie's cousin Amanda. He still didn't know Amanda's address, but it had to be somewhere in the trailer. He headed home.

10

The following Thursday, Buster invited Jolie to ride to Abilene with him to shop for fresh fruits and vegetables at the farmers' market. "Thursday's the best day to go," he said, "'cause you catch the vendors when their stuff's just been brought in fresh and you miss all them weekend shoppers."

They left as soon as lunch was over. As they made the hour-and-a-half drive, Buster asked how things were going in the kitchen now that she had gotten her feet wet. "Just fine," Jolie told him, and for the entire trip they talked about cooking.

At the market, they found fresh vegetables and Jolie picked up an assortment, plotting in her head what she would do with the squash she bought, the melons and berries, the tomatoes and cucumbers. She had already fallen into the routine at the Circle C of having freedom in the kitchen. She loved creating meals. And the family was so generous in their praise. Jude had called her dishes "kinder and gentler" than what the previous cook had prepared. Jolie didn't know what that meant, but she took it as a compliment and was thrilled by it.

Buster bought bushels of potatoes and a huge bag of dried pinto beans. "I cook beans and taters and corn bread with every meal," he said. "In my kitchen, you can even have 'em for breakfast if you want to. And some of the boys like to."

Jolie laughed. She loved working with Buster. She was

used to camaraderie with the male cooks at the Cactus Café. Buster was one of the most entertaining people she had met in a long while. And she liked being privy to the man's world the cookhouse was. The only women in the kitchen were Buster's two helpers.

On the way home, she said, "Jude's trying to put together a wedding reception for her friend Suzanne. She said you might be barbecuing in that big pit on the patio."

"I might. They're waitin' to see if the sheriff's gonna say he'll come to it."

The mention of Jake set off a little squiggle in Jolie's stomach. Having her mind and body react to everything related to him was becoming annoying. "I don't understand this family," she said. "There's all this talk about whether or not Sheriff Strayhorn will come to the ranch. If Jude and him are first cousins, it seems strange that he wouldn't."

"There's a lot of family history there, darlin'. And where Jude and her cousins are concerned, most of it ain't good."

"Did something bad happen?"

"It was before my time. All I know is what I heard."

Jolie couldn't resist the story, even if it was second- or even thirdhand. And she could tell that Buster was itching to tell it. "What happened?"

"Well, there was three of them Strayhorn boys, you see. And all of them and their families lived in the big house. Hell, why not? You could bivouac a small army in that ranch house. J.D.'s the oldest. Ben was the middle boy and—"

"Was?"

"He's dead. He went off to Vietnam and got hisself killed. Then his wife, who disappeared after the funeral, turned up dead in California. Killed herself with drugs." Buster shook his grizzled head. "I wasn't here when all that was goin' on, but it must've been a helluva mess back then. Windy told me a little about it. Ben and his wife was both just kids, but they had a little boy. Old man Strayhorn went to California and got him and brought him back here. Jeff and his wife, Ella, raised him. They call him Cable, but his real name is some combination of all these Strayhorn family names. I forget what it is now."

"Where is he?"

"He lives off back in East Texas or someplace now, but back then, him and J.D. and Ike and their families all lived at the ranch."

"Ike is the sheriff's father?"

"Was. He's dead, too. He was the youngest."

"And all of those people lived in the ranch house at the same time?"

"Yep. 'Til the trouble started."

"I can tell a big family once lived here just by looking at that huge pantry behind the small one," Jolie said.

Buster gave an old man's heh-heh-heh. "Oh, yeah. Darlin', when Miz Penny Ann was alive, that room was packed full of everything imaginable from home canning to stuff imported from overseas. The Strayhorns have always had high taste in food."

Penny Ann instantly translated into the name Jolie had seen on the old leather cookbook, Penelope Ann. "Who is that?"

"Old man Strayhorn's mother. Jude's great-grandmother. Died just a few years ago. She was ninety-four."

"Was she a cook?"

"Lord, girl, that woman was everything. She *was* the Circle C, more than any of the men. I admired her deeply."

"You knew her?"

"And what's more important, she knew me. And every other hand at this ranch. And their families. She was one fine woman."

"My goodness," Jolie said, feeling a reverence for a woman she would never know. "I found one of her cookbooks in that big pantry. I didn't know who she was, but her recipes look good. I've been thinking of cooking some of them."

"I don't know about Jude, but if you cooked a dish out of that book, I guarantee you J.D. would recognize it. And it would bring him some good memories."

Jolie was more intrigued than ever about this pioneer family into which she had fallen. "You were telling me about the trouble."

"Oh, yeah. Got sidetracked there for a minute. Well, the story is that Ike, being a rounder and a hell-raiser, got tangled up with J.D.'s second wife. Then one night while they's drinkin' and havin' a good time, they had a car wreck that killed the both of 'em."

"Oh, my God. Jude's mother?"

"Naw. Jude's mother was J.D.'s first wife. She was from back East. She took a powder early, when Jude was a baby. I never knew her. Far as I know, she never came back here, neither. Not for any reason. Some folks say the old man paid her to stay away. With him being dead and all, I don't s'pose anybody'll ever know fer sure if that's true."

"What happened after the car wreck?"

"I can only imagine, knowin' J.D. like I do. Story is he didn't even want Ike planted in the family cemetery. J.D.'s an even-tempered man, but he ain't nobody to mess with. If he thinks he's gettin' screwed over, and he gets his hackles up, there's usually hell to pay.

"Fer sure, what Ike and J.D.'s wife done was a scandal that tore the family apart. Jake's mother took him away from the ranch and they never came back. Fact is, from the way the talk is, it sounds like Jake ain't set foot on the Circle C since he was a kid."

Jolie sat in silence for a few beats while the Strayhorn family and its stories and their consequences sank into her consciousness. This must be what Jake had meant that day they had coffee in Maisie's, when he said that sometimes things happen out of your control. "I don't get it. Jude seems to be friends with the sheriff."

"Jude and Jake *are* friends. But Jude's daddy prob'ly can't look at Jake without thinkin' 'bout what happened, even though he ain't got no truck with Jake personally."

"That makes me sad for the sheriff. He would've been just a boy when that happened. It wasn't his fault."

"You don't need to feel sorry for him. He does all right. They all keep their distance and that seems to be the best. Things is easier around the ranch right now than they've been since I been workin' there. Old man Strayhorn dying and Jude getting married to Brady changed the air. In all the years I've cooked for 'em, this is the first time I've ever seen J.D. act like he's a happy man."

"Gosh," Jolie said, feeling like a part of some big family soap opera, which was ridiculous because she had her own drama to worry about. She was living on borrowed time. Any day now she expected Billy to appear or some kind of issue to crop up over her license plates.

At the city limits sign, Buster slowed his speed and they passed through town. Maisie's Café was located on the corner of the main street and some other street that intersected it. The café was housed in a two-story brick building. The back of the building was visible from the street, along with a long string of stairs leading to a second floor. As Buster picked up speed leaving town, Jolie, remembering her coffee klatch with Jake, glanced toward Maisie's and saw a familiar person coming down the stairs: Mr. Strayhorn.

"What's on the second floor of the café?" she asked.

"Maisie's apartment. She lives up there. Why?"

"I just saw Mr. Strayhorn going down the stairs."

"You sure?"

"It was him. Is he friends with Maisie?"

"Ever'body's friends with Maisie, but I doubt if J.D.'s been to her apartment. You must've seen somebody else, darlin'."

Jolie said no more, but she was certain the person she saw was her new boss and she was equally sure Buster had just blown her off. He knew as well as she did that it was Mr. Strayhorn that she saw. Now her curiosity was aroused. When the opportunity arose, she would just ask Jude, she decided.

The Circle C ranch house was two miles from the massive front gate on the highway. The school bus picked up the children of the ranch's families at the gate every school day morning and let them off in the afternoon. Once Danni had started riding the bus to and from school, Jolie had driven her to the gate in the mornings and picked her up in the afternoons. Having expected to be in Abilene all afternoon at the farmers' market, Jolie had arranged for Irene's husband to pick Danni up and bring her back to the ranch house. When Jolie reached the kitchen, Danni was there, telling Irene in Spanish about her school day.

Jolie had planned an uncomplicated supper—chicken-fried steak with mashed potatoes and cream gravy, fresh corn on the cob and green salad. Irene had already floured tenderized cuts of round steak and had them laid out on a large platter.

As Jolie began putting away her purchases, Danni accompanied her into the small pantry and helped her. "Mom, I told everybody at school what a good cook you are."

Jolie was preoccupied with stashing potatoes in their bin in the pantry. "You shouldn't tell people that, Danni,"

"I told them you'd make cupcakes for the party. With icing."

Jolie straightened, bumping her head on a shelf. "Ow! What?" She found and rubbed a knot on the back of her head. "What party?"

"When school's out. I told them about the chocolate ones with the chocolate icing. You know, the ones you put the chocolate chips inside?"

"Danni, I don't know if I can do that. How many cupcakes would they need?"

"There's twenty-two in our class and we want to invite the third and fourth graders. There's thirty of them."

Jolie added the number in her head. "Danni, that's fifty-two cupcakes. Are the other mothers making some, too?"

"Nooo, Mom," Danni whined, frowning. "Your cupcakes are best."

Just then, Jude came into the kitchen and stuck her head into the pantry. "Hey, Jolie, did Danni tell you about the school's-out party?"

"Yes, she volunteered me to make cupcakes."

Jude laughed. "Do you want to?"

"Well, I haven't thought about it. Danni thinks I make some kind of secret recipe, but what she doesn't realize is I just use cake mix. I sort of try to make them better by adding chocolate chips and frosting them with chocolate buttercream. They aren't really special at all."

"Sounds pretty special to me," Jude said, smiling. "They sure have made an impression on Danni. She told everyone at school about them. If you want to do it, the ranch will furnish the stuff to make them. School won't be out for two more weeks, so the party won't take place until the last week."

"How many cupcakes would that be?"

"Umm, let's say eight or nine dozen. Some of the parents usually show up."

Jolie blinked at Jude and nodded. "Okay."

But she didn't feel that it was okay. Cooking a meal for three people was one thing, but baking and frosting eight or nine dozen cupcakes and keeping them fresh was another.

"You can use the cookhouse ovens and equipment. I'm sure Buster and Juanita and Mary will help you."

Jolie nodded again.

"Oh, by the way," Jude said. "Brady cut some firewood and some kindling for you. He stacked it at the corner of your house earlier."

"Brady cut wood?"

"He likes doing things like that. Says it keeps him in shape."

"I don't know what to say," Jolie said. "Danni and I were wondering where we would get wood. We've, uh . . . never had a fireplace."

"Do you know how to build a fire?"

"Uh . . . I don't know. Do you have to do something special?"

"When Brady comes in from the barn, I'll ask him to

come show you how. It's going to be a cool evening. A fire will feel good."

"Okay," Jolie said.

While she waited for the potatoes to boil, she put the floured steaks in the big cast-iron skillet to fry. She found a store-bought pound cake in the freezer, then hulled some of the fresh strawberries she had bought at the farmers' market. When Mr. Strayhorn heard she was serving chicken-fried steak with potatoes and gravy, he brought the man who was the horse wrangler to eat. Everyone raved over the meal. As soon as it was over, she and Danni went to their cottage. She was worn out.

When they arrived, she saw a pile of wood stacked at the end of the house. Soon, she heard a tap on the door. Brady came in carrying some wood pieces he said were kindling and showed her how to make a fire. He said he was headed back to the house to build a fire in the fireplace in his and Jude's bedroom. Jolie couldn't imagine. She didn't know how many fireplaces were in that ranch house, but there had to be several.

After Brady left, Jolie and Danni sat shoulder to shoulder and watched the flames for a long time. She had never been near a fire in a fireplace. Trailers didn't have fireplaces. The world was full of so much she had never seen and never done. She intended better things for her only offspring.

"It's like a campfire, isn't it?" Danni said.

Jolie pulled her daughter close into her embrace. "A little. When were you ever around a campfire?"

"I've seen one in the movies. It isn't very warm, is it?"

"I think you'd have to stand closer."

"How long will we live here, Mama?"

"I don't know. As long as the Strayhorns like my food, I guess." *Or until Billy shows up and ruins everything for us*, she thought but didn't say.

"I like it here. Everyone's nice."

"You're right, Danni. We're in a good place."

"The sheriff came to school today."

That familiar little squiggle darted across Jolie's stomach. "He did? Why?"

"He talked to us about safety this summer, after school's out. Our teacher invited him."

"Oh," Jolie said, relieved he wasn't there seeking information about Danni.

"But my friend Madison said the real reason she invited him is 'cause she's got a crush on him."

"Isn't Mrs. Gibson married?"

"Madison said she got a divorce and she's looking for a man."

Jolie suppressed a grin. Another single female with a crush on the sheriff. "Did he know who you are?"

"Uh-huh. I'm the only new kid."

Jolie swallowed. "Did he . . . talk to you?"

"Uh-uh. He asked me about school in Grandee. And he asked me how you are."

"He did? What did you tell him?"

"I told him just fine. I think he likes you, Mama."

A laugh burst from Jolie's throat. "Why would you say that, Danni?"

"'Cause he asked me sort of privatelike, so none of the other kids heard him. The teacher didn't hear him, either." She drew a great breath. "He's nice."

Jolie thought he was nice, too, and she didn't even know why.

She thought of Buster's words: *Jake ain't set foot on the Circle C since he was a kid.*

She couldn't imagine living every day forever in luxury like that in the ranch house. If the sheriff had lived there once as part of the family, he must carry a terrible hurt not to ever go back.

11

As if they were neon, every time Jolie walked from her little cottage to the carport, ready to drive to the ranch house, her license plates glared at her from the back bumper of her car. Even with all that was going on in her life—learning her new job, helping her daughter adjust to a new school environment, getting acquainted with more new people than she could count—the two small metal rectangles lurked in the background. Until now, she had known of no one she could discuss the situation with. Buster's name had floated in her mind every day since they returned from the trip to the farmers' market and he had talked to her so freely about the Strayhorn family. She felt positive she could ask him how much trouble she was in over exchanging her plates with a car back in Grandee.

She waited until the lull after dinner, the dead time before supper had to be started, and made her way to the cookhouse. Entering without knocking, she found Buster cutting dough into strips, his hands covered with flour, his gnarly fingers lifting the delicate strips as if they were fine china. The big dishwasher hummed in the background and Buster's two helpers were at the sink washing pots and chatting in Spanish. They had just finished serving the big meal of the day and the two women were cleaning up.

She loved the huge kitchen in the cookhouse. It always smelled wonderful. It reminded her of a restaurant kitchen, and in many ways that was what it was. Probably plenty of restaurants didn't serve the number of meals every day that Buster and his helpers did.

"Hey, young'un," he said with a big grin.

"Whatcha making?" she asked, grinning back.

"Puttin' together a little cobbler for tomorrow's dinner. Ya see, I put it all together today, slap it in the freezer, then bake it tomorrow in time to serve hot for dinner. It'll be larrupin'. What's goin' on in the big house today?"

She saw a huge bowl of peeled and sliced applies on the counter. "Well, I'm not making apple pie. But I did make a pie from a recipe I found in that old 'Penelope Ann's Favorites' cookbook. I made it out of plum jam. I never heard of a pie made out of jam before."

"And how'd it turn out."

"It was good. Different."

"I bet J.D. loved it."

"He said so anyway." She lowered her voice and said, "Listen, Buster, can I talk to you about something personal?"

"Sure you can, darlin'." He wiped his hands on his apron. "Want a cup of coffee? A glass of sweet tea?"

"Tea would be fine."

He turned and spoke to the women at the sink in Spanish. While Juanita pulled a large tumbler off the shelf and filled it with ice cubes and tea, Buster poured himself a cup of coffee. Juanita handed her the glass and Buster gestured toward the long dining room, now empty of diners. "Let's go in there where it's quiet."

Jolie thought the dining room a pleasant place. Today, all of the windows in the long room were open and green smells from the outside wafted in. They sat down opposite each other at one of the varnished tables. Buster dragged over an ashtray and lit a cigarette and listened while she told him about exchanging the license plates with a car parked in the Cactus Café's parking lot.

"How much trouble do you think I'm in?" she asked at the conclusion.

"Darlin', you're askin' the wrong person." Looking past her as if he were thinking, he took a drag off his cigarette and blew out a plume of smoke. "Guess you could go ask somebody in the courthouse in town."

She frowned. A courthouse, *any* courthouse, was the last place she wanted to go for information. "I was hoping not to tell anyone official about it."

"If they don't already, sooner or later, those folks that own that other car are gonna know 'bout it. Even if they ain't memorized they own license plate number or don't notice they got a different one all of a sudden, all it'll take is one little stop by the po-lice. Then *boom!* The whole thing blows up on ya." He jerked both hands up to indicate an explosion. "Why'd you do such a thing anyway?"

She leaned forward, speaking in a low tone, not wanting to chance that anyone, even the two women in the kitchen who supposedly spoke only a smattering of English, might overhear. "My ex-husband—his name's Billy—has done some things that are illegal. I was afraid he might've used our car. I was afraid the cops might have a record of the license number and I could get stopped and arrested."

"Hmm," Buster said, drew on his cigarette, then dumped the ash in the ashtray. "Look, here's what you do. Next time you go to town for something, stop by the sheriff's office and fess up to ol' Jake." He picked up his mug and sipped.

"No! . . . I couldn't do that. Jude said he's a hard-nosed cop. He might arrest me. At the very least, he'd tell her or Brady and I'd get fired." The thought caused tears to rush to her eyes, but she blinked them back and cleared her throat. "And, Buster, if I lose this job, I've got nowhere to go. Danni and I'd be homeless."

Buster ground out his cigarette. "Darlin', Jake's tough, but he's not mean. I've run into him m'self a couple of times when I had a little too much hooch. I can tell you for sure, he's more interested in helpin' than hurtin'."

"Really? He seems so . . . well, stern. He makes me so nervous."

"Don't think like that about him. He's a good man and a smart man. Knows more about the law than anybody I know. Just go tell the story you just told me. He'll help you fix things."

"Well . . . I don't know . . ." She shook her head.

But after what Buster had said, the idea of discussing the problem with the sheriff of an isolated small town was starting to seem like a good idea. She was far enough removed from her escape to look at it more clearly. And weren't people always saying cops were supposed to help people?

"You think about it," Buster said. "I'd be surprised if liftin' a license plate's a bad crime."

That was possible, she supposed, and wished she was smarter about things. When she left Grandee, she had been so focused on getting away and so fearful of getting caught, her thinking had been clouded.

Buster rose from the bench seat with his coffee mug as if the matter was settled. "Wanna help me finish up this apple pie?"

Maybe the issue *was* settled. Maybe the right thing to do would be to go talk to the sheriff.

"Okay," she said, and followed him into the kitchen.

Jake's Wednesday turned out to be a busier day than usual. Chuck and Amanda both had taken personal days, leaving him alone in the office, and some damn fool had broken into Lockett's only coin-op laundry. The burglar had used a tool to jimmy the locks on the five dryers and stolen the quarters. Silas Belcher, the laundry's owner, estimated about two hundred dollars was missing, but Jake could tell three or four times that much damage had been done to those dryers.

Being the only game in town, Jake had to do his own crime scene work. He took two dozen pictures, dusted for fingerprints around the coin boxes inside the dryers and told Silas to come in and leave his own prints to compare to the ones lifted from the coin boxes. After studying the damage, he concluded the tool had probably been a tire iron or a crowbar.

He stopped off at the bank, told the manager about the robbery and asked her to be on the lookout for someone who had an extraordinary number of quarters he or she wanted to convert to dollars. The bank manager laughed and said, "You don't really think a burglar would come in here to trade his quarters. He'd know we'd suspect him."

"Beverly, criminals aren't the smartest people I ever met," Jake told her. "If he can't figure out there's not much money in a small-town laundry, he most likely won't figure out that you might put two and two together."

"I'll alert everyone," she said, still laughing.

He returned to his office to eat lunch and catalog what little bit of evidence he had and file it away.

On Wednesday afternoon, Jolie made a grocery list of items to pick up from Lucky's. She had spent the entire night talking herself into taking her problem of the license plates to the sheriff. She hadn't seen him since the day they'd had coffee together in Maisie's Café. But just because she hadn't seen him didn't mean he hadn't been on her mind. She couldn't stop thinking about him, how wise and strong he seemed. And she thought she could see in him what Buster had described—that he was a helpful person. She even feared she might even have joined the posse of local women who had a crush on the sheriff.

She wrote the stolen license plate number on a piece of notepaper and stuck it in the pocket of her jeans. Because grocery buying was part of her job, she drove the pickup Jude had told her to use. She wasn't about to drive the car into town and take a chance the sheriff or his deputy would spot her crime and impound the car.

At Lucky's, when she rolled her cart up to the cash register, Suzanne was waiting for her with a big smile. "Hi, there."

Jolie really liked Suzanne and almost felt a kinship with her. The enthusiastic blonde reminded her of some of the friendships she'd had over the years with different employees at the Cactus Café. She smiled back. "Hi."

Suzanne began to check the groceries in the cart, quickly scanning bar codes and bagging the items as she talked. "How's your daughter getting along in school here?"

"She loves it. She's made friends with every kid in the elementary grades. And she really loves hanging out with sixth graders. It makes her feel so grown up she's starting to treat me like one of her peers instead of her mother." She finished the comment with a laugh and Suzanne laughed with her.

Somehow the conversation veered to Suzanne's upcoming wedding. She talked as if she and Jolie were old friends, which made Jolie feel as if she were part of the festivities. Suzanne said that she and Pat had been to Abilene over the weekend to buy Pat a new blazer. The plan at the moment was that he would wear a modified Texas tux and a silver and turquoise bolo tie.

Jolie had never seen a tux of any kind except in pictures. "What's a Texas tux?" she asked.

"Starched and ironed jeans and a tuxedo jacket," Suzanne answered. "Most guys wear Wranglers or Cinch jeans. But Pat isn't wearing a tux jacket. He's just going to wear a black blazer."

"Oh," Jolie said, thinking after Suzanne described it that she had seen men dressed like that before on TV. "What are *you* wearing?" she asked.

"I'm planning to wear an ivory prairie dress, tan cowboy boots and a retro Queen of the Rodeo hat with a big turquoise-colored bow."

"That sounds so pretty," Jolie said, thinking about her own wedding. She could barely remember it, but she recalled that her mom had bought her a green flowered dress on sale at Walmart and a pair of black shoes. The fact that green wasn't a good color for her was low on the list of considerations. Back then, Jolie hadn't known she looked awful in green, nor had she worried about it. She was just glad her mother had been willing to buy the dress. Otherwise, she might've had to get married in worn jeans and flip-flops.

Mom had also bought Billy a pair of black pants and a white shirt. At that time, Billy was nineteen, working as a clean-up man wherever he could find a job. He barely had enough clothes to cover himself day to day and had none that even came close to being a wedding getup. She hadn't known it then, but Billy had already been playing with drugs for several years.

Knowing Suzanne lived with her father, she asked, "Where will you live after you get married?"

"We'll live at Pat's. He's got a nice house. He rebuilt the old house that was on his place to suit his ex-wife, but she didn't like it. Dumb woman."

"It doesn't bother you that he built it for someone else?"

"Lord, no. I don't get het up about stuff like that. What's he gonna do, tear it down? It's a good house. Big and roomy. We're thinking about adding another barn and starting to board horses."

"Wow," Jolie said. "That's so cool. Pat gives horseback riding lessons, doesn't he?"

Suzanne laughed. "Yeah, but he doesn't have many students. This is West Texas, forgodsake. Everybody who's got a horse knows how to ride it. He does work with a couple of barrel racers and calf ropers, though. Why do you ask?"

"I've been thinking about something my daughter could do this summer after school's out. She wants to learn to ride. She's ten, but will soon be eleven."

"Good Lord, girl, you couldn't be in a better place for her to learn. There must be somebody around the Circle C who'd teach her."

"I don't know who it'd be. Everyone's so busy. Besides, it's something I want to do for her on my own. How much does Pat charge?"

"I don't know what he'd charge for teaching a kid to ride. Probably not much. I don't know if he's ever done it. But I'll ask him for you."

"Thanks. Does he have a horse that would be good for that?"

"I'm sure he does. He's got a lot of horses."

"Great. I'll check back with you when I'm in town again."

"Next time you come to town," Suzanne said, "I'll take a break and we'll go to Maisie's for a Coke. We can visit and get better acquainted."

A little ball of excitement burst inside Jolie's chest. Every friend she had ever had had been an employee at the Cactus Café. And those women came and went like passing through a revolving door. "Really? That would be so much fun. I'll be sure to make extra time."

She gathered her sacks and said good-bye. She left the grocery store in an upbeat mood and started for the sheriff's office. At least Amanda would be there for moral support.

Buster had told her the sheriff's office wasn't in the courthouse, but was in a separate building across the highway. He had also told her it was the sheriff's living quarters and the jail.

Lockett had a town square of sorts, with the courthouse sitting in the middle. It was a new one-story building and Jolie wondered if it had replaced one of the old fancy courthouses that existed in so many Texas small towns. She drove all the way around it, but saw no building that looked like a sheriff's office or a jail, either. Just when she was about to go inside the courthouse and ask directions, she spotted a small brown wooden sign with white letters that said SHERIFF'S OFFICE →.

She followed the arrow's direction to a one-story wooden building that didn't even look like a good house, much less a government building. It was pink, although it had probably started out as some kind of brown. The intense West Texas sun could bleach the color from anything. The only thing that helped her recognize the building as the sheriff's office was loops of razor wire atop a tall fence on one side of it.

Parked near the door was the white SUV she had seen at the Dairy Queen on her first encounter with the sheriff. She didn't see Amanda's pickup.

She entered a reception area, but still didn't see Amanda. She heard footsteps coming in her direction and looked toward a doorway that led to what looked like a hall. Her stomach began to tremble. And then, before she could catch a good breath, the sheriff appeared in the doorway.

"Good morning," he said, smiling as he stepped into the reception area.

For a full five seconds, she was speechless. He was so tall. And so handsome. And he seemed to fill the room.

"Is—is Amanda here?"

He placed his hands on his hips. "She's off today. Had some personal business to take care of."

"Oh." Jolie felt awkward that she didn't know that about her cousin. In fact, she didn't know Amanda well enough to be privy to what was going on in her life other than surface information. Since the hamburger they'd had together right after Jolie's arrival, she had talked to Amanda on the phone only twice. Jolie hadn't pushed the relationship, feeling her cousin had already done enough for her.

"How's it going?" the sheriff asked.

"Fine. . . . I, uh . . . I—I need to talk to you about something."

"Come on in," he said, smiling as he stood aside and gestured toward the hallway.

He led her into a small office and offered her an armchair. She sank to the cushioned seat woodenly, sitting on the edge, her purse balanced on her knees. He took a seat behind his desk and rested his forearms on his blotter, obviously waiting to hear what she had to say. "What can I do for you?"

She drew a deep breath and blurted, "If a person took

someone's license plate, what would happen to them?" The question didn't come out of her mouth even resembling the one she had rehearsed a hundred times in her mind.

He cocked his head to the right, his eyes narrowed. "Depends on the circumstances. Somebody take your license plates?"

"No. I just wondered if—if it's a bad crime."

He sat forward, picked up a pen and began turning it in his fingers. "Technically, no. It's property theft. And petty theft at that. A set of license plates for a car usually costs under a hundred dollars."

"Oh," she said as a flood of relief washed over her. "So a person wouldn't go to jail?"

"Like I said. Depends on the circumstances." His head tilted again. "Maybe you'd better tell me what you're really talking about."

All of the tension she had carried for weeks exploded inside her like a breaking dam. Tears rushed to her eyes and spilled onto her cheeks. "It's me," she sobbed. "I'm the one who did it. I stole someone's license plates."

12

Having seen many upset criminals, Jake was mostly immune to tears. But something about this delicate-looking woman had attracted his attention the first time he saw her, something besides the fact that she was good-looking. She looked fragile on the outside, but he detected a well of inner strength. *Whoa!* He didn't usually think of weeping women making confessions as either pretty or ugly or strong or fragile. He simply thought of them as suspects, tried to maintain objectivity and obtain the needed information.

Somehow this young woman had gotten under his skin and aroused his instinct to protect something softer and weaker than he, not as an officer of the law, but as a man. And he had to admit that he hadn't met many women lately who made him feel that way.

He came to his feet, dragged a chair that sat against the wall to her side and offered her a box of Kleenex. He was close enough to catch a faint whiff of a clean-smelling scent that he liked. "Now. Tell me what you're talking about," he said. "All the details."

She snatched a couple of tissues and dabbed her eyes. Between sniffling and weeping, she told him of taking the license plates from a fellow employee's car in the parking lot of a café where she used to work in East Texas, and replacing them with plates from her old Ford. Worrying over going to jail and leaving Danni without a mother had been in her thoughts day and night.

Once she started talking, the whole story spilled out almost in one long sentence. She also told him about sneaking away from Grandee in the wee hours of the morning in a raging storm. He listened without comment, finding it unnecessary to prompt her. She hadn't looked at him once through her whole confession. He leaned forward, bracing his elbows on his thighs so he could look at her at eye-level. "First things first. Let's deal with the license plates. I'll have to cite you for stealing them."

"I know," she said, her eyes downcast, her fingers shredding her tissue into confetti. She made a deep sniffle.

He plucked another tissue from the box and handed it to her. "But since I don't believe your motive was to commit a greater crime, it'll be like a traffic ticket."

She blew her nose and looked at him over the Kleenex. "Really?"

"You'll have to see the judge, but I'll talk to him about meeting with you in his office. You won't even have to go into the courtroom. With my recommendation, he'll levy a fine, you'll pay it and that'll be the end of it."

"I don't have any money," she said, looking down at her hands clasped in her lap. "I mean I've got a little that I've been saving to buy Danni a desk." He detected a faint quirk at the corner of her mouth. "I don't get paid much at the Circle C," she added.

Jake knew that to be a fact. It was the same with most of the Circle C employees—not much cash, but a lot of benefits. Jake believed that was how his grandfather and his uncle kept employees for life at the Circle C Ranch. It was almost as if they adopted people and gave them an allowance rather than hired them. "It won't be a big fine. But Danni might have to wait a little while on the desk."

She nodded. "Will—will everyone know?"

"You'll have to reregister your car."

She nodded. "That'll cost money, too, won't it?"

"Yes, ma'am, it will."

She heaved a great sigh and looked off to her right.

He was tempted to offer to pay for the registration for her, but he shoved that idea from his mind. He couldn't engage in such a glaring conflict of interest. She would have to find the money to pay the fine and register her car on her own. The most he could do for her was not throw the book at her for lifting someone else's plates.

He was more concerned with what she hadn't told him about the husband. Amanda hadn't been an encyclopedia of information, either. He had to wonder how or why Billy Jensen had intimidated such a sweet gentle woman to the point where she had felt a need to handle leaving him as she did.

Jolie had already told him the day they'd had coffee at Maisie's that the guy was a substance abuser and she had feared more serious domestic abuse loomed ahead of her. Those two violations were the most common crimes most cops dealt with and they frequently went hand in hand. He knew the stages of escalation in domestic abuse: A nudge became a shove, a shove became a slap, a slap became a punch and on and on until some stoned or drunk asshole, left unchecked, put his wife or girlfriend in the hospital with grave injuries. Or picked up a gun.

If Jolie was going to live in Willard County, in all likelihood, sooner or later the husband she had left behind would come looking for her, which could turn into a law enforcement matter.

Jake usually knew if and when new people came to town. That same day they had shared coffee in Maisie's, Jolie had given him a description of the husband. If Billy Jensen showed up in Willard County, he should be easy to spot, especially if he tried to find a job. Little or no employment existed except at the Circle C Ranch. The few drilling and oil field servicing companies that had recently moved in typically brought their own people, and drifters weren't welcome in their ranks. He personally knew most of the county's permanent citizens and even a few of their relatives from out of town. He made a mental note to keep his eye peeled for a skinny, blondish, thirty-one-year-old man who would probably have "trouble" tattooed across his forehead.

"Would you like a Coke?" he asked Jolie.

She finally looked up and at him, her nose and eyes red and swollen. "I guess so. But my eyes are all red. Where would we go?"

"I live here. I've got some Cokes in my refrigerator."

She nodded.

"Just stay where you are. I'll be right back." He got to his feet and left the office for his apartment, where he filled a glass with ice cubes and Coke. He carried the glass and the Coke can back to the office and handed them to her. Then he took his seat again and said, "Okay now, tell me everything about your husband and what he's been up to."

As they sat side by side, their knees almost touching, she told him how Billy had been in trouble his whole life. But only minor trouble until he got into drugs, she added, defending him. Jake knew human nature. He knew she was really defending her own bad choices. That was common.

Billy had been in jail, but not prison, she said. She didn't know everything he had done. Jake would be able to look up his record, and even if his wife didn't know what he had done, Jake would. She said Billy had never known either of his parents, had been in and out of the foster system in Dallas his whole life, had run away and lived on the streets several times as a boy. Jake saw all of that as a grim harbinger of things to come.

Before they finished their conversation, the phone rang. He told the caller he would call back. When he hung up, Jolie was on her feet, her purse in her hand. "I have to go," she said. "I have to fix dinner. I'm already late. Now I'll have to throw something together in a hurry."

His connection with her had been broken by the phone, but he believed he had her trust. Sooner or later she would tell him the rest of the story. Jake asked her to wait while he wrote her a ticket. He went behind his desk, found a form in a drawer and wrote out the citation. "Get your car reregistered as soon as you can," he said, handing it across the desk to her.

"I will," she said, taking the ticket. "Although I really haven't driven it off the ranch. When I come to town, they let me drive one of the ranch's pickups."

He reached for a notepad and pen on his desk. "Give me your phone number. I'll call you and tell you when you can meet with the judge."

"I only have a cell."

"That'll do."

She spoke the number and he jotted it down. He plucked a card with his phone numbers on it from the card holder on his desk and handed it to her. "Promise me you'll let me know if you hear from Billy, if he threatens you in any way or if he comes to town. You can call me anytime." He moved from behind his desk, placed his hand on the small of her back and escorted her to the front door. "I don't want you to worry. Everything's going to work out."

She nodded. "My worst fear is that if he does find out where we are and come here, he'll go to the school. That's why I wanted Danni to have a different last name."

"The school let you do that?"

She nodded again. "I know they don't usually. I think Jude had something to do with it."

"What name is she registered as?"

"My maiden name. Kramer."

Jake walked back to his desk to where he had a notepad. "What's her whole name?"

"Danni Marie."

"I'll check on her every once in a while."

"Oh, would you? I'd be so grateful."

"It's my job to look out for Willard County's citizens. And that includes you and your daughter."

For the first time since she came into the office, she smiled. And what a smile it was. She looked like a different person.

He stood in the doorway and watched her drive away. For some reason, he was sorry to see her go. He instinctively knew she was a good woman who'd had bad luck in life, but she had apparently risen above it. He admired that, knew how hard it was. He had seen too many women who had started out as responsible citizens married to or living with men who were losers of Billy Jensen's caliber. Before long, the women sank to the same low level as their partners. But that apparently wasn't true of Jolie. Jake could see she had fought to stay out of the gutter her husband had provided his wife and daughter.

He decided to take a drive around the school. He set his hat on and went out to his SUV.

Jolie didn't go back to the Circle C right away. She couldn't let the Strayhorns see her red eyes and face. She drove out the highway a few miles to the north, then turned around and came back. She drove through the drive-up window at the Dairy Queen and ordered a Coke. The teenager at the window gave her a bright smile, which gave Jolie a lift. She sat in the parking lot drinking her Coke and watching people come and go.

Soon she pointed the pickup toward the Circle C. As she drove, all she could think of was Jake Strayhorn. In her mind, he was no longer "the sheriff." Instead, he was an attractive, heroic man. He was older. Older than Jude or Brady, she suspected. But he wasn't *too* old. After the story Buster had told her about the Strayhorn brothers, she tried to reason through the maze of them and their children to figure out Jake's age, but she couldn't come to a conclusion. She made a mental note to ask Buster the next time an opportunity arose.

She tried to imagine what it must be like to be married to someone like Jake, someone who was strong and would always be responsible and always take care of his family. She had no experience to draw from, so no vision came to her.

When she reached the ranch, she hurried into the kitchen intent on starting supper immediately. She had baked a chicken yesterday, planning on making a chicken salad for dinner tomorrow, using a recipe that had been served in the Cactus Café. Now it would become supper tonight. She set Irene to cutting the chicken into bite-size pieces, chopping celery and pecans while she, Jolie, quickly whisked together a dressing. After she put the salad together, she went to the pantry in search of some dried cranberries.

When she came back to the salad, Irene offered her a handful of washed green grapes. "What, for the salad?"

Irene smiled, pushing the grapes toward her. "*Sí*. You try. Is good."

"Okay," Jolie said. "I'm game." She carefully stirred the green grapes into the salad, then put together plates with toasted sourdough bread slices and cranberry sauce, just the way they served it in the café in Grandee.

While she worked, she couldn't help overhearing Brady and Jude and Mr. Strayhorn talking in the dining room. "We haven't had a break-in in Lockett in years," Mr. Strayhorn said. "As upset as Silas is, you'd think he'd lost thousands."

"I was in the bank today," Jude said. "Beverly told me they're looking out for someone with too many quarters."

Everyone at the table laughed.

"Who do they think did it?" Brady asked.

"Haven't heard of anyone," Jude said. "I know practically everyone in Willard County, but I sure can't think of anyone to accuse."

"We've got a lot of people coming and going, working on the oil rigs," Mr. Strayhorn said. "Could've been one of them, I suppose."

"I don't know," Brady said. "Those fellas seem like pretty good citizens. I'd be surprised if one of them did it."

Jolie's heartbeat had become a flutter. Curiosity was killing her. As soon as the men finished the chicken salad, she walked into the dining room and served dessert herself—

chunks of red velvet cake with rich cream cheese frosting. She had made it yesterday from scratch. "I didn't mean to be eavesdropping, but something was broken into in Lockett?"

"The coin-op laundry," Brady said. "Odd business to break into."

"I can't imagine someone thinking he could get much money out of a small-town laundry," Jude added.

"How much money did they steal?" Jolie asked.

"Not much," Jude said. "According to Beverly, probably not more than a couple hundred dollars. He broke into the dryers and there's only five of them."

Jolie swallowed past the anxiety skittering across her midsection. A crime like that sounded exactly like something Billy would do.

But it couldn't be him. No way could he find out where she and Danni had gone. In the first place, no one knew. And even if he did, she was banking on him not knowing where Lockett, Texas, was.

13

For days after hearing about the laundry break-in, Jolie was a wreck. She jumped or caught her breath at every unexpected noise, dreaded going to bed for fear of waking up to find Billy in her room. Every night before turning in, she walked out onto her small porch and looked in all directions.

She had already observed that there was really nothing to keep Billy from showing up at her door. No guard stood at the Circle C's gate. If Billy came onto the ranch, all he would have to do was spot her car; then he would know where she and Danni lived. Even if someone saw him and questioned him, if he said he was Danni's father or Jolie's husband, she believed no one would interfere with him, because Jude had told her she could have her privacy. She lay in bed every night staring at the ceiling wondering if she should, or could, somehow hide the car.

She plodded through the daylight hours trying to concentrate on her responsibilities and not wanting to reveal that she suspected Billy could be somewhere around Willard County. Jake's words haunted her: *". . . if you hear from Billy, if he threatens you in any way or if he comes to town, promise me you'll let me know. You can call me anytime."*

And she would do that, too, if she felt threatened. Or maybe she should do it anyway. The debate became so burdensome that the next evening, in the middle of breading pork chops for supper, she had to sit down at the breakfast table and gather herself, smearing flour all over her cheeks when she buried her face in her hands.

On Friday when she drove to the front gate to pick up Danni, her daughter dragged from the school bus with heavy steps and plopped into the passenger seat, morose. Only one fifth grade student had been allowed to skip sixth grade and go to seventh and it wasn't Danni. All of the fifth graders had taken the test, but only the one had scored high enough.

Being able to mingle as an equal with older kids was all Danni had talked about ever since she had heard about the possibility, so Jolie knew her disappointment. But like the tough little trouper Danni was, she didn't break down in tears. They talked about her setback all the way from the gate to the ranch house kitchen where Jolie was ready to start supper.

Danni followed her to the pantry, doing what she could to help. "You've made so many new friends," Jolie told her as she studied the pantry, looking for the items she needed. "You don't want to leave them behind, do you? If you went to seventh, you'd have to start over and make new friends again."

Jude came in just then and heard them talking. Jolie had noticed that Jude always came into the kitchen and went to the refrigerator for a cold drink after she came home from the school. Jude agreed with Jolie's comments about skipping sixth grade and Danni seemed mollified, if not ecstatic. In the same conversation, Jude elevated Danni's mood by telling them Brady's ten-year-old son, Andy, would arrive in June to stay until August.

"He probably won't like me," Danni said.

"I don't understand why you always say kids won't like you," Jolie said. "Why do you think that?"

"'Cause I'm a girl."

"I'll bet you and he will get along just fine," Jude said. "He's a nice boy. He's like his father. Quiet and easygoing."

"Does he have a horse?" Danni asked.

"He doesn't have one of his own, but there are a couple around here he can ride."

Jolie thought she saw a hint of Danni's mood plummeting again, probably at the idea there was no horse for *her* to ride. "Guess what, Danni," Jolie said quickly. "I spoke to someone about you taking riding lessons after school's out."

Danni's eyes grew round with interest. "Really?"

"If you don't mind my asking, who did you speak to?" Jude asked.

"Your friend Suzanne. I asked her if her fiancé taught kids to ride."

"What did she tell you?"

"She said she didn't know, but he might."

"I don't think Pat has ever given riding lessons to kids. His expertise is in horses, not riders. Brady will be working with Andy. I'm sure he'll be glad to teach Danni, too."

"Can I, Mama?" Jolie asked.

"Danni, you don't have a horse." A flush crawled up to Jolie's face as she realized Jude might think she was hinting that the Circle C should furnish a horse for her daughter to ride.

"We have some horses gentle enough for kids to ride," Jude said.

Jolie finally looked at Jude. "But it's still dangerous, isn't it, even if a horse is gentle? For a kid Danni's age, I mean? I had second thoughts about it after I mentioned it to Suzanne."

"It depends on how you look at it. Any animal that outweighs a human by a thousand pounds has the potential to hurt you in some way. You have to learn how not to let that happen. That's what Brady will teach Andy and Danni, too, if you let him. I promise you there's no better horseman anywhere than my husband."

"Can I, Mama?" Danni asked again. "Please?"

Jolie bit down on her bottom lip. Another worry. She wished she hadn't mentioned the idea to Suzanne and she wished Jude hadn't brought it up.

As if Jude knew her thoughts she said, "Most things worth doing have some risk to them, Jolie. Learning to ride and care for a horse is a wonderful experience for a child. It teaches a sense of responsibility and builds self-confidence. I had a horse to take care of my whole life. But Danni's *your* daughter. If you don't—"

"Please, Mama, please don't say no."

Hearing a sermon from Jude, or anyone, about the risks life presented wasn't necessary for Jolie. If anyone knew a person couldn't live risk free, Jolie did. What could be riskier than living every day with an alcoholic drug user with unpredictable temperament and behavior, then escaping him in the middle of the night?

Everything Jolie was, everything she had ever done in her adult life, including having lived with Billy longer than she should have, had been for her daughter. "I know I'm overprotective. It's just that Danni's all I've got. I don't mean to be ungrateful. If Brady wants to teach her, I know it'll be fine."

Unexpectedly, Danni rushed at her and wrapped her arms around her, nearly knocking her backward. "Thank you, Mama. Thank you, thank you."

Danni's simple gesture brought moisture to Jolie's eyes and nose, but she sniffed it back. "You just be careful, okay? If you got hurt, I don't know what I'd do. We're not going to worry about it today anyway. It's still a long time until June."

Jolie always made up her face every day. Keeping her hair clean and styled and her makeup neat was something she had done to maintain her self-esteem in a negative environment that had tried to drag her down every day. For her meeting with the judge, she dressed in one of the few dresses she had, put on the only pair of shoes she owned that even resembled dress shoes, a pair of plain black flats. A good appearance seemed particularly important for the coming meeting. As Jake had instructed when he called her and told her the appointment time and date, she had removed the license plates from her car to take to court with her. All the way to town, driving the Circle C's pickup, she wondered if the Strayhorns knew what she had done.

To her surprise, Jake met her on the wide sidewalk in front of the courthouse. "I'll go in with you," he said, "in case the judge wants to ask me any questions."

Her heart almost wouldn't hold the gratitude she felt as Jake walked into the courthouse with her. Having him beside her chased away the butterflies that had been dancing in her stomach all morning.

The meeting was short and unnotable and the judge didn't ask Jake a single question, which only confirmed Jolie's hope that Jake had been there to lend moral support to her personally. The very idea gave her goose bumps.

She paid her fine to the clerk, then walked outside with Jake still beside her. They stopped at the end of the sidewalk and she looked up at him, tenting her hand above her eyes against the brilliant sunlight. "Thank you so much for going in there with me. I've never had a meeting with an official before."

That wasn't entirely true. Indeed, she had bailed Billy out of jail twice in the past and scraped the money together to pay his fines. She had met with court-appointed counselors and defense lawyers. She hesitated a few seconds while she talked herself into correcting the fib she had just told. "Well, I should say, I've never talked to officials about myself. I've talked to someone about Billy a few times."

He smiled. He had such a beautiful smile. He seemed to be unaffected by the information she had just given him. "You did just fine," he said. "Told the judge just the right things."

"But I was really nervous."

"It's all done now. What about registering your car?"

"I can't right now. Not until I get some more money. I don't want to leave myself completely broke. Like I told you the other day, I don't drive the car anywhere anyway."

"That's okay. Just don't forget to do it as soon as you can."

"I don't think I can forget. The car has no license plates at all now."

"I guess that's true," he said, and laughed.

"I was going to drop by your office today," she said. "I have something to tell you."

"Let's walk over to the café." He gestured toward Maisie's, which was across the street and less than a block away. "We can get some lunch and you can tell me."

She nodded and they started toward the café. "I haven't eaten a meal out since before I went to work at the Circle C," she told him as they strolled. "The last time was that day Amanda and I had hamburgers at the Dairy Queen, the day I first saw you looking at my car. In fact, I haven't been to town except to go to the grocery store for the ranch."

"How long have you been out there now? Three or four weeks?"

"About that. But it seems like we've lived there forever. The Strayhorns are so open and accepting. They treat my daughter and me like we're part of their family. Jude has volunteered Brady to teach Danni to ride a horse."

"If there's a man who knows how to do that, it's Brady Fallon."

"You've known Brady a long time?"

"Since we were kids. Brady used to come visit his aunt and uncle in the summertime. He, my cousin Cable and even Jude roamed Willard County's prairies in blissful childhood ignorance."

Jolie couldn't imagine that Jake Strayhorn was ever ignorant. She cocked her head and looked up at his profile, his strong straight nose, his heavy brows and dark eyelashes. "When you lived at the Circle C, did you live in the big house?"

"Yep. My room, along with my folks', was on the third floor."

"I've only gone up to the third floor once, when Lola

Mendez showed me around the house. Jude said no one uses it."

They reached the café and took seats at a narrow rectangular table with one end shoved against the brown wood-paneled wall. As he placed his hat on the chair seat beside him, the waitress came over with two glasses of water. "Hey, Jake. Don't see you in here much for lunch. Is the Dairy Queen closed." She gave a snorting laugh.

"How's it going, Nola Jean?" he said, smiling at her.

"Dairy Queen's still open. I just decided to vary my menu today."

"Today's a good day to come in. Got chicken and dumplings. Maisie made it herself."

"Oh, that sounds good," Jolie said.

"Great," Jake told Nola Jean. He waggled his finger between Jolie and himself. "She and I both will have chicken and dumplings. And some iced tea."

As Nola Jean strode away, Jolie leveled a look at Jake. "You must eat lunch at the Dairy Queen every day."

He sat forward, smiling, his forearms on the narrow table, which brought him within two feet of her. Her gaze landed on his hands—strong masculine hands, with a smattering of brown hair on the backs and long fingers with short, neat nails. Everything about him was neat, from his crisply pressed and creased jeans to his spotless white shirt, to his neatly trimmed wavy reddish hair. She thought of all the times she had sat across the table from Billy when he had been wearing a filthy T-shirt and hadn't even combed his hair, much less had it cut.

"Not every day," Jake said. "I eat at home when I can talk myself into my own cooking."

Jolie laughed. "I know you're a bachelor. I should come and make you a meal. To thank you for all you've done for me."

She couldn't believe she had just said something that forward.

"I haven't done anything special or anything that I wouldn't have done for anybody else," Jake said. "I don't just arrest people, you know. I'm supposed to help people out if I can."

Nola Jean reappeared with two tall glasses of iced tea, then hurried away again.

Jake sipped; then his mouth tipped into a big grin. "Let's get back to what you were saying about cooking."

Jolie busied herself stirring Splenda into her iced tea. "It was nothing. I just said I'll come and cook you a meal. Or I could bake you something. I'm a good baker."

"I wouldn't turn down a home-cooked meal. Or a home-made cake."

His answer surprised her. She hadn't expected him to agree. An involuntary smile crawled across her mouth. "Then I'll do it. I take Mondays off, so any Monday's okay for me."

"Sounds good. After you've been cooking all week, you sure you want to spend your day off cooking a meal for somebody else?"

Jolie had never experienced a feeling as uplifting as the one being with Jake gave her. She hadn't often enjoyed a man's company, or even had the opportunity to. She had been loyal to Billy, though many, including herself, questioned why, and she had been a hardworking waitress with a household to support and a child to raise single-handedly. Most of her exchanges with men in the Cactus Café had consisted of quick empty conversation about nothing. "I like cooking," she told him.

"Then how about next week?"

"Good. What do you like to eat?"

"Everything. Surprise me."

"Okay, I will." She couldn't keep from giving him a huge grin. Without thinking she placed her forearms on the table, too, putting their arms within inches of each other's and their faces a foot apart. When she realized what she had done, she sat back quickly. "Oh, I'm sorry. I didn't think."

"No problem," he said, and made no effort to move back. "You said you want to tell me something. What is it?"

Just then, Nola Jean showed up again carrying two plates of steaming chicken and dumplings and a basket of rolls. Jolie and Jake both straightened and sat back, allowing the waitress to set the dishes in front of them. As soon as she left, without touching her meal, Jolie sighed and said, "I just want to say I might know who broke into the laundry."

A roll in one hand, a knife in the other, Jake looked at her, his eyes narrowed. "Yeah?"

She nodded. "I think it could be Billy." Oddly, she felt no guilt over ratting out the man with whom she had lived ten years.

Jake sliced open the roll and buttered it with nimble fingers. "What makes you think so?"

"Because it sounds like something he'd do. He's—he's done things sort of like that before. He's . . ." She swallowed and looked away. "When he was sent to jail the last time, it was for breaking into a little grocery store in Grandee."

"I'll look into it," Jake said, placing his roll on the side of his plate and picking up his fork, "but I don't think it's possible."

She felt her eye twitch as a sudden spear of fear of the unknown passed through her. "Why not?"

"He's in jail now, darlin'. Got picked up in a drug bust in Dallas." Jake dug into his food. "He's been in a week. Can't make bail."

Her mouth pursed into a silent "oh."

This was a good-news-bad-news turn of events. Good news that she could temporarily stop worrying about his whereabouts and bad news that sooner or later he would get out of jail. Still, she breathed a sigh of relief.

"Aren't you going to eat?" Jake asked, looking up from his food.

"Uh, yes." She picked up her fork and sliced a dumpling in half. "How did you find out he's there?"

"I looked up his sheet. Made a couple of calls."

Now she wondered just how much he knew about Billy—

and not for the first time, about her and her and Billy's life together. Most people thought they were still married. More important, *Danni* thought they were. She hesitated, trying to decide which question to ask next. "Did, uh . . . they say how long he'll be there?"

One of Jake's shoulders lifted in a shrug. "Until he either makes bail or gets his day in court. Then they'll either sentence him or let him go."

"Did they say which one?"

"No way to know at this point. Depends on how good the case against him is, how good a lawyer he's got. I assume the court appointed somebody."

She nodded as she swallowed another bite of food. This was similar to what had happened the last time when Billy had been sentenced to six months in the county jail. "Then who stole the laundry's money?"

"I've got my eye on somebody," Jake said, and smiled. He held her gaze until she returned to her meal. "Tell me something. You're a real sweet, pretty woman. How'd you get mixed up with a guy like Billy?"

She didn't like talking about the origin of her relationship with Billy, had shut it out of her mind to the point where she barely remembered it. She dropped her gaze to her plate. "It seems like I've known him forever. He worked construction and I had a part-time job washing dishes in this little café. He came in all the time to eat. He started asking me to go places. And I went. . . . Then I got pregnant." She looked up and could tell Jake was calculating.

"At what, seventeen?"

She shrugged, then concentrated on eating and trying to appear casual.

"How old were you?" he asked.

There was no mistaking an angry note in the question. "Sixteen," she answered, without looking at him.

"And he was nineteen."

Had she told him Billy's age? She couldn't remember. She knew he was saying Billy was guilty of statutory rape. Others had said it to her before. She might not recall much about those teenage years, but she well remembered her mother's rage and her threats. "My mother wanted him to marry me. She told him she'd get the law on him if he didn't."

She paused, unwilling to go further. The bottom line was her mother hadn't been nearly as worried about Jolie's future welfare as she had been about being stuck with paying for and helping raise a baby. Jolie had somehow known that even as a teenager. But though she had thought it, she had never said it, as if speaking it aloud would confirm that her mother would have rather have her married to a loser than have to put up with her and her baby. Thus she had never called on her mother for help of any kind.

When Jake didn't say anything, she felt a need to explain. "You have to understand how it was, Jake. . . . How it *is* for people like me and Billy. We're white trash. We're—"

"Jolie, that's a description I never use. I've seen people rise above their circumstances."

A burn passed behind her eyes. She had tried so hard to do that very thing. At sixteen, she had naively thought that being with Billy, with his being older, was a step up.

Before she could respond to Jake's comment, he said, "I've been a cop my whole life, Jolie. Do you think I've never run across bad boys like Billy Jensen?"

"No. No, I don't. I know you see a lot of bad people in your job."

"Well . . . not so much anymore, but I used to."

She looked past him, blinking back tears that still threatened. "I always dreamed of having a better life, but if Billy ever had any dreams, they'd been beat out of him before I ever knew him. Then later, I only dreamed of escaping."

"There's a lot of guys like Billy. Too many. They're all sad stories. But they're still lawbreakers. It's all about choices and bad judgment, you see? Now, the social engineers will argue it's all about environment, about poverty, about poor education and so on and so forth. There's some of that, but in the end, it's about personal choices and bad judgment."

No one had ever said so plainly what she already knew instinctively. Indeed Billy did have the worst judgment of anyone she had ever known and his choices were always made on impulse. "Do you believe there are people who are born doomed?"

"Sometimes it seems that way."

"I believe Billy's one of them. One of the social workers told him his mother was a crack addict the whole time she was pregnant and perhaps he had been born addicted to crack himself. I've often wondered if that's why he can't seem to think straight. He's not dumb, but he can't reason things through and make good decisions."

"Drug use changes people," Jake said. "Some are able to fight back from it, but too often, too many don't."

"Even if that were a possibility for Billy, I don't believe he could do it alone. If someone doesn't save him, I don't know what will happen to him. He has no chance and no hope. He never has, really. That's part of why I stayed with him so long. In the beginning. I naively thought I could make a difference in his life. I might have kept trying if it hadn't been for the drinking and the drugs. I'm not strong enough to deal with him and them both. And I have Danni to think about. I don't hate him. I feel sorry for him. But I'm still afraid of him. And I'm even more afraid of his friends."

Jake shook his head, sighed and returned to his food. "Just remember what I told you. If you hear from him, let me know."

14

Jake Strayhorn stayed in Jolie's mind daily and nightly from the moment she left the café. He was so strong and decisive, fearless even. She had never known anyone like him. All she could think about was the coming Monday when she would go to his apartment, cook a meal for him and just be around him for an hour or two. She loved his company.

And while Jake filled her mind, she had to summon her concentration to make edible meals for the Strayhorn family and keep order in the kitchen.

And she had to bake cupcakes for the school's-out party. The number required had grown to ten dozen. Somehow, in the initial tally, someone had forgotten the teachers and teachers' assistants. Jolie made herself concentrate on the logistics of how to make so many cupcakes, frost them and keep them fresh until the day they were needed. The school's-out party was ten days away and she had eight working days. Meanwhile, while the Strayhorn family dined on Wednesday evening, they discussed that Jake had made an arrest in the laundry break-in. A local family's nephew who had just been released from federal prison had been charged. Jolie's ears perked up. Hearing that information should have been a relief, but all it did was remind her that Billy would get out of jail someday.

* * *

As daylight sneaked above the horizon, Pat Garner awoke alone. He missed Suzanne. They usually awoke together and started the day with slow and easy lovemaking. He hadn't seen her since yesterday morning when she went to work. Her dad had worked a short week and she had expected him to come in off the road yesterday, so she slept at home last night, as she always did when he was in town. Then, with her being off work today, she had gone to Abilene early this morning to run errands and do some shopping.

Pat lay in bed a few extra minutes enjoying the fact that he was happier than he had been in years. He and Suzanne had set the wedding day to be on July 10. Two months from now he would be a *married* man and there would be no more mornings waking up alone.

He rose and dressed in his work clothes, downed a couple of cups of coffee along with two hot dogs for breakfast, then left his house for his barns and arena. He planned to work with four horses today.

On his mind as he worked was the fact that he still hadn't done the one thing everyone wanted him to do. And that was to ask Jake Strayhorn to be present at the wedding reception at the Circle C Ranch.

Pat didn't know why he had agreed to do that. He knew Jake hadn't been to the Circle C once since returning to Lockett six years ago. Pat didn't know exactly what the reasons were, but being a live-and-let-live kind of person, he was content to let Jake deal with his family in whatever way he chose.

He knew that Jake had had no relationship with his uncle, J. D. Strayhorn, nor had he had one with his deceased grandfather, Jeff Strayhorn. Jake had been present at the old man's funeral last year, but not as a family member. He had been there as a law enforcement officer managing traffic, along with two state cops. It had seemed as if everybody in Texas had come to Jeff Strayhorn's funeral, but Pat suspected that if Jake hadn't been a cop, he wouldn't have been there at all.

Jake's only communication with the hierarchy at the Circle C was with Jude. So why didn't *she* ask him to come to the reception? After all, she was his cousin. Despite Pat's reasoning, the dilemma with Jake had been on his mind every day since he and Suzanne declared they would get married and she had asked him to talk to Jake.

"I am really nervous about this, J.D.," Maisie said.

Sitting on her blue frilly bed, J.D. watched her fold a frilly blouse and neatly place it in her suitcase. J.D. thought of Maisie as a frilly woman. No matter when he saw her, she always looked feminine and pretty and well put together. Being a plain but meticulous man himself, he liked that. "Why? It's a couple of days in Amarillo."

"But we'll see people who have no idea who I am. No telling what they'll think."

Digging into his jeans pocket for his pocketknife, J.D. couldn't keep from grinning. "We don't care what they think, do we?" He opened the knife and began to trim his fingernails. "My meeting at the quarter horse association will be over by five o'clock this afternoon. We'll have a nice steak dinner tonight, go to the horse show tomorrow and come back home Saturday. No big deal."

"I feel like a schoolgirl going out on a date," she said. "In all the years we've been seeing each other, how many times have we gone somewhere together where there were people who know you?"

"I told you, I want us to be open. I'm tired of hiding."

"You can rest assured that with you running willy-nilly up and down my stairs, we won't be hidden much longer. When I think back on it, I have a hard time remembering why it was necessary for us to hide in the first place, especially after Jude got grown and went away to college."

J.D. sighed, closed his pocketknife and stuffed it back into his pocket. He was in no frame of mind for this conversation. He had wanted to take her with him on this business trip and spend an extra couple of days enjoying each other's company and checking out the performances of two of Sandy Dandy's offspring. But she seemed hell-bent on digging up old arguments they'd had for years. He knew his shortcomings, didn't need to be reminded. "It was my fault, Maisie. I guess I was a coward."

She came to him and leaned down, flooding his space with her flowery fragrance that had become so familiar to him. She placed her cool palm on his cheek and kissed him. "You're an emotional mess, Jasper, but I've never seen you as a coward. If I believed that, I wouldn't have stayed here all these years."

J.D.'s mouth quirked at her calling him Jasper. Only a few of his family members had ever called him by his given name and they had all passed on. "So then why are you picking on me?"

She straightened, heaving a great sigh, a bad sign. "I wasn't going to bring this up until after this trip." She returned to the suitcase and added a folded pair of pants and began sorting through other items lying on the bed. "Since I can't put it out of my mind, I might as well tell you. Glenn's decided not to reenlist. He and his family are coming back to the States."

J.D.'s stomach made a little dip, knowing this was leading to something he wouldn't like. Maisie's oldest son, in the army, and his family had lived in Germany for years. "What's he going to do back here?"

"He's gotten a job at Lockheed in Fort Worth."

"Isn't that the company that makes airplanes?"

"Yes, but he's going to be doing something with security. He's already bought a house west of Fort Worth not too far from his sister's." She paused, keeping her eyes trained on a necklace she was fiddling with. "He wants me to move over there so I can be closer to all of them."

The last thing J.D. had expected was to hear at this late date was that Maisie would leave Lockett. This news was a surprise. Maisie had never had a close relationship with either of her children. They rarely brought their families to visit her in Lockett and stayed only a token amount of time when they did come. She had never visited her son in Germany, though a few times in the past J.D. had offered to pay for her trip. J.D. knew for a fact that Maisie and her daughter had never gotten along, which was one of the reasons Sarah had left home at eighteen and rarely returned to Lockett. He concentrated on keeping an even reaction. "What did you tell him?"

She closed her suitcase and straightened, giving him a look he could only call a glower.

"My children are my only family, J.D. Their kids are my only grandchildren and I barely know them." She lifted the suitcase off the bed and set it on the floor, then stood there looking down at him, her hands planted on her hips. "My God, Glenn and his family have lived overseas since before his babies were born. And I don't see nearly enough of Sarah and her girls. Sarah's been gone from here since she left to go to college, and with the café to take care of, I've hardly had a chance to even go see her. She has a beautiful new home and I've been in it only once. At my age . . ."

Her words trailed off and she shook her head, still not looking at him.

J.D. found himself uncharacteristically nervous and his throat had grown thick. He had always believed Maisie had stayed in Lockett to be near him. But he also knew she hadn't had much choice. Until now, spending time with her kids had never been an issue. Nor had it been an option, really.

He got to his feet and picked up her suitcase. "Let's don't talk about it now, sugar. We'll be late. Ed will have the plane ready and he's expecting us."

She gave an even more exaggerated sigh. "This is how it's always been, J.D. Every time something difficult arises, you don't want to talk about it."

He walked over, and looped his arm around her shoulder and gave a little squeeze. "We'll talk. I promise."

* * *

By noon, without a cloud in the sky and a temperature approaching ninety, Pat was hot and hungry. He hadn't heard from Suzanne and wondered why. When she made a trip to Abilene, she usually called from her cell and chatted while she was on her way. He unhooked his own cell and speed-dialed her number, but the call went to voice mail. "Hey, sugar, call me," he said, and disconnected.

In no mood to go back to the house, clean up and fix a lunch, he decided to go to town and grab a burger at the air-conditioned Dairy Queen. After he ate, if Jake was in his office, maybe he would drop by and talk to him.

At the Dairy Queen, he visited with a couple of small ranchers like himself who were also having burgers. They talked about the usual subjects: cattle prices, high taxes, government telling them what to do with what was theirs. After lunch, he drove to the sheriff's office.

He met Amanda Mason headed out the door on her way to lunch. He found Jake looking in a file cabinet behind the receptionist's desk. "Hey," Jake said when he walked in. "What's going on?"

"Wedding planning," Pat said sheepishly, almost embarrassed to talk about something so froufrou with another man.

Jake grinned and closed the file drawer. "You'll survive it."

"I wonder," Pat grumbled, and at the same time he recalled hearing that Jake had once been married. Somewhere in his former life, a former wife existed. "How long since you were married?"

"Um, fifteen years or so." He started back toward his office. "Come on back and sit down."

"You never had any kids?" Pat asked, following him.

"Nope."

"If you don't mind me asking, what happened to your marriage?"

"Nothing much. Got married too young. Both going in different directions mostly." Jake rounded the end of his desk and sat down in his desk chair. "Sit down." He gestured toward one of two guest chairs across from his desk.

Pat sat, tipped his hat back and crossed his ankle over his thigh. "That could apply to a lot of people," he said.

"I suppose. She had ideas about a career. About the time things started getting really rocky, I got sent overseas. That finished it off. I was in Kuwait when I got the divorce papers."

That was more than Pat had ever heard Jake say about his past, but he still didn't know much more than he had known in the first place about what had happened to the man's marriage. "And you've really never wanted to try it again?"

"Haven't had time."

"I didn't think I'd ever get married again," Pat said, shaking his head, "but I'm looking forward to starting over with Suzanne."

"She's a good gal. Y'all will be happy. Her dad's a good guy, too."

Pat nodded, trying to find an opening to bring up the reason he had come here. He fixed a look at Jake and blurted, "Jude wants to have the reception out at the Circle C."

He saw absolutely no discernible body language coming from Jake. Nor did he get a reply or comment from him. Jake had a reputation for being almost clairvoyant, so Pat suspected he already knew what Pat was going to say next. Still, he said it. "We'd, uh . . . we're wondering if you'd be willing to go to the reception."

"No," Jake answered. He sat forward, his forearms resting on the desk. "You don't need me at the reception."

"Yeah, we do," Pat said. "Suzanne wants you there and I'd like to see you there, too. You're supposed to make a toast."

Jake shook his head and Pat felt like a fool. "Okay. If you feel you can't do it, we'll find another place to have the reception. The church basement is where most people have wedding receptions anyway."

"I don't want to be the one to throw a monkey wrench in your plans, Pat," Jake said. "It won't hurt my feelings if you want to get somebody else to stand up with you. The Circle C's a nice place and if Jude puts on a big party, it'll be first class."

"There's no one else I want to ask to be best man. And personally, I don't give a shit if we even have a reception, period. I guess I'm asking you for Suzanne's sake, with her and Jude being best friends and all."

"I just don't want to do it, Pat. I can't. I've stayed away from there and cut out my own little piece of turf in Willard County. I don't want to rock that boat. My name might be Strayhorn, but I'm the people's man and I believe most of the Willard County citizens see me that way. That's why they elected me."

Pat snorted. "Well, you did win by a landslide."

"But that might change if I started showing up at the Circle C. It would be too easy for folks to start looking at me as the Circle C's man. The Strayhorns control enough already. I don't want the public to think they also control the sheriff."

Pat didn't claim to have Jake's ability to read minds, but he had seen a rodeo or two. And what Jake had just told him was an excuse, not a reason. Jake's reasons for having nothing to do with the Circle C went far deeper than negative public opinion. If Jake Strayhorn *wanted* to be social buds with his family, he wouldn't care about public opinion.

"I think I know what you mean," Pat said. "Come to think of it," he added, "I don't have much of a relationship with the Strayhorns, either. Since I didn't grow up in this county, I don't feel the connection. I'm one of the few people around here who's never worked out there as a ranch hand. I've done a little training with a few of their horses, but I've never gone past that big round corral attached to the big barn."

"Hmm," Jake said. "I've never thought about your not growing up here. You've never told me what you're doing in Willard County anyway."

Pat chuckled. "When I decided to go into the horse business, I was mostly looking for good and cheap pasture. And Willard County's where I found it."

"Well, you've got a good place."

"It is now, after I've spent every dime I've made on it. If I wanted to sell it, I probably never would get my money back. So I guess I'm stuck with getting married and raising a family on it."

"Family usually follows weddings," Jake said, grinning.

Having done what he came to do, Pat placed his hands on the chair arms and sat forward. "Well, I've got two horses waiting on me, so guess I'll run along." He got to his feet and started toward the door. Jake followed him and they stepped outside together. "I'm gonna tell Suzanne we'll just plan the reception at the Methodist church. That's a lot easier anyway."

Just then a roar and grinding of gears from an eighteen-wheeler caught their attention. With the sheriff's office being only a block off the square, they could see the main highway that ran through town. They both looked toward the sound. A dark blue Peterbilt truck tractor growled its way through town, headed north. Painted in an arc of white letters on the door was TRUETT BREEDLOVE.

Pat's mind suddenly became a jumble as facts crashed into each other. If Truett hadn't been at home last night, where the hell had Suzanne been? Pat still hadn't heard a word from her.

The truck driver lifted his fingers in a gesture of hello and Pat and Jake both waved. "Looks like Truett Breedlove's back," Jake said.

"Yeah," Pat said. Not wanting Jake to see his consternation, he turned toward his truck. "Well, I gotta get going."

"See ya," Jake said.

Back in his truck and driving through town, Pat jerked his cell phone from his belt and started to punch in Suzanne's number. "Wait a minute," he mumbled, and snapped the phone shut. Something he had tried not to do since he had been with Suzanne was hang on too hard. He had already left a message for her. Something had held her up. She would call him when she started home from Abilene. By seven, he had finished out the two horses he had planned on working in the afternoon. He checked his cell for messages from Suzanne, but saw none. He went to the house, showered and put on old jeans. He usually went to Truett's house for supper when Truett was in town, but tonight it looked as though a frozen dinner was on the menu at Pat Garner's house. He shoved one in the microwave, then watched the news on TV while he ate. After the meal, he checked his cell again.

At nine, he was worried. Had she had a wreck? Or car trouble? She had a fairly new truck, but anything could happen. He punched in her number, but the call went to voice mail.

"Hey, sweetheart," he said. "I'm getting worried about you. Call me."

He called Truett but didn't get an answer. Had he and Suzanne gone somewhere together? He returned to the TV and surfed for a movie. Usually, he was getting ready for bed by this time, but he knew damned well he wouldn't be able to go to sleep. At ten o'clock, he was dishing up ice cream when his cell warbled. Caller ID showed Suzanne's name. "Hey," he said. "You got my message?"

"Yes, I got it. You don't need to worry about me."

"Where are you?"

"I just got home. I didn't get to the mall until late. I wanted to finish my shopping, so I just grabbed something for supper in the food court."

Her words seemed to come in a breathy rush and in an unfamiliar tone of voice. Was she lying to him? "Well, at least you're home safe. I tried to call your dad and didn't get an answer."

"Oh, he was probably in the shower or something. Listen, I'm working tomorrow, but I'm putting a roast in the Crock-Pot and making a pie. You're coming for supper, right?"

He managed a chuckle he didn't feel. "Like I've got something else to do. Sure, I'll be there."

"Miss you," she said.

"Yeah, me, too."

"See you tomorrow."

"Yeah, tomorrow."

They disconnected and he laid his phone on the kitchen counter, bewildered. That whole conversation had sounded wrong and felt worse. What in the hell was going on?

15

As expected, Pat ate supper at the Breedlove home on Friday night. As expected, the meal had been delicious and he had eaten his share. Suzanne was a great cook. Her dad was his usual friendly self, telling stories about his adventures trucking from one coast to the other. Suzanne was quieter than usual, but clingier.

After the meal, Pat helped her clean up in the kitchen. She said little about the wedding, so Pat debated whether he would even bring up that he had talked to Jake about attending the reception and the resulting answer. But finally, she asked.

"He said no," Pat told her, rinsing plates under the faucet and handing them to her to put into the dishwasher. "I think we should just have it at the Methodist church and be done with it. The location's not that big a deal."

"Why is he being so hardheaded?" she said, irritation roiling in her tone.

"It's the family issue that goes back a long way. I'm sure you know more about it than I do. All I know is it has nothing to do with you or me. I think we should leave it alone."

"But Jude—"

"This isn't about Jude." Pat turned off the faucet and picked up a dish towel. Drying his hands, he turned to face Suzanne. "If she wants to engineer a family reunion with Jake, she should do it on her own and not use our wedding."

Suzanne let out a little huff of exasperation and straightened. "Well, that's a tacky attitude."

"It's not an attitude. I'm just saying that Jake has his reasons for not wanting to show up at that ranch."

"Did you ask him what his specific reasons are?"

"He said he doesn't want to be seen as Strayhorns' lackey. I respect that."

"Well, I don't. He's being silly and childish. That bullshit with his dad and J.D.'s wife happened more than twenty years ago. He's supposed to be your friend."

Pat suspected Jake and the wedding reception weren't the real bee in Suzanne's bonnet, but he couldn't even guess what was annoying her. "Suzanne, why are we having this conversation? The man has spoken his intentions. I'm content to let it go at that."

"Then you should ask somebody else to be your best man."

Pat clenched his jaw. He knew she was stubborn and hot tempered and he went out of his way not to stoke her ire, but he would let her push him only so far. As much as he cared about her, he still had to maintain his self-respect as a man. "No. Number one, I don't know that many people around here. And number two, of the few I do know, I can't think of a one of them I'd ask to be best man at my wedding. And it's probably too late to get my cousins or my brothers-in-law involved."

Suzanne sighed and slammed the dishwasher door. "Shit. This is stupid."

"You got *that* right," Pat retorted.

Suddenly, going to his own home alone took on a huge appeal. He had never been good at thinking on his feet in confrontations. Suzanne was always way ahead of him. He needed privacy to sort things out in his mind. He threw the dish towel onto the counter. "I'm gonna go on home," he said, and walked out of the kitchen.

Truett had settled in front of the TV in the living room and paid no attention when Pat walked through and picked up his hat off a table by the front door. Suzanne followed him outside, all the way to his truck. A full moon hung in the east, making the night lighter than usual.

At the truck door, she said softly, "Don't be mad at me. I'm stressed out."

He could see her pretty blue eyes shiny with tears even in the darkness. "Why? What's got you uptight?"

She shook her head and looked away. A zing darted across his gut. "What's going on, Suz? Getting cold feet?"

"No," she answered quickly, and turned back to face him. "No, I'm not."

He still couldn't read her. "C'mere," he said, and pulled her to him. He wrapped his arms around her and held her close, breathing in the clean scent of her hair. Her arms wrapped around him tightly and she buried her face against his shoulder. He cupped her head gently and held her. "Let's forget about Jake and Jude and all of it," he said softly, his throat aching with feelings he couldn't express, questions he didn't know to ask. "Who says we have to have a big-ass reception at all? If you don't want to use the church basement, hell, we can have a small group at my house. The reception's just not that important, Suz."

"I know," she said, and sniffled, then pulled away. "I'm just stressed out. I'll be okay."

Now he no longer wanted to go home alone. He wanted to take her with him, wanted to hold her in his arms all night, but with her dad at home, he knew she wouldn't go. He hung on to her fingertips. "Wish I could take you home with me," he said anyway.

She gave him a weepy smile. "Dad'll be leaving Monday."

Pat nodded.

Monday. A helluva long weekend loomed ahead. But maybe by Monday he would figure out what was going on or she would tell him.

He drove the fifteen miles home slowly, thinking all the way. Entering his quiet house, he went directly to his bedroom and opened the top drawer of his dresser. Digging under his socks, he pulled out a sack that held a black velvet box and opened it. He backed to the edge of his bed and dropped to it, opening the velvet box and staring at the diamond-encrusted wedding ring inside.

He and Suzanne had decided against spending the money on an ostentatious wedding ring set, but one day, after he had sold a trailer load of steers at the auction in Abilene, for a helluva lot more money than he had expected, he had a fat check burning a hole in his pocket. He wanted to give Suzanne a pretty ring she would be proud of, wanted her to be proud to be his wife. He had spent that whole check on the friggin' diamond ring that glittered back at him now. He had intended to surprise her with it at the ceremony.

He had little experience with women, had always been too shy to put himself forward. He thought he had chosen a good one when he married Becky, who was from his hometown. From the beginning their relationship hadn't been great. The fact that he hadn't seen that before their wedding was reinforcement that he didn't know what the hell he was doing when it came to the fairer sex.

Hell, so that Becky could have a nice house to live in, he had sold livestock he should have kept and used the money to rebuild the old house that had been on his place when he bought it. He had bought her a new car that he rarely had ridden in. She had shopped as if he were a millionaire. At some point he realized he would never be able to make enough money, never be good enough at anything to please her. His thinking must not have been wrong, because she just up and left for what he thought was a trivial reason.

He had just recovered from the marriage breakup, the divorce and the money it had cost him when the vivacious Suzanne came along with a broken-down old horse she wanted him to teach. He had fought his attraction to her, had told himself he didn't need a woman in his life, especially one like her who was so good-looking she caught the eye of every hard-leg around.

On a sigh, he snapped the ring box shut. He had learned a lesson in dealing with Becky. Giving women *things* got you nothing.

He rose to his feet and returned the ring box to the sack it had come out of. He checked to be sure the receipt was still inside the sack. Just an hour and a half's drive tomorrow and he could have back the thousands that ring had cost him. Before he had bought it, he had made sure he could return it.

Jude had been so busy with winding up the school year, she hadn't had a chance to talk to Suzanne all week. Saturday was a good day for dinner out. As soon as she ate her usual bowl of cereal for breakfast, she keyed in her friend's cell number. When Suzanne answered, Jude said, "Hi. I was thinking of coming to town today to buy you dinner. What do you think?"

"Okay, I like free food."

Jude detected a lack of ebullience typical of Suzanne. "Uh-oh. You don't sound good. Everything okay?"

"Sure. Just tired. Yesterday was a long day."

"Oh, that's right. You went to Abilene shopping. Busy day, huh?"

"Boy, I'll say."

"Well, I'll see you about eleven thirty. You can tell me all about it."

Jolie and Irene were busy making something. "Jolie," she said, "I just want to tell you again how much we loved those enchiladas you made for supper last night. Best homemade enchiladas I've ever had. And that salad was delicious. Brady was still talking about it when we went to bed."

"Thank you," Jolie said, and her cheeks reddened.

Jolie was such a sweet person and she tried so hard to please. Jude had not one misgiving about having hired her. Daddy and Brady were pleased, too.

"I won't be here for dinner," she went on. "Since Daddy isn't here, either, Brady would probably be willing to eat with the hands in the cookhouse. I'll ask him to. Then y'all won't have to make dinner."

"Okay," Jolie said. "I'll just put extra effort into supper. I'm going to town, too, to pick up the stuff to make the cupcakes. I'll go ahead and start on them and freeze them, then frost them on Thursday before the party."

"Great," Jude said. "See you tonight."

She left the house for the barn. Brady's highbred grullo mare, Sweet Sal, was due to give birth in June. She had been bred to Patch, Jude's paint stallion. She and Brady both were thrilled—almost as thrilled as they were about their own baby. Patch's lineage went all the way back to the original paint horse that had been given to Jude's great-great-grandfather by the Comanche chief, Quanah Parker. Once the foal was born, she intended to work with it every single day until it became a superior performance horse.

She met Brady in the middle of the round corral. She hadn't seen him since he left their bed this morning before daylight. He enclosed her in an embrace. "How you doing?" he asked softly.

"Okay."

"Not sick this morning?"

"Uh-uh. I might make it. Did Daddy tell you when he'll be back?"

"This afternoon."

"I'm going to town to eat with Suzanne. I told Jolie you'd probably be willing to eat dinner in the cookhouse."

"No problem," Brady said.

They were sharing a long, sweet kiss in the middle of the corral when a voice interrupted. "All right, you two. Cut it out." Clary Harper, the ranch's horse wrangler, walked out of the barn, his arms full of gear. "You're embarrassing the horses."

Brady chuckled and kissed the tip of her nose. "Love you."

"Love you more." Jude pulled away. "Let's go check on Sal before Clary has a heart attack."

*   *   *

J.D.'s small Lear jet touched down at the airport in Abilene and rolled to a stop. He unfastened his seat belt, got to his feet and walked to the back where Maisie was belted into a leather armchair. She had sat apart from him all the way from Amarillo. Now she was looking at something outside and didn't turn her head toward him.

"Ready to go?" he asked.

Without speaking, she unfastened her seat belt, gripped her chair arms and got to her feet.

"I figured we'd stop by Vance's and eat dinner before we go back to Lockett. That okay with you?"

"I need my suitcase." She began opening overhead cabinets.

"They'll get it. Let's just go."

He offered her his hand. She hesitated, looking down, then took it. He couldn't guess what she was thinking. She had been in a pout ever since he had told her at dinner that he had no desire to get married again and never would.

They deboarded and walked slowly toward his truck without a word. A steward hurried past them carrying their bags.

The two days in Amarillo hadn't gone well. Both of the colts J.D. had been interested in watching had given superb performances and scored high marks in the horse show, but even that hadn't been enough to salvage the trip. After the show, he had taken Maisie to dinner and after too many drinks they had fallen into the discussion of her leaving Lockett.

What followed was a long diatribe on how he had disrespected her all these years by sleeping with her, treating her like nothing more than a prostitute, keeping their relationship a secret as if he were ashamed of her and at the same time, demanding that she, too, keep it a secret.

He had countered with the same reasons he always did: with all that had gone on inside his family with him and his brothers, his two former wives and with the responsibility he had shouldered for most of his existence on earth, he couldn't let his life appear to be a soap opera. In self-defense, he couldn't keep from bringing up the money he had sunk into the black hole known as Maisie's Café for no reason other than to help her out. He knew that without the café, she had no means of support and he cared about her. Her kids hadn't kept in close touch with her over the years. Until now, they hadn't demonstrated much concern for her. She certainly had never been able to call on them for financial help.

Somehow, in the labyrinth of slightly drunken conversation, the truth had finally wormed its way through. She wanted to get married. She had never said so before, which flabbergasted him. No matter. As much as he felt for her, marriage was out of the question. After the passing of his two brothers, his father had never let him forget that he was destined to be the steward of the Strayhorn empire.

The foreordination was so interwoven with who he was, forgetting the fact was impossible. But even if he wanted to get married again, which he didn't, no way would he ever marry a woman with children. No way would he ever do anything that would raise inheritance issues at the Circle C and give lawyers and courts the opportunity to lay claims on its future or tear it to pieces. If he had learned nothing else from his dad, he had learned that much. It had taken a while, but he had finally come to understand why his dad had never remarried after J.D.'s mother died.

It worried him greatly that Jude's husband had brought a child from another marriage into the family, a child who might someday, somehow, believe he had a claim on the Circle C. Even now J.D. was working with the Abilene law firm that represented the ranch's interests in dealing with that issue. It had nothing to do with his regard for Brady. It had to do with keeping the Circle C ranching empire whole, as the single undivided family entity it had always been.

Jude left the Circle C early enough to reach Lucky's Grocery by noon. She didn't see Suzanne when she walked in, so she made her way to the storeroom where Suzanne sometimes worked. Suzanne came out and met her in the aisle. Jude was shocked at her best friend's appearance. Her eyes were swollen as if she had been crying. Dark circles showed underneath. Her usually well-kept long blond hair was tied back with a large clip.

"Are you okay?" Jude asked cautiously.

"Yeah. Let's go eat."

As they left Lucky's and walked toward Maisie's, Jude couldn't imagine the source of her friend's anguish. "Are you and Pat quarreling?"

"Not yet. I haven't seen him since day before yesterday."

Not yet? What in the world did *that* mean? Jude was stunned. She knew Suzanne slept at Pat's house every night that her dad wasn't home. "Okay, what's going on?"

They reached Maisie's plate-glass front door. Suzanne led the way inside and to the table in the corner where they usually sat if it wasn't occupied. A few diners sat at tables in the center of the room. The waitress, a teenager unknown to Jude, came to take their orders. She wore low-cut jeans and a cropped top that showed her navel, pierced with a silver ring. Bright red streaks had been dyed into her dark brown hair and stood up in spikes. A tattoo of dark blue thorns encircled her neck, a tiny silver ball perched on her upper lip and a tiny arrow pierced one brow. Jude could think of no Lockett teenager she had ever seen with such body adornment.

"You must be new here," Suzanne said.

"I'm not from here," the kid said. "I live in Dallas. I'm just helping my aunt out. My mom and dad wanted to get rid of me for the summer."

"School's already out in Dallas?" Jude asked, studying the deep blue tattoo, wondering if it had a meaning. She knew some tattoos did.

"No, but *I'm* out."

Suzanne saved Jude from pondering that answer by saying, "I'll have a cheeseburger and iced tea. And tell Maisie it's for me so she'll know how to fix it."

"Aunt Maisie's not here," the teenager replied as she slowly wrote the order on a pad. "A lady named Arlene's doing the cooking. Do you still want the burger anyway?"

"Must be Arlene Wood," Jude said. "How bad could she screw up a cheeseburger?"

"Um, I guess so," Suzanne said to the kid. "Tell Arlene I want everything on it and mayonnaise and mustard both and to be sure and toast my bun."

"I'll have a cheeseburger, too," Jude said, "without the onions. And I'll have a glass of water with it."

"Did Maisie go shopping or something?" Suzanne asked the teenager.

"Nah. She went somewhere with her boyfriend. He's rich."

"Her boyfriend? Maisie's got a rich boyfriend? Who is it?"

The teenager shrugged. "I dunno. Do you want any dessert?"

Suzanne looked quizzically at Jude. "Who knew? Did you know Maisie had a boyfriend?"

"Nope," Jude answered.

"Just the cheeseburgers," Suzanne told their waitress. As soon as the teenager returned to the counter, Suzanne said, "See? I told you Maisie had a boyfriend. Well, at least Arlene's not a bad cook. Hope you didn't want dessert."

Jude shook her head.

"So, how're you feeling?" Suzanne asked.

"Oh, no. This isn't about me. We're going to talk about you and what's going on with you. Why have you been bawling?"

Suzanne planted her elbow on the table and propped her chin on her palm. "Sometimes fate is so damn cruel."

"As in what? C'mon, Suzanne. You know I'm sitting here on pins and needles."

Suzanne leaned forward, both forearms on the table. "Do you know how many days—and nights—I waited and prayed to hear from Mitch McCutcheon?"

A warning bell sounded in Jude's brain. "Oh, hell. He called you?"

"Better than that. He's here. In Texas."

A recollection of Suzanne's reckless side popped into Jude's mind. "But not in Lockett," she said cautiously.

"Abilene. I saw him in Abilene."

"Oh, My. God. Where did he come from?"

"Wyoming. That's where he's from, you know. His family has a ranch up there."

"Does Pat know?"

Suzanne shook her head.

"What's he doing in Texas?"

"He's headed for Dallas, well, Mesquite, really. To ride in that PBR rodeo over there. You know the one that's on TV sometimes. He wants to revive his career."

"That is awful, Suzanne."

"I know. I told him he's too damn old to be riding bulls. It's a kid's game. Hell, he's a year older than I am."

"I wasn't talking about it being awful that he's riding bulls. I meant it's awful that he got in touch with you. How'd he find you?"

"He just called. Out of the blue. I've still got my same cell number I've had for years. I nearly fainted when I saw his name on caller ID."

"And that's what you were doing yesterday? Hanging out with him? You know, I might be naive about men, but I'm not dumb about geography. If he's going to Mesquite by way of Abilene, he's taking the long way to get there."

"He called me from the airport. He wanted me to come to Dallas, but I told him it was too far. So he rented a car and came to Abilene."

The teenager returned with their drinks. As soon as she left again, Jude leaned forward and whispered, "Please tell me you didn't sleep with him."

Suzanne sat back in her chair, her eyes focused on the paper wrapper she had removed from her straw. "Oh, *hell*, no. I wouldn't sleep with him. We just talked." Her mind seemed to wander to another place and she said softly, "We just talked."

Jude unwrapped her own straw and crammed it into her glass, unable to mask her irritation. "But I know you. Even if you didn't sleep with him, you're thinking about it."

"What can I say? That magic never goes away. Even after a long dry spell, it just comes zooming back like it's never been gone. There are those moments you just never forget. Just stop and think how it is when you're with Brady."

She had a point, Jude had to acknowledge. She couldn't imagine ever finding a man to replace her husband, in bed or otherwise.

"He's still good-looking and sexy." Suzanne's eyes took on a glister of tears and she touched the inside corner of one eye.

"Come on, Suzanne. Magic or not, he beat you up. He cheated on you. Numerous times. With a bunch of different women. He surely doesn't really expect you to come back for seconds."

Suzanne turned her head and sniffed away tears. "He said he's sorry for the way he treated me."

Jude's attitude softened, remembering the hole of depression Suzanne had spent months climbing out of. "Did you tell him you're getting married?"

Suzanne shook her head.

"You should've told him."

Suzanne shrugged. "The right moment never came up."

"He wants to get back together with you?"

"That's what he says."

Jude couldn't hold back a huff of disgust and frustration that she felt. "More important, what did *you* say?"

"I said I don't know."

"Oh, my God, Suzanne, you're making me crazy. Abusers don't stop abusing. They get worse. Pat Garner adores you. He treats you like a queen. Plus, he's smart and responsible. He's one of the few men in Willard County with a college education. He's making a good living in a place where more than half the population lives below the poverty level. You and Pat—"

"I know, I know, Jude. Trust me, I *know* all that. But there's one thing wrong."

"There's more than one. But which one are you talking about?"

"Pat ain't Mitch."

16

Even after they were in his truck and embarked on the hour-and-a-half drive back to Lockett, the discussion J.D. and Maisie had had through dinner continued to weigh on him. "You said you want to be around your grandkids," he said. "How would our getting married resolve that?"

She gave a great sound of patience, as if he were the dumbest man on earth. "Because we'd live somewhere besides my apartment, Jasper. Surely in that ten-bedroom ranch house there would be room for my kids to come and see me or even stay with me and visit. Maybe I could even have my grandchildren stay for a spell in the summer."

J.D.'s first thought was *Oh, Jesus.*

In all the years with Maisie, he hadn't known she had designs on living at the Circle C or bringing her family there. He couldn't even imagine it, especially now with Jude pregnant and Brady's son and stepson probably spending more time there. He had never so much as hinted to Maisie that her moving to the Circle C was possible. In fact, he thought he had made that clear from the beginning and throughout their relationship that it was *not* an option.

He had worked day and night his whole life to make life at the Circle C tick along like a fine watch. The ranch's future ownership and management had been set up by his dad years back after the passing of J.D.'s two brothers, a process that hadn't even involved him directly. Eventually, Jude would take over and her coming child or children would inherit from her and so on. He didn't know Maisie's children or their children and he wondered, no more than Maisie had seen of them, just how well Maisie knew them. He did know what the sudden access to substantial wealth wrought in people who hadn't enjoyed it before.

Money—especially money people hadn't earned with their own two hands—changed more than lives; it changed personalities. He had seen it in both his ex-wives and in his brothers' wives. Beyond that, even in his most colorful imagination, he couldn't envision outsiders and strangers coming to the ranch and having free run of the place. The Circle C wasn't a vacation spot. It was a serious business with hard work under way every day.

"Evan Carter's house is for sale," he said. "It's a nice big place, big enough for your kids and grandkids to come visit. And it's in town. I'll buy it. I'll give you a deed for life. You won't have to live in that apartment above the café anymore."

"J.D., if all I wanted was a house, I would've asked you for one a long time ago."

"When I said I'll never get married again, I meant that, Maisie. You know what my family's been through. It seemed like Ben wasn't cold in his grave before Ike and Karen—"

"I well remember those days, Jasper. And I remember when your mother passed away and your dad's depression. I know the whole place was dropped in your lap overnight."

She might remember, J.D. thought. Everyone in Willard County probably remembered. The future of Strayhorn Corp had teetered and all of West Texas knew what the collapse of one of the largest and most successful old ranches in the state would mean to the regional economy. Maisie had been married back then. Though she had eventually buried her husband, his accidental death hadn't been steeped in scandal. She had been allowed to grieve in peace. She couldn't possibly *know* the agony and turmoil of the months after Ike's and Karen's deaths, followed by J.D.'s mother's death, followed by his dad's depression and withdrawal from the ranch's daily demands. "Maisie, I promised God that if He'd just let me get through all of that and hold the Circle C together, I'd never get married again."

"Do you honestly think God expects that of you?"

"I don't know what He expects. I just know that since all of that settled out, things have been good. I also made a silent promise to more than God. I vowed to my dad, to the Circle C, to my daughter, but most of all to myself. There's just been too much water over the dam."

"J.D., do you think I hung out here in Lockett all these years looking forward to my old age all alone? I thought that once you had yourself and the ranch firmly in hand again, you'd marry me. But I guess that was erroneous thinking on my part, especially given the fact that you wouldn't even allow us to be seen together in public."

J.D. felt beleaguered. He believed he had been good to Maisie. Besides helping her pay her bills, he had given her expensive gifts, had made some solid investments in her name. Christ, she could sell the jewelry he had given her and live off the proceeds for a few years. This conversation was worse than quicksand and he was starting to feel like a mouse in a maze. The talk always went somewhere he didn't want to go and threatened to ruin the good relationship he'd had with Maisie, the only relationship he had ever had that endured. He thought her a special woman, but that didn't mean he wanted to get married. "Maisie. Let's stop this. We're repeating ourselves. I've *never* said I wanted to get married again. I'm too old to be a bridegroom. But I'm willing to provide for you and take care of you. I know you haven't been close with your kids. I know you're facing an uncertain future. I'll buy you that house. That's the best I can do."

"It isn't enough, J.D. This isn't about *things*. There comes a time when a woman wants to belong to someone." She shook her head and stared out the window.

J.D. heard a break in her voice, but he steeled himself and they rode in silence until she finally dropped off to sleep.

*   *   *

Pat walked out of his arena after one o'clock in the afternoon, starved. He felt as if a boulder had settled inside his rib cage. After last night's unsettling conversation with Suzanne, he had risen from bed determined not to call her. It was her move. She was the one in a snit about something he wasn't comprehending.

He was on his way to the house to get something to eat when he heard her truck. He stopped and waited beside his round corral. As she parked and slid out, he stayed where he was, resting his elbow on the top rail. She walked over to him, carrying a brown paper sack, rose to her tiptoes and kissed him on the lips, then handed him the sack.

"Hope you haven't eaten. I figured you'd have crap for lunch, so I brought you something."

"Thanks." He took the sack and looked inside, saw a covered foam dish. "What is it?"

"Jude and I ate lunch in Maisie's today. She had those barbecue chicken nuggets she makes that I know you like. I also brought you some fried okra and coleslaw."

He dredged up a smile, though the tension between them might be even thicker today than it had been last night. "Sounds good."

"I've got to get back to the store, but I get off at five. I could come back."

"I thought your dad wasn't leaving town until Monday."

"I can't spend the night, but I can stay a little while. I want to talk to you about last night. I feel like we didn't finish what we were trying to say."

Finally. Maybe he was going to find out what the hell was going on. But a little buzz still zinged through his gut. He shrugged. "Okay. It goes without saying you're always welcome."

She nodded and gave him a smile that wasn't exactly a smile. "I know."

After she drove away, he continued to his house carrying his lunch. He appreciated that she brought him food, but if all she wanted to tell him was that she would come back later, she could have saved a ten-mile trip and called on the phone.

He poured himself a glass of milk and set up a tray in front of the TV set. Some kind of sports was always broadcast on Saturday afternoon. He surfed until he landed on ESPN and a PBR bull-riding event. He could tell from the commentary the show was coming from Dallas. The next thing he knew, he heard the name Mitch McCutcheon. The camera zoomed in on a stocky cowboy wearing red leather chaps with foot-long fringe and loaded down with gear. He had just made a ride good enough to put him in tonight's finals. Pat stared at the TV screen, his glass of milk suspended between his plate and his mouth. The interviewer, a woman, talked about McCutcheon's age—thirty-three was old for a bull rider—and making a comeback, blah, blah, blah. The guy looked and behaved like any typical bull rider—short, but stocky and muscular. And cocky. He had stark blue eyes and a short haircut, but before Pat could observe more, the interview ended and the camera moved on.

Like a venomous snake, reality slithered into Pat's psyche. Now he knew why the woman he was planning to marry had been out of touch for an entire day. "Fuck," he muttered.

He watched the rest of the broadcast, but no one beat McCutcheon's time. In replay after replay of his ride, Pat could see the sonofabitch was an athlete, could see he was fearless and gutsy, could see all the reasons he was a champion at a sport as challenging as bull riding, all the reasons women drooled over bull riders.

He keyed off the TV, got to his feet, carried what was left of his meal to the kitchen and dumped it in the trash. He no longer had an appetite.

Late in the afternoon, Jolie put together a grocery list and drove to town. She had called ahead to Lucky's to make sure they had all the cake mix she needed. She had taken her own money with her to also buy what she intended to cook for Jake on Monday. She had made enchiladas with homemade salsa and black bean salad Friday night and the family had raved over the meal and she had decided to repeat the menu for Jake.

As she passed in front of Maisie's Café, she saw Mr. Strayhorn's pickup parked on the side street. She thought he was out of town. Just then, she saw Maisie get out the pickup and start up the stairs. Mr. Strayhorn followed her, a suitcase in his hand.

Oh, my gosh, she thought. Was the owner of the café Mr. Stayhorn's girlfriend? Jolie hadn't heard one word about that though she had now been in Lockett more than a month. She had meant to ask Jude when she saw him leave Maisie's upstairs apartment a couple of weeks back but had forgotten about it.

As she entered the grocery store, she looked for Suzanne but didn't see her at the cash register. She claimed a basket and rolled it through the maze of aisles, selecting items she needed. She had started for the cash register when she saw Suzanne coming up the same aisle. "Hi," Jolie said.

"Oh, hi, Jolie," Suzanne said. She wasn't her usual cheerful self.

"What's wrong?" Jolie asked.

"Oh, nothing. Just not feeling that chipper today."

"Oh, I'm sorry," Jolie replied. "Anything I can do to help?"

"Yeah. You can shoot all the men on the planet."

Jolie laughed. "I'm laughing," she said, "but something tells me you might not be kidding."

Jolie returned to the Circle C kitchen and unpacked the groceries she had bought. Brady came into the kitchen and told her they were having three overnight houseguests who would be eating supper, along with Clary Harper and Dr. Barrett, the vet. Fortunately, she had put a big roast into the oven before she had gone to town. Expanding the menu to include five extra people wouldn't be difficult.

As soon as Brady left, Jolie asked Irene, "Who's here?"

"Is horse people," Irene answered.

"Horse people?"

"*Sí*. They talk about the horses."

"Oh."

"Is different. Before Grandpa die, no one stay."

"Why? People didn't like Grandpa?"

"Grandpa no ask."

"Oh. You mean he didn't invite guests to stay overnight." Jolie was pleased at how well they were communicating, in spite of the fact that she couldn't speak any Spanish. Irene's English was strong enough to make up for her own shortcomings.

"*Sí*. He no want in the house."

"You're saying Grandpa didn't want houseguests?"

"*Sí*."

Jolie couldn't imagine what kind of man Jude's grandfather must have been. The ranch house was huge. It could accommodate many guests and the Strayhorns certainly had enough money to entertain. It felt strange that a dead man wielded as much influence in the family as Grandpa seemed to.

Following a routine Irene had already established before Jolie arrived at the Circle C, she and Irene took a break before starting supper. Irene's husband came and picked her up and they went to their cottage for a couple of hours' rest—or as Irene called it, "the *siesta*."

Jolie drove to the front gate and picked up Danni, then returned to their cottage. She and Danni were relaxing on the sofa discussing Danni's school day when Jolie's cell phone warbled. She picked it up and checked caller ID. The screen showed a local number, but no name. Her stomach dropped to her shoes. The number wasn't Amanda's. Who else would call her from a local number?

Billy? Had he found her?

She had to know. She drew a breath, opened the phone and cautiously said, "Hello?"

"Jolie?" a deep male voice said.

Definitely not Billy. . . . But who? "Uh, yes, this is Jolie."

"This is Jake Strayhorn."

Utter joy unleashed in her chest. "Oh. Gosh," she said breathlessly. "I'm so surprised to hear from you." She scooted to the edge of the sofa cushion, leaning forward and bracing her elbow on her knee, working to untangle her tongue. "I—I didn't recognize your number. The caller ID—"

A deep but soft chuckle came across the line and she envisioned the fan of fine lines at the corners of his eyes when he smiled. "I'm using my cell phone. It's more or less my private number."

She felt a little spurt of satisfaction at the notion that after they disconnected she would have his private number on her cell phone. "Oh, I see."

"Just following up to see if Monday's still a plan."

"Yes. Yes, it is." She heard her excitement in her own voice and scolded herself to calm down.

"I called for you to give me a list of what I need to buy," he said. "As you might guess, I don't have a fully stocked kitchen."

She heard herself laughing like a schoolgirl. "Actually, I just came from the grocery store. I've already bought what I need."

"You bought food?"

"Well, yes. This was my idea. The dinner's supposed to be a thank-you gift, if you recall."

"I won't hear of you paying for a dinner for me."

"But I don't expect—"

"Jolie. I appreciate what you want to do. Just your effort is thanks enough. I'll buy the food."

"Honestly, it isn't necessary. It's already done. . . . When do you want to eat?"

"Well, let's see. Your daughter probably gets out of school around three, right?"

"Yes, but she doesn't get to the ranch on the school bus until closer to four."

"Let's make it lunch and give you time to get home before four. How about we eat at one o'clock?"

"Sure. I'll have to come over a couple of hours early, to make sure I have enough time."

"That'll be just fine. I'll make sure Chuck's got the office covered."

"The office? . . . Oh, your office. I didn't think." A new concern rose in Jolie's mind. "Will, uh . . . will Amanda be working that day?"

"She'll be in the office all day. Is that a problem?"

"No, no. Not a problem. It's just that I hoped I could get by without her seeing me come there. She'd ask questions about what I'm doing and I'd have to go into a long explanation. You know what I mean."

"Then come to my front door. It faces the street on the other side of the block. Nobody ever uses it. In fact, I doubt most people even know I have a private entrance to my apartment. There's a carport. My personal truck's parked in it. It's a silver Ford. Just park behind it. Will you be driving a Circle C truck?"

She laughed. "I have to. My car doesn't have license plates, remember?"

"Just checking," he said, and she heard amusement in his voice. She was sure he was teasing her. A pause followed and she wondered if they had lost their connection. Then he said, "I'll see you Monday, then."

"Yes. I'll be there."

They disconnected and she sat there a full minute, her mind a blank except for the image of Jake Strayhorn's face less than two feet across the table in Maisie's Café.

"Who was it, Mama?" Danni asked.

"The sheriff."

Danni's breath caught, her narrow shoulders scrunched and she giggled. "See, Mama? I told you he likes you."

"It isn't like that. I'm going to cook him a thank-you dinner because he did a favor for me."

"What did he do?"

"It was nothing important. Just a small favor. Listen, Danni, please do not say anything about this at school, okay? It could cause gossip we don't need."

"Okay. Is it a secret?"

"Yes. It's a secret between you and me. No one, absolutely no one else, needs to know. Now, it's time to go cook supper." Even as safe as Jolie felt at the Circle C, she still didn't want to leave her daughter alone.

"Okay," Danni said, her shoulders lifting in a sigh. "Maybe Jude will come and talk to me."

Usually, Danni watched TV in the family room or did her homework while Jolie worked in the kitchen. Sometimes Jude would see her watching TV and go in and talk to her about school or something else. Jolie could see they were becoming fast friends. "Maybe so. Don't say anything about the sheriff calling to Jude, either."

"Okay. I don't know what the big deal is."

As Jolie returned to the Circle C to prepare the evening meal, she felt as if she were floating on a cloud. The hours flew by. She loved the talk about horses and kept her ear tuned to the conversation going on at the table. She had never been around people who turned horses into show animals, or who bred them for money and knew their histories and bloodlines and could talk endlessly about them. There was an air about it that she liked.

The next day, she and Irene prepared a huge breakfast for the Strayhorns and their guests, followed by a big dinner. Jolie usually didn't make a dessert until the evening meal, but she threw together a pineapple upside-down cake for the guests to have after a dinner of baked chicken and salad.

On Sunday evening, before going to her home, Jolie asked Jude if she could drive to town for a personal errand in the ranch's pickup. She explained that she didn't have the money to register her car, which wasn't a lie. She still believed Jude knew nothing of her dilemma with the license plates or just how afraid she was of Billy showing up.

"Of course," Jude said, and mercifully didn't ask what Jolie was going to be doing in town. She did ask if Jolie needed an advance on her pay, but Jolie declined.

17

Pat checked the time. Five p.m. Suzanne's earlier visit had shattered his concentration. He had been unable to make himself spend the rest of the afternoon grappling with the mind of a knot-head horse. He had spent the time cleaning his barn instead. A simple physical task was all he could handle. Now he was filthy with barn dust and dirt. He returned to his house, showered and shampooed his hair, then put on old jeans and a T-shirt, all the while steeling himself against behaving like a jealous asshole when Suzanne showed up after work. The last thing he wanted to do was alienate her by being too possessive. At the same time, he was just plain pissed off that she would lie to him about where she had been all day Thursday.

He heard her truck at five fifteen. He walked outside and waited on the front porch. She parked in his driveway, slid out and came to him with a phony smile. She looked like hell. She had dark circles under her eyes and had been crying. He suspected she intended to kiss him, but he knew he couldn't respond in the usual way, so he clutched her arms and held her away.

"What's wrong?" she said, looking up at him.

Fury zinged through him. How dare she play with their future and be casual? "Can't play this game anymore, Suzanne. Saw your old friend on TV a little earlier."

With anger, emotions and his own insecurities riding at

the forefront of good sense, the statement had just popped out of his mouth. He had intended to be a little more subtle.

He couldn't describe all of the expressions that played across her face in a matter of a second. He saw a tiny twitch in a facial muscle, saw her eyes grow wet, but she didn't cry.

"Can we to inside?" she said finally. "It's hot out here."

He released her arms and gestured toward the front door.

They entered his pleasantly cool living room. "Want a drink?" He walked toward the kitchen. Whether she wanted one or not, *he* needed one.

"Do you still have some Crown?" she asked from behind him.

"Jack Daniel's."

He reached into the cupboard, pulled out a half-full bottle of black label Jack and set it on the breakfast bar with a clunk. A couple of glasses followed. He poured a shot into his glass and threw it down without tasting it, grimacing as he felt the burn all the way down. He poured a second shot for himself, then poured one for her. "Want something with it?"

"Water, maybe."

She placed her purse on the table, pulled out a chair and eased down to it as if she were exhausted. He thought about all the meals they had shared at that table, the laughs they'd had, the conversations they'd had, the plans they had made, the good times. He had shared *everything* with her. He turned on the tap, added a splash of water to her glass and handed it to her.

"Thanks." She took a swallow that reddened her cheeks and made her cough.

"Take it easy," he said. "Jack Daniel's is sipping whiskey."

"I hate it." She fanned her lips with one hand. "I don't know why people drink the nasty stuff."

Still standing behind the breakfast bar, Pat sipped from his glass, clenching his teeth as he swallowed the fiery liquid. "So he showed up."

She looked at him without comment for a few seconds. "He, uh . . . he's riding in the PBR show in Mesquite."

Pat thought about the beginning of his acquaintance with Suzanne, when he scarcely knew her. He thought of all the hours he had listened to her talk about Mitch McCutcheon, had even let her weep on his shoulder. Hearing about the guy now after all that had happened seemed surreal. To think the sonofabitch was within a few hundred miles seemed even more surreal. Pat almost couldn't bear to think of Suzanne sharing her heart, soul and body with the ungrateful fucker.

He set his glass on the counter and crossed his arms over his chest. "So to get down to basics, you were in love with him a couple of years ago, he treated you like shit and now he's come back for another go-round."

"No," she said, frowning. "Not necessarily. Mitch still doesn't know what he wants. Maybe he never will. In some ways, he's like a little boy."

Pat had had enough of Mitch McCutcheon to last a lifetime. He had no interest in an analysis of the guy's psyche. "But if he did know, and if what he wanted was you, you'd go with him."

"No," she said too quickly, then drew a breath and looked away. "I don't know."

Pat felt as if she had punched him in the gut. Reflexively his head shook. "Jesus Christ, Suzanne."

They stared at each other for a full minute. He braced one hand on the counter, the other fist on his hip. "So let me see if I've got this timetable figured out. I know he made the finals. Saw it on TV. He'll ride tonight and you're going to meet him somewhere tomorrow." He threw a palm in the air. "Or hell, I don't know, maybe you'll meet him tonight."

"No, I won't. I mean, I'm not."

Pat held her gaze, accusing her with his eyes, until she turned her head. "I'm . . . I'm supposed to see him in Abilene tomorrow," she said.

Pat hadn't expected to have gotten the scenario so right.

Hearing that he had caused an even tighter kink in his gut. "Look at me," he said, and she turned her head back and faced him. He looked her in the eye. "Thursday, when you spent the day with him. Did you fuck him?"

She glowered at him. "No!"

Should he believe her? He didn't know. "But there's a fifty-fifty, or maybe a sixty-forty, or maybe even a hundred percent chance you will when you see him tomorrow?"

"No. There isn't. He and I—we just need to talk. My God, Pat, I left him in the middle of the night. I—"

"And you feel guilty about that? Give me a fuckin' break. Forgodsake, Suzanne, when I first met you, you had a black eye. What kind of damn fool do you take me for?"

She slashed the air with both hands, her words thick with tears and emotion. "I have to do this, Pat. I'm trying to be honest here. I have to find out what my feelings are."

"And you think you can do that in one more meeting in Abilene."

"I don't know. I just know I have to try. I have to settle it in my mind. . . . And in my heart."

This was getting worse. Pat could hear his blood swishing in his ears. "Your heart? Bullshit. Do you hear yourself? We were planning on getting married, Suzanne. That's a lifetime promise. Jesus Christ, you've stopped birth control so you can get knocked up."

"Pat, I know. Believe me, I know."

He inhaled deeply, trying to calm himself. "And I know this. No self-centered sonofabitch who didn't have the guts to make a commitment back when he had the chance gets to come in here now and fuck us up. It's not right."

She winced, rose from her chair and walked back to the living room. He followed, leaving his drink on the breakfast bar. She sat down on the edge of a sofa cushion, propped her elbows on her thighs and looked up at him. "I know, Pat. I know how it sounds."

He could see her anguish, even felt a weird sympathy for her. He walked over and sat beside her on the sofa, schooling himself to speak calmly. "I believe I'm a better man than he is, Suzanne."

"Oh, Pat, you *are* a good man. I've told you."

"And because I'm a better man, I'm not gonna say you can't see him. But while he's filling your ears with bullshit promises, just don't forget—"

She broke into tears and buried her face in her hands.

He couldn't stand seeing her cry. "Shit, Suzanne." He sat back on the sofa and pulled her against him, bringing her head to his shoulder. "Don't cry." He stroked her hair. "C'mon now. Don't cry, Suz. Hell. Go on and see him. Get it over with. Go on and—"

His words were halted by her mouth finding his. She kissed him as if there were no tomorrow, thrusting her tongue deeply into his mouth. He couldn't help himself. He kissed back just as savagely, his need driven by anger and jealousy and adrenaline. He had never wanted to fuck her as much as he wanted it at this moment. She was his. She had claimed she wanted his child. No other man had a right to her.

They began to tear at each other's clothing. She was rough, tugging off his T-shirt, unbuttoning his fly; he was rougher, dragging her T-shirt over her head and throwing it aside. Then her soft warm hand was inside his shorts and her fingers were wrapped around his rock-hard dick and desire was thundering through his body. "Gotta get this off . . ." He levered himself up and shoved his pants and shorts past his hips. His cock stood tall and swollen and red, his balls drawn up into his belly, as if every last ounce of his blood had drained from his brain.

Her head lowered to his crotch. "No, Suz, don't . . ." Her mouth covered him with wet warmth and new sensation shot through him. "Aw, shit, Suzanne . . ." His head fell back to the sofa back, his eyes closed as he got lost in the titillating tongue flicks, the rhythmic sucking motions.

She licked and nipped, teased and sucked. He grew dizzy. His hips began to undulate involuntarily. He was on the edge. He gripped her head with both hands and dragged her mouth away from his groin, despite his overeager pecker thinking he had gone crazy. "Suz . . . don't," he huffed out, his breath coming in grating pants. "Let me get inside you."

"Pat . . ." she whimpered.

He sat up and went for the rest of her clothes. "Wanna be . . . inside you." He yanked off her boots, then clawed at her fly, opened her jeans. Together, they frantically peeled her jeans and panties off one leg. He reached for her naked thigh, brought it across his body until she stood on her knees astraddle his hips, her knees sinking into the cushions, her pussy only inches from his face. Her scent came to him, only making him hotter and he almost came. He knew that at this point she would be oozing creamy moisture and ready to take him. His hips lifted, his cock jerking and nudging as if it had a mind of its own, seeking her opening like a starved animal. She reached between them and guided it.

"That's it . . . that's it," he choked out, shuddering as the sensitive head pushed into her flaming flesh. She slid all wet and steaming onto him. On a grunt, he thrust upward, buried himself deep, demanding that she take all of him.

She yelped. Her fingers dug into his shoulders. "Yes . . . yes . . ." She began to move up and down, but her motion was hampered by the sofa cushions. "Oh, yes . . . Pat . . . I can't . . ."

His dick was on fire. He gripped her ass tightly with splayed fingers, helped her pump. Animal grunts escaped his chest. He sought her mouth again and filled it with his tongue, desperate to meld every part of him with every part of her. Every thrust took him deeper into a hazy profound need to possess, to own.

She tore her mouth away. Her head tilted back, her breasts thrust to him. "Suck me . . . suck me . . . help me . . ."

He shoved her bra up, heaving for breath as he devoured her flesh with no mercy, scraped her nipples with his teeth.

"Hard," she said, now riding him fast and frenzied.

He complied, bucked hard, pushed deep with every thrust.

"Oh, Pat . . . oh, Pat . . ."

He reveled in the noises and pleas that filled his ears, but he was losing control, knew he couldn't last. He slid his fingers between them, wet them with her juices and found her clit.

She began to pant and hiss through clenched teeth, her fingers digging into his shoulders. He felt her first faint contractions, then ripples, then clutches. She cried his name through sobs and tears as her vaginal muscles milked him with sweet powerful pulls. His own orgasm boiled through him like a volcanic eruption. His body went rigid, his teeth gritted. His only vague thought was of filling her womb with his semen, planting his seed. Nothing else mattered. He spurted and spurted, a dozen times, more, until he was empty.

Then it was over and they were spent and drenched in sweat and she was still weeping. His heart was thundering in his chest, his whole body shaking. They clung to each other, her face buried as she sniffled against his neck. A full minute, maybe two, passed before he could speak.

"Did I hurt you?" he choked out.

"No," she said, and sniffled.

"I didn't mean to be so rough."

"No, no. You weren't." She caught his jaw with her palm and pulled his face close. "I love you," she whispered, and covered his mouth with hers.

I love you, too, he thought, but he couldn't say it. He could only say it aloud when the moment felt perfect, with no barriers and no baggage. And this wasn't the moment. "I wish you didn't have to go home," he said instead.

"I don't have to."

"But your dad—"

"I'll call him and tell him I'm staying at your house tonight. It isn't like he doesn't know we sleep together."

Pat awoke the next morning well after daylight with Suzanne's tousled head resting on his chest under his chin. He was sore. He felt as if they had made love all night. And they had. He had come more times than he thought possible.

At one point in the night, she had told him she had come to his house to confess she had spent most of Thursday with

Mitch, then returned home to Lockett confused and frustrated. She admitted Mitch had asked her to go back to Wyoming with him, had made her a promise that they would get married. His parents remembered her and adored her. She revealed that she and Mitch had never been married. She told people in Lockett who asked they had been because she didn't want to bring embarrassment to her dad. Pat wasn't surprised they hadn't been married. He had already concluded just from watching the cocksucker on TV that Mitch McCutcheon wasn't the marrying kind.

Coming fully awake, he remembered he had horses to feed. He eased out of bed, dressed quietly in the bathroom, then went into the kitchen. His partial glass of whiskey still sat on the breakfast bar and hers still sat on the table. He picked up both glasses and poured the contents down the drain. Then he put coffee on to brew and trekked to the barn.

He saw the mares in the distance, heading toward the barn. Since it was breeding season, he kept them separated from his stud. He didn't want to risk an unsupervised pasture breeding episode where one of his horses might get hurt or pick up a reproductive tract infection.

He put out flakes of hay and watched the horses approach, the younger mares following the older one because they instinctively knew she was wiser and more knowledgeable of survival, which is how it went in horse society. Simple. Every animal knew its place and its role. His mind veered to human relationships, which were complex and nobody ever knew for sure what the hell was going on. His education in agribusiness and animal husbandry had taught him nothing about that.

He believed he had figured out something, though, by watching his own parents and his two older sisters. In every human coupling there seemed to be a giver and a taker, one who loved more and gave more. With his parents, his dad was the giver and his mother took and took, but it was his dad who was the stronger. The same appeared to be true in his sisters' marriages. He believed he was the giver in his relationship with Suzanne, as he had been in his relationship with Becky. And he believed he was the stronger. Suzanne was the fun, vivacious one, but at the end of the day, she needed him.

For a flicker of an instant, he let himself wonder if when Suzanne had been with McCutcheon, *he* had been the strong one. *Don't go there*, Pat told himself, and started back to the house.

When he reached the kitchen, she was up, standing in front of his refrigerator, coffee mug in hand. His robe enveloped her, striking her at her ankles. Her long blond hair was tied back with one of his bandanas. He thought she looked beautiful. Her eyes were still swollen. She had cried half the night. Once when they had made love, she had wept all the way through it.

"You've got eggs and bacon," she said. "Hungry?"

He went to her, wrapped both arms around her and pulled her close. She smelled like soap and water and toothpaste. "Starved."

She looked up at him, rose on her tiptoes and kissed him. "We didn't get much nourishment last night."

Indeed they had bypassed supper altogether. He smiled down at her. "That's a matter of opinion. You okay?"

She gave a low chuckle. "A little tender. It was a wild night, cowboy."

He chuckled, too. "Tell me about it."

"I'll cook." She left his embrace, rolled up the sleeves of his robe and started gathering things from the refrigerator—eggs, bacon, butter. While she fried eggs, he made toast. Sharing the morning with her felt right. He wanted to do it forever.

They took the food to the table and sat down. "Are you going to be mad if I go to Abilene today?" She wasn't looking at him. Instead, her eyes were focused on cutting her eggs with the side of her fork.

His gut clenched, but he tried not to show a reaction. He could make himself deal civilly with this situation with her old lover. He could make himself talk about it casually. He could give her space. Besides, if she wanted to go meet the sonofabitch, how could he stop her? At least she wasn't lying to him. He set down his mug. "No. I think you should go."

She looked at him, her fork stopped between her mouth and her plate. "You do?"

"Yeah. I think you should go down there and settle it with him once and for all."

She picked up her mug, sipped and set it down. "I can't believe you said that. You don't really feel that way."

"It doesn't matter how I feel. If you made a plan to meet him and you don't do it, if you don't clear the air, you'll always wonder about him. And what's worse, I'll wonder about him, too. It'll be like a loose end forever dangling."

She lowered her eyes and fiddled with her mug handle. He couldn't tell what she was thinking. "Then I think you should come back," he said, "and we'll get married and have the life we planned on. We'll never talk about him again."

She left her chair, came behind him and wrapped her arms around his shoulders, placed her mouth near his ear. "We can have the reception at the church," she said softly. "Jude won't mind. I know how much your friendship with Jake means to you."

A lump flew to his throat. He clasped her forearm and gently squeezed.

"I was afraid I'd lose you," she said. "I thought you'd send me packing."

He brought her around to his side, scooted his chair back and pulled her onto his lap. "When you said you didn't know how you felt about him, Suz, I came close to doing that very thing. But I must not have been ready to give up on us." He clasped her jaw and kissed her fiercely. "Lady, I'm yours. There ain't no way you're ever gonna lose me."

But later, as she drove away, headed for home to get ready to go to Abilene, he still wondered if she would decide on a life with Mitch McCutcheon.

18

The air in the Circle C kitchen was thick with mouthwatering aromas. Jolie and Irene had prepared a huge breakfast of fried eggs, sausage and bacon both, biscuits with cream gravy and fresh melon. Now they were putting the finishing touches on dinner for the Strayhorns and their guests. With Danni home from school, even she had helped in the kitchen. A pork loin Buster had cut for her was almost done. She worked at making a brown gravy while Irene mashed potatoes.

After dinner, Jude and one of the guests came into the kitchen and heaped compliments on her and Irene. As soon as the guests followed the others back to the barn, Jude lingered behind and said, "After two huge meals today, we won't need supper. Y'all take the evening off and rest. Daddy and Brady and I can fend for ourselves for supper."

Once the kitchen was clean and sparkling again, Irene and Reuben left for home, but Jolie stayed and used the food processor to grate a block of cheese she intended to use to make tomorrow's enchiladas. She had few kitchen tools to work with in the cottage. She put the grated cheese into a plastic storage bag and took it home with her.

At home, she still couldn't rest. While Danni watched and kibitzed, Jolie stirred up a devil's food cake from a gourmet recipe she had learned from the baker who supplied the

Cactus Café with desserts. Waiting for the cake to bake, she put ground meat and onions and spices on to cook for the enchilada filling.

"Whatcha making, Mama?" Danni asked.

"It's enchiladas for the sheriff's thank-you dinner," she said. "Remember I told you about it."

"Can I help?"

"Um, this is all I'm doing today. Soon as I finish, we'll watch a movie." She had rented *Bolt* for Danni at the grocery store. Lucky's seemed to have a little of everything.

By the time the meat concoction was done, so was the cake. While it cooled, she and Danni sat down on the sofa and watched the movie. Then all of a sudden, the day was gone. Danni bathed and Jolie tucked her into bed, reminded her that the meal for the sheriff was a secret. Then she set out to frost the cake.

Using a hand mixer she had borrowed from the ranch house's kitchen, she whirred a chocolate buttercream frosting together and slathered it on the two-layer cake. She even added some little frosting swirls and curls as decoration. It looked delicious. She had done a fine job, even if she did say so herself.

And she was exhausted. She was also so excited she probably wouldn't sleep a wink. But she had to. She had to look her best tomorrow.

The next morning Jude was in her office studying bull statistics when Suzanne called. "Hey, girlfriend, whatcha doing?" Suzanne said.

"The usual," Jude answered, relieved at hearing from Suzanne. She hadn't seen her since Friday when they'd had lunch at Maisie's. With Suzanne's old lover in the area, anything could have happened over the weekend.

"Got the coffeepot on?"

"I don't know. But if it isn't, we'll put it on. You're coming out?"

"Yep, I'm on my way."

"Obviously you aren't working."

"I'm not going in until after lunch. I just wasn't up to being my old jolly self this morning. Sometimes that facade is hard to maintain. Especially after a long, hard weekend."

Uh-oh. Now what's happened? Jude wondered.

Suzanne soon arrived and entered the ranch house through the back door, as did everyone except strangers. Jude met her and they went into the kitchen where the coffeepot was tucked into its spot on the counter and clean as a whistle.

"Where is everybody?" Suzanne asked.

"Lola and I are the only ones here on Mondays. We've finally got a routine going. Jolie and Irene and Reuben take off on Mondays. Daddy and Brady are eating breakfast almost every day in the cookhouse with the hands and on Mondays they eat dinner out there, too. And I sort of graze here in the kitchen. Then Brady and I usually throw something light together on Monday night. Now that I'm pregnant, heavy spicy food like what Windy used to make doesn't set well."

"Oh, I forgot. You're not drinking coffee, either. I don't have to have coffee. It's too hot anyway. Just give me something cold."

"Tea? Dr Pepper?"

"Dr Pepper sounds great. I'll help." She dragged a tumbler from the cupboard. "Are you drinking?"

"Apple juice."

Suzanne dragged down another tumbler and proceeded to fill both with ice cubes. She carried the glasses to the breakfast room's round glass-topped table. "Okay to sit here?"

"Sure. So, what happened over the weekend?" Jude pulled a jug of apple juice and a can of Dr Pepper from the refrigerator.

"Somebody was looking out for me, that's what happened."

Jude followed her to the breakfast room, handed her the Dr Pepper and poured apple juice for herself. "Are you and Pat still engaged?"

"We sure are." Suzanne popped the aluminum can top and filled her glass with the fizzing drink.

"Don't keep me in suspense," Jude said, screwing the lid back onto the apple juice bottle.

"Somebody or some thing kept me from making the biggest mistake of my life," Suzanne said. "Sit down and I'll tell you all about it. The trials and tribulations of Suzanne Breedlove's love life."

Jude sank to a chair and for the next fifteen minutes, Suzanne kept her mesmerized with the tale of her emotional meeting with Mitch on Thursday, her emotional episode with Pat on Saturday night, then going to Abilene yesterday and meeting Mitch for yet another emotional encounter of a different kind.

"I'm drained," Suzanne said in conclusion, gathering her long blond locks onto the top of her head, then letting them fall.

"I don't wonder," Jude said. "I'm surprised Pat stood still for you to go back to Abilene and meet with Mitch a second time."

"I was, too, at first. But the more I thought about it, that's the way Pat is. He likes things clear. No gray areas."

What Jude knew of Pat was mostly what Suzanne had told her. Though he had worked with some of the Circle C horses, his relationship was with Clary Harper, not Jude. "All I know, Suzanne, is he's been good for you. I don't know how you could find a better guy."

"Me, neither." She sipped her Dr Pepper, then grinned mischievously. "The sex ain't too bad, either. Now, instead of Mitch, it's Pat who sends me to the moon."

"Oh, you," Jude said. "This is about more than sex. This is about the rest of your life."

Suzanne chuckled. "I know. But you can't discount good sex. You know it's important to me." She gazed out the window wall onto the sun-drenched patio, a faraway look in her eyes. "Mitch and I talked for a long time. Talked about stuff we never discussed before. He begged me to go back to Wyoming with him. Made me a lot of promises." She turned back to face Jude. "Can you believe it?"

Jude lifted a shoulder in a shrug. "I don't know him. But I believe anything you tell me."

"After all was said and done, I asked him not to ever be in touch with me again. Hell, Jude, I don't even want him to send me a Christmas card."

"Wow," Jude said softly, amazed after hearing all she had previously heard Suzanne say about Mitch. "You told him that?"

"Not the part about the Christmas card."

"Was it hard?"

Suzanne nodded, her eyes showing a glimmer of tears. "Yeah, it was, Jude. He's changed. I could see I hurt him. It was upsetting. He and I shared a lot. But the more I thought about it, the more I realized that at this point, he and I don't share much more history than Pat and I do. And what I've got with Pat is a helluva lot better and more promising for the long haul. Besides all of that, it was hard to concentrate on anything Mitch said when I knew I could be pregnant with Pat's baby."

"Are you kidding me?" Jude asked. "I thought you took birth control pills."

"I quit. A few weeks ago. After I told Pat I wanted us to have a baby and he said okay if we got married. I told you I Pat and I are planning to have kids."

Jude shook her head. "Good Lord, Suzanne, you're a surprise a minute. Have you missed a period or something?"

"No. But I'm hoping."

"What have you told Pat about Mitch?"

"Everything. I told him everything. Even the stuff I didn't want to tell and he didn't want to hear. Nothing hidden between us." Suzanne blinked back tears. "And he still wants me."

Jude already had a good opinion of Pat Garner, but it lifted another notch. She felt for Suzanne. At one point, before Jude and Brady had confronted their feelings for each other, Jude thought she had lost him. She leaned forward and covered Suzanne's hand with her own. "I am so glad, Suzanne. I was so afraid you were going to do something stupid."

Suzanne sniffed and managed a damp smile. "It was tempting when Mitch first called. But I've learned something about myself in this whole thing. You know what was wrong with him and me?"

Jude blurted a laugh. "Well, I could think of several things, but what are *you* thinking?"

"When we were together, I loved him more than he loved me. That's why he treated me bad. I allowed it. I always felt like he was more than I was." She splayed the fingers of both hands for emphasis. "I mean, he was this famous, good-looking, all-macho bull rider who, drunk or sober, was on his way to becoming a world champion. I was afraid that if I stood up for myself, he wouldn't love me. Or wouldn't love me as much. I mean, a lot of women wanted him, like a trophy or something."

"You should have thought better of yourself," Jude said, but as she said it, she remembered what Suzanne had left behind in Lockett. Back when they were younger and still in high school, Jude had heard Suzanne's mother berate her for the smallest of things and criticize most of what she did. Leaving Lubbock, Texas, with Mitch, was Suzanne's form of rebellion.

"Yeah," Suzanne said. "I've always been the person who loved the most. It was that way even between Mom and me." She shook her head, dabbed under one eye with her finger, then drew in a deep sniff. "Is it that way between you and Brady?"

"You mean which one of us loves the most? It's me, of course. Brady would get along just fine without me. He *did* get along without me. I was the one spinning like a top and going nowhere. That doesn't mean he didn't want me or love me or that I wasn't important to him. It just meant he isn't

the kind of person who would commit suicide over losing
me or any woman."

"And what about you? If you lost Brady, would you be
suicidal?"

"Of course not. I'd somehow go on just as he would. But
honestly, I can't stand to think of what it would be like without him. He's everything to me. And I believe that I'm everything to him."

"Pat and I had this very conversation last night—"

"You stayed at Pat's with your dad in town?"

"Oh, hell, Dad knows Pat and I sleep together when he's
out of town. We aren't teenagers, you know. In fact, I've
already told Dad I'm going to go ahead and move into Pat's
house. Hopefully, I'll get everything moved and unpacked
and straightened up before the wedding. Then we can go on
our honeymoon and come back to our home."

"I'll help you," Jude said. "Go on with what you and Pat
talked about."

"Well, he has this belief that it isn't possible for two
people to love each other equally. He thinks that between
him and me, *he's* the one who loves the most."

Suspicious, Jude asked, "Is he?"

"He thinks he is, but I don't think so. He's the strong
one. I'm just the loud one. Pat's like Brady. I think if I disappeared he would go on with his horses and keeping his
place up and doing what he was doing when I met him. Oh,
he'd miss me and maybe think about me, but his life would
go on."

"All life goes on, Suzanne," Jude said, donning her teaching hat. She hadn't studied biology for six years for nothing. "It's what nature intended."

"For that whole trip to Abilene yesterday," Suzanne said,
"I tried to bring up a mental picture of how things might be
with Mitch if I went to Wyoming with him, but it just wouldn't
come to me. I couldn't imagine it. All I could think of was
what if I lost Pat? What would I do? Being with him is like

being with a rock and I've gotten used to that security. He's not mercurial and exciting like Mitch, but he's strong as iron and I know he'll always be there."

"There's something to be said for strength and reliability," Jude said.

"You remember what I said to you when we went to lunch the other day?"

"You said a lot. Refresh my memory."

"I said the bottom line is Pat ain't Mitch. Well, the *true* bottom line, Jude, is Mitch ain't Pat."

Jude laughed with delight and the belief that Suzanne had made the right decision.

"Oh, and I should tell you, Jude. Pat mentioned the reception to Jake. Jake just won't attend a party at the Circle C." She stared out at the large limestone barbecue pit. "Too bad. I know it would be great, and I appreciate your offering to do it, but I think we have to have it at the Methodist church. Jake's the only person Pat wants to be his best man. He would be fine with skipping the reception altogether, but if we're going to have it, he wants his best man to be there."

Jude couldn't keep from being a teeny bit hurt. Not at not hosting the reception, but because one of her only two cousins refused to set foot on the place where he was born, even at the request of a friend. "Oh, that's okay," she said. "It was just an idea. I'm not surprised Jake won't come to the ranch. Lord, he's been back in Lockett six years and he hasn't been here yet, so why would he come to a wedding reception?"

Suzanne nodded. "Right. I wonder if he'll ever get past that."

19

After getting Danni off to school, Jolie dressed with care. She wore jeans every day in the ranch kitchen, so she liked an opportunity to wear something feminine. Everyone had always teased her about being a girly girl. Even when she had worn a plain green uniform in the Cactus Café, she had often added a tiny floral pin or a bow in her hair or a pair of pretty earrings to dress it up.

Today, she had put on a floaty summer skirt with yellow sunflowers on it and a knit top. She styled her newly colored hair in a casual flip and put on her makeup, all with extra care. She recognized the behavior, had seen it many times in other women who worked with her in the Cactus Café when they had a boyfriend they wanted to impress. Jolie didn't understand why she was doing this. Jake Strayhorn wasn't her boyfriend and never would be.

She arrived at Jake's apartment slightly before eleven o'clock. Standing on his front porch, hanging on to her purse and her sacks of goods, she buzzed his doorbell.

Though she had been counting the hours until this moment, she was so nervous she had forgotten the cake in the pickup. Before she could organize her thoughts to go back for it, his front door opened and he stood in the doorway, tall and imposing and dressed in a gray snugly fit short-sleeve T-shirt instead of the long-sleeve dress shirt he had been wearing every time she had seen him. He was without his gun, she noticed. His body was lean, but muscular, as if he worked out, and he had a dusting of brown hair on his forearms. She wondered what he did in Lockett to stay in such good shape. He smiled his glorious smile. "Hey," he said.

"Hello," she said with exaggerated enthusiasm, trying to overcome the sudden discomfort she felt in her chest.

He invited her in and at the same time, reached for the two sacks in her hands. His scent surrounded her and she couldn't keep from noticing the bunch of his biceps as he gripped the sacks. "Hope you're hungry," she said, and stepped inside his living room.

"I am."

With no sacks to hold, she interlocked her fingers in front of her and looked around to get her bearings and make her pulse rate settle down. The room was lit by natural sunlight. Though muted by the overhang on his porch, it streamed through one large window and cast a rectangle of light onto spotless tan carpeting. The apartment's interior wasn't nearly as shabby as the building's exterior, she noticed. It was clean and well kept, but decidedly utilitarian. And masculine. But then, the same things could be said of its occupant.

She identified one concession to self-indulgence. A large flat-screen TV appeared glaringly out of place against a brown-paneled wall and a DVD storage cabinet was full of DVDs. The sheriff was a movie fan?

"Kitchen's this way," he said with a tilt of his head. Carrying the grocery sacks, he led her to the kitchen. It was a galley-style kitchen, smaller than the kitchen in the trailer she had left behind in Grandee, and infinitely smaller than the brightly lit Circle C's cavernous kitchen. The cabinets were old and painted white, but she saw a newer-model stove and refrigerator and a dishwasher. Everything was as neat as the living room and it was sparkling clean. It even smelled clean. The only object that sat on the white-with-gold-speckled Formica counter was a Mr. Coffee.

He placed the sacks on the counter. She put her purse on one end of the counter and began to unpack the sacks. Lifting out a small box of tea bags, she said, "I remembered that you drank tea that day in Maisie's, so I brought some tea bags to make sweet tea." She stopped her task, looked at him and shrugged. "I didn't know if you'd have tea bags."

"You're right. I don't."

"You wouldn't have a large pitcher, would you?"

"Might have." He opened a cupboard and produced a large plastic pitcher.

"Great. Do you have sugar?"

"Always have sugar," he said, grinning. "Sometimes I like a little in my coffee. What do you want me to do to help you?"

"Well, I need a couple of little pans."

"Coming up." He squatted on his haunches at one of the cabinets and found two small saucepans.

"Does one of these have a lid?"

"Lid?"

"Oh, that's okay. I can use a saucer."

"One saucer, coming up," he said, and opened the cupboard.

She filled one pan with water and set it on the stove to boil. "I make tea the way we brewed it in the Cactus Café where I used to work. It's really good."

"Tea's fine. I like tea."

"Then after I get the tea going, I'm going to chop some things for a *salsa cruda*. I intended to do it back at the ranch, but I ran out of time."

"Good. I like that, too."

She glanced at him across her shoulder. "You know what *salsa cruda* is?"

"Darlin', I'm from Texas. I know a little bit of Spanish."

"Right," she said, and laughed. "You probably have to speak Spanish in your job. I've learned a little since I've been working with Irene. Do you have a good knife and a chopping board?"

"I do have the knife, but afraid not on the chopping board. How about a plate?"

"A plate's fine."

"I'm good at chopping," he said, taking a plate from the cupboard.

She smiled at him. Billy had never helped her in the kitchen a single day that she could recall. "Okay, does it make you cry to chop an onion?"

"Don't think so."

"Good. Then you can chop this." She handed him a white onion from one of the sacks. "I always cry when I chop onions."

"Well, we don't want the cook crying," he said, taking the onion and lifting a big knife from a drawer. He placed the plate near the sink and tackled the onion with fast, nimble fingers. She paused for a minute, watching him. Her eyes moved from his hands to his strong facial features. Though his brows were brown and his eyes green, his lashes were black and thicker than a girl's, a unique and striking combination. She caught herself looking too closely and returned her attention to taking cans out of the grocery bags. "I brought canned sauce so I don't have to take the time to make it."

"Fine with me."

She handed him two tomatoes, a jalapeño pepper and a little bunch of fresh cilantro. "These need to be chopped, too. You can just put them all together in a bowl."

"Can do," he said, continuing to chop.

The water began to boil, so she placed tea bags in it, removed it from the burner and covered the pan with a saucer. When she looked again, he had a small bowl full of finely chopped tomatoes and onion.

"You're really fast," she said.

He gave her a wink and a thumbs-up, then turned to the sink, turned on the faucet and rinsed off the knife.

Lord, she liked him. Too much. And it was insane. She couldn't be distracted by liking *anyone*. She was trying to survive.

She shook herself mentally, grabbed a spoon and gave the ingredients he had chopped a quick mix, added some seasonings and shoved the bowl into the refrigerator. She turned to the enchiladas and the black bean salad. He wanted to help again, so she set him to opening cans, which took him no time at all.

Once he had finished, he leaned his bottom and the heels of his hands on the counter edge and watched her assemble the enchiladas. She had brought an aluminum foil pan for the enchiladas, assuming he wouldn't have a pan she could use. "Where'd you learn to be such a good cook?" he asked.

"Seems like I've been cooking forever. But where I learned to do it right was at the Cactus Café. We didn't have chefs, but we had supergood cooks. It was a busy twenty-four-hour place. Sometimes I helped in the kitchen if we were shorthanded or if we were busier than usual. The cooks always taught me things. And I watch the Food Channel. Or I did when I had TV, that is."

"You don't have TV in your house?"

"The reception's awful. There's a tall antenna on the roof, but the reception's still bad. There's no cable channels anyway, even if we had good reception. The ranch house has satellite TV, though."

"Don't feel put upon. TV reception's the same all over this area. The county pays for Internet service via satellite for my office, but not TV. That's why I buy movies."

"I noticed your DVD collection," she said, preoccupied with dipping the tortillas in warm sauce, then spooning the seasoned meat and grated cheese onto them.

"I bought that fancy TV in the living room, thinking I needed it for entertainment," he said. "But I don't have much time to watch it. Don't like the programs anyway, so if I watch, I usually tune in to the news and weather."

A silence fell between them. Her hands were busy, but her mind was scrambling for something to say. He saved the day by saying, "Busy week at the Circle C?"

"Yes, actually, it was. There were some horse people there over the weekend. I think they were talking about breeding horses."

"Ah. This is breeding season. And the Circle C has some of the best horseflesh in Texas. Or the whole Southwest, for that matter."

"I tried to eavesdrop on the conversations, but I didn't understand what I was hearing. I've never been around animals of any kind. Did you know they have their own vet? And their own clinic?"

He smiled. "Yes. I did know that."

"I was blown away when I found that out. I can't imagine having so much money."

"Horse breeding's big business at the Circle C. They produce a lot of winners of all kinds."

"They've got that one horse they're really proud of. Sandy Dandy. He's the one everyone's interested in. I've seen him in the corral. Jude says he looks so regal because he knows how important he is. I swear it seems like Jude knows how horses think."

Jake laughed. "Jude's been on a horse or around horses her whole life."

"Do you have a horse?"

"Not at the moment. Someday, when I give up this job, I might like to have a couple of pleasure horses."

"Danni's going to learn to ride."

"That seems logical, living where you are."

"She's really excited, but I can't keep from worrying about her getting hurt."

"I'm sure that's what any good mother would do. But she'll probably do just fine."

Jolie had filled the aluminum pan with enchiladas and reached for the pan of warm sauce. "I try to be a good mother, especially since I'm really the only parent Danni has. Billy has no interest in being a parent. He can't even take care of himself, much less a little kid. In some ways he's like a little kid himself."

She topped off the pan of enchiladas with the rest of the sauce and grated cheese and slid it into the oven. Then she started on the black bean salad. "I hope you like black bean salad. I made it a couple of nights ago for the family. Jude said Brady loved it."

"Brady was a bachelor for a while. He's probably like me. Just about any food he doesn't have to fix for himself tastes good."

A laugh burst from Jolie. "Thanks a lot."

He looked at her with puzzlement; then as he realized what he had said, his expression changed to one of apology. "Oh, hell. I didn't mean it like that."

She laughed again. "I know what you meant."

Then the oven timer buzzed. The tea was made and the black bean salad was finished. They had been talking nearly an hour, but it seemed like a few minutes. She pulled the pan of enchiladas from the oven, filling the small kitchen with delicious spicy aromas.

"Oh, man," Jake said. "I can't remember the last time this kitchen smelled this good."

Suddenly she remembered the chocolate cake. "Oh, my gosh. I left the cake in the pickup. I hope the frosting hasn't melted. I'll be right back." She hurried to the door, berating herself for being such a nervous ninny that she forgot the cake.

While Jolie was gone, Jake brought out a couple of plates and silverware and carried them to his small round table in the tiny eating area off one end of the kitchen. The space and the table barely accommodated two people. Not since he had been living in the county's facility had he had a female guest in it to eat. Not even one.

She came back into the apartment carrying a cardboard box. "I think I got it just in time. The frosting's soft, but it's not melted. Thank goodness it isn't that hot outside."

He took the box from her and looked down on a round chocolate cake that looked as good as any he had ever seen in a bakery. It had little curlicues of frosting around the edge and little flowerlike things made out of frosting here and there. "Wow. That looks too pretty to eat."

He set the box on the counter and she lifted out the tall

cake. He felt his eyes widen. It looked even better out of that box.

"It's a layer cake," she said anxiously. "Devil's food."

"You made that?"

"Well, yes, I—"

"Man, oh, man. Darlin' I can't remember the last time I had chocolate cake."

"Really? But you like it, don't you?"

She seemed to be waiting for his reply. "I love it. I just never have it."

"The plate isn't mine. It belongs in the house where Danni and I live, so I'll have to get it back from you."

"No problem."

She lifted her arms and let them drop to her sides. "Well, I guess we should eat."

They sat down at the table and Jake let her place two enchiladas on his plate and a helping of the black bean salad and they dug in. The meal was the best he had eaten in a long time. He didn't often get homemade food. Hoping he was showing his appreciation, he raved about it throughout the meal. After he had cleaned his plate, he had no room for cake. "I'll probably have a big slice of that cake and a glass of milk for supper. You are going to leave it behind, right?"

"I made it for you," she said. "I'm going to leave all of this food with you."

Then they were out of things to say. And Jake felt he had said enough about the food.

She looked around. "This is a nice apartment."

He looked around, too. "It's not a bad place, considering its age and the county's lack of funds. I added a few things on my own, such as all the new appliances in the kitchen. The old ones that were here weren't safe." He lifted a shoulder in a shrug. "It'll do. My needs are simple."

"You certainly keep it clean."

"Military training. And a local woman comes in and cleans for me once a week."

Jake was having a good time. Much better than he'd had

the last few times he had taken women out on dates. Jolie was down-to-earth and without guile. He detected no agendas and no axe to grind. He felt comfortable and unthreatened. "Want to see the rest of it?"

"Sure."

They picked up their plates and placed them on the counter, and then he walked her through the apartment. "There's three bedrooms," he said as they walked from room to room. "The last sheriff had a family. But to tell you the truth, I don't know why a man with a family would want to live here."

Jolie didn't know, either. Where would children play? Even where the beat-up trailer she had shared with Billy was located, there was a place for Danni to play outside.

One bedroom held weights and workout equipment. Now she knew why he looked to be in such good shape. One bedroom held a desk and bookshelves. Of course he would read books. He was smart.

They reached a room where a king-size bed almost filled the small space. A person would have to walk sideways around it. It was covered with a blue spread and pillows. Everything in the place was either blue, tan or brown, just like the living room.

"And this is my bedroom," he said.

She looked at the bed, then looked up at him. She couldn't hold back a laugh. "It's almost wall-to-wall bed."

"I'm a big guy," he said sheepishly. "I like having room to stretch out."

Instantly she thought of him sprawled on the bed and wondered if he slept in pajamas. Of course not, something told her. He wasn't a pajamas kind of guy. Her next thought was of his big powerfully-built body and she couldn't keep from imagining him naked.

"It's a little crowded," he was saying, bringing her back to earth. "But since I'm the only one who lives here, it's fine for me. Obviously, if I had a family, I'd live somewhere else."

"Why don't you live out at the Circle C?" she asked. "No one uses even half of that big house."

"Not a good place for me," he answered. "Since there's only three of us in the sheriff's department, me living close to the office and the jail is more convenient anyway. So, tell me about your family."

Oops. He slid past that question about the Circle C in a hurry. She shouldn't have asked it. She made a mental note to avoid talking to him about the ranch. "My family? There's not much to tell. My mom lives in Terrell, but she works in Dallas. Last I heard of my sisters, one was in California and one was in Bossier City. She works in one of the casinos. After all of us got grown, we sort of drifted away from each other. What about you? Do you have brothers and sisters?"

He shook his head. "Only child."

"Gosh, you don't have family, either. Guess we have that in common."

"Do you mind if I ask how old you are?"

Why would he want to know? She cocked her head and frowned. "I don't mind. I don't care about age. I'm twenty-seven, but sometimes I feel like I'm a hundred."

"Why?"

"Because I've never fit in with girls my own age. Why do you ask?"

Jake was disappointed. He knew Billy was nearly thirty-one. He had hoped she was the same age, which would make her only seven years younger than he. "No reason. You do seem older."

"A lot of people tell me that. It's probably because I sort of grew up early. I've been holding down a job for as long as I can remember. I quit school a little before Danni was born. I started working full-time when I was seventeen. And I sort of raised my sisters. I've always had responsibilities."

He could tell that about her. Responsibility, if one assumed it, made a person grow up fast. He knew that much from his own experience. After his mother and he left the Circle C, she suffered a breakdown and never quite recovered. Jake had gone to high school and run their household until he graduated.

They had made a full circle and were back in the kitchen. "It's almost time for me to go," she said. "I'll clean up my mess and—"

"No, no. You don't have to bother. I'll do it and if I don't get finished, the woman who cleans for me will do it."

"But I hate leaving a mess behind."

"It's not a problem."

"Well, uh, just let me know when you're finished with the plate the cake's on and I can drop by and pick it up."

"I'll do that."

Jolie hated to leave, but she picked up her purse from the end of the counter. "You mentioned age. Could I ask how old you are?"

His eyes leveled on her face. "I'm thirty-eight."

Eleven years. He was eleven years older than she. Their gazes locked for a few seconds; then she turned away and started toward the living room. "I, uh, enjoyed the visit."

"So did I. And it was a real nice meal."

"I could do it again," she said quickly, hating to leave even more now that she knew his age. "I mean since you don't have anyone to cook good for you and—"

"I'd like that. But I don't want to impose—"

"It's not imposing. I like doing it."

"Jolie. You don't owe me anything."

"I know. But I'm grateful for your looking out for me and Danni."

Their gazes locked again and she saw the hint of a frown line between his thick brows. She couldn't tell what was going on inside his head. "Damn," he finally mumbled, and looked at the floor.

"It isn't that I don't feel safe where I am, but . . ."

When she didn't finish her thought, he looked up. "He's going to show up. You know that, don't you?"

She swallowed. "How—how do you know?"

"I know his type. You're the closest thing to grounding he's got. And I know they won't keep him in jail in Dallas forever on a low-grade drug beef. If you know any more about him than what we've already discussed, or what he might try when he gets out, it'll help if you tell me."

She felt as if all the blood had drained from her body. Her life had been so calm since she had come to Lockett, a part of her had deluded herself into believing Billy would never find her. "Well, I don't know. He's, uh . . ." Her voice trailed off as she remembered she was speaking to a cop. As much as she trusted Jake Strayhorn, she couldn't bring herself to tell him about her strange relationship with Billy.

"When you left him, did you leave clues behind that would indicate where you might be?"

"I don't know. I tried not to, but I just don't know."

20

Jolie barely made it to the front gate before the school bus. Instead of going home—she had started to think of the cottage as "home"—she and Danni went to the Circle C's kitchen. Monday might be her day off, but she still had to start on the cupcakes. Irene and Reuben were off also and the family was out of the house as well. With the exception of the housekeeper, Lola, she and Danni had the whole place to themselves.

"Do you wish this was our house, Mama?" Danni asked, her small fingers gripping the counter edge as she watched Jolie mix up chocolate batter.

"Heavens, no," Jolie said, thinking of parts of the huge mansion she hadn't even explored yet. "Look how hard Lola works keeping this place up."

"It's like a palace," Danni said wistfully. "But it's scary, too, especially the third floor."

Jolie looked at her daughter with astonishment. She didn't disagree with Danni's assessment. Nothing was on the third floor but fully furnished bedrooms and bathrooms that were never used. The vast emptiness had given Jolie a haunted feeling. She had heard Lola complain about the bathrooms up there having to be cleaned every day. "Danni!" she stage-whispered. "When did you go up to the third floor?"

"One day when you were cooking. I didn't do anything. I just looked at everything."

"This isn't our house. You can't just go everywhere you want to without asking someone. Don't do that anymore."

"Jude showed me her rooms."

Jolie hadn't been to Jude and Brady's suite, though Lola had told her they occupied an area on the second floor that was larger than the cottage where she and Danni lived. "She did?"

"Uh-huh. She showed me where the baby's gonna live. Jude and Brady's rooms are pretty."

"We'll make our little house pretty. Next payday, I'm going to get some things for your room."

"Are we going to stay here forever, Mama?"

Riding a high after spending several hours with Jake, Jolie was happier than she had been in months or even years. She abandoned her cupcake batter, sank to her knees in front of Danni, clasped her narrow shoulders and looked into her face. "Oh, I hope so, Danni. I really like it here."

"Me, too," Danni said. Then she added with a huge sigh, "But the wind blows all the time."

Jolie laughed, pushing back a tendril of Danni's long hair. "You're so funny. What would I do without you?" She pulled her daughter into a hug, then set her away and said, "Jude says that's because we're almost in the mountains. This is what they call the high plains. We're a lot higher here than we were in Grandee. Cooking isn't even the same. When you bake something, it takes longer and sometimes it doesn't turn out."

"Does that mean the cupcakes will be bad?"

"No, no. I've got it all figured out. The cupcakes will be fine. I promise."

Jolie felt so good she baked four dozen cupcakes before calling it a night.

Even with all Jolie had to do, she thought of Jake constantly. Every hour a new little thing to wonder about him cropped up in her mind. Among the things she pondered was if there were other men like him in the world. Surely there were, but she had never met them.

She casually knew a few of the cops who came into the Cactus Café. Were all of them like Jake? Was Jake's personality and demeanor a cop thing? She doubted it.

She thought about the funny warm squiggle that passed through her system at just the sight of him. She couldn't think of any guy she had ever met who affected her that way.

Like a little song, the words "Jolie and Jake" and "Jake and Jolie" played in her head. Their names fit, as if they were a couple. She felt silly, like back in school when kids would write "someone plus someone" on their book covers. But silly or not, she couldn't stop the thoughts.

And the largest question of all was, would she ever again have the opportunity to spend time alone with him? To her great regret, she couldn't imagine how she would.

The day before the school's-out party, she started early and as she cooked three meals for the family, she sandwiched in between the frosting of the cupcakes with thick creamy chocolate icing and candy sprinkles. She now had twelve dozen. Buster had gotten into the act. Last week, he recognized the challenge of transporting so many cupcakes to the school all at one time, so he had ordered some bakery boxes from one of his sources. Irene pitched in, added the sprinkles and set the cupcakes in the bakery boxes as Jolie finished frosting them.

On Friday, Jolie dressed in jeans and a plain orange knit shirt and arrived at the school after dinner with twelve boxes of a dozen cupcakes each, one of which she intended to deliver to Jake. More than a hundred students and teachers came to the party in the school's community room. To her relief, cupcakes were not the only goodies that had been volunteered. Everyone had plenty to eat. Between Jude and Danni introducing her, Jolie met the parents of most of Danni's friends. She felt welcomed. She called the day a success.

As the crowd began to disperse, she gathered her purse

and the box of cupcakes and walked out of the building looking for Danni. All afternoon, she had kept the cupcakes for
Jake hidden under her purse. To her surprise, instead of Danni,
she saw Jake striding up the sidewalk, giving her a full-body
view of him and his get-out-of-my-way gait. He was wearing his usual starched and ironed jeans and a pale green dress
shirt and tie. The gold badge on his shirt pocket glinted in
the sunlight. She paid no attention to the badge. Instead, an
awareness of him as a man slithered through her. Her heart
began to dance and her face broke into a smile. When they
met she said hello, then added, "I didn't realize you'd be at
the party."

He smiled at her, too, the green color of his eyes en-
hanced by his tanned skin and his green shirt. He said hello,
but his expression quickly turned serious. "I'm not at the
party," he said. "I came here hoping to run into you. I want
to let you know Billy's out of jail."

Her dancing heart stumbled and her libido calmed down.
"Oh?"

"He got released a few days ago."

She knew Jake had looked up Billy's record, but she had
no idea he had been keeping up with him so closely. "He
wasn't there very long."

"I don't know his circumstances and the Dallas jail's
crowded. I take it he hasn't been in touch with you?"

She squinted against the sun and tented her eyes with
one hand. "No. But then, he doesn't have my cell number. I
changed it before I ever left Grandee."

"Hmm. That's good and that's bad. It's good that he can't
harass you by phone, but bad that now you won't know if
he's trying to call you. If he can't call you, he might be more
inclined to try to confront you personally. Does he know
Amanda?"

"Not really. He's only seen her once or twice."

"Would he make the assumption that she's someone who
would help you?"

"Even if he did, I'm not sure he knows where she lives."

Jake planted his hands on his hips and looked at the sidewalk, as if he were thinking. "After getting out of jail, it might take him a day or two to get reoriented."

"If it's like the past, he won't start drinking or drugging right away. He won't have any money. He might try to find a job of some kind. Last time, one of those community services places found him a job."

"What does he usually work at?"

"Laborer. He works on construction sites, cleaning up and stuff like that."

"I imagine jobs on construction sites are hard to come by right now," Jake said, "even around Dallas. Building's cut back everywhere."

"What should I do?"

"Nothing much you can do but wait. Just keep your eyes sharp. Be sure your doors are locked. Observe your surroundings so you don't get surprised. Does he have a car?"

"An old pickup. But it doesn't run half the time. If he's been locked up, it's been sitting somewhere undriven. It probably doesn't run now. I'd be surprised if it could make a trip from Grandee to Lockett."

Jake nodded and pulled a small notebook and pen from his shirt pocket. "Describe it to me."

"It's a Chevy. I forgot the year, but it's around twenty years old. It's supposed to be tan, but it's faded and rusted in places."

"License plate?"

"Oh, my gosh, I don't know it. I just always recognized the pickup, so I never bothered with learning the license plate number."

"I'll be able to find the number," Jake said, closing the notebook and sliding it back into his shirt pocket.

Just then Danni and one of her girlfriends bounded up to where they stood on the sidewalk. "Mama," Danni gushed, her whole small body alive with excitement. "Madison wants me to spend the night and go to the movies in Abilene tomorrow."

Jolie hesitated. She had rarely allowed Dannie to do sleep-overs. "Well, I don't know, Danni—"

"Hi," a fortyish woman said, following behind Danni and her friend. Jolie thought she had just met the woman inside, but couldn't remember her name. "We just met. I'm Janelle Wilder and this is my husband, Mike."

The chunky balding man removed his cowboy hat, held it to his chest and offered his right hand. "How do you do, ma'am?" Jolie shook hands with him. The man then turned to Jake and offered his right hand to him, too. "H'lo, Sher-iff. How's it going?"

Jake smiled and took his hand. "Good, Mike. Everything's quiet."

"Haven't seen you in a while. Just want to tell you again how much we 'preciate the job you're doing. I sleep better at night knowing it's you who's looking out for us."

"Thanks, Mike," Jake replied.

Jolie's chest swelled with pride, as if she and Jake were together, as if he were hers to be proud of.

"We'd love for Danni to spend the night," Janelle Wilder said. "We've been promising Madison that she could have a friend over and we'd all go to the movies."

"Please, Mama? Please, please?"

"Well, I—"

"We'll take good care of her," Mike Wilder said. "Have her back home by tomorrow evening before supper. In case you're worried about who we are, I'm the manager of the cat-tle auction. Been around here forever. Everybody knows me. Just ask Jake here."

Jolie looked up at Jake. "That's true," he said.

"Please, Mama?"

"But you don't have any of your things. You don't—"

"We'll get her fixed up with what she needs," Mike said. "We've raised four kids. We've got all kinds of kid stuff."

Janelle Wilder smiled again, an open, friendly smile. "Mad-ison's our youngest and our only girl. She came along late.

If she wants a friend over to go to a movie, that's usually what we do. I admit we spoil her."

On a sigh, Jolie relented. The two girls raced off together. Everyone said, "Nice meeting you," and then the Wilders were gone, too, and Jolie was left standing there alone with Jake. She looked up at him.

"Mike and Janelle are okay," he said. "Danni will be fine. I would've said something if I thought there was a problem."

Jolie nodded, though she wasn't sure how she felt about allowing her daughter to go with strangers. Still, she trusted Jake, a fact that startled her. She couldn't identify at what point she had ceased to think of him as just another cop and started to want his personal opinions and approval. "Where do they live?"

"In town, over behind the bank. Redbrick house. The only one on the street."

Deciding she was worrying unnecessarily, Jolie nodded and dredged up a smile. "Would you like a dessert? I brought extra." She offered him the box of cupcakes.

"Yeah?" He took the box, looked inside, then grinned. "You made these?"

"Danni volunteered me to make a couple of dozen for the end-of-school party, but before I knew it, the number had grown to ten dozen. Making more didn't matter, so I made some for you, too. I was planning on coming by your office after the party and dropping them off so I could pick up the plate I brought the cake on."

"Oh, yeah, the plate. It's all clean and sitting on my kitchen counter." He was looking at the cupcakes in the box as if he could devour all twelve of them.

"You already ate that whole cake?" She laughed, covering her mouth with her hands.

He was still grinning. "I told you I don't get chocolate cake that often. Look, I'm going back to my office. You can come on by and pick up that plate like you planned."

"Okay. I'll be right behind you."

Jolie's heart pounded all the way to the jail. Approaching the run-down building, she saw Jake's county SUV parked in front of the sheriff's office. Amanda's Toyota was parked there, too. Jolie's heart sank. She did not want to walk into the sheriff's office and run into her cousin, who would surely ask her personal questions. She drove around the block and parked behind Jake's personal pickup; then she walked to his front door and pressed the doorbell. To her relief, he opened the door and invited her in.

She moved on to the kitchen and saw the open box of cupcakes on the counter.

"Those look great," he said.

"They've got chocolate chips inside. They're a little bit messy. You should probably eat them with a fork."

"Want to share one with me? We could sit down at the table here." He gestured toward his tiny table.

"Okay. I guess I've got time."

"Good. I've got milk or tea, either one, to go with it."

"Tea would be good."

He dragged two small plates out of the cupboard and two forks out of a drawer. Then he filled two glasses with ice cubes and took a jug of tea he had bought somewhere from the refrigerator. "I ran out of the tea you made," he said.

"I could make more," she said quickly. "I left the tea bags here and it only takes a few minutes." As if she were in her own kitchen, she went to the cupboard where she knew a pan was kept, filled it with water and put it on to boil.

They sat down at the table with cupcakes and the store-bought tea. "I noticed that tall fence with the razor wire," she said.

"Exercise yard," he replied, slicing off a bite of the chocolate confection.

"Oh, of course. Do you often have people in jail here?"

"Not very often. Lockett's a law-abiding place." He slid the bite into his mouth, then closed his eyes and let out a long hum.

"Is it okay?" she asked nervously.

"It's great. Better than the cake. Although I didn't figure anything could be better than that cake."

She fanned her hand in front of her face and leaned back in her chair. "Whew. I'm glad you like it. I wouldn't want to get a reputation for being a bad cook."

A few beats of silence passed. She cut a bite of the cupcake on her plate and slipped it into her mouth, searching her mind for something to say. Finally, "How many people will the jail hold?"

"It's got two cells. Want to tour it? I could—"

"No, no. No tour. At least not while Amanda's here."

He looked puzzled for a few seconds, then said, "Oh. I gotcha. . . . Well, I'll just tell you about it. It used to have four cells, According to the old-timers around here, back in the forties when the jail was built, farming was booming and they'd just started drilling for oil. Lockett was a bigger town and needed a bigger jail. Nowadays, the county's got less than half the population it used to have. When I took over as sheriff, we were paying for storage on some records. Turning two of the cells into storerooms saves the taxpayers that expense."

"That makes sense," Jolie said.

The water in the pan began to rustle and she got to her feet and set it off the burner. "I just thought of something." Frowning, she bit down on her lower lip. "I hope not too many people see the Circle C's pickup parked in your driveway." She found the box of tea bags in the cupboard, along with a saucer. "They might wonder what's going on." She dunked two of the large tea bags into the hot water and covered the pan with the saucer, then glanced at the clock.

"They might," he replied. "But I doubt it. Hardly anybody ever drives down that street. You might have noticed there aren't any houses. Nobody wants to live close to the jail."

Jolie returned to her seat at the table. "I guess not. I don't blame them."

"Most people think it would be pretty easy to get out of."

"Would it?"

"I don't know that anybody's ever tried. Most of the people we arrest are locals. Drunk or involved in a family fight. Or both. They don't want to add jailbreaking on top of the problems they've already got. They're rarely here more than a day or two. If we arrest a perp I'm worried about, we take him down to Abilene to the Taylor County facility. It's a real jail." He smiled and dabbed a crumb of chocolate from his lip. "That's why we need only two cells."

Discussing jails and criminals reminded her of Billy. "If Billy should come here, what would you do?"

"Depends on what *he* does."

"I don't want to see him, but I don't know how I could stop it if he knows where we are. With so many people living on the ranch, people come and go whenever they want to. No one would ever question Billy or anyone who came to see me."

"The Strayhorns might be open-minded, but if somebody drives onto that ranch that they don't want to be there, it's still trespassing. Do J.D. and Jude know about Billy and your situation?"

She shook her head. "I've been meaning to tell Jude. At first I didn't tell her because I was afraid she wouldn't want me working there, but now that I know her better, I think she wouldn't be mad if she knew."

"Jude's a good woman. Feels guilty because she's rich. She's generous hearted and likes to help people. You probably should tell her."

Jolie nodded. "I need to just make it a point to talk to her about the whole thing. Funny, but I thought with Billy and me not being married, he'd eventually—"

"You're not married?" Jake's eyes focused intently on her face.

That little squiggle darted across her stomach again. "No. Not anymore. Last year, Billy stayed in the jail in Grandee for six months. That was the last straw. I divorced him."

"While he was in jail?"

"Yes. And I got full custody of Danni. He didn't object."

"But your name's still Jensen."

"Well, yes. I couldn't very well change it. It's Danni's name, too, even though she's going by Kramer right now in school."

"And you still lived together after you got divorced?"

Now she was nervous again and fearful of what Jake would think. She got to her feet and stepped to the stove to check the steeping tea. "I sort of got stuck in the situation. I intended to move before he got out, but I had a hard time getting enough money together and my car needed tires. On top of that, they released him early. I didn't even know he was out until he just showed up one day."

Jake still sat at the table, watching her. "I need that pitcher we used the other day," she said, glad to change the subject. "For the tea."

"Oh, sure." He got to his feet, went to the cupboard, dragged it off a shelf and handed it to her.

She poured the warm tea into the pitcher. "As soon as this cools, you could add some water to it."

"Okay." He was standing within an arm's reach.

She looked up at him, into his wise eyes. "I intended to leave, even after he was back."

"I'm not judging you, Jolie."

"But I want you to know why I didn't." A sudden burn of tears passed through her eyes and she fought not to cry. "He became possessive and threatening. Like he was before he went to jail. After he got back this last time, he seemed to hang on harder. He thought I was plotting against him. I guess the divorce caused him to think that. The counselor the county had him talking to told me meth users get paranoid. I've been afraid of him for quite a while. He's a mess. Sometimes he looked at me more like his mother than his wife."

"What did he threaten you with?"

"Different things. Sometimes he'd tell me how he was

going to kill me. Other times he threatened to take Danni and disappear. He doesn't want Danni, but he knew threatening her could get to me." She drew a deep sniff.

Jake placed a hand on her shoulder. His touch was so gentle, yet so strong. A long breath left her lungs.

"A lot of people threaten things they never do, Jolie."

"Oh, I know." She cleared her throat. "I hear people say things all the time, like 'I'll kill you' or something like that. My mother used to say, 'I'm gonna knock your head off,' but no one ever believed her. And I can't recall that she ever even hit anyone."

"Then again, sometimes somebody means it," Jake said. "I know you say you're afraid of him, and I'm not saying you shouldn't be, but do you really believe he might harm you?"

"I don't think he would when he's clean and sober, but when he's drunk or stoned, I think he'd do anything. That meth turns people into animals."

Now both of Jake's hands cupped her shoulders. He pulled her closer and placed a kiss on her forehead. A strange warmth radiated through her, as if his touch was magic. She almost shivered as she savored his gentleness. She had experienced little gentleness in men.

"I won't let him hurt you, Jolie," Jake said softly. "Or your daughter."

But you're not always around, Jolie thought.

21

Jake watched Jolie drive away. She wasn't wrong about meth users. And Billy Jensen sounded like a head case all right. High on meth, perfectly sane people became head cases. It was entirely possible that Jolie was in danger.

Hearing her say she was a free woman had affected him. He felt disturbed and unsettled and at the same time relieved. He didn't understand it. Her marital status was none of his business.

He also felt uncharacteristically aggressive, even hostile, toward Billy Jensen. He didn't understand that, either. He had confronted and arrested many of the Billy Jensens of the world. Most of the time he had felt sorry for them. Yet he had a suspicion that if ever confronted by a man who could mistreat a woman and little girl as nice as Jolie and Danni, any sympathy Jake might feel would fly right out the window.

As soon as Jolie was out of sight, he walked from his apartment into his office, slid his glasses out of his pocket and wrote Jensen's particulars on a piece of notepaper. He carried the information to Amanda's desk. "Where's Chuck about now?" he asked her.

"Who knows?" Amanda answered. "You know Chuck. He probably got thrown off course helping somebody feed their chickens or something and forgot what he's supposed to be doing. He's due in here any minute."

Jake glanced at his watch. Four o'clock. He handed Billy

Dean Jensen's information to Amanda. "Get this out to the towns around us."

She glanced at the note, then looked up at him, frowning. "A BOLO? On Billy Jensen? That's my cousin's husband's name."

"Yeah. What do you know about him?"

"Only what I've already told you. He's a badass. Drinks too much. Does dope. Has he found my cousin?"

"Not yet. He's been in jail in Dallas, but he's out now. Make sure Chuck gets this information. Just in case Badass Billy decides to put in an appearance around here."

"But how did you—"

"I'll be in the apartment if you need me before Chuck gets here." He started back up the hallway toward his apartment. The last thing he wanted to do was discuss Jolie's problems with Amanda.

Except for a couple of warnings to speeders and paperwork earlier, his day had been uneventful. Well, not entirely uneventful. His afternoon with Jolie Jensen couldn't be called ordinary.

She and the fact that she wasn't married wouldn't leave his head. He couldn't think of the last time a woman had dominated his thoughts. He couldn't even put his finger on what specific thing made her stick in his mind. It was mostly what he sensed. She was honest and loyal. He couldn't keep from being amused that she worried about getting the Circle C's cake plate back to where it belonged. Hell, out at that ranch, probably nobody even knew they owned a cake plate. Or cared. And she was courageous. He knew that climbing out of the box life had built around her long before she had the ability to influence her destiny was hard, even impossible for some.

He also sensed that she and her daughter needed him. He wanted to be needed. That was why he had been a cop for so many years.

But lately, something new had taken root within him and he didn't know where it came from. He now realized he wanted more than to be wanted, which had nothing to do with being a cop. He wanted a companion—a woman to be thrilled to see him drive up in front of the house, wanted to be thrilled himself about going inside and finding her there, waiting for only him. He could picture Jolie in the kitchen preparing something delicious that they would share, could picture her daughter excited about her school day. He wondered if he was too old to have kids of his own. Not that he hadn't known plenty of men his age who had infants, but was it responsible to bring a kid into the world when you would be nearly sixty years old when that kid hit twenty?

He made himself a sandwich, poured a glass of milk and sat down to watch the news, which usually depressed him. For years, he'd had a feeling that society wasn't winning the war on crime and his confidence that it ever would had dissipated to nothing long ago. He was the first to admit he had become a cynic, even a curmudgeon, both characterizations of himself he didn't especially like.

While he watched reports of war and mayhem overseas, corrupt politicians and murder and disaster in the U.S., his thoughts drifted to the place he had recently bought from old Glenn Petry out on the canyon rim. Petry's wife had passed on a few months back. His kids who lived in Lubbock had talked him into selling the place and moving closer to them.

The house wasn't great, but it was livable because Petry and his wife had lived in it. The land was good—six hundred acres of pasture that was leased for grazing and three hundred twenty acres in maize, also leased. A full section and a half of land. And the place had a good water well that supplied drinkable water, an important asset in West Texas.

Jake had no great aspiration to have cattle or horses other than pleasure horses as he had told Jolie. He knew little about farming. What he desired was space and a change from the overdose of reality that had been a part of his life since he was fourteen years old. Running from his life was one of the reasons he had left Dallas and the homicide division of Dallas PD, where he could have named his own future in law enforcement if he had chosen to. He had left Dallas behind and come back to Willard County.

The Petry house was twenty miles from town, perched on a canyon rim ten full miles from the front gate. What could give a man a greater feeling of space than ten empty miles stretched out in front of him and a deep canyon behind him? Jake figured he could live out his days right there. He had all the money he needed. He could afford to do anything he wanted to. He had spent some time in Colorado while in the army. He wanted to return to the Colorado mountains to fish and hunt, wanted to buy an RV and travel the country. He had seen more of foreign countries than he had seen in the good ol' U.S.A. As a lover of history, he knew there was plenty to be seen. For the first time in a long time, it occurred to him that it would be nice to have someone to share it with him. And his next thought was of Jolie Jensen. It was amazing that just as he was thinking of giving up law enforcement, he should run into a woman who awoke something inside him.

He sighed, turned off the TV and pulled a book from his bookcase—*Historic Sites Along the Oregon Trail*. He loved the Old West. As much as he enjoyed the book, he couldn't concentrate on it. His concentration was focused on Jolie and her daughter and the confrontation with her former husband that was bound to come.

Jude stayed behind after the school's-out party broke up to help tidy and straighten the community room and visit with other teachers. She left late in the day, intending to catch Suzanne at the grocery store.

Sure enough, she found her friend in Lucky's back room sitting at the computer. Suzanne looked up. "Hey, girlfriend. Looks like you survived the party with those little crumb crunchers. It's late. Is it just now over?"

Suzanne seemed to be in much better spirits than when Jude had seen her on Monday and she looked better in general. "I stayed behind to talk to some old friends. It's kind of bittersweet since I won't be going back to teach in the fall."

"Yeah," Suzanne said, smiling. "Just think how your life's going to be changed by this time next year."

Jude gave a huff. "I just hope I can handle it."

"Sure you can. You've raised baby horses. Taking care of baby people can't be much harder."

Jude felt her brow crease in a frown. "Actually, baby horses are smarter than baby people. Odd, isn't it?"

"You could hire a nanny, you know."

"Brady and I talked about it, but we decided we wouldn't. Why have a baby if you aren't going to take care of her? I don't want her to grow up without me."

"Just a thought," Suzanne said.

"I might consult with Lola or someone who has raised kids, but mostly I want to do it myself." She placed her hands on her hips and looked over Suzanne's shoulder at the computer screen, but didn't recognize the program. "Whatcha doing?"

"Entering bar codes into the POS system. Gotta keep up with inventory, you know."

"I'm thinking of going by Jake's office and trying to arm-twist him into coming to the reception. What do you think?"

"Honestly, Jude, it isn't that big a deal to Pat and me." She turned her swivel desk chair and looked up at Jude. "Sit down," she said.

Jude sank to the armchair beside Suzanne's desk. "I know, but it would be fun and I'd like to do that for you."

"I know you would and Pat and I appreciate it. But I've already told the pastor we'll probably want to have the reception at the church. The only big difference will be that we won't be able to have booze. But it's a wedding reception. Nobody needs to get snockered. Pat and I can celebrate with champagne later." She grinned wickedly. "We might come up with an innovative way to enjoy it even more, given a little privacy."

"No doubt," Jude said. "You've made a sex maniac out of Pat."

"I have not," Suzanne said indignantly. "He always liked sex. But before me, he never had a good opportunity to express himself."

Jude laughed and Suzanne laughed with her. One of the traits Jude enjoyed about Suzanne was that whatever popped into her head fell out of her mouth without inhibition.

"But I have a selfish motive, too," Jude said. "Besides wanting to have a big party, it's such a good opportunity to try to get Jake to come to the ranch. I have to believe Daddy would be receptive."

"Well, good luck," Suzanne replied, and laughed again. "But don't pester Jake on our behalf."

"Speaking of Jake, I have to tell you what I saw at the school's-out party. He met Jolie out in front of the school. They were standing—"

"Jolie Jensen? The gal you hired as a cook?"

"I saw her give him a box of cupcakes and they were standing really close and looking at each other plumb cow-eyed. I couldn't believe my eyes."

"You are shitting me," Suzanne said. "Do you think she has something going on with him?"

"I don't know how she could. Or when. She works all the time. I am giving her Mondays off, but I haven't kept up with what she does with her free time. Besides, you know Jake. Ever since that business with that schoolteacher, he'd never have something going on in Lockett."

"This is too delicious," Suzanne said with a mischievous giggle. "Wouldn't it be something if the elusive Jake Strayhorn got flanked and hog-tied by your ranch cook?"

"Stranger things have happened. She's a really nice person. And she's so pretty."

"Be sure to keep up with that and keep me informed," Suzanne said.

* * *

When Jude reached home, she learned from Jolie that Daddy wouldn't be home for supper and Brady had volunteered to grill steaks for everyone, including Jolie, Irene and Reuben, on the red limestone fireplace grill out on the patio.

Jude hurried upstairs to dress. Dressing for supper had always been her custom. Appearing at the table clean and neat had been demanded by her grandfather.

Soon after she stepped into the shower, Brady opened the door and stepped in, too.

"Hmm. Where'd you come from, cowboy?"

"Just passing through, ma'am," he answered between languid, luscious kisses. "Slaughtered a couple steers. . . . Got meat for the table."

They soaped each other sensuously. She loved the feel of his smooth skin and perfect sinewy body covered with silky bubbly suds. "Is that so?"

"Hmm." He kissed her.

His large capable hands glided over her, his fingers finding all of her most sensitive places. "You're a devil," she said. "If you're cooking for everyone, we don't have time for this."

"I know."

"If we're late, everyone will know what we've been doing."

"Sweetheart, you're pregnant. I think they know what we've been doing."

"Okay, but we still don't have time."

They gave up on sex and left the shower. As they dried each other, he held her away and looked at her stomach.

"It's too soon. You can't tell," Jude said. But she could tell. Her tight jeans felt extra tight. She dropped her towel and turned toward the mirror.

"Yes, I can," he said. "See?" He grasped her waist with both hands. "I used to be able to almost put my fingers together around your waist. Now look."

"You could not," she said, though she could see his fingers were inches apart. She turned in his arms, ran her hands over his hard, powerful shoulders.

"Could, too," he said softly, and again enveloped her with his brawny arms for a long kiss.

"We've got to stop. We'll never get to the barbecue," she told him.

"Shit. I'm so horny now I won't be able to cook."

"Don't think about it. But eat hearty. You're going to need your strength."

They parted and he left for his own dressing area. Jude put on a loose-fitting black gauze dress, fancied it up with turquoise jewelry and tied back her hair with a rawhide string. Brady came back into her dressing room smelling marvelous and kissed her silly one more time. When he lifted his mouth from hers, he said, "Later, Mabel. We've got a date. I'm gonna make you come 'til you scream."

"Uh-huh," she agreed. "Can't wait."

Downstairs in the kitchen, Jolie had put together some tomatoes, green peppers, mushrooms and onions, even some peaches, for the grill and made a salad that included everything but the kitchen sink. She had also made a homemade dressing in the blender. Jolie was a wonderful cook and she and her daughter were starting to become like members of the family. Not seeing Jolie's daughter, she asked, "Where's Danni?"

Jolie explained that Danni was spending the night with Madison Wilder.

"Oh, that'll be fun," Jude said. "I know the Wilders very well. Danni will have a great time. Mike Wilder can do voice imitations of animals and he tells the funniest stories. I've had his two oldest boys in my classes. They're good kids."

As they ate, Jude said to her husband, "These steaks are perfect. All this time you've been telling me you couldn't cook anything but bologna and cheese sandwiches."

Brady chuckled. "I've moved up a notch."

After the meal, while Irene and Jolie fussed about cleaning off the table, Jude and Brady sat talking. "I love this patio," she said. "I was so looking forward to putting together Suzanne and Pat's reception here. We haven't had a party since before I finished college. I'd even found a band from Lubbock to play."

"Uh-oh. Jake must have decided not to come here," Brady said, picking up her hand and enclosing it inside his own.

"I don't mean to interrupt," Jolie said, the empty salad bowl under her arm, "but why won't he come here?"

A visual of Jolie and Jake on the sidewalk in front of the school came to Jude, but she pushed it aside. Of course Jolie knew nothing of the enigmatic Strayhorn family. "Waaay too much family history," she said. Then she turned to Brady. "Have you said anything to him about the reception?"

"Haven't seen him," Brady said. "But I don't think we should push it. Jake has his reasons. They're deep and personal. If he makes up with the Strayhorns, it'll have to be in his own good time."

"But it just seems so sad. I always felt like Grandpa could've said something or done something that would have fixed the problem with Jake, but he refused to. He wouldn't even talk about it. So much time has passed now. I don't think Daddy would get upset if Jake came here, do you?"

"Don't know. J.D.'s not a man who wears his feelings on his sleeve."

"It's too bad Mr. Strayhorn missed supper," Jolie said. "The steaks were so good. Did he have supper with his girlfriend?"

"Oh, Lord, no," Jude said, laughing. "Daddy doesn't have a girlfriend. I can't remember a time when he's *ever* had a girlfriend. There used to be a widow in Abilene he went to see occasionally, but he hasn't even done that in recent years."

"Oh," Jolie said. "I thought his girlfriend was the lady who owns the café."

"Maisie?" Brady asked.

"Why would you think that, Jolie?" Jude asked.

Jolie's expressive brown eyes grew even larger and she didn't answer right away. "I just assumed it. I've seen him a couple of times coming and going from the apartment where she lives."

Jude blinked several times, mulling that statement over, then turned to Brady. "Why would Daddy be coming and going from Maisie's apartment?"

"Couldn't tell you," Brady said, then turned his attention to Jolie. "When did you see him?"

"Uh, last week. . . . And the week before that."

Now Jolie was obviously nervous. Jude hadn't meant to make her feel as if she were being interrogated.

"You're sure it was him?" Brady asked.

"Well . . . yes, I'm sure." She shrugged again. "Or at least I was when I saw him."

Jude felt oddly blank. She had known Maisie Thornton since childhood. Never, not once, had she heard an inkling of any kind of relationship between her and Daddy. Jude felt her brow knit. "I cannot imagine. Now curiosity is killing me. I'm going to have to ask Daddy what he's doing at Maisie's."

At ten o'clock, Jolie came back to the patio. "We're all finished. Irene and Reuben have left and I'm going home, too."

"Good night, Jolie," Jude and Brady said in unison. "Wonderful salad," Jude added, and watched Jolie climb into the Circle C pickup and drive home.

"Have you noticed Jolie's car has no license plates?" Jude asked.

"Haven't paid attention," Brady said.

"Why do you suppose that is? She and I had the briefest conversation about it once, but if she told me, I don't remember why."

"Beats me. Is that why she's been driving the ranch's truck on her days off?"

Like her husband, Jude hadn't paid attention, either, to what vehicle Jolie drove. She had to admit she wasn't a tough-minded supervisor. "She's doing that?"

"Every time she goes to town," Brady said. "I haven't seen her in her own car in quite a while."

Jude didn't want to jump to conclusions or entertain negative thoughts about Jolie, but she hesitated. "Well, she can't really drive a car with no plates, can she? I did give her the keys and tell her to feel free to use the pickup."

"Good idea," Brady said. "Let's go to bed. "Four o'clock comes early."

Since he rose at four every morning, Brady usually went to bed before now. They moved into the house, locked the doors and started upstairs.

The conversation from just minutes before about Daddy and Maisie preoccupied Jude all the way up the stairs. The information, if true, was strangely disturbing. Jude thought she knew her father, and the father she knew was a stoic individual whom, in her wildest imaginings, she couldn't picture as a lover. If he was secretly seeing some woman, a side of him she had been totally unaware of had suddenly manifested itself.

They reached their suite and went inside. Jude moved directly to her dressing room and changed into a thin, short gown, tied her long hair back with a ribbon, washed off her makeup and brushed her teeth. When she returned to the bedroom, Brady was already in bed. "You're clothed," he said, deadpan.

Her gown wasn't see-through, but it was revealing enough. "Hardly."

"I like you better naked."

Jude walked over to the side of the king-size bed. She placed a hand on her hip and studied a nail on the opposite hand. "Listen, Brady, I've been thinking."

"Uh-oh. That statement has an ominous ring to it."

Now she planted both hands on her hips and gave Brady a direct look. "I've been thinking about Daddy and Maisie. Do you really think she could be his . . . well, his convenient woman?"

Brady rose on his elbow. "Something tells me we're gonna talk about this."

"We have to."

"I can't imagine your dad with a convenient woman. There's probably a logical explanation for him to be walking up the stairs to Maisie's apartment."

"What could it be?"

"I don't know. Maybe Jolie was mistaken about who she saw."

Jude gave a little gasp of exasperation. "Oh, you men. You have no appreciation for nuance."

"Right on," he said.

She sank to the edge of the mattress. "I'm trying to decide if I should approach Daddy and ask if he's seeing Maisie. . . . Or should I approach Maisie and ask her?"

"Why not think about it tomorrow? You might decide you want to leave the lid on that box."

That could be good advice, Jude thought, but once an idea entered her head, she was loath to step back from it. She had heard more than once that when she got something on her mind, she was worse than a dog with a bone. That component of her personality had proved to be both blessing and curse at different times. She didn't try to deny it. Could she help it if she was curious? She was a scientist. Surely all scientists had curious minds.

Indeed, her track record for weaseling personal information out of her father was sorely lacking. In their relationship over the years, he had always been eager to give her his opinion and try to direct her life, but had rarely mentioned his own personal activities.

"I just can't imagine Daddy with a girlfriend. I always thought if he had a female companion, he wouldn't be so eager to pry into *my* life. But whenever I've so much as hinted at the idea, he's always cut me off and changed the subject."

"Uh-huh," Brady said, now lying on his back, his arms cocked behind his head.

"I mean, look at him. He's a virile, handsome man. He's at home anywhere, whether he's riding herd with the hands or dining with Austin politicians. I think he would be attractive to women, don't you?"

"I have no idea," Brady said.

Jude heard the dismissive tone in his voice, but she refused to be deterred. "Maisie is an open, friendly person. Approaching her might be easier and more productive. I've known her forever."

Yet all Jude really knew about the woman was that her two kids, both older than Jude by a few years, had gone to Lockett school and Maisie had owned the café for more years than Jude could calculate. "Lord, when I was little," she said, "I used to go into the café and Maisie would make me ice-cream cones."

"Hmm," Brady said.

"I've taken Maisie for granted." Frowning, she looked across the room at the crocheted lace curtains. "I mean, she *is* an attractive woman and she's been a widow for years. I've never given much thought to her and Daddy going to school together. They must be about the same age. They might have been in the same grade."

"I think you should let sleeping dogs lie."

Jude turned to him. "Brady, why do I feel like I'm having this conversation all by myself? You've thrown two clichés at me, but haven't said diddly-squat about a thing I've said."

He rose to his elbow again and opened the covers, inviting her to come inside. "I just think you ought to stay out of your dad's personal business."

She gave a little huff. "After all the years he's meddled in mine? Not a chance."

He reached for her hand and urged her into bed. "I know you," she said, stretching alongside him and snuggling close to him. "You're going to try to throw me off track with sex."

"Good plan, huh? Will it work?"

She grinned up at him. "It might."

"We did have a date, remember?"

22

Jude awoke the next morning on a mission and Brady wasn't in bed to distract her. His plan to prevent her confronting her father had only worked short-term. She dressed and put on her makeup, then went down to the kitchen, where she found Jolie and Irene working on the noon meal. Irene was flouring quail breasts. "Oooh, quail. Are we having company for dinner again?"

"Mr. Strayhorn came in and said there would be three guests," Jolie said.

"Ah. More horse owners." Jude prepared a bowl of cold cereal, then leaned her bottom against the counter edge and munched. "Did Daddy say where he was going from here?"

"The vet barn," Jolie said.

Jude gulped down her cereal and a glass of apple juice and headed for Doc Barrett's clinic. She found her father and her husband in the office Brady now used at one end of the building. Before Brady came to work at the ranch as GM, the office had been Jude's. Giving it up to Brady had been a bone of contention between her and her father, as well as her and Brady, at the time. Now all of those bitter emotions had disappeared as if they had never occurred.

Brady and Daddy stood when she entered. "Hey, sweetheart," Brady said. "Got a couple horse owners in from Lubbock. They're meeting with Doc now. They like the looks of Sandy Dandy."

"Of course they do," Jude replied. "He's so handsome and bossy. Typical male animal." She went to Brady and slid her arms around his middle. "Did you have a good breakfast?"

"Sausage and eggs," he said. "Can't beat that."

Jude turned her attention to her father. "Daddy, can I talk to you about something?"

She felt the pressure of Brady's hand on her shoulder, knew he was warning her to back off. She ignored the message.

"Shoot," her father said. "But make it quick."

"You might prefer that we talk privately."

Brady dropped his arm from around her, an indication he was not pleased with what she was determined to do. "I'm gonna go see what Doc's doing," he said, and headed for the door. He stopped in the doorway, caught her eye and shook his head. She ignored him. This was between her and her father. She intended to find out once and for all if the man had a girlfriend and if the relationship was serious.

"What's the big secret?" her father asked.

She walked over to him and straightened his collar. "You won't believe the gossip I heard."

He gave a humorless heh-heh-heh. She sensed that he had tensed and gone on alert. "This is Lockett, punkin. I'd believe just about anything. What is it?"

"I heard that *you*"—she pressed her finger into his chest—"have something going on with Maisie Thornton."

He said nothing for several beats, then planted his hands on his hips. "Like what?"

"Daddy, please. I'm not a child." She backed away from him and rounded the end of Brady's desk. She began straightening things. "I'm not criticizing you. You know I've always thought you should have someone in your life."

"I do have someone. I have you. And Brady. And soon I'll have my grandson."

She looked up and at her father. "And what if it's a granddaughter?"

"You know what I meant."

Now it was her turn for the humorless heh-heh-heh. "I'm afraid I do." Her hand instinctively went to her stomach. "If my baby's a girl, no way will I stand for her to be manipulated and treated the way I was treated growing up. For that matter, Brady won't stand for it, either."

"You think he doesn't want a son?"

For a troublesome, fleeting moment, she thought of the fact that when Brady referred to their baby, he did not say "she" or "it"; he always said "he." "I believe he doesn't care. I believe he wants a healthy child. Of either sex."

"You might not know Brady as well as you think."

She gave an exaggerated gasp. "Thanks a lot!" The burn of tears rushed to her eyes, but she swallowed them back, something she had done for as long as she could remember in conversations with her father. "Daddy, how can you say something like that to me?"

"Now, now. I didn't mean to sound so blunt. You know I wasn't trying to hurt your feelings."

She believed that. Their relationship had been going so smoothly lately she had forgotten how tactless he could be. Then she realized he had keenly sidestepped her question. "I know, Daddy. You'd think I'd be used to those tacky remarks after all these years. . . . So, what about Maisie?"

He raised his hands, palms out, and shook his head. "Jude . . ."

That was one of his favorite not-going-to-talk-about-it gestures, but she had no intention of letting him escape. She, too, showed him her palms. "So you're having an affair. It's no big deal. Lord knows, you're old enough. I'm just trying to find out if what I heard is gossip or if it's true. Have you been . . . well, going around with her long?"

He shook his head again, looking at the floor. He thumbed back his straw Stetson.

"Jude . . ."

Now she was becoming annoyed. "You've already said that," she said crossly.

"I've known Maisie since we were kids," he said.

"But you haven't been sleeping with her since you were kids. . . . Or have you?"

He was ruddy complexioned from years of exposure to the relentless Texas Panhandle sun, but when he was embarrassed or angry, his face turned a red-brown color. Like now. "Jude . . ."

"Well, have you?"

More hesitation. "For a long time," he finally said, his shoulders discernibly sagging. "I'm not going to lie to you. But I'm not going to discuss it with you, either."

Jude stared at him, blinking. "How long?"

"Jude, I said I wasn't going—"

"You haven't hesitated to pry into *my* private life. How long?"

"Twenty years," he snapped. "That's all I'm going to say."

"Twenty years?" Jude said, stunned. "As in two-oh? Are you kidding me?"

"Jude, please . . ."

"How have you kept it a secret for so long? And why? It isn't like you had a reason to hide it."

"I did have reasons. My own reasons."

"What? What are they?"

He dropped to the armchair in front of the desk, sitting on the edge of the seat as if he might get up and walk out at any minute.

"Was Grandpa one of the reasons?" she asked.

On a frown, he removed his silver-rimmed glasses, ducked his chin and pinched the bridge of his nose with his thumb and finger. She had seen him do that often when he was upset or frustrated.

Jude, too, sank to Brady's desk chair, hoping she and her father were going to have a meaningful talk.

He slid his glasses back on and leveled a serious look at her. "I've never allowed anything to come before the ranch," he said. "You know that. And that includes women and any other personal indulgences I might have had. You don't know the details, I realize, and I don't intend to go into them.

Suffice to say that in the past, I made two major mistakes with women by putting my own desires first. In terms of both money and pain, my bad judgment has cost this ranch and this family enough."

Instinctively Jude knew he was speaking of her mother, who had left Lockett when Jude was an infant. Jude had rarely had conversations with anyone about Vanessa O'Reilly, including Daddy, and no one had ever said to her point-blank that her mother's abandonment included money. She leaned forward, resting her forearms on the desktop. "You gave my mother money?"

"I didn't. . . . But I've always believed Dad did."

"That's why she never came back here. Never called, never wrote. Grandpa paid her off."

Her father didn't reply, just continued to look at her.

It was a perfectly logical conclusion. Why Jude hadn't thought of it before, she didn't know. "Surprise, surprise. My manipulative grandfather never gave any consideration to the fact that I might like to know my own mother."

"Jude, it just wasn't that simple. Your grandfather *did* know your mother. He was better at detecting her motives than I was. He thought everyone would be better off if she simply stepped out of the picture and went back to where she came from. And he knew I wouldn't have confronted her on my own."

Jude knew her father's reputation for ruthlessness. She couldn't imagine him being unable to confront anyone about anything. He leaned forward, his palm braced on his knee, his face thrust closer. "Strayhorns take care of their own, daughter, and always have. Dad didn't want her taking you back East and neither did I. We might have never seen you again." He punctuated the words with taps of his finger on the desktop.

"I assure you, she didn't put up much of an argument," he added. "Money was why she married me. But in those days, I was too naive to know it. Or maybe I was too proud to admit it."

Jude didn't even have a snapshot of her mother. Her issues over the woman's abandonment had been settled in her mind and heart long ago. She had to wonder about her own child. After it was born, would she be able to abandon it and never see it again? She knew that in the animal kingdom sometimes females rejected their young. She shook her head to clear it, determined not to be distracted from the subject. "We're getting off track. What happens now? With Maisie?"

"She wants to get married."

Instinctively Jude's mind flew to the ranch and its stability, the conversations she had heard, ad infinitum, about the ranch's future; the intricate prenuptial document that had been presented to Brady before she married him. Her father's affair took on a new dimension. "Married? You're going to get married?"

"No. I told her no."

Jude stared at Brady's desktop, which was now neatly organized. Unconsciously she had put it in perfect order. "My God. I can't believe this." She looked up at he father. "Why did you tell her no?"

"Marriage is a contract that opens closed doors unexpectedly. No one can know what lies behind them. I don't intend to do anything that might cause problems for you and Brady and your children on down the line. The Circle C and Strayhorn Corp has always been a family enterprise and must be kept that way. Maisie has two kids of her own and I don't intend for them, or any uninvited outsider, to ever think he has so much as a remote claim on the Circle C or any part of it."

"But that's ridiculous thinking. My God, we have a flock of lawyers. Don't you think they can defend the Circle C's ownership? They certainly managed to tightly truss up Brady. And his son. Against my wishes, I might add."

"I just know that the whole damn country is sue-happy and once lawyers get involved in a thing, it goes on forever and costs somebody a bunch of money that could be better spent on something else. I can't help but think of the Double Diamond that's been in litigation for eighty years. And during that time, attorneys and the courts have scalped the heirs. Besides that, there's a movement out there that believes that grazing cattle are a blight on the earth and wants big and old ranches like the Circle C broken up."

Jude couldn't argue with any of that. She could think of a number of times Strayhorn Corp had been sued for the most frivolous reasons and she was confronted with evidence of her father's last statement every day.

"There's an old saying, Jude," her father continued. " 'The road to hell is paved with good intentions.' I've learned the truth of that the hard way. At one point in my past life, though I tried to be a good and fair man, I was not a cautious one. But thanks to my dad's tutelage, I eventually came to be one. I don't see myself changing at this late date."

Jude didn't need to be reminded of her grandfather's *tutelage*. She had lived with it for more than thirty years. "Grandpa wasn't like you, Daddy. He preferred living as a hermit."

"No, Jude. That's not true. You don't know all that he faced in his life. He was the heir to an empire and a dynasty, to which he eventually dedicated all of himself. In his mind, he had no other choice. He was the only living child, the only son. Fate handed me that mantle and I've worn it gladly. I'll continue to wear it until the day I turn this operation over to you entirely. And I expect, though you don't believe it now, in the end, you'll do the same thing."

"I won't be chained to provincialism like you and Grandpa," she said fiercely. "I will not."

"This ranch is a part of your soul, daughter. If and when the time comes, you'll do what you have to."

Jude could see the conversation was veering into battleworn territory. She softened her tone. "We're not talking about me right now, Daddy. I want you to be happy. I know you must be lonely. If a life with Maisie would make you happy, I don't see why—"

"It's already settled, Jude. Too much has happened. You might say I'm a victim of the Campbell Curse as much as my brothers."

"That's superstitious nonsense. I loved Grammy Pen, but even when I was a little kid, when she talked about that Campbell Curse stuff, I thought it was malarkey. I don't believe our family is cursed."

"Jude. Let it be. It's settled."

"You're the one who's kept Maisie's Café going, aren't you?"

"What do you mean?"

"Daddy. Nobody believes Maisie's Café is a moneymaking business. In fact, everyone in town wonders how she's managed to keep it open for so many years when she has no more customers than she does."

"She's a good cook. She's—"

"That doesn't matter. There are only so many people in Lockett who can or will go out and eat in a café of any kind, whether the food's good or not."

He looked away and gave her no answer.

Memories had been worming their way to the front of Jude's mind—stories she had heard in town over the years, conversations she'd had, something she knew that involved her best friend. "I know something," she said. "If I'd been aware you were . . . *involved* with Maisie, I would've already told you."

Her father looked at her warily. "What?"

"When Suzanne first came back from Wyoming, and didn't have a job, she talked to Maisie about buying the café. Truett was going to help her with the money. They got far enough along in negotiating that Maisie let them look at her financial records, but she was adamant that Suzanne and her dad had to keep their talks confidential. She told Suzanne and Truett she was afraid she would lose business if people knew she wanted to sell the café. Suzanne took me into her confidence and told me about it.

"After Truett saw Maisie's records and her tax returns,

he speculated that Maisie was keeping the place afloat with outside help. Suzanne and I concluded she must have a sugar daddy. We figured it had to be someone from out of town. Neither of us ever thought once that it was you."

"Suzanne came back here two years ago," her father said. "Are you telling me that Maisie, that long ago, talked to Suzanne and her dad about selling the café?"

"She's still talking to her. Maisie approached her again maybe six months back. But Suzanne was already with Pat by then. She told Maisie she was no longer interested. Truett and Pat both are businessmen. Neither of them would sit still for Suzanne to buy into such a money-losing proposition."

Her father's face took on an expression Jude had never seen. "What exactly was Maisie talking about selling?" he asked. "Besides that old building, all she owns are the fixtures and the kitchen equipment. And those aren't worth that much."

"She'd like some blue-sky money. Because the café's been in business for so long and has an established customer base."

"How much is she asking?"

"I don't know what the latest number is. But it doesn't matter. Suzanne finally told her the price she was asking made no sense. If Suzanne wanted to own a café, she could start one from scratch a lot cheaper."

"Well, as I said, my, uh . . . *relationship* with Maisie is a settled matter. Looking back on it, I wish I'd never started it."

He rose from the chair and walked out. Jude could see he was upset, but not because his secret had been discovered. Jude believed what had upset him was learning that Maisie was trying to sell out. She wondered just how much money her father had invested in Maisie's Café, which most of the local people considered to be nothing but a hole in the wall.

Jude's opinion of Maisie Thornton, which had already been colored by what had happened between her and Suzanne, took on yet another shade. Who knew a femme fatale lived in Lockett, Texas?

23

Jude's revelation that Maisie had discussed selling the café with someone as far back as two years ago had stunned J.D. and left him with a disquieting anger, though he wasn't yet sure what he was angry about. Maisie had never mentioned selling the café and she'd had plenty of opportunity. The notion gnawed at him. Before Suzanne Breedlove, how many others had she tried to sell to that he didn't know about, or would never know about?

Last night, wanting to patch things up after they had parted on a sour note a week ago, he'd had a pleasant supper with Maisie in her apartment. They hadn't discussed her leaving or marriage or anything related, though he had sensed both issues loomed like an elephant in the room. After supper they had watched a movie on TV, which required no conversation, and then he had come home.

Now he entered the ranch house through the back door as usual and was met by the aromas of the upcoming dinner being prepared. He laid his hat on the harvest table in the hallway, then stopped off in the kitchen for a cup of coffee. In his office he fished a tiny key from under a stack of notepaper in a small wooden box on his desk. He unlocked his right bottom desk drawer, pulled out an unlabeled file and opened it flat.

Lying in front of him were the notes and records of every penny he had given to Maisie over the years out of his personal funds. He scarcely missed the money. Since he had never expected her to pay him back, if someone asked him why he kept the figures, he wouldn't have been able to give a logical reason, except to say that he had done it out of habit. He was basically a numbers man—numbers of cattle, numbers of calves, numbers of horses, numbers of dollars things cost, so on and so forth. He sipped his coffee as he sifted through the various bits of information—figures jotted on the backs of receipts, some written on notebook paper, others on napkins. He had never added them up.

He glanced at the calculator on the corner of his desk, but stopped short of pulling it closer and starting to make entries. He didn't need a calculator, because being a numbers man, he knew the total would be well into six digits. Twenty years of gifting was a long time.

His thoughts drifted to specifics. He had bought her a new ventilation system for the café kitchen, had bought new carpet for the café two or three times, had bought new furniture. He had paid for countless plumbing and electrical repairs in the hundred-year-old building that housed both the café and her apartment. Hell, she had redecorated the café and the apartment a couple of times and he had paid for most of that.

He had teasingly told her once he would get off cheaper if he built her a new building. But she had insisted on keeping the old one for sentimental reasons. She and her husband, Mike, the father of the daughter who rarely so much as called her mother, had bought it together. Never mind that J.D. had invested more in it than Mike Thornton had.

And after he had done all of that, she hadn't respected him enough to tell him she intended to sell the place? Had she kept it a secret because she feared he might expect a payback out of the sale proceeds?

Nothing had ever confounded him as much as women.

He closed the file, removed his glasses and laid them on the desk. He leaned back in his chair and rubbed his hands down his face. He believed he had only two choices. He could either marry Maisie and deal with the legal and financial consequences . . .

Or not.

How could he marry her when he no longer trusted her? That fragile strand had been broken by her planning behind his back without regard to all that he had done for her.

And if he chose not to marry her, he had to make a clean break and let her go on her way.

He reached for his coffee and sipped, barely noticing it was now cool. He set the cup back on the desk and rose from his chair, walked over to the window that overlooked the big round corral. He stood there for long minutes watching Brady and Jude and three visitors from Lubbock checking out Sandy Dandy, the best stud the ranch had bred in years. He let out a long breath. He knew what he had to do.

He left his office and went back to the kitchen. "If anyone wants to know where I am, I've got to run an errand in town," he told Jolie. "What time are you serving dinner?"

"I told Brady to bring everyone about twelve thirty," she answered.

"How many guests did Brady say will be here?"

"Including Mr. Harper, nine."

"Fine. I'll be back to eat dinner with them."

For the first time in his life, J.D. left an important meeting with horse owners in someone else's hands. As he walked out to his truck parked outside the big barn, he considered that just two short years ago, no one could have convinced him he would ever see the day he could do that. But now he had the greatest confidence that his daughter's husband was more than capable of handling it. Half an hour later, he walked into Maisie's Café and sat down on a red vinyl stool at the gray Formica lunch counter. He gave it a second look. He had paid for that, too.

Nola Jean Hart said hello and poured him a cup of coffee. "How are you today, Nola Jean?"

"Real good, Mr. Strayhorn."

"Your family?"

"Everybody's okay. Kids getting out of school pretty soon. So we'll have plenty of summer help."

"Right. Next week, isn't it?"

"Yessir."

"Is Maisie here today?"

"Yessir. Want me to get her?"

"Tell her I'm out here if you don't mind."

Maisie came out of the kitchen and took a seat beside him, her usual flowery scent filling the space around them. Her face was flushed and a sheen of sweat showed on her forehead. J.D. knew that came from her working in the kitchen.

"What brings you to town today?" she asked. "I thought you had horse breeders to entertain."

J.D. heard the guarded tone in her question. "You got time to go upstairs for a minute? I want to talk to you about something."

"Okay," she answered. "Long as we don't take too long. People will soon be coming in for lunch."

He left his coffee on the counter and they walked outside, rounded the corner and tramped up the long stairway attached to the side of the redbrick building. She led him through the living room into the kitchen. "Can I fix you a glass of tea?"

"Yeah." He lifted off his hat and set it on one end of the kitchen table, then took a seat. He removed his glasses and rubbed his eyes, dreading the coming conversation.

She filled two large tumblers with ice cubes and tea, brought them to the table and sat down opposite him. "Okay, I'm listening," she said.

He slid his glasses back on. "I came here for some answers, Maisie." He sipped the tea and carefully set the glass back down, then looked her in the face. "I just heard that Suzanne Breedlove and Truett have been talking to you about buying the café."

She didn't say anything right away, only blinked, her hands clasped around the glass of tea. Then her shoulders lifted in a shrug. "We've talked."

"For about two years, as I understand it."

Again she said nothing immediately, but a frown creased her brow. "What's this about, Jasper?"

"That's what I'm wondering. At what point were you going to tell me you're trying to sell this place?"

She turned away from him, gave him her profile and raised her chin. "It's mine. I can do anything I want to with it."

"You're right. It's yours. Even with all the money I've put into it, I've never asked for any ownership rights. I could have. I *should*'ve filed a lien on the building. I know better than to be that negligent, but I believed you were an honest woman—"

"I am an honest woman," she snapped. "And don't you dare say I'm not."

"Okay, I didn't mean that you aren't. I trusted you, Maisie. I believed we were friends." He propped his elbows on the table and opened his palms. "Why, forgodsake, wouldn't you tell me you wanted to sell?"

She turned back to him, fire in her blue eyes. "You got what you paid for from me, J. D. Strayhorn! So don't come in here with bullshit about being friends and all that crap. Screwing was all you ever wanted from me."

"That's not true," he said, taken aback at her ferocity.

"It is true." She slapped the table with her hand, the diamond cocktail ring he had given her several Christmases ago glinting in the morning sunlight streaming through the kitchen window. "There's nothing wrong with me wanting to make a change."

"You're right, Maisie. There's nothing wrong with people wanting to change their lives. Were you planning on saying good-bye before you left town?"

"Don't you dare accuse me of anything."

"It's a simple question."

She leaned back in her chair, her face set in a scowl. He could see a faint throb in her temple. She crossed her arms over her chest. "This town is nothing, J.D. I was dumb not to leave it a long time ago. You and your family and your precious money dictate every damn thing that happens, then shower your manna on the whole county like you're God or something."

"If you felt so put upon, why didn't you say something? Why did you stay?"

"Because I didn't have a lot of choices," she snapped, looking away from him again. After a few seconds passed, she said quietly, "I never did have any choices." Her chin began to quiver and she dabbed tears with her fingertips. "Mike left me nothing but this place and a bunch of bills. You know that. Hell. We didn't even own the tractor that killed him. A damned finance company had a lien on it."

J.D. refused to fall into that conversation. He had no responsibility for her marrying a man who had never had two nickels to rub together and no prospect of elevating his station in life. He shook his head and got to his feet. Suddenly he was just tired. "I'm disappointed is all."

She, too, stood. "Disappointed? You don't know what disappointment is, J.D."

"You might not think so, Maisie, but I assure you I'm well acquainted with disappointment."

"You're a self-centered bastard," she said, her voice breaking. "You could have married me after Mike died. You could've taken care of me. I loved you, J.D., ever since high school. I would've done anything for you. I kept hoping you'd love me back, but *you* and *your* family and *your* ranch, what *you* wanted were always more important than I was. Or than anybody was. Pretty soon I started to figure I'd better start worrying about myself because I couldn't count on you."

J.D. didn't want to waste the energy denying it. He found it unbelievable that after all these years, Maisie still didn't understand him or his situation. He looked at the floor, his hands on his hips.

"If you would've married me, maybe I could've done some things for my son and daughter," she said, now weeping. "Things I've never had the money to do. Maybe they would've thought more of me."

J.D. looked up and stared at her, amazed. What she meant was maybe *J.D.* could have done some things for her children. "That's baloney, Maisie. No amount of money, yours or mine, would've bought you the affection of those kids."

"Just shut up. You don't know anything about my kids. You don't even know your own." Sniffling now, she walked over and snatched a tissue from a box on top of the refrigerator. "I would've been a good wife to you. Now I don't know what's going to happen to me."

J.D. had nothing else to say. For him, the question had been answered. She had confirmed what he had suspected and even feared when Jude told him she was trying to sell the café. He pushed his chair back under the table, picked up his hat and started for the living room and the front door.

"Where—where are you going?"

He stopped in the doorway, but didn't turn toward her. "Home, Maisie. I'm going home."

"When will I see you again?"

Not trusting his voice, he shook his head.

"Call me? We can talk some more when I don't have to worry about getting lunch together."

He shook his head again and resumed his trek through the living room.

"You're a selfish bastard," she yelled behind him. "And I mean it!" The last words he heard from her as he eased through the front door were "Self-centered asshole!"

Back in his truck, he checked his watch, then started back toward the Circle C. After abandoning the horse owners this morning, for sure, he had to be present when they came into the ranch house for dinner.

He usually drove the twenty-eight miles from town to the Circle C at eighty. Today he slowed his speed, thinking over the conversation he had just had with Maisie. Two sentences stood out:

You got what you paid for from me, J. D. Strayhorn. . .
Screwing was all you ever wanted from me.

Was that true? Was sex really all he had ever wanted from

her? He didn't think so. He enjoyed her company, liked the familiarity of a lifetime acquaintance. He had to admit that without the sex, the relationship probably wouldn't have lasted. Hell, he wasn't a monk. In his younger days, sex had certainly kept him seeking her company. In bed, Maisie was apt to say the least. J.D. had often wondered where she had learned all she knew about sex.

Women . . . Sex . . . Shit. If anyone should know how the sex game was played, he should. He saw it every day in animals. Routinely, he watched good reliable stallions go nuts over the scent of a mare in estrus. And it wasn't all that unusual for her to tease him into wildness, then reject him. He had seen bulls injure themselves trying to mate while cows continued to idly graze through the process. Bulls would literally screw themselves to death if pastured with too many cows in heat. J.D. had always believed humans weren't much different from animals. Having better-developed brains didn't necessarily ensure that intelligence overrode instinct.

He cursed himself, fearing he could look in the mirror and recognize a grown man who was supposed to be smart guilty of the same behavior as dumb animals.

His thoughts veered to Jude. And Brady. And their coming child. Family. They were the ones to whom he owed his loyalty. Seeing Jude happy with Brady meant more to him than anything. Just watching them together was a balm to his soul. He could already see she would be a wonderful mother. She would be like his grandmother and her great-grandmother, Penny Ann—wise and patient.

Looking back, he couldn't believe that he and his dad had tried to make her marry Webb Henderson and Jason Weatherby, both of whom were less than she was. The fact that she hadn't held a grudge against him and her grandfather was proof of her tolerance and her affection for them.

He wondered if he should leave the Circle C and turn the whole operation over to Jude and Brady. He had enough money to live in luxury anywhere he wanted to. He was a rich man, rich with wealth that had nothing to do with the ranch operation or the salary he drew from it. Like all of Penelope Ann Campbell Strayhorn's progeny, he had his own trust fund. He had rarely dipped into it, had left it in the care of the Mercantile National Bank in Abilene, the institution that shrewdly managed all of the Strayhorn trust funds. His had grown to a fabulous amount of money.

But he didn't want to leave. The Circle C and his family were all he had. He remembered how his dad used to tell him family were the only people you could rely on. That sermon had started a long time ago, before Ike's betrayal and the fatal escapade that had made J.D. question the family loyalty tenet. But even after that gut-wrenching accident and discovery, as soon as the sharp edges of grief dulled, his dad and his grandmother had resumed the litany of family loyalty and declared that Ike had been the exception to the rule.

J.D. made a right turn and passed through the Circle C's rock stanchions, his mind now on his kid brother Ike, who had been gone more than thirty years. During all that time, J.D. had hated him, wouldn't even utter his name except rarely.

A weedy two-track road veered off to the left, leading to the Campbell-Strayhorn cemetery. As if an alien being had taken a grip on the steering wheel, before J.D. knew it, he was headed in that direction.

He hadn't been to the cemetery since his dad's funeral. The gray granite double stone had already been placed years back when Mom had expired from a pulmonary embolism after gall bladder surgery. More of the Campbell Curse.

The whole place looked to be well maintained. Reuben Asaro was responsible for the maintenance, and it appeared he did a good job. A neatly trimmed deep green plant with yellow flowers grew at the corner of the stone at the head of Mom's grave. He and his dad had personally planted it there.

Beside his mother's grave lay his younger brother, his parents' middle son, Ben. J.D. removed his hat and held it over his heart as he read the stone.

Bennett Campbell Strayhorn
American Hero
September 20, 1950–March 14, 1972

A small holder on one side of the tombstone held an American flag. J.D., two years older than Ben, had been in college when Ben was killed by sniper fire in a remote jungle in Vietnam. With Strayhorn clout in Willard County, Ben could have avoided military service. But he had wanted to go, as their father had gone in World War II. Always a scrapper, Ben had wanted to be the first to the fight, so he had enlisted in the Marines.

J.D. still vividly remembered the grim phone call from the ranch, made by Windy; the coming home and finding the pall in the ranch house, seeing his parents beside themselves with grief.

Ben had had a wife. He had met her in California and married her before shipping out to Asia. Soon after his death, she had succumbed to a cocaine overdose. Her remains were somewhere in California. Her passing had brought Ben's son, Cable, to grow up at the Circle C.

J.D. strolled along the white caliche footpath that divided the older occupants from the newer ones, his eyes scanning the stones of the generations of Campbells and Strayhorns who lay at rest. He stopped at the pink granite memorial stone Penny Ann had had installed years ago. The inscription appeared under a tiny, carved lamb:

Judith Ann Campbell
Asleep in the arms of Our Lord
April 10, 1863–March 18, 1866

No remains lay beneath the stone. Judith Ann, Jude's namesake, had drowned in the Red River when Alister Campbell brought his family from Missouri. Her small body was never found.

J.D. bowed his head, his mind on the magnificent history

every Campbell heir carried in his soul and bore on his shoulders. No one was more aware than he that he was no more than a grain of sand in the Campbell dynasty. Nothing he had done or would ever do came close to what the Circle C's founder had done. The best J.D. could hope to accomplish was to keep intact and in good standing what Campbells before him had struggled for and some had died for. Long ago, J.D. had dedicated his life to that proposition.

He looked up and in his line of vision was the farthest corner of the cemetery. Apart from the rest of the graves lay his brother Ike. J.D.'s memory spun backward. Ike had been buried there as a compromise, separated from the family in death as he had been in life. J.D. hadn't wanted him buried in the family cemetery at all, had had an acrimonious quarrel with his parents over that subject. In the end, he had been persuaded but not assuaged when Dad had promised him Ike would be buried away from the rest of the family group.

J.D. had never stood at Ike's graveside. He had never been to his deceased wife Karen's grave somewhere in Abilene.

He felt a flush. He was ashamed. Now that he was approaching the sunset of his own life, he knew that where a person's earthly body rested made no difference. He got to his feet, set his hat on and walked to Ike's grave, noticed that Reuben showed no prejudice. Ike's grave was as well maintained as the rest of them. He looked down on another gray granite stone that read:

Isaac Maris Strayhorn
Son
February 11, 1951–July 10, 1985

For the first time in years, J.D. remembered that Ike's middle name was the same as their mother's maiden name. He had forgotten what Ike looked like. His most vivid image of him was seeing him come barreling up the driveway to the ranch house in his red Corvette, the only Strayhorn who had ever driven a Corvette, a useless extravagance on a cattle ranch. Ike had always been out of step with the rest of the family.

J.D. had also forgotten what Ike's wife had looked like. He remembered her name was Faye but not much more except that she had cried a lot and never seemed to mesh with the family.

His next thought was of Jake.

Jake.

Ike's son who was still alive and a better man than most.

All these years, J.D. could have had a relationship with his brother's son and he had not. He had been so consumed by his own pain and pride, he had not bothered to even know where Jake was or what he had been doing until the man had returned to Lockett.

Dad must have felt some guilt, too, because when Jake announced his run for Willard County sheriff four years ago, together, Jeff and J.D. Strayhorn had contributed hugely and anonymously to his campaign. That was the Strayhorn way: cover with money what you couldn't bear to feel.

J.D.'s chest filled with emotion and his throat burned. He knelt on one knee, covered his heart with his hat, closed his eyes and thanked his Maker for keeping him sound in mind and body and able to fulfill his destiny.

And he asked for forgiveness.

24

Being an experienced waitress, Jolie knew two people, namely her and Irene, could only do so much in terms of serving. To feed dinner to nine people, she decided to lay out a buffet on the long mahogany antique sideboard that sat against one dining room wall. She found an intricate lace runner in one of the drawers and spread it the length of the elegant piece of furniture. Then she placed a heavy oval platter piled with breaded and fried quail breasts in the center. She surrounded it with a ceramic dish of steaming scalloped potatoes, a large bowl of steamed fresh snap beans with lemon and dill, a salad of crisp field greens and baby spinach leaves with Feta cheese and a tray of assorted finger vegetables.

For dessert, early this morning she had put slices of fresh peaches and kiwi and some fresh blueberries into a bowl to macerate with lemon and sugar. While the guests ate, she would spoon the fruit into large clear wineglasses she had found in the cupboard, drizzle it with a dressing she had made of sweetened yogurt and poppy seed, and top it off with a fresh strawberry.

One of the guests she recognized from a previous visit came into the kitchen and told her that knowing he was going to be eating one of her meals was what had spurred him to return to the Circle C and stay for dinner. She accepted his compliment with a huge smile. Having been in this job almost two months, she was starting to hit her stride with creative cooking and loved having the freedom and the utensils to make anything she chose, no matter the cost.

Mr. Strayhorn arrived from town barely in time to join the meal. He came into the kitchen for a glass of water. His face was flushed and he seemed agitated. "Are you okay?" she asked him.

"Just a headache," he said. "I'm going to my office for a minute. Don't serve the meal until I get back."

Reuben came into the kitchen. "Senor Strayhorn, he come back?"

"He's back from town, yes," Jolie answered.

"No. Not town. *El cemetario.*"

Holding a spoonful of fruit over a wineglass, Jolie glanced at Irene. "Cemetery?"

"*Sí.*" Irene nodded her head.

"What cemetery? Where is it?"

"This family," Irene said. "They have their own graves."

"You mean a family cemetery?"

Irene nodded again. "*Sí.*"

"What was he doing at the cemetery?" Jolie asked Reuben.

"He sad. He go to the one they no like. Far away. He pray."

"Senor Strayhorn's brother," Irene explained. "He grave no with others. He by hisself."

"You're saying that Mr. Strayhorn's brother isn't buried with the rest of the family?" Jolie said.

Instantly she thought of the story Jake had told her. But he hadn't told her of the Strayhorn family cemetery. Before her thoughts could travel further along that path, Mr. Strayhorn returned looking more like himself and took his place at the head of the table. While the main course was being eaten, Jolie continued to spoon the macerated fruit into the wineglasses, keeping her ear peeled to the conversation going on in the dining room. She didn't mean to be an eavesdropper, but she found everything that went on at the Circle C fascinating.

After the meal, Mr. Harper took everyone back to the vet barn, but Jude and Mr. Strayhorn both came into the kitchen. "Jolie, that was an outstanding meal," Jude said. "Just exquisite."

"I second that," Mr. Strayhorn said. "If we aren't careful, girl, we'll have people hanging around just to eat."

Delight gushed through Jolie.

"If we were going to have Suzanne's reception here, I'd hire you to prepare the food," Jude said. "I'd rather pay you than a caterer."

Mr. Strayhorn gave her a pointed look. "Why aren't you having Suzanne's reception? I thought that had been decided."

"Oh, Daddy, it's one of those things. I didn't mention it to you because something different has already been arranged. Jake is going to be Pat's best man."

"The sheriff?"

"Yes, Daddy, my cousin. Your nephew. Remember him? If he's going to be best man, naturally Pat wants him to be a part of the reception. But you know how Jake feels about us. He won't set foot on this ranch. But it's already taken care of. They're going to have it in the Methodist church basement."

Mr. Strayhorn said nothing for the longest time. Then he cleared his throat and walked out of the kitchen.

Jude gave a huge sigh and rolled her eyes. "As much as I love my father, I'll never understand him." Then she smiled and said, "Thanks again, Jolie, for the great food." She, too, left the kitchen.

Jolie didn't know what she had witnessed in Mr. Strayhorn, but now she was determined to ask Jake what was going on with Suzanne's wedding reception.

After she and Irene and Reuben and Lola ate, Jolie helped Irene straighten the kitchen, then went to her cottage to rest. Her head was filled with thoughts of Jake.

As Billy Jensen motored west in his newly repaired old truck, one thing consumed his concentration. He knew where his fuckin' bitch of a wife was, or at least what town she had run off to. That cousin, Amanda, had sent Danni a birthday card with her return address on it. He would find Jolie when he got to Lockett, Texas, and he would get even. Just because she had divorced him didn't mean she wasn't his wife.

He was happy to have his truck running again. Being without wheels and bumming rides had been a sonofabitch. This time, he had paid a real mechanic to fix it. Hell. For a few days, he'd had money to burn, though it hadn't lasted long.

The money had been unexpected riches—more than he would have earned in months at that chickenshit job back in Dallas. After he got out of jail, some do-gooder agency had helped him get on with a yard maintenance company, working his ass off in the hot sun every day. Fuckin' rich people had to have their goddamn lawns and flower beds looking perfect. The bastards paid him minimum wage and somebody chewed his ass out every day.

But he really shouldn't complain, he reminded himself. If those do-gooders hadn't gotten him that chickenshit job, he wouldn't have run across that rich blonde named Melissa. While he was down on his hands and knees digging in her backyard flower bed, she had walked out her back door butt-naked and asked him if he wanted to fuck.

For a few seconds he had thought about the days he had spent in jail and the fact that he had gotten out on probation. For a flicker of an instant, he thought about the differences in her status and his and suspected she could get him into trouble big-time. With all of that swirling inside his head, he had almost said no. Then she had come closer and rubbed herself all over him and talked about his "fantastic hard body" and his "package" that had gotten harder than his body, something that hadn't happened in a while.

On the spot, he had quit that chickenshit yardman job and spent three days and two nights in Melissa's bed. That woman knew how to fuck and, high on meth, she couldn't get enough of Billy Jensen's cock. At first he had resisted joining her in smoking, knew it was the root of most of his problems, knew it could get him sent back to jail. But he couldn't keep up with her without some help. Turned out, she had some first-quality shit that she had been extremely generous with and once he got a whiff of it, the "flash" and the good old times came back to him. He could fuck as long as she could, something else that hadn't happened in a while.

But three days and two nights was too much. He had run out of steam. He vaguely remembered that a counselor somewhere had told him that's what the drug did—made you feel as if you were going off a dozen times at once. The extreme pleasure was part of the trap. But after a while, the counselor had said, you wouldn't be able to get hard at all.

Even if Melissa hadn't kicked him out, he would have left anyway. He had somewhere to go.

But before he pulled out of that rich bitch's driveway, he stopped by the dining room buffet where he had noticed her purse. He had seen a softball-size wad of cash loosely lying in it. She hadn't even tried to hide it. He had walked out of that bitch's mansion with that purse.

Once he got home and dumped the contents on the living room floor, besides the wad of cash, he found a pile of credit cards and those gift cards that looked like credit cards and half a baggie of crank. He shoved the gift cards into his pocket, tucked the credit cards into a drawer, to be used only as a last resort. They could get him sent to the *big* jail. He counted the cash and discovered he had three thousand dollars, mostly in hundreds. So as not to call attention to himself—no one would ever believe he would legitimately have hundred-dollar bills—all he had to do was stop by some grocery store with one of those self-checkout things, buy a pack of gum or a drink and bingo—he had twenties. Spendable cash.

She-it!

He had never known another living female who even had three thousand dollars, much less carried it around in her purse. Only dope dealers had that kind of money. And for a while, less what he had paid to have his truck repaired, he'd had it. But unfortunately, he'd lost track of it somewhere. Or maybe somebody had stolen it from him. Now he barely had enough to buy gas to get him to West Texas. Fortunately the State of Texas had provided him with a Lone Star card so he didn't have to spend his money on food.

Jolie was glad to see Monday come. She needed a day off. Horse people had been at the ranch all weekend and extra people had been present at every meal, including breakfast.

She hadn't been cooking breakfast since Jude always ate cereal and Mr. Strayhorn and Brady ate in the cookhouse with the hands. Over the weekend, even visitors who hadn't slept at the ranch had been present to eat the morning meal.

Jolie was learning new things every day. She now knew that the summer months were the prime breeding months for horses. Horse owners from everywhere came to discuss breeding their mares to the Circle C's stallions. It appeared the coming months would bring many guests for meals.

Once she got Danni off to school, she collapsed on the living room sofa. And that's where she was when her cell phone warbled. She recognized the number. Jake. A giddiness came over her and she pressed the TALK button and said, "Hi."

"Hey," he said in his soft, deep voice.

"How are you today?" she somehow asked.

"I'm good. Are you still off on Mondays?"

"Yes. In fact, I was just collapsed on the sofa," she said on a girlish laugh. She scolded herself. She wanted him to see her as a woman. "It was a really busy weekend around here."

"Horse breeders?"

"Yes."

"It's that time of year. Branding will be coming up in June. That'll be another busy time, but it probably won't affect you much."

"It might. Buster already asked me if I wanted to go with him and help him on the chuck wagon. I didn't realize they had a real chuck wagon that they took out into the pastures."

"They've done it for as long as I can remember. As I recall, it was a good experience."

"I think Danni would love it. Buster says he sleeps out there with the chuck wagon, but I'd drive one of the pickups back and forth. I haven't asked Jude and Brady yet if I can go."

"Listen, I've got Chuck talked into taking care of the office today. Want to take a drive?"

A feeling of warmth and well-being gushed through every cell of Jolie's body. "Sure. Where to?"

"I want to show you something. Meet me at the Dairy Queen about eleven. We'll have lunch first."

She had to be in the middle of a dream or at the very least, having an out-of-body experience. "Okay. I'll be there."

She floated to the bathroom to bathe and dress.

25

The Dairy Queen at noon was a gathering place for Lockett citizens. As they ate burgers, Jolie had no doubt many people were watching them and were talking. She couldn't make herself worry over it, though she was sure the sighting would get back to the Strayhorns sooner or later. Jake seemed not to be concerned about it, either.

"You're taking your gun?"

"I'm always armed, even in Lockett."

"But you weren't the day we ate enchiladas."

"I'm always armed, darlin'. See, cops don't always know where the bad actors are, but the bad actors usually know where the cops are."

He carried a hidden gun? That fact served as an even more invasive reminder of who and what he was. Even if she went on a worldwide search, could she ever find anyone more opposite from Billy? "I guess I've never looked at it that way."

The only other anxiety Jolie had was leaving the Circle C's pickup parked in the Dairy Queen's parking lot while she took a ride with Jake.

"Drive it to my apartment and park it in the driveway," he told her. So she did.

As she belted herself into the passenger seat in his pickup, she noted that no more than two feet spanned the space between them. She had never been inside a pickup cab with any man other than Billy and not often with him. The scent of something woodsy and masculine filled the small space. She would love to ask him the name of his cologne, but she wouldn't. "Where are we going?" she asked.

"About ten miles out."

She kept silent as he drove and so did he, but she stole glances at him, admired his strong profile, his straight nose, his efficient hands on the steering wheel. "Have you taken those driving lessons?" she finally asked.

"Driving lessons?"

"I watched a program on TV that showed cops learning special driving skills."

He smiled. "I've done some of that. Not much call for it in Lockett, though. My job here is mostly administrative. When I first got elected, the sheriff's office was a big mess. Amanda and I worked hard cleaning things up and bringing everything up to date. There might not be much crime in Lockett's population, but you never know who's going to pass through town."

People like Billy, Jolie thought.

Soon they came to a run-down gate. Jolie recognized it as a "cowboy gate," made of barbed wire and wooden posts, one of the many things she had learned in the short time she had been in Willard County. Jake scooted out and opened the gate, then came back and drove through the opening. He scooted out again and closed the gate. Jolie had also learned that in livestock country, opening a closed gate and not reclosing it could turn into a catastrophe.

They proceeded slowly along a dirt road. The day was warm and bright, the sky a brilliant blue with only small puffy clouds in the distance. Black and russet-colored cattle grazed at the green grass growing on both sides of the road. Looking ahead, she saw a hawk floating in the air against the blue backdrop.

"See that hawk?" Jake said, looking up and out the windshield. "He's probably hunting field mice."

A feeling of peace and freedom and happiness filled Jolie's

chest, as if she had no worries about her and Danni's futures or about the uncertain arrival of Danni's father. "Poor mice," she said.

"Everything has a purpose," Jake said. "If it wasn't for the field mice, those hawks might get awful hungry."

They reached an older one-story brick house that had an almost flat roof. It screamed *neglect*. Jolie couldn't guess its age. What had been a lawn was grown up with weeds and knee-high grass going to seed. A wooden gate of vertical slats with swatches of white paint here and there hung by one hinge. Jake stopped in front of it and scooted out of the pickup, so Jolie got out, too, the slam of her door clapping loudly in the hush that surrounded them. No sound penetrated the deafening silence save a distant birdcall. A gentle breeze touched her cheeks and ruffled her hair and she thought of Danni's comment about the wind blowing all the time. Something else she had learned since being here was that even in this modern age, the Texas Panhandle was a vast, raw and untamed silence. Maybe it would never be tamed. Maybe that was part of its mystique.

Jake walked over and lifted the gate to the side. "Don't know what this gate is protecting," he said. "The cattle are fenced off."

"Whose house is this?" she asked.

"Mine. I bought it a couple of months ago."

She looked around, could still see the cattle grazing in the distance. "I don't think I've heard you have cattle," she said.

"I don't. Those you're looking at belong to somebody else. The land's leased out for grazing."

He led her over a crumbling sidewalk to the house's front door, dug a key from his jeans pocket and opened the wooden door. They stepped into a stuffy empty living room with a floral-patterned linoleum floor. Dust motes swirled and danced in the bright light coming through the windows. Patches of sand showed in places on the floor. The room smelled dusty and unused. "Needs a little cleaning," Jake said, "but nothing major."

She walked from the living room into the kitchen and was confronted by old and well-used appliances and scarred cabinets.

He followed her. "Kitchen needs some upgrading."

They moved out a door on the opposite end of the kitchen and into a hallway that led to an empty bedroom. "It's got three bedrooms," he said, leading her from one room to the other, his boot heels thudding softly on the linoleum-covered wooden floors. "Believe it or not, it's got two baths."

"It could be nice," she said, though she couldn't imagine how much work would be required to make it so. "Are you going to move here?"

"Eventually." He started back to the kitchen. "Let me show you the view from the back."

He led her out of the kitchen onto a large covered wooden porch, also in need of painting. Along a wooden rail, a row of scraggly bushes grew, showing tiny buds. She hardly knew one plant from another, but she thought she recognized them as rose bushes. A short distance away, below the measureless blue sky, she could see one wall of a deep canyon showing variations of rusty red and yellow layers. Scrubby dark green plants she couldn't identify grew along the rim on the opposite side. Jake raised his arm and pointed to his right. "At this time of year, the sun sets right over there."

Jolie braced the heels of her hands on the porch rail and looked out. The panorama of sky, canyon walls and endless open space was almost too much for her eyes to take in. "Do you come out here and watch the sunset?"

He stood beside her, also leaning on the porch rail. "I have a few times since I bought it. It's beautiful."

Jolie saw no sign of a tree. "Here, it's a lot different from East Texas."

"Do you miss the pine trees?" he asked.

For the first time, it dawned on her that she hadn't even missed the tall pines that were part of the landscape where she had grown up. She looked up at him and smiled. "Not really. Now that I think about it, I suppose I had so much to do back there, I hardly noticed the trees. I'm busy at the ranch, but compared to what I left behind, cooking for Jude and Brady and Mr. Strayhorn is almost like a vacation. I have a lot more time to appreciate things now. Every day makes me realize more that it's a blessing I was able to come here. I'll probably never go back to East Texas."

"I'll probably never leave here, either," Jake said.

"I'm hoping I'll be like the Strayhorns' last cook," Jolie said, straightening and laughing.

"Windy? He died from a sudden heart attack."

"I know. I'm hoping I'll just keep living in that little cottage and working in the Circle C's kitchen until I drop in my tracks like he did."

"There could be worse things," Jake said.

"I know. I've lived through some of them."

"So you like being out at the Circle C, then."

She looked up at him. "This is the first time I've ever lived in a house."

Jake didn't reply, only appeared to be studying her face.

"You might not know what that means to me," she said. "From the day I was born, I lived in a trailer house. Or several trailer houses, really. I think I've already mentioned my mom moved us around quite a bit. When I married Billy, all I did was move into a different trailer house, smaller and rattier than the trailers I grew up in. My mom bought it for us off a used-trailer lot in Terrell. She didn't want us living with her. It didn't cost much. In time, Billy and I were able to pay her back."

When Jake still didn't say anything, she looked him in the eye. "I wanted you to know what I come from."

"Everybody comes from something somewhere," he said. "Just because you started in a place doesn't mean you have to stay in it."

As their gazes held, a stillness grew between them, which was fine with her. She was happy just standing near Jake Strayhorn without saying a word. Besides, she didn't want to talk much about her life in Grandee or about Billy, especially on such a beautiful day in this exquisite place that obviously meant a lot to the man who was coming to mean something to her. She was grateful he didn't ask her any more questions about herself. She turned her attention back to the landscape.

"Have you thought about me being eleven years older than you?" he asked.

"A little," she said, hoping and praying that question meant all that she interpreted it to mean. "Have you thought about it?"

"Yeah, I have. Eleven years is a lot of time."

"Do—do you think it's a problem?"

"Not for me. Is it a problem for you?"

"No. I just know you're the best man I've ever been around. Your age doesn't matter."

"I've got a lot of flaws, Jolie. I'm hardheaded and set in my ways. I've lived alone a long time."

"I've lived alone, too. I wasn't alone, but I *lived* alone." Then she laughed, lightening the moment. "Just so you'll know, I'm not the least bit hardheaded. And I'm a pushover. I can be talked into anything."

His brow arched. "You're no pushover. I saw that much right away."

He picked up her hand and stared down at it, rubbing the top with his thumb. Her breath caught, but she tried not to show how his touch affected her.

"I've been single fifteen years," he said.

"What are you trying to tell me, Jake?"

He looked up, his beautiful eyes serious, his square jaw set. "It's just that in that length of time, a single man gets to know quite a few women. It just happens."

Was he talking about sex? Was he making a confession? Should she tell him she had never been with a man other than Billy and that she hadn't been with even him for more time than she could say without thinking about it? Sex had never been as important to her as keeping a roof over their heads and food on the table, both daily challenges for most of her life. She felt a flush crawl up her neck. "I, uh . . . well, I guess that's just the way life is," she said.

He gripped her hand. "Come on. I'll show you the canyon."

He led her off the porch, through the rustling grass to the canyon's rim, where they stood and looked into the deep chasm. "Oh, my gosh. It's a lot deeper than it looks from back on the porch."

"Couple hundred feet probably. The canyon floor's sandy and damp a lot of the time. If you go down there, you've got to look out for quicksand."

"Quicksand?"

"Wet sand with no bottom. It can engulf a person or an animal. Even a vehicle."

"It sounds dangerous."

"It is. You can't get out of it. It'll eventually suck you under."

"Like life," she said, staring down at the canyon's sandy floor.

He gave her a look but didn't comment. Then he said, "When Brady Fallon and Cable Strayhorn and I were boys, we used to come here and play. We crawled over every foot of this canyon."

"It's a wonder you weren't swallowed."

"We knew where we shouldn't go," he said. "A hundred fifty years ago, this was Comanche country. There are lots of stories about them and this canyon. It was a sacred place for them. When we were kids, Cable was into that history. He knew their stories and he used to tell us."

She looked up at him, squinting and tenting her hand to shade her eyes from the bright sun. "Cable's your other cousin besides Jude?"

Jake nodded. "He and I are the same age."

With no warning, he lifted off his hat and placed it on her head. "There," he said. "That'll give you some shade." He grinned. "You look cute."

The hat sat on the top of her ears and eyebrows. She

touched the edge of the brim with her fingertips. "But what about you? The sun doesn't bother you?"

His lips quirked. "I'm used to it."

"I've seen your cousin's picture in the ranch house and I heard his name from Buster in the cookhouse. Buster said his daddy was killed in a war."

Jake nodded. "Vietnam. My uncle Ben. He was in the Marines. Jeff could've used his influence and kept him out of the military like he did with J.D. and my dad, but the story is Ben wanted to serve. So he joined the Marines."

"I only went to the tenth grade, so I don't know much, but I had customers in the Cactus Café who were Vietnam veterans. They used to wear those caps that said so. I've heard them talk about it. Your uncle's wearing a uniform in the picture I saw of him and there's a flag in the frame with it."

"One of the things I remember from living at the Circle C," Jake said, "is Ben had war hero status. Even though Cable never knew him, Jeff and Penny Ann taught him that his daddy was a war hero. For that matter, they taught us all."

"I've never heard of anyone with the name Cable before."

"It's a nickname. It came from Jude. When she was a little girl, she couldn't say 'Campbell,' so she said 'Cable.' Everybody picked it up." Jake bent and plucked the top from a stalk of grass and ran it through his fingers. "His real name is Campbell Davis Strayhorn. Davis comes from Jefferson Davis. The whole damn family's named after him, you know."

Jolie tried to think if she had ever heard the name Jefferson Davis. Jake had said it as if she should know who that person was. Her brow knit. "Who's that?"

"The president of the Confederacy. During the Civil War, the founder of the Circle C was a dyed-in-the-wool, loyal-to-the-bone Southern sympathizer."

Jolie did know a little something about the Civil War, even if she hadn't known who Jefferson Davis was. "I guess I hadn't heard that. So, what's *your* name? Are you named after him, too?"

"Nope. My name is Jacob Campbell Strayhorn. Guess my folks didn't feel that much loyalty to the South."

"Oh, my gosh. Your name's Campbell, too? Like your cousin's? Then who are you named after?"

"Everybody named Campbell is named after Alister Donahue Campbell. He came from Scotland. He was a farmer in Missouri. In 1866, he took his family to South Texas and homesteaded. His son, Jefferson Davis Campbell, didn't want to be a cotton farmer. He had a dream of being a cowboy and a cattle rancher. When he was nineteen years old, all alone, he drove a hundred head of strays and mavericks up here from South Texas, lived in a dugout here in the middle of Comanche country and started the ranch where you now cook. He must've had his share of guts and ambition."

"Something tells me you know who's in that picture in the dining room."

"That picture's been hanging in that house since it was built in 1899. That's the man I'm talking about. Mine and Jude's great-great-grandpa. He's standing beside the Comanche chief, Quanah Parker."

"Wow," Jolie said, awed. "All that history. And I don't even know my daddy's name."

"Don't worry about it. I believe kids need a father, but sometimes fathers drop the ball."

He squatted and plucked two small clusters of rust-colored flowers with gold-tipped petals and dark brown centers, then stood and offered them to her. "Indian blankets," he said, smiling, a fan of fine lines at the corners of his eyes. No one had ever given her flowers, even *wild* flowers. "Oh," she replied softly, taking the little clusters. She touched the petals delicately, then raised a flower to her nose. "It doesn't smell."

"But it's so pretty to look at, it doesn't need to smell. Those dark centers remind me of your eyes."

Her heart swelled so, she could hardly swallow. She had an urge to cry. She looked up at him. "I know it probably isn't the right thing to say, but I'm so glad I met you."

He smiled and took her hand again. They walked together back to the porch, sat down on the old porch swing. She returned his hat and he set it on the porch rail. He continued to hold her hand and she hung on to the cluster of flowers. They sat there quietly, arms touching, hands joined, easily moving back and forth in the swing. Eventually, she put her head on his shoulder; he touched his cheek to her hair and they continued to swing slowly.

She sensed she was experiencing something with Jake Strayhorn that few people had. "If you know so much about the Circle C and its history," she said, "why won't you go there? Someone said you haven't been there since you were a kid."

"That's true. I haven't."

"But if you don't want to associate with them, why did you come back here?"

"I said before, this is home, which doesn't have anything to do with the people who live here."

She straightened and looked into his face. "I guess I don't understand."

Jake laid an arm along the swing back behind her. He gave a great sigh. "It's a long story, Jolie. I've never talked about it with too many people."

"Couldn't you talk to me about it? You know a lot about me and my life, but I don't know hardly anything about you."

He shook his head. "The man I am now is what's important, not what happened years ago."

"But what happened years ago is what made you the man you are now. I learned that much about people from living with Billy and listening to the people who used to try to counsel him."

A chuckle came from Jake, but it wasn't an expression of amusement. "You're too wise for your years, Jolie. That must be what I like about you."

She looked down at the flowers in her hand. They were already wilted. "Gosh. Wildflowers don't last long, do they?"

"They're like some people. They need a connection to the land to stay alive."

"Mr. Strayhorn and Jude are like that, aren't they?"

"They see the land as permanent and static, something greater than they are. It's embedded in their souls. In their deepest places, it's all they care about."

"But Jude doesn't love the land more than she loves Brady. Every day I see how much she cares about him."

"If she ever has to make a choice between him and the ranch, it's my guess she'll choose the ranch. It's an unconscious thing, you see. Something Jude doesn't yet know she has. I suspect J.D. has made choices his entire life with that philosophy in mind. So did my grandfather. Remember what I said once about life being about choices? It doesn't make any difference if you're rich or poor."

"Buster told me about your father and Mr. Strayhorn's wife. Was that about choices, too?"

She was prepared for him to blanch, but he remained relaxed and quiet. "Without a doubt. Did he also tell you about my mother?"

"No. He didn't act like he knew anything about her. Where is she?"

"In a cemetery in Dallas. You might say she could be included in all that *Campbell Curse* bullshit that my great-grandmother used to spout."

"You mean the woman everyone calls Penny Ann."

"My mother killed herself. Accidentally, I suspect. Booze and tranquilizers. Bad combination. She wasn't strong. She was surely no match for the Strayhorns. I still can't figure out how she managed to end up married to my dad.

"When she and I left the Circle C, we went back to Dallas so she could be close to her two sisters. Not long after we got resettled, a check started coming from Penny Ann every month. I'll always be grateful to Penny Ann for that because Mom wasn't educated to work at a job that would pay enough to live on, nor was she in any shape emotionally to hold down a job. I was a kid, but I gave her as much support as I could. By the time I turned eighteen, she was going to some doctors and seemed to be better. I joined the army. I figured she'd be okay there near my aunts."

"She wasn't?"

He shook his head. "When I got back from overseas, that's when I realized how much she was drinking and I learned she was getting prescriptions from half a dozen doctors. My aunts had given up on her. I liked the army, had some thought about staying in for twenty years, but with Mom in the shape she was in, I didn't reenlist. I got a job with the Dallas PD, bought a little house and moved her in with me. I thought it would be enough if she was with me. It wasn't. You remember asking me if I thought people were born doomed?"

Jolie nodded.

"I've had similar thoughts about my mother. Something was missing inside her. She never got over what happened with my dad and J.D.'s wife. Never was able to put it behind her and move on. I came home from work one day and found her dead in bed."

Jolie's hand flew to cover her mouth reflexively. "Oh, my gosh, Jake."

He raised his palm and shook his head. "I blame myself for being so blind to her needs and her weaknesses and not making a greater effort to figure out how to help her. But I also blame the Strayhorns and all their goddamn money and power. The Strayhorns call the shots in the cattle and horse business in Texas, and to some degree the oil and gas business. They own the necessary politicians in Austin. Even own a few in Washington."

All at once Jolie realized she had bit down hard on her bottom lip. "But why blame them? They didn't—"

"Do anything? Not directly. I've thought about it many times. I've come to some conclusions. My old man apparently was a worthless, spoiled asshole who ran roughshod over everybody. He'd had everything he ever wanted and had been required to do damn little to earn it. He didn't care about anybody but himself. A lifetime of too much money and being part of a family with too much power made him that way.

"According to my mom, J.D.'s second wife, Karen, was a gold digger. She married J.D. thinking marriage to a Strayhorn was a ticket to do anything she damn well pleased. So with two people with the attitudes she and my dad had, both living under the same roof, I suppose it was inevitable they'd get together."

"Does Jude know about your mother?"

"I've never told her. I doubt anyone else has, either."

"Does Mr. Strayhorn know?"

"I've never told him and I don't think my aunts ever did. My dad's buried in the Strayhorn family cemetery, but the idea of burying my mom beside my dad didn't even come up for discussion. I believe Penny Ann knew about her death, because the checks stopped coming."

"She wouldn't have told Mr. Strayhorn?"

"Possibly not. From what I've heard, J.D. didn't want to hear it. The Strayhorns have cast-iron constitutions, you see, and wide shoulders. I don't think any of them spend a lot of time dwelling on past events and their causes. No matter what happens, they keep moving ahead. If any member of the family epitomizes that notion, it's J.D."

Jolie's eyes had welled with tears. She had problems, but they were obvious and unhidden. She couldn't imagine how Jake had kept his pain secret for so long. "Did your grandpa ever get in touch with you?"

"Not personally. He took care of me with money through his lawyers. Made my life easier than it might have been otherwise. I can't complain about that. I rejected his help at first, but his lawyers never let up on me. Nagged me constantly. Eventually, I gave up and stopped resisting. Now, thanks to him, I have no financial worries."

"Oh, Jake, that's all so sad. Mr. Strayhorn's your uncle. I don't even have an uncle. Haven't you ever wanted to make up with him?"

"No. I've made my life without him."

26

On Monday, after her school day ended, Jude stopped by Lucky's. When she had passed through town this morning, the first thing that had caught her eye on Main Street was a big CLOSED sign on Maisie's front door. Was that what Daddy had meant when he said it was all settled?

Looking for the latest gossip on the subject, she found Suzanne uncrating produce in the grocery store's back room. "Hey, girlfriend," Suzanne said, peeling big leaves off heads of lettuce and dropping them into a trash can.

"Hey, yourself. Listen, when I came through town this morning, I almost hit a car when I got sidetracked by the sign on Maisie's door. Have you seen it?"

"Oh, yeah. Everybody in town's talking about it. The word is, she's gonna go live in Fort Worth with one of her kids."

"Holy cow," Jude said, trying to reconcile this bit of information with what her father had told her on Saturday. "She's already left town?"

"Not yet. I haven't seen her myself, but people say they still see her lights in her apartment at night. They say she's packing."

"Wow. That happened fast. What about her café? She's just going to leave it?"

"That's the story."

"What about her building? Is it still for sale?"

"Haven't heard. I suppose so. If she moves away from here, she won't need a building, right?"

Now Jude wondered, after the conversation she'd had with her father, whether he, in fact, owned Maisie's building. "So, when you and your dad were looking into buying the café, did you also talk about buying the building?"

"No. We never got that far. Dad said if the café can't make it on its own, what's the point of owning the building? He didn't need an apartment and I didn't, either. I mean, let's face it. Real estate in Lockett is not a gold-star investment."

"Then you aren't interested in buying it now. I mean, it's already got a restaurant kitchen set up in it."

Suzanne shook her head. "That whole idea is dead. This town won't support a café. There just aren't enough people here. And the people who do live here can't afford to eat out. Lord, the county barely supports this grocery store. Why are you so interested?"

"Oh, no reason. Just nosy. You know how it is when something gets sprung all of a sudden."

"Yeah, I know what you mean. When something's unexpected, it's just that much more interesting. Now that Maisie's leaving, I guess we'll never find out who's been keeping her going all these years, huh?"

Suzanne was Jude's best friend and a long-term friend, but some things Jude couldn't share with her. "No, I guess not."

Jude was determined to again take up Maisie with her father. But, for the moment, feeling a need to change the subject with Suzanne, she said, "So. Have you heard any more from Mitch?"

"Nope. And I don't think I will."

"I'll bet Pat's thrilled about that."

Suzanne snickered. "Yeah, he is. The Mitch episode was a serious roadblock, but we got past it. And now things couldn't be better between us."

"I'm glad." She leaned forward and gave Suzanne a hug. "Well, I have to get home," she said, straightening. "I just stopped by to see what you knew about the café. If we want to eat lunch out in the future, I suppose we'll be stuck with hamburgers at the Dairy Queen."

"Oh, shit. I hadn't thought of that. Now Lockett has only one eating place."

"As you say, it probably can't support any more. Oh, by the way, while I was at school today, it occurred to me that we should wait until after the school year ends and have your wedding shower in the school's community room. With the ranch being twenty-eight miles out of town, some people might not want to drive out there. I know the community room is kind of sterile-looking, but I can decorate it and make it look festive."

"Fine with me," Suzanne said.

"Since you've invited everyone in town and the surrounding counties to the wedding, I'm inviting all of them to the shower. So you'll get lots of loot." Jude laughed.

"Suits me. I don't plan to do this ever again. Be sure to invite all of my relatives from down around Austin. They all know my mother was crazy. They'll want to make it up to me by giving me good wedding presents."

"You're such a cynic," Jude said.

"There's nothing cynical about facts, girlfriend."

Driving home, Jude sifted through what she knew about Suzanne and her relationship with her mother. She would never treat her child the way Lavelle Breedlove had treated Suzanne.

At the ranch, Jude saw Brady's pickup in front of the vet barn. She parked beside it and went inside, found him in his office. He rose when she entered, rounded his desk and drew her into his arms, kissed her soundly, his end-of-day stubble rasping her chin and sending a new surge of desire down her spine. "Busy day?" he asked softly.

"Hmm. You?" She traced one of his thick brown brows with a fingertip.

"Nice to have all the visitors gone, though we did have good meetings."

Jude nodded. And as much as she enjoyed being in his arms, she stepped back from his embrace. "Brady, did you know Maisie has closed the café?"

He hitched a hip up onto the corner of his desk and rested an elbow on his thigh, his fingers still clinging to hers. "I haven't heard that. Haven't been keeping up."

"Do you think Daddy knows?"

"Uh-oh. If he doesn't, something tells me he's about to find out."

She frowned. "Don't scold me. I have to tell him, don't you think? Especially after our conversation this morning."

His brow rose. "Oh, yeah. How'd that little daughter-father talk turn out?"

Jude's mouth twisted into a horseshoe scowl. "Now you're being sarcastic. It wasn't bad. Or good. You know how close-mouthed Daddy is. I know you think I shouldn't have brought it up. He did tell me, more or less, that Grandpa paid my mother to never darken the doorway again."

Brady's eyes narrowed. "How does that relate to J.D. and Maisie?"

Jude laughed. "It doesn't. But it came up while Daddy and I were talking. I had a scary thought during that conversation. If my mother took a check from Grandpa and walked out, her female nurturing instinct must have been absent. What if that's a genetic thing? What if I've inherited it?"

"What do you mean?"

"Well, look at how I grew up. I don't exactly have striking examples of perfect parenting to mimic. No mother's influence at all and Daddy was like a prison warden for a lot of years."

Brady stood, reached for her and drew her close. "You've got plenty of nurturing instinct. I've seen you with my son and with Jolie's daughter. And those kids at school. I've never seen anybody better with foals than you are."

"But horses aren't the same as people. You love them

and take care of them, but you only bond with them up to a point. What if it's like that with the baby? What if I don't connect with it? It's something to think about, don't you think."

"No, I do not. And I don't want you worrying about things like that. Tell me what else your dad said."

"Nothing of earth-shaking importance. We can talk about it tonight. Right now, I have a lot of other things on my mind. Where is Daddy anyway?"

"He went to his office. Said he had to make some calls."

"In his lair, huh? I'm going to the house and trap him."

Ignoring her husband's groan, Jude rose on her tiptoes, gave him a quick kiss and an "I love you." She stopped in the doorway and looked back at him. "It's time for Daddy's cocktail hour. Want to come with me?"

"Not if you're gonna try to make J.D. do something he doesn't want to."

She left the vet barn, keeping close the image of her husband standing there scowling, with his hands propped on his hips and his elbows sticking out like batwings. The men who surrounded her were such alpha chauvinists, but she had to admit that Brady supported her in all things, even when he didn't agree with her. But time and circumstances had proved she wanted nothing less from the males in her life. In the past, she'd had choices of softer, gentler men and they had revolted her.

Inside the house, she stopped by the kitchen and poured herself a glass of apple juice, said hello to Jolie and Irene, then went to her father's office, which was the office Grandpa had used for all of his life. As she made her way up the hallway, she thought of how few times she had been in this part of the house until her father had moved into this space. At a dark brown oak door, she tapped with her knuckle and stepped inside the sanctum that smelled of leather, Aramis cologne and Daddy's cigars.

Her father had transferred most of his favorite things

from his former office on the opposite end of the house—his oversize furniture upholstered in buttery tan and burgundy leather, some wild game heads and horns, a huge stuffed wild turkey, some cowhides—so his office still looked like a wolf's lair. "Hi, Daddy. Came to have a drink with you."

He placed the phone receiver in its cradle, a cigar stub resting between his thumb and finger. He looked at her with an expression of alarm. "Jude, you're not drinking—"

"Don't get excited. It's apple juice. But the color's right." She dropped into a cushy wingback chair.

Her father left his big leather arm chair behind his desk, walked over to the bar and opened the bifold doors that kept it hidden. Grandpa hadn't been a drinker, so originally, a bar hadn't existed in his office. Daddy had had one built when he took over the space. He liked his cocktail hour.

He lifted a heavy crystal glass off a glass shelf and filled it with ice cubes from the undercounter refrigerator. In his previous office the bar hadn't had its own refrigerator. Lola had had to bring in ice cubes from the kitchen every day. In redoing Grandpa's office, Daddy had remedied that inconvenience.

He poured a splash of Crown Royal over the ice cubes. "You haven't come to have a drink with me for a long time," he said.

He was right. For a time, they had been on the outs; then she had married Brady. Now it was Brady who shared the cocktail hour with her father more often than not.

He returned to his chair. "You don't have a drink with me anymore. This visit makes me think you've got something on your mind."

With an opening like that, Jude saw no point in waltzing around the issue. "Daddy, did you know Maisie's Café is closed?"

He gave her a look she could only describe as wary. "What do you mean?"

"What I said. There's a big Closed sign on her front door. Suzanne said everyone in town is talking about it. They're saying she's going to Fort Worth to live with her kids. Is that true?"

He didn't answer right away, just sipped his whiskey. Then, clearing his throat, he said, "That's what she said. But I didn't know she was going so soon."

Jude knew she was nosing into something that, as Brady had said, was none of her business, but she couldn't stop herself. If her father had hung out with Maisie for years, he must surely have deep feelings for her. "Did you ask her to stay?"

"If I'm not willing to get married, Jude, I can't very well ask her to stay."

"Then you don't care if she leaves?"

"I didn't say that." He leaned forward, resting his forearms on a tan desk blotter. His circumspect gaze leveled on her. Daddy had never had any problem looking someone in the eye. He knew he was powerful and his word was usually the last one with most of the people he dealt with. But she wasn't most of the people. "Look," he said, "if it will end the talk about this, I'll tell you this much. I offered to put her up in a house in town."

Like a mistress! Jude thought, still unable to quell the feeling that this thing, whatever it was, between her father and Maisie Thornton was unbelievable. "She wouldn't go for that. All or nothing, huh?"

"I offered that before you told me about Suzanne and Truett negotiating on the café. Hearing she had been trying to sell it without telling me, I changed my mind. Sometimes the price of a thing is just too high. And not just in dollars and cents. She broke the trust. And you and I have already talked about this as much as I'm willing to." He threw back the remaining whiskey in his glass.

Jude felt dizzy. She would never understand her father. She knew he wasn't an unfeeling man, but this wasn't the first time she had seen him shut off his emotions as if he were shutting off a faucet. Her thoughts headed off in a new direction, one that had little to do with emotion, but a lot to do with business sense, an area where he would definitely be more comfortable. "So, if you're ending the relationship and she's leaving town, what about the money you've put into the café? What will happen to that?"

"It's a gift."

"You don't own that building where the café was and where she lived, then?"

"I do not own a square inch of it." He stood and walked to the bar again, replenished his drink.

Confounded, Jude only stared at him. He must have spent a ton of money on this woman. "Lord, this is baffling, Daddy. It just looks to me like if you've been spending time with someone for twenty-something years and supporting her financially, it's almost like being married. I don't understand how you can let it—and the money—go so easily."

"Who said I'm letting it go easily? But the operative phrase, daughter, is I *am* letting it go. And I do not want to keep talking about it. I've got what I want. What I've always wanted. And it's right here. This ranch. My family. And now you're blessing me with a grandchild. And I'm grateful. Only a greedy man could ask for more."

Family. Jude thought of Jake being Pat Garner's best man, a fact that was restraining Suzanne and Pat's wedding reception from occurring at the Circle C. Frowning, Jude touched an ice cube floating on top of the liquid in her glass, carefully forming her next comment. "Oh, yeah. Family. Tell me something, Daddy. Do you consider Jake family?"

"He's my brother's son. I've always considered him to be family. As did your grandpa."

"But you don't even talk to him. Haven't you ever wanted to just, you know, talk to him? Good Lord, what happened, whatever it was, wasn't *his* fault."

"I've left it up to him. He knows where the ranch is."

"His mother was your brother's wife. She lived here one day; then the next day she didn't. She went away as if she was never here. Haven't you ever wondered what happened to her?"

"I know what happened to her. She passed away a few years ago."

Jude felt her eyes widen. "You kept up with her?"

"I did not. The truth is, Jude, for years I didn't *want* to know anything about her."

"But that doesn't make sense. What happened wasn't her fault, either."

"No one will ever know if that's true. I don't know what was whose fault. I don't know what her and my brother's marriage was really like, but in his defense, where Faye was concerned, he did the right thing."

"Which was?"

"She was already several months pregnant when they married. Remembering my brother as I do, I doubt if he was happy about that. You can't know what goes on between a man and a woman in private, but being a married man hardly changed Ike's lifestyle. I suppose he resented being a shotgun bridegroom."

"Does Jake know about all of that?"

"Of course he does. My God, he can add."

Jude tried to recall whether she had ever seen a picture of Jake's mother. Hell. Come to think of it, she had never seen a picture of Jake as a baby. "Guess Jake and his mother haven't earned a place in the gallery on the credenza behind your desk," she said.

Her father expelled a great sigh, as she had seen him do many times in their conversations. "His mother was a beautiful woman, as I recall, but she had her own problems. I don't believe she was ever happy living here. All of her family was somewhere around Dallas and that's where she went when she left here. At the time, I wasn't terribly interested in where she went or what she did.

"I've told you how it was in those days. Ike and my mother passed away within months of each other. When that car wreck happened, we were in the middle of one of the worst droughts we'd seen in many years. My God, we were buying and hauling water by truck to keep the stock alive. We were forced to sell some of our best mother cows and even our broodmares. Range fires followed the drought. Dad lost it. Checked out to the point where he couldn't even be consulted. Penny Ann and I were the only ones left to try to save this ranch. . . . And I had you, Jude. You were a little girl, seven years old. I'm not making excuses, but at that time, I had all I could handle. If Penny Ann hadn't been here, I don't know what would have happened. After it all settled down, I wanted to absolutely erase that phase of my life. Keeping pictures of my brother's widow and son and maintaining a relationship with them was no way to do it."

Jude felt chastened. She also felt a slew of conflicting emotions, including a reluctant pride in her father's strength and an intense gratitude that she was his daughter. She had never known great personal grief, but she knew what drought did to the ranching industry, had seen with her own eyes the hand-wringing worry over parched pastures and the desperate, almost superhuman effort to provide thousands of cattle with a simple drink of water. And range fires. She knew the horror of thousands of acres of pastureland consumed in a matter of minutes and cattle and horses with no escape, burned to death in the path of the fires. All of the money in the world couldn't remedy either of those catastrophes. She had almost been a victim herself of a range fire. Brady had rescued her.

"Penny Ann kept up with Faye and supported her," Daddy went on quietly. "I didn't know it at the time, but after Dad died, I found the evidence in Penny Ann's personal accounts that Dad kept in his office."

A sudden flash of anger at the whole tacky situation overtook Jude—at her deceased uncle who apparently had been an irresponsible fool, at her grandfather and father's stoicism, even at Jake and his stubbornness. "You know something, Daddy? That's all history and we're living in the present. It's ridiculous that we have family floating around outside the perimeters of this ranch and the only time anyone ever sets foot in this house is when someone dies. Jake didn't even do that much. He didn't come when Grandpa died. Maybe now would be a good time for you and him to talk. Because I'd really like to give my best friend a wedding reception and I can't unless Jake agrees to show up."

27

Jolie had never been so glad to see anything as she was Tuesday night. After getting almost no sleep the previous night, she was exhausted. Worrying over Billy's possible appearance in town or Danni's safety was not what had kept her awake. All night, images of Jake had roiled in her mind. He was attracted to her. She believed it. Otherwise, why would he have let people in town see them together? Why would he have taken her on a drive and shown her the house and land he had bought? She believed that to him, the house and land purchase was private enough to be intimate.

She imagined herself in that old house on the canyon rim waiting for him to come home every night, as Billy never had. She imagined him taking her on long, quiet drives through the countryside and in his soft, deep voice, telling her things she didn't know, as Billy never had. And she imagined him coming to her at night and holding her, thrilling her in ways she had only read about in novels, as Billy never had.

As soon as she tucked Danni into bed, she went to bed herself. But she spent another restless night, her fantasies of Jake Strayhorn and a new worry about Danni revolving in and out of snatches of sleep. School would be out in a week. What would Danni do all summer? They lived twenty-eight miles from town. Jolie couldn't expect a ten-going-on-eleven-year-old girl to while away her days in front of TV in the ranch house's family room. With Brady's ten-year-old son soon to come for the summer, she had to worry over what kind of mischief he might drag Danni into. Or what if he rejected Danni as a friend altogether?

Jolie's alarm buzzed at six a.m. She rose from bed knowing she had to go to the grocery store after the noon meal to pick up the few odds and ends to take her through the rest of the week. She wished she wasn't hoping she might see Jake in town, but she couldn't help herself. She took the time and endured the inconvenience of washing her hair in the cistern water. Because of the inconvenience factor, weeks back she had given up on the rainwater and resorted to using the softened well water to wash her hair. Now, looking in the mirror, she had to admit her bleached hair looked like a haystack and was hard to manage. She did the best she could with it and gave up. After doing her hair and makeup, she put on jeans and a plain red V-neck tee and added gold hoop earrings.

She wore a butcher's apron over her clothing all morning, being careful not to get food stains on her shirt. She made a hearty soup of leftover ham and navy beans and a cast-iron skillet of cheese and jalapeño corn bread. Only Brady and Mr. Strayhorn came in for lunch, so she left the serving to Irene and passed up eating lunch herself.

She stopped off in the half bath just inside the door coming from the garage and made sure her makeup looked as fresh as possible. Then she drove to Lucky's.

She shopped in Lucky's less often than she had when she first started working at the Circle C. She had now established a routine and gotten organized to the point where she was planning better and coordinating food buying with Buster. Now she received deliveries from the supplier that serviced the cookhouse and the ranch supply store.

Seeing the CLOSED sign on the Maisie's Café door caused her a moment of anxiety and she wasn't sure why. At the grocery store, she mentioned the sign to Suzanne, who made jokes about it. No comment was made of Mr. Strayhorn in association with the café owner, so Jolie was careful to dial back her own words. Who her boss saw or what he did was none of her business.

As she left the grocery store with her bags, parallel-parked directly across the street from the door was Jake, his butt pressed against the passenger side of his silver pickup, his legs crossed at the ankles, his arms crossed over his wide chest. Was he waiting for her? Daring to acknowledge that he was, she felt a stone dropping inside her stomach, but a grin quirked the corners of her mouth.

He came across the street and reached for her bags. "Had lunch?" he asked as he began to lift the bags of groceries into the bed of the Circle C's pickup.

It was insane how his very presence made her tongue-tied. "No, uh, I haven't. I didn't take the time to eat before I left the ranch."

"Got anything perishable in these sacks?" He placed the last plastic bag in the pickup bed.

"No. It's all dry stuff."

He flashed a breath-stealing smile. "Then it'll be okay until we get back, right?"

She looked up at him and lost herself in the pool of his green gaze. In all ways he was unlike any other man she had ever known. "Right."

He took her elbow and steered her to the passenger door of his pickup, her feet hardly touching the ground. He opened the door and held it while she climbed inside. Watching him briskly round the front end, she was almost giddy with joy, but sneaking through her happiness was the reminder that even if she didn't have all of the problems she had, Jake Strayhorn was out of her reach.

He scooted behind the steering wheel and belted himself in, his big body and his woodsy scent filling the cab. She felt only slightly less nervous than she did the day she went for a drive with him. "Is your deputy minding your office?" she asked.

He glanced across at her and smiled. "Yep. It's his turn."

His perfect face was made for a cowboy hat, she thought. "Where are we going?"

"Dairy Queen. That's all that's left." He fired the engine and, checking his side-view mirror, pulled from the curb.

As they drove away, she shot a quick glance at the grocery store's plate-glass front door. Suzanne was standing there watching them. "Oh, hell," she mumbled.

Jake turned to her, smiling. "Suzanne see us?"

"I think so," Jolie answered.

"I figured she was watching," Jake said, chuckling. "It's not a problem, darlin'."

"But she's Jude's best friend."

"It's still not a problem. People around here don't have much to keep them entertained, so they like being nosy. Suzanne's harmless, but even if she did tell Jude and Brady, they wouldn't care."

"I don't want to have to explain myself to anyone." She dredged up a smile. "But I agree. I doubt if they would care."

Jake reached across the cab of the pickup and covered her hand with his. That little squiggle zipped across her midsection. She hesitated a moment, then intertwined her fingers with his.

"I was surprised to see the Closed sign on the café door," she said as they rode toward the Dairy Queen holding hands. "Do you know why it's closed?"

"Owner's leaving town."

"I used to think the café owner was Mr. Strayhorn's girlfriend."

"Why did you think that?"

Jolie laughed. "Brady asked me the exact same question almost word for word. I saw Mr. Strayhorn and her together two different times on her stairs." She lifted a shoulder in a shrug. "And they looked like a couple."

"Well, I'll tell you confidentially that they are. Or at least they were. How they managed to keep it quiet in a place like this I don't know. I've known about it a long time."

"Oh, my gosh. Jude told me that couldn't be true. She and Brady must have no idea."

"I agree. I think Jude would have said something to me if she knew. I suspect others in Willard County know it, too, but people around here gossip about the Strayhorns and the Circle C only up to a certain point. They know who their benefactors are."

"If Maisie is Mr. Strayhorn's girlfriend, why is she closing and leaving town?"

Jake grinned impishly. "Lovers' quarrel?"

Jolie couldn't keep from laughing. The idea of the unapproachable Mr. Strayhorn engaged in a lovers' quarrel, or even an affair, was funny. And she was starting to see a side of Jake Strayhorn she wouldn't have guessed was there. She cocked her head and gave him a look that, coming from her, was flirty. "In your job, you find out everything about everyone, don't you?"

"Sooner or later. Whether I want to or not. How much time do you have?"

"Two or three hours. Until I have to pick up Danni."

"We could get a couple of burgers at the drive-through, then go to my apartment and watch a movie. What do you think?"

Something was happening between them, something she wasn't sure she knew what to do about. Common sense told her to decline. "Well, I—"

"I know that's not much of a date, but there aren't a lot of choices in Lockett. And you're on a tight schedule."

Date? This is a date? Indeed her schedule *was* tight. So far, she had one day a week and a few hours in the afternoons off work. Period. "Okay. We probably have time."

At the Dairy Queen's drive-through window, the plump order clerk was friendly, but she did a poor job of trying to hide her curiosity about Jake's passenger. Jake behaved as if her tilting her head to get a better view of Jolie were nothing unusual and ordered cheeseburgers with everything. Jolie rarely ate burgers of any kind, but she kept silent about it. A couple of minutes later, the clerk closed the window and disappeared.

"I wonder if she thinks I'm under arrest," Jolie said on a nervous laugh.

Jake turned toward her and grinned. "She's just curious. No one ever sees me with a woman in Lockett."

"You don't like the women here?"

"I've never thought it was a good idea to mix my social life with being the sheriff in such a small town. Of course, the locals all think I should be married, so occasionally, some well-meaning citizen has tried to marry me off."

"I don't blame you for not being married," Jolie said. "I've known people who claimed to be happy, but for me it was mostly drudgery and worry."

Jake gave her an intent look. She didn't know what to add. That was how she felt.

The heavyset order clerk appeared at the window with a puffy paper sack. Jake lifted his butt off the seat and dug into the pocket of his tight jeans, pulled out a money clip and peeled off several bills. He handed the money through the window and told the clerk to keep the change and at the same time, handed Jolie the sack of food.

As he eased away from the order window, she said, "I don't think I should leave the Circle C's pickup parked downtown."

"We can handle that. I'll drop you off and you can drive it to my apartment."

She followed him to his apartment and parked behind his pickup as she had done before. As she scooted down from the seat, he joined her and reached for her hand. They held hands all the way to his front door. Inside the apartment, he carried the sack of food to the kitchen. While she stood back and watched, he dragged plates from the cupboard and arranged the burgers and fries on them. He looked up at her with a boyish grin. "Want to find us a movie?"

"Okay," she said, and went to the storage shelf in the living room. Her fingers were so unsteady, she almost couldn't flick through the DVD selections and her concentration was so fractured, she couldn't focus on the titles. Finally, she just picked one at random.

Jake came in carrying the food and a couple of cans of Coke and set everything on the heavy coffee table. "This is pretty poor pickings compared to what you're used to."

"It's fine. Really."

"What did you find for us to watch?"

She handed over the movie.

"*The English Patient*," he said. "Didn't know I had that one. I've never watched it."

"Me, neither."

They sat on the sofa, their arms almost touching, munching their burgers as the movie began. The apartment felt cool and pleasant and soundless except for the music and dialogue from the movie. Lack of sleep caught up with Jolie and after she'd eaten half her burger, her eyelids grew heavy. She sat back, her head against the sofa back, and let her lids flutter closed. As she relaxed, she felt her shoulder sag and touch Jake's arm and she felt the warmth and size of him. *Security*, her fuzzy mind thought as repose stole through her.

"Tired?" he asked.

If he only knew thoughts of him had kept her awake for two nights, she thought with amusement. "A little. I haven't gotten much chance to slow down the past couple of weeks. So many people have been at the ranch and they all eat."

"Well, you cook about the best meal I've ever had."

She smiled, not opening her eyes. "Why do I have the feeling you could eat a rubber tire and think it was good?"

She heard his soft chuckle near her ear, felt his arm slide across the sofa back. "I'm an easy keeper, Jolie," he said in his velvety baritone voice. "I want you to know that."

No matter how she sorted through that remark, the implication couldn't be misconstrued and a tiny panicky joy burst through her. "I shouldn't be dozing," she said, trying to ignore her heartbeat pounding in her ears. "I should be watching this movie. I really wanted to see it when it came out." She opened her eyes just in time to see the blond female star climbing naked into a bathtub with the male lead. She swallowed a gulp and her pulse shot to a cadence that made her dizzy. Other than with Billy a long time ago, she had never watched an explicit love scene in the company of a man. She felt a flush crawl up her neck, was too aware that Jake's solid, sinewy body was only inches away, couldn't keep from imagining what he would look like without clothes.

She turned to look at him, saw his green eyes even more intense than usual and before she knew it was coming, his head lowered and his mouth brushed hers. When she didn't flinch or pull away, his mouth brushed again, then squarely covered hers. His lips were warm and soft, unthreatening. They exerted a sweet pressure. The room seemed to be spinning around them and as much as her head believed this could be a bad idea, she had no intention of stopping him or herself. She kissed him back.

He broke the kiss and his hand tenderly cupped her jaw. His mouth began to taste hers in little silky nibbles that felt so wonderful she opened her lips for more, relished his tongue touching hers. When an unfamiliar heat began to course through her and her insides began to shake, she pulled back, looking wide-eyed into his face. "Jake, I—"

"Jolie," he murmured, stroking a tendril of her hair back from her face. "Pretty, gentle Jolie."

"I've never . . ." She stopped. Should she tell him she couldn't remember the last time she'd had sex, that she had never had sex with any man other than Billy, that she had never even been kissed by anyone else?

"Never what?" he asked, his fingertips trailing down her jaw.

"I'm not an experienced woman," she blurted.

"I know that."

"How—how do you know?"

"Darlin', I've spent a good part of twenty years knowing more about people than they know about themselves."

Feeling exposed and vulnerable in a way she never had

been before, she drew a quivery breath. "But I don't understand. Why me? You must know a lot of women. They must surely have more—"

"They don't. Trust me."

She covered the back of his hand with hers and peered into his beautiful eyes. "Oh, I do trust you, Jake. I'd trust you with anything. Even my life."

"Then we don't have anything to worry about."

His mouth covered hers again and this time, she had only one question when their lips parted. "Are—are we going to have . . . to sleep together?"

"I hope so," he said softly, his eyes locked on hers, his mouth only inches away. "But I don't want you to think that's the reason I asked you to come here and have lunch."

That thought hadn't even crossed her mind. "We should hurry. I don't want to waste any time."

His lips tipped into an easy smile. He reached up and pushed a tendril of hair behind her ear. His touch on her face sent a frisson of excitement through her. "We don't have to be in a hurry," he said softly. "We can wait until you're sure."

"I'm sure. I don't want to wait. There's so much I've missed, Jake."

He took her hand and looked down at it, circling the top with his thumb. "I know you're treading new ground. I want you to be sure I'm the one."

She took his hand between both of hers and kissed it. "Oh, Jake, I've never been more sure of anything in my life. I never dreamed I would meet someone like you. I want to be with you. I want you to . . . to . . . I want you to make love to me."

"You humble me, Jolie."

"Can we go to your room? We still have time, don't we?"

A soft laugh burst from his throat. "As much time as you want."

He stood and pulled her to her feet. Neither of them spoke as he led her to his bedroom. While he turned back the covers on his king-size bed, she stood behind him, her fingers tightly interlocked, her emotions raw, her heart racing. Her mind was as busy as her heart, trying to decide what Jake would expect. Should she remove her clothes herself or wait for him to do it like lovers in the movies? Though she had feelings for Jake she had never had for anyone and she wanted this, she had no experience with how she should behave in an intimate tryst with a man she hadn't yet learned to be at ease with.

And she tried to remember what underwear she had put on and whether she was wearing one of her better bras. She couldn't have felt more clumsy and awkward.

While all of that danced through her mind, Jake came to her and placed his hands on her shoulders. He lowered his head and kissed her neck beneath her ear. She closed her eyes and relished the feel of his warm lips moving over her neck. He seemed to be searching for a good place and in no time he found one. "Oh," she said, on a shiver as little prickles tingled over her skin. His strong arms came around her and she placed her arms around his neck. "You're the sweetest woman I've ever known," he said.

"Really?"

"I mean that."

His lips settled on her mouth again and reflexively, she pressed against him. They kissed for the longest time, with the world spinning around her and an odd craving building within her. Mere kissing just didn't seem to be enough. She thought she would go crazy if they didn't move on. His hands began to glide over her body and soon she felt his touch on her bare skin beneath her top. He pulled back and looked down at her. He must have felt her shaking all over, because he said, "Don't be nervous. We're gonna go slow."

She looked into his eyes that were now hooded by his eyelids. "I'm . . . not," she said. "We don't have to go slow, unless that's what you want."

He lifted her top and peeled it over her head. She hadn't thought about how her body looked in years. She knew she was in fairly good shape because she physically worked and she had walked miles waiting tables. "I'm—I'm not tanned," she said self-consciously.

He smiled and drew her close in a hug. "Oh, Jolie," he murmured against her hair. "You're beautiful."

She pushed back from him. "I'm inexperienced at this. When Billy and I went to bed, we just got undressed and climbed into bed. Should we do that? Just take off our clothes and get in bed?"

"Eventually."

He reached behind her, unhooked her bra and freed her breasts. Her breasts weren't especially large, but they filled his hands. He touched them as if she were something precious, stroked her and caressed, murmured wonderful things against her skin.

"I should take off my shoes," she said.

He gave a little laugh. "Me, too."

Catching her hand, he sank to the edge of the mattress and brought her down to sit beside him. He began to pry off his boots. Her arm touching his, she untied her sport shoes and rid herself of them and her socks before he got his second boot off. She stood then and unzipped her jeans. He took the task from her and peeled them off, leaning forward and placing warm soft kisses on her belly. "Do you take birth control pills?" he asked.

"No."

He opened a drawer in the bedside table and pulled out packages of condoms. "Let's get in bed," he said, and urged her between the covers. In seconds he was undressed and she couldn't keep from staring. His body truly was all that she had imagined it would be.

Then, limbs entwined, hands venturing everywhere, they wallowed naked and wanton across his huge bed, their bodies sliding together in a sensual embrace. He took his time, kissing her and caressing her, but she was eager and ready for what came next. "Now, Jake," she whispered. "Now."

Together they rolled until she was on her back and he

was kneeling between her thighs, rolling on a condom. He eased into her. Clutching at his shoulders, she frowned and bit down on her lower lip at the size and newness of him, while he murmured words like *relax, sweetheart . . . that's it . . . easy . . .*

As he moved inside her, she sought his gaze, found his eyes a deep green, almost brown. Their gazes held trancelike as he moved in and out and in again. She lifted her hips to him again and again, seeking the strength and weight of him. His lips caught hers and he kissed her deeply, gently pushing up into her, tenderly coaxing her to another level. Her breath began to sough. That funny squiggle had moved down from her stomach to low in her belly. She didn't recognize it for what it was, knew she had never felt it before. A tiny panic passed through her and she gripped his shoulders tightly, digging in with her fingertips. "Jake?"

"Just relax," he whispered. "Let it happen."

And it was happening. Jolting spasms swept through her, drove her to a heightened plane.

At the peak of it, her inner muscles contracted against him, out of her control. He stayed with her until the last tiny spasms went away. "Oh, Jake," she whimpered against his neck.

"Hold on to me," he ground out, sliding his arm under her bottom and holding her tightly against him.

She hooked her heels around his bottom, cradled his hips with her thighs and held him fiercely. He thrust hard and fast, then went rigid on a groan. And just like that it was over.

They lay quiet and trembling. She felt a need to say something, but she was speechless. After a few beats, he rose and went to the bathroom. He soon returned, crawled between the covers and scooped her into his arms. "You're wonderful," he said softly, his gaze solemn, his fingers trailing over her cheek.

She closed her eyes, savoring his every touch. "Is it always like this?" she asked.

"What do you mean?"

"It was never like this with Billy. I didn't know it could feel so good." She snuggled closer to him, laid her cheek on his furry chest, dared to place her arm around his middle.

"It makes a difference when you care about someone," he said.

"You've been single a long time. Why haven't you found someone to care about?"

"I've always wanted someone special. Someone who was open and honest and wanted me for who I am."

"I believe everyone wants that."

"It's harder to find that you might think."

She smiled and kissed his chest. "Someone told me you're hardheaded and iron-willed. They said that's why you've never found someone who would put up with you."

He chuckled, creating a gentle rumble in her ear. "I don't deny it for a minute."

She wriggled against him, loving his soft warm skin, traced the shape of his hairy thigh with her instep. "You can be hardheaded with me as long as you aren't mean to me."

He rose to his elbow and looked down at her gravely. "Jolie, I will never, ever be mean to you. Or to your daughter."

"I know that, Jake," she said softly. "One of the very first things I heard about you when I came here is that you aren't a mean person."

Jolie felt as if she had found a home. She let her eyelids flutter closed. They dozed for a while until she remembered to check the time. "I suppose I should get up and put my clothes on. It's probably getting close to time for me to leave."

"I wish you didn't have to go."

"I wish it, too, Jake."

By the time Jolie reached the Circle C's front gate, she was so nervous and distracted she was talking to herself. She couldn't believe she'd had sex with Jake. And now that she had, she couldn't stop thinking about it and wanting more of it. Where was this going? What might happen next?

She had to pull herself together. She couldn't let Danni see her in this state. And she sure couldn't cook an edible meal if she didn't find a way to push Jake and the whole afternoon out of her mind. Then it dawned on her she had spent hours without worrying about where Billy was or what he might be doing.

The grind of the school bus's engine yanked her out of her thoughts and soon the big yellow vehicle lumbered to a stop and Danni tramped off. She and the daughter of one of the hands parted and Danni came to the pickup and climbed in. "How was your day?" Jolie asked her.

"It was okay. . . . Mama, I saw a pickup like Billy's today."

Jolie's breath stuck in her throat. "Wh—where did you see it?"

"It was driving down the road by the gym."

"The person driving it wasn't Billy, was it?" Jolie's voice had come out reedy and thin.

"I couldn't see good. But I don't think so."

Like a mound of ants scattered by a footprint, Jolie's mind raced in all directions and she had to force herself to think rationally. Most of Willard County's population was poor. There would be plenty of twenty-year-old pickups here, wouldn't there?

"I'm hungry," Danni said. "Did you make a cake to-day?"

"There's still some carrot cake," she said shakily, trying to compel her breathing to a normal rhythm. "And there's some strawberries. You can have something when we get to the house."

"What's wrong, Mama? Are you scared?"

"No, no. I've just had a busy day. And I've still got a lot to do."

"What're you cooking for supper?"

Jolie was dumfounded. She had forgotten what she had planned for supper.

But she hadn't forgotten the last face-to-face encounter she'd had with her ex-husband. Jake's advice rushed at her. . . .

Do J.D. and Jude know about Billy and your situation? . . . You probably should tell her. . . .

She *should* inform Jude and Brady, even if she might not find the courage to tell Mr. Strayhorn. She owed it to them because she didn't know what Billy might do.

Should she also tell Jake what Danni had reported? It might be nothing and she hated the idea of going to Jake like a nervous ninny whining over nothing.

She parked the pickup in its usual spot. Before she got out, she said, "Listen, Danni, I want you to be very cautious. I don't want you going back to the cottage without me and I don't want you going around the ranch unless Jude or Brady is around, okay?"

"I never do, Mama."

"I know. I'm just reminding you to be cautious."

Jolie wished school was already out, wished Danni didn't have to be away from her all day. "You need to be cautious when you're at school, too."

28

Pat was working in his arena when he heard the sound of a vehicle he recognized coming up his driveway. Suzanne coming home from work. She had moved into his house ten days ago. Now that she was here, he loved getting up in the morning and going to bed at night. They both had changed in subtle ways in the aftermath of the Mitch episode. Suzanne seemed to need him more, which made him work at being closer to her. Their relationship had changed, too. Believing Mitch had vanished as a threat, Pat felt more relaxed, freer to be himself. The need to defend his manhood had disappeared. He no longer felt Suzanne was leading him around by the nose. They functioned as a unit. He was a happy man.

He began to wind down his workout with Blue Streak. An hour later he entered his house to the aroma of Italian spices. Country music played from the kitchen. He found Suzanne stirring something in a pot on the stove. She looked casual and at ease, wearing boxer shorts and an oversize T-shirt, her feet bare and her long blond hair in a ponytail. "Hey," he said.

She gazed up at him with a huge smile. "Hey, yourself, cowboy."

"Whatcha making?" he asked, glancing into the pot.

"Spaghetti. Quick and easy."

He looped an arm around her shoulder, bent down for a

kiss, which turned into more than just a peck. His interest veered from food to something else entirely. "I'm gonna get a shower," he said. "Wanna join me?"

She grinned. "I just got out. I still have to make a salad. We can eat as soon as you finish."

He squeezed her bottom and trekked to the bathroom. He showered away the sweat and dust of the day and shampooed his hair, made a quick pass with his electric razor to knock down his end-of-day stubble, pulled on sweatpants and a T-shirt and returned to the kitchen. Suzanne was at the sink washing lettuce under the faucet. He walked behind her, wrapped his arms around her and pressed himself against the cleft of her bottom. She smelled of soap and water and Suzanne. Almost instantly his dick turned to stone.

"Hmm," she said. "You must be really glad to see me."

"Left over from this morning," he murmured against her ear. With both of them having overslept, they hadn't had sex this morning. He cupped her breast with one hand, gave her neck a nip, then soothed the spot with his tongue.

"If there's anything I like, it's a man with a one-track mind," she said with a low giggle.

He slipped his other hand inside the elastic waistband of her shorts and caressed her flat belly, learned she wasn't wearing panties. "Hmm, soft," he whispered, and moved his fingers down. She made a little noise and leaned back into him. He parted her sex with his fingers and found her wet and hot.

"Pat," she said in a tiny voice.

"Shut the water off," he said, his own voice coming out hoarsely. "Let's go to bed."

"Are we talking a quickie?"

"Only if that's what it has to be."

"There's no such thing as a quickie with you, Pat Garner. Wait a minute."

She pulled away from him, turned off the faucet and the burner under the pot on the stove and he led her to the bedroom. In no time they were skin to skin, sensually rubbing against each other. If he lived to be a hundred, he would always be amazed at how well they fit together. Limbs and mouths entangled, they rolled together over his king-size bed until he was behind her, his body curved around hers, his hands caressing her breasts, her belly, his fingers sliding between her thighs and stroking her into little kittenish whimpers. "There . . . yes, there . . . oh, Pat . . . don't tease me. . . ."

Running his hand along her firm hip, he hooked her knee and pushed it high, positioned his cock and eased into her. She moaned softly and her hot muscles latched on to him. Sensation whooshed through him. He gritted his teeth and held his breath to keep from coming. On a grunt, he seated himself all the way to the hilt, then hesitated and drew a deep breath, fighting for control. "God, Suzanne . . ."

She fidgeted against him. "Pat . . ."

"Shh-shh . . ." He splayed his fingers over her belly and pressed her closer to him.

"I need . . ."

"I know," he murmured. He moved his fingers down and began to stroke.

"Oh . . . oh, Pat . . ."

"Easy, now," he whispered against her neck. "Nice and slow." He took control and with great effort, kept the pace excruciatingly measured, losing himself in the smooth slide of his hard flesh against the walls of her slick, hot channel.

Her hips began to move against him. "I don't want slow," she said in a tiny, desperate voice.

"Relax," he whispered.

"I can't," she said, but she stopped struggling against him.

"That's it . . . sweet, sweet baby . . . that's it." He stroked her nape with his tongue, gently bit into her shoulder while he blindly played with the tender petals of her sex, deliberately avoiding the core of her.

Her breath began to hiss between her teeth. She gripped his wrist tightly, trying to move his hand. "Pat . . . touch me."

He resisted her effort, didn't want her to come yet. When

she did, he would, and he wanted to enjoy her as long as possible. He sensed she was on the edge and pulled out. She gave a frantic little gasp, but he quickly turned her to her back, crawled between her thighs and pushed into her again. She lifted her knees, clutched his biceps and peaked at once, sobbing out and panting. He barely lasted through her contractions powerfully pulling at him. After she finished he let go, too, breathing her name as his own orgasm tore through him and he filled her with his semen.

They lay silently, clinging tightly and soothing each other with gentle caresses and tender words. In time, he tilted his head back and looked into her clear blue eyes. "Your eyes are like the Texas sky," he said. "Sometimes, when I'm outside and there's not a cloud in the sky and all I can see for miles is blue, I think of your eyes."

She kissed him. "I love you," she said softly.

"I love you, too," he said.

She traced his lower lip with her fingertips. "You're terrible, you know that? When we were doing it, you were talking to me like I've heard you talk to your horses."

He smiled, covered her fingers with his hand and kissed the tips. "Sometimes you're like them. Sometimes you need gentling just like they do."

"Is that so? Now I have to decide if I do or don't like being compared to a horse."

"You know how much I love my horses."

"I do. And I'm glad I'm part of what you love. . . . You hungry?"

"Uh-huh."

"We should get cleaned up and eat before that spaghetti turns into garbage."

Later they sat at the table, eating. "Oh, I meant to tell you something as soon as you got home," she said, "but you distracted me." She looked up from her plate and gave him a mischievous look.

He gave her a wink. "Tell me what?"

"Today, when Jolie Jensen came to town and bought groceries, Jake Strayhorn was waiting for her in broad daylight across the street from the grocery store."

"What does that mean?" Pat asked, not quite getting it and knowing he was being obtuse.

"I thought you might know since you're friends with him. In front of God and everybody, she got in his pickup with him and they drove away."

"The hell," Pat said, puzzled.

"Later he brought her back," Suzanne said, "and she got in the Circle C's pickup and drove toward the sheriff's office. Never have I seen Jake associate with a woman in Lockett."

"Me, either. Not since that schoolteacher, which was before you came back here. But what the hell? Jake likes women as much as the next man."

"I'm amazed, aren't you? I mean I'm amazed about him picking Jolie. She's a really nice person and really pretty, but I just never expected Jake would go for her. She must be a lot younger than he is."

"Jake's thirty-eight."

"And I'll bet she's under thirty."

"That doesn't matter," Pat said. "I get the feeling Jake's a lonely guy. Maybe he thinks it's time to settle down. His friends are getting hitched. First Brady, now me. Maybe he feels left out."

Suzanne huffed. "That's no basis for a relationship. You make it sound like he would just pick anybody out and say, 'Okay, I'll take this one.' "

"That isn't what I mean at all, Suz. All I'm saying is Jake's not the kind of guy who would dive off a cliff over a woman, but that doesn't mean he'd be cavalier about his feelings for someone."

"You mean he'd take up with somebody just to have somebody around?"

"Not at all. But he's a planner. He would be thoughtful and decisive about what he wants. Then he'd make a decision."

"Well, he must be serious about her. He didn't seem to mind at all that everybody in town probably saw her get into his pickup."

Lying in the dark in his king-size bed, his fingers interlocked behind his head, Jake pondered the afternoon with Jolie. Lord, she was something. Her total honesty and openness were as refreshing as a drink of cool water. And she was a pretty woman. He had thought so the moment he saw her. A man could get lost in those searching deep brown eyes. A few years ago, he would have called her "hot," but words like that no longer came to his mind when he thought of women. Not that he didn't enjoy a sexy, good-looking woman, but nowadays, he sought specific characteristics, such as loyalty and a companion he could trust. Affection and unselfishness. In terms of relationships, it was a relief to finally know what he wanted.

Since half the world was female, the qualities he required should have been easy for him, or any man, to come by, but until Jolie Jensen, he hadn't found them all in one person. In Jolie, he saw even more than he required. She was brave and strong. He had always respected bravery, always admired those willing to push the envelope and take personal risk to break away from a bad hand life had dealt them. But Jolie, even while being brave, retained a vulnerability that pierced him deeply and made him want to love and protect her and her daughter. Originally, he had hoped that the woman he finally chose to spend the rest of his life with would be a little closer to his age, but now he had concluded that a thing like age wasn't quite so important.

He couldn't identify the moment his wants had evolved from "just sex" with a hot woman. God knew he had found sex whenever he wanted and to whatever erotic degree he fancied, but that evidently hadn't been enough. Not since he was a kid and had married at twenty-one had he desired to take a relationship further. Maybe he had simply grown up and started looking for something different.

Odd that from out of the blue, someone would turn up in Lockett who seemed to be all that he wanted. But that was the way life was, he had learned. Unplanned things happened at unexpected moments. Now that he had found Jolie, he had to figure out how they could spend more time together.

He dropped off to sleep, but after spending a restless night, awoke before daylight. He would be alone in the office most of today, so he had no time for his run, nor would he be able to go out for breakfast. He brewed coffee and nuked a frozen egg and sausage burrito in the microwave, then went to his office.

He had no sooner arrived than the phone rang. He picked up to hear the driller from AmDril Drilling Company, one of the drilling companies in town temporarily, reporting that all of the company trucks parked in their yard had been broken into overnight. Jake locked the office and drove out and investigated. He found few clues that would lead him to make an arrest. A vandal had obtained entry to the trucks by smashing the drivers' and passengers' windows. Missing mostly were small electronic items that could be sold for quick cash, though not anywhere in Lockett that Jake knew about. He returned to his office with the evidence he had gathered, but suspected finding the guilty party would be an accident. Nevertheless, back at his desk, he wrote a report, laid a copy on Chuck's desk and gave a copy to Amanda.

"Now, who do you suppose did this?" she asked disgustedly, scanning the report and shaking her head. "I can't think of a soul around here who would. Not even kids."

"Somebody passing through, I suspect," Jake told her. "The yard's right on the highway and they don't have security night lighting. After this, they probably will."

He returned to his office. Glasses perched on the end of his nose, he sat at his desk shuffling through the faxes that had come across while he had been out. Most of them were BOLOs out of various Texas cities. Most severe crime in Texas occurred in and around the population centers. Most rural people were too busy to be criminals. His pulse rate escalated when he saw Billy Dean Jensen's name. He hadn't expected it, but he couldn't say he was surprised, either.

He pulled the sheet out of the small stack, sat back in his chair and studied Jensen's picture, recognized the dead-eyed look of a drug user. Jake read further—known drug user, history of mild violence and domestic abuse, a few more facts typical of young men like Jensen. He was alleged to have stolen money from an individual several days back and since he was on probation, the Dallas PD wanted him ASAP.

Every one of Jake's cop instincts told him Jensen couldn't be found in Dallas because he was headed for Willard County and his ex-wife. He plucked his cell phone from his belt and keyed in Jolie's number. She didn't answer, so he left a message for her to call him.

He strode to the front office and showed the BOLO to Amanda, took a seat in a chair beside her desk while she studied it. Her eyes widened as she read down the page. "Oh, my God," she said. "I knew Jolie had problems, but I had no idea she was married to someone like this. I thought they just had a few fights."

"Exactly how are you related to Jolie?"

"My mother and her mother are cousins. Jolie's actually my distant cousin and I don't even know her that well. I'm ten years older than she is. I just remember hearing my mom say it was shameful all the work and responsibility Evelyn shoved off on Jolie while she gallivanted around with this man and that. Jolie practically raised her two sisters and she's had a job for as long as I can remember. Mom always said Evelyn treated Jolie more like her slave than her daughter."

Jake already had the picture of how Jolie had been raised, but Amanda's conversation only redoubled his admiration for her as well as his determination to protect her. He pulled his notebook from his shirt pocket and read her the description of Jensen's vehicle. "Have you ever seen Jensen's truck?" he asked.

Amanda shook her head, still studying the picture on the BOLO.

Jake handed her his notebook. "Here's the description of it. Either make a copy or write it down and be sure Chuck gets it."

While Amanda jotted down the notes from his notebook, Jake checked his watch, made a mental note that school would let out soon. "We need to keep an eye on the school," he said, getting to his feet.

"You think he's coming after her, don't you?" Amanda said.

"Just being cautious."

"Do you think he'd hurt her?"

"All I know is she's afraid of him. And that tells me he could hurt her."

Jake returned to his office, plucked his cell off his belt and tried Jolie's number again. Still no answer. He didn't want to alarm her, so he left another message for her to call him, telling her nothing about the reason for his call. He weighed just how much potential danger there could be for her and Danni, if it was worth him driving to her cottage on the Circle C Ranch, a place he hadn't been in twenty-four years. For all he knew, he could be wrong about Jensen. Even though he was an alleged thief, the guy could have been tamed by the system. Perhaps he was now harmless as a lamb.

But not likely.

Jolie had been busy all day. She and Irene had thoroughly cleaned the appliances in the kitchen.

She was dirty and tired, but she still had to prepare supper. She had never paid much attention to her cell phone, but hoping Jake might call and invite her to spend Monday with him again, she pulled it from her apron pocket and turned it on.

She saw two messages from Jake, which chased away her fatigue. She walked into the big pantry and speed-dialed his private number. She heard only two burrs before he picked up. "Jolie, you okay?"

She gave a low laugh. "Of course. Why wouldn't I be?"

"I've called you a couple of times today."

"I just now saw your messages. I've had my phone off all day."

"Jolie, a fax BOLO on Billy came into my office today out of Dallas County."

"BOLO?" Her heart began a quick tattoo.

"It means be on the lookout. He was out of jail on probation, but now he's accused of stealing some money and he's in violation of his probation."

Jolie closed her eyes and drew in a deep breath. "I was afraid it meant something like that. Did it say where he is?"

"They don't know. If they did, they'd pick him up."

"Right," Jolie said, feeling as if a band had tightened around her lungs.

"Jolie, does Billy have a gun?"

"A gun? N-no. I mean he never has. Does he have one now?"

"I just asked because I hadn't heard you say if he has one. Did you tell Jude and Brady your circumstances?"

"No. Everyone has been so busy, including me. I haven't had a chance."

"What time do you go home?"

"Usually by nine. I don't like for Danni to get to bed later than that on a school night."

"Are you afraid to stay alone?"

"I wasn't, but I might be now. If Billy's got money, he's probably smoking meth."

"How would you feel about me talking to Brady and telling him you need to sleep in the ranch house until we resolve this?"

"I don't think I can do that. Danni has to get ready for school tomorrow and I have to get ready for work, too. I've been through a lot with Billy, Jake, but I've always tried to not let it affect Danni's routine. I don't want to change that.

Besides, I'm not sure I'd be comfortable sleeping here in this house."

"Well, keep your cell phone close by. When you get home, call me and let me know you're there. Be sure to lock your doors. I'll be waiting for your call."

"If I have a problem, can't I call 9-1-1?"

Jake chuckled softly. "Sweetheart, I *am* 9-1-1."

"Oh," she said. "I hadn't thought of that." She heard Reuben come into the kitchen and begin speaking to Irene in Spanish. "I—I guess I should get off the phone. I'm in the pantry and I need to help Irene finish up."

"Be sure to tell Jude and Brady what's going on."

"Okay."

"I'll be thinking about you. If I don't hear from you by ten o'clock, I'll assume something's not right."

"Okay," she repeated.

And then what? she wondered.

They disconnected. She stood in the pantry a few minutes, organizing her thoughts. *Stay calm*, she told herself. After all, she had known the day was coming when Billy would show up, hadn't she? And hadn't she dealt with him and his antics for years?

She went through the motions of finishing supper, left the serving of it up to Irene and Reuben. She was so rattled she might spill something on someone. After supper, Mr. Strayhorn went to his room, as he always did. Jude and Brady sat at the table talking, which wasn't unusual. They rarely watched the huge TV in the family room or used the study, she had noticed. She couldn't imagine having so many wonderful things and never using them.

Irene went to the family room and brought Danni in to eat supper with them at the round breakfast room table, but Jolie had no appetite. She walked into the dining room and said to Jude and Brady, "Can I speak to the two of you for a minute?"

"Of course," Jude said.

"Is something wrong?" Brady asked.

In a matter of a few minutes, Jolie blurted the sorry tale of her life with Billy Jensen, including the fact that he might be on his way to Willard County. And if he was stoned enough, a simple barrier like a barbed-wire fence would do nothing to keep him from coming onto the Circle C. She even told them about exchanging her license plates with another car's.

Brady laughed. "Jude wondered what happened to your license plates."

"Have you talked to Jake?" Jude asked.

She nodded. "He's keeping an eye out. But I understand he can't be everywhere at once."

"You and Danni are welcome to stay in the ranch house," Jude said.

Jolie shook her head. "I don't want to disrupt Danni's life any more. I've always gone out of my way to make sure everything for her is as normal as possible. Billy doesn't know where we live. I don't think he'd start knocking on the door of every house on this ranch. . . . And besides, we don't know for sure if he'll come here."

29

Early Saturday morning, sitting in his office, Jake was startled by a loud voice he didn't immediately recognize. "Goddammit, Chuck, don't tell me to calm down. I been robbed. How would *you* feel if it happened to you?"

Jake sprang to his feet and dropped his glasses on his desk. He strode to the outer office and saw Lucky Henson, the owner of Lucky's Grocery, pacing and ranting at Chuck.

"What's going on?" Jake asked.

Lucky turned to him, his square face vivid and shiny with perspiration. Everything about Lucky Henson was square, even his Hawaiian-print shirt.

"Goddammit, Jake, some bastard broke in my back door. Got my week's take and all my extra cash." Lucky threw a hammy hand in the air and began to pace again. "Jimmied the lock, tore up the door, trashed my office."

"Let's go take a look. Gimmee a minute." Jake returned to his office for his hat and glasses; then he and Chuck followed Lucky out of the sheriff's office.

Lucky's building backed up to a large caliche parking lot that eventually merged with an open grassy pasture. The back door, which opened into the storeroom, was a weathered three-panel wooden door with an aged knob tarnished to brown and a flimsy lock. Jake could see the door had been forced open by a powerful blow. The wooden frame and jamb were splintered and separated from the brick wall.

"Look at this shit," Lucky shouted. "It'll cost me five hundred dollars to get that door fixed."

Jake didn't disagree. He could see that an entire new door and doorframe would have to be installed.

Lucky went on to explain that the door was always dead-bolted from the inside and at the end of the workday, he and his employees left through the front door.

Jake examined the door and the area around it, but found nothing but wood splinters and pieces. He walked around inside the storeroom. Boxes of merchandise had been opened, the contents scattered. Various display items were strewn over the floor.

"Just look at this," Lucky growled, only slightly calmer than he had been in Jake's office. He pointed at a desk with nothing on it but a mug of pens and pencils, a box of tissues and a few overstuffed file folders. "Assholes even took my friggin' computer." He clasped his head with both hands. "This is a fuckin' disaster. That computer's got my whole damned inventory in it and my bank account numbers."

"Lordy, Lordy," Chuck said, obviously awed by the damage.

"Where did you keep the money?" Jake asked.

Lucky gestured toward a closed door. "In my office."

"How much did they get?"

"I figure they got a thousand in cash out of my deposit bag. And all the change I keep around in case we run short. About five hundred dollars."

"So we're talking fifteen hundred dollars total cash?" Jake said.

"About that," Lucky replied.

"Let's take a look," Jake said. He walked through the chaotic storeroom, glancing in all directions. Lucky trailed behind him, still ranting. Inside the office, Jake saw no safe. "Where was the money?"

"In that drawer." Lucky pointed to a massive wooden cabinet.

Jake observed a drawer with a splintered front, as if something heavy had hit it a hard blow. The drawer's lock looked to be strong, but it had been no match for some heavy tool. A crowbar, Jake surmised.

Lucky walked over and gestured toward the ruined drawer. "This is where I keep what I'm gonna deposit. I take it down to the bank in Abilene every Monday. This is Saturday. That means they got every friggin' dime in cash from this whole week. Thank God for credit cards and checks."

"They didn't take the checks?"

"Nope. Just the cash."

"If you bank out of town and don't go every day, why don't you have a safe?" Jake asked, frowning.

"'Cause this is Lockett. Who's gonna break into my store? Everybody knows I ain't got any money."

Jake squatted to more closely examine the drawer. "If you're going to keep money in here, Lucky, you need to get a safe. A heavy one."

"This drawer didn't have my cash stash in it," Lucky said from behind him.

Jake got to his feet, dusting his palms on his jeans. "Where was it?"

Lucky pointed to a heavy steel file cabinet, saying the locked top drawer was where he kept extra bills and coins for emergency change. The drawer had been caved in by a blow and the lock destroyed. While Lucky babbled to Chuck, Jake examined the file cabinet drawer. "Who's around here at night?" he asked.

"Why?" Lucky said, a hopeful expression on his face.

"These are heavy blows. There had to have been some noise."

"Hell, there ain't nobody around Lockett at night. You know that. The only person there ever was in town at night was Maisie, but she's gone. You know that, too, right?"

"Yeah, I heard."

Chuck came in with a fingerprint kit and began dusting for prints.

Jake had already concluded that Lucky's thief was ex-

perienced at breaking and entering and had likely worn gloves.
Not seeing a heavy tool lying loose, he suspected the bad
actor had brought one with him. But none of the obvious
evidence was what had Jake preoccupied. The earlier theft
at AmDril Drilling Company had taken on new signifi-
cance. He tried to remember when, if ever, he had known of
two robberies in one week in Lockett, or for that matter, in
one month or even one year. In Lockett, two burglaries in a
week was a crime wave. "Anything missing besides your
computer and money?" he asked Lucky.

"Well, I ain't sure, but I think there could be a few groceries missing."

A hungry burglar. Jake nodded. "You got any new people working for you?"

"Lord, no. I only got three people total. You know 'em
all. They've been with me for years. The newest employee I
got is Suzanne Breedlove. And hell, she's been here more
than two years."

"When will your employees be in?"

"Probably be here any time."

"We'll need to talk to them."

Jake's mind began to churn. A strong suspicion had been
building inside him, one of those eerie hunches. Instinctively
he knew the identity of Lockett's serial thief. Riding a high,
Billy Jensen needed quick cash to keep it going. At some
point he would flame out and crash, but where the hell was
he at the moment?

Jake gestured for Chuck to follow him outside. "I'm going back to the office," he told him. "I've got an idea who
did this. Finish up here and wait for the employees to show
up. Take their statements."

When he reached his office, he saw his friend Brady
Fallon's truck parked in front. He walked inside and found
Brady himself sitting beside Amanda's empty desk.

Brady rose and put out his right hand. "Hey, Jake."

Brady looked different, Jake noticed. He looked older and
more serious somehow, even had a few gray hairs. Talk

around town was that J.D. Strayhorn's new son-in-law was assuming more responsibility daily for the operation of the Circle C. Jake was happy to see that Brady wore authority and influence well. He grinned and shook his hand. "Long time no see. How's the ranching life?"

Brady grinned, too. "Fine. Just fine. Had a good calf crop this year. Getting ready for branding."

"Jude?"

"She's good, too. Starting to get a little round. You must have heard she's expecting. October, the doc says."

Jake hadn't seen Jude in weeks, but the local grapevine had been abuzz. He couldn't imagine his tomboyish cousin pregnant. "I did hear. Congratulations," he said. "Come on back to the office." He headed up the hall. Without breaking stride he stepped behind his desk.

Brady followed and closed the door behind him. He took a seat in front of Jake's desk.

"Haven't seen you in a while," Jake said. "What's up?"

"I'll get right to the point, Jake. Last night our new kitchen manager, Jolie Jensen, told Jude and me about her ex-husband. I got the impression you're aware that he's some kind of hoodlum."

"Small-time criminal. In and out of jail. There's a hot warrant on him out of Dallas for probation violation." Jake had no reason to mention the theft allegation to Brady.

"Jolie's pretty shaken up. She's afraid of the guy. After hearing Jolie talk, Jude's worried, too. I told her I'd come to town this morning and discuss it with you. So level with me, buddy. Is this something we need to be concerned about? You think this dude will come to Lockett?"

Jake didn't doubt Jolie was upset. She knew her ex-husband better than anybody. But Jake also knew Jolie was tough. She had been surviving life with the guy for years. "I don't know much. His name's Billy Dean Jensen. We don't know where he is at the moment. It's purely suspicion, but I wouldn't be surprised if he's headed for Lockett. He might be here already."

"Intending to do what?"

"I don't know. He's a meth user. If he's high, he's probably paranoid and unpredictable. If he's like most of those folks, his muddled mind's probably got Jolie all mixed up with the reasons for his problems."

"So he's dangerous, then?"

"Hard to tell. Anybody's potentially dangerous when he's hopped up and out of his head. I recommended to Jolie that she ask you to let her stay in the ranch house, just until we get this straightened out."

"We offered her that," Brady said, "but she didn't want to. She's putting up a brave front, but I think she's scared to death."

"Like I said, Jensen is probably unpredictable and I'm sure she knows it. I don't want to disrupt your operation or your life. Chuck and I'll be patrolling the highway along the ranch's gate. I'm going to alert the DPS and our Ranger, although I don't know if the Rangers will enter into it. Jensen isn't the kind of criminal they typically pursue, but since he's wanted by Dallas PD, they might. Don't worry, Brady. We'll get him."

Brady sat forward, his elbow propped on Jake's desk. "Jake, don't BS me. That ranch covers more than four hundred square miles. Randomly watching the front gate looking for one guy is like looking for a flea on a dog."

"I know it looks that way. But we'll get him. Jolie just needs to be sure she keeps an eye out and watches what she and her daughter are doing."

Brady drew a deep breath and sat back in his chair. "Tell me what you want *me* to do."

"You do the same." Jake picked up a piece of paper on which Amanda had typed a description of Jensen's truck and handed it across his desk. "Here's a description of the rig he's most likely driving. If you see it anywhere, call me at once. Chuck and I'll be doing some double duty to make sure the phone's covered twenty-four hours."

Brady sighed. "Too bad we don't have a 9-1-1 service here."

"Got to have the money to put it in place and hire the people to man it," Jake replied.

"I might give that some thought. After this is over, let's get together and come up with some figures. I'll take it up with J.D."

Jake shrugged. He didn't doubt the Circle C could buy a 9-1-1 system, but the long-term maintenance was another matter, another strain on the county's overstretched budget.

"Jude said something to me last night that raised a question in my mind, Jake."

"What?"

"She said she had often wondered, given how you feel about the Circle C, what you'd do if the need for a cop should surface out there. I gotta ask you, Jake, what if this Billy Jensen somehow finds his way to the ranch? Will you be able . . . or willing . . . to do anything about it?"

Jake sat forward, his forearms resting on the desk, and looked his friend in the eye. "I was elected to serve the people, Brady. *All* the people. You don't have to worry. I'll do what has to be done."

Brady nodded. "I told Jude that. And that's all I need to know." He got to his feet. "I gotta get going. Jude and Jolie both will be mad at me if I hold up dinner." Brady put out his right hand. "I trust you, Jake."

Jake shook Brady's hand. "Thanks, Brady. Take care."

As soon as Brady left, Jake sat back in his chair, thinking of Jolie and deciding what to do next. He wasn't fond of the idea of going onto the Circle C to deal with Billy should things come to that. So that meant he had to arrest the bastard before he ever got to the Circle C Ranch.

He plucked his cell phone from his belt and keyed in Jolie's number, hoping she wasn't in the middle of preparing dinner. She answered at once.

"Hey," Jake said. "I didn't think I'd get you."

"Irene's about to serve dinner. We're waiting for Brady."

"He just left here. Should be home in ten or fifteen minutes."

"Brady was at your office? What was he doing there?"

"He came to talk about Billy."

"Has something happened?"

"Not yet."

"I'm going to town soon to pick up some things at the grocery store. I could come by and say hello and you could tell me what you talked about."

"Good. Oh, and you don't have to worry about Amanda. She doesn't work on Saturday. I'll be waiting for you."

As soon as Jake disconnected, his thoughts returned to robbery. Now believing a connection existed between the drilling company theft and the grocery store burglary, he drove back to the drilling company, intending to take another look around their premises.

As he pulled into the caliche-covered yard, he saw little activity, couldn't tell if the office was open. No CLOSED sign hung on the door, so he parked and walked up to it. Inside, a local young woman he recognized sat at the receptionist's desk. "Hey, Molly, your boss around?"

"Hi, Mr. Strayhorn. Him and his wife went to Vegas for the weekend."

"What about your driller?"

"He's out with the drilling crew."

"I was out here a few days ago investigating some break-ins into your trucks. I'd like to take another look at the ones that are parked over at the edge of your lot."

"Sure," she said. "I don't see why not." She stood and went to a key board on the wall, lifted off two sets of keys and handed them to him.

Jake touched his hat to her and walked outside. All of the trucks he had checked out a few days ago weren't here, but two were. He ambled across the parking lot toward them, surprised to see that the broken windows he had seen when he had been here previously had already been replaced.

He had just approached the first truck when he happened to glance toward the far back corner of the yard at an old tan pickup truck. The hair stood on the back of his neck, as it often did when intuition wouldn't be denied. He grabbed for his shirt pocket and pulled out his notebook, reread the description of Billy Jensen's truck. His blood began to hum in his veins.

He returned to the front of the office and his own SUV. He drove back to the truck and compared it to his notes, which by now included Billy's license plate number. Knowing he dared not search the truck without a warrant, even if it were unlocked, he walked around the outside and peered inside. He saw empty fast-food sacks, papers and food wrappers, a little mud and general debris and dishevelment. The cab looked as if someone was living in it.

He had to get a search warrant, had to dig into the truck, but unfortunately, he had no idea where Willard County's only judge might be found on a Saturday afternoon.

He returned to the office and asked the receptionist who owned that particular truck.

"New guy," she said. "I can't remember his name. Do you want me to look it up for you?"

"Please," Jake said.

She opened her right bottom drawer and pulled out a file, ran a manicured nail down a list of names. "His name's Bobby Jones," she said. "He just went to work a few days ago. He's one of the roustabouts."

"Did he show you a Social Security card or a driver's license?"

"No," she answered, suddenly looking nervous. The law required her company to examine both. "He said he misplaced his wallet, but he'd find it and bring that stuff to me later."

Jake nodded, deliberately not asking if she or somebody had asked to see the two documents. "When are you expecting him back?"

"Oh, gosh, they just went out. I'd be surprised if they're back before midnight."

"Where are they working?"

She assumed a blank look. "I have no idea. I just know it's about an hour's drive from here."

The lack of a Social Security card or driver's license convinced Jake of what he suspected. Bobby Jones was Billy Jensen. Frustrated, he returned to his office to prepare a search warrant and look for the judge. He also had a plan to be back at Jensen's truck before midnight.

Jolie was so eager to see Jake she decided to put off her shopping until last. As soon as she was able to get away from the ranch's kitchen, she drove straight to the sheriff's office. Only Jake's SUV was parked in front, so she parked beside it and went inside. She found him digging in a file cabinet drawer. He came over to her at once and kissed her cheek. She hadn't expected that and felt her face heat up.

"I want to talk to you about something," he said. "Sit down." He gestured toward a metal armchair located at one end of Amanda's desk. He pulled out Amanda's desk chair, sat down and rolled over to her. Jolie sat with her hands in her lap, her eyes intent on his face, anxiously waiting to hear what he had to say.

He leaned forward and picked up her hand. "Has Billy ever been known to use the name Bobby Jones?" he asked quietly.

"Not that I know of."

"I'm pretty sure Billy's in town. I think he's working at AmDril Drilling Company. His truck's parked in their yard."

She felt her eyes widen. "Oh, my God."

"The drilling company's trucks were robbed a few days ago. The grocery store was robbed last night."

Jolie's palm flew to her cheek. "Oh, my God. Do you think it was Billy?"

"I don't know yet, but I've got my suspicions."

"Of course it was Billy. I know it was. If he's drugging, he needs money. More than he can make at a job."

"Listen, I don't want you to panic, but I want you and Danni to be extra cautious. In Lockett, it wouldn't be hard for him to find out where you live. I alerted Brady about my concerns."

Tears burned behind Jolie's eyes. She had become relaxed in her daily life, almost able to make herself believe a confrontation with Billy would never come. "I hate this. I hate having the people I work for affected by my personal problems. It was like that in Grandee. My boss and his wife put up with far more than they should've had to because of me."

"Don't be upset about Jude and Brady, Jolie. They're good people. They want to help you."

She sniffed. "I know and I'm grateful. But that doesn't undo anything."

"I want to help you, too. And I'm going to. I'm gonna arrest Billy and send him back to Dallas. He'll go back to jail and serve out his sentence. He's also been charged with theft back there and it's possible that will get him more jail time. But meanwhile, I don't want you to be afraid."

"I'm not when I'm with you, Jake."

Still holding her hands, Jake got to his feet and pulled her up and close. The next thing she knew his arms were around her and her arms were around his middle and they were kissing and her mouth was open and letting his silky tongue slide against hers. They kissed for what seemed like forever. Finally, he broke away, his breathing shaky. Hers, too.

"I know we shouldn't do this here," she said in a small breathless voice. "I know it would be bad if someone came in."

He placed his forehead against hers. "You've been on my mind night and day since Wednesday," he said softly. "As soon as this business with Billy is over, Jolie, I've got a lot of things I want to talk to you about."

"Okay."

"I want to take this further, Jolie. You and me and Danni."

"You do?" she almost squeaked.

"Don't you?"

She looked into his expressive eyes, saw their sincerity, wanted to match his commitment with her own. "I think so."

He leaned back and smiled down at her and she could see the bristle on his jaw. "You *think* so? Darlin', you need to *know* so."

"But how can I? I don't know what I'm doing. Or how I'm supposed to behave."

30

Jolie left the sheriff's office in a rush. She barely had time to stop by the grocery store before going back to the ranch to start supper. She breezed through the aisles, picking up the items she needed. At the cash register, she heard the female employees chattering about the robbery Jake had already told her about.

"How much money was stolen?" she asked, recalling that Jake hadn't mentioned an amount.

"Lucky said around fifteen hundred," Suzanne answered.

Jolie willed herself not to catch a breath. Good Lord. With that much money, no telling what Billy would be up to. She suddenly felt an overwhelming urge to be at home with Danni. She had already arranged for Reuben to pick Danni up from the school bus, but all she could think of now was how much she wanted to be home.

"I've got to get back to the ranch," she said, now in a hurry to get out of the grocery store.

"Let me help you with those bags," Suzanne said, grabbing a couple of the plastic sacks and walking beside her to the front door. Suzanne followed her outside. "I saw you with Jake the other day," she said, lifting the sacks of groceries into the Circle C's pickup bed.

Jolie felt a clench in her midsection. *Damn!* She concentrated on loading her own bags into the pickup bed and didn't reply.

"Hey, I'm not criticizing," Suzanne said. "I'm just being nosy. Jake's a great guy."

Jolie turned to her antagonist. "I was, uh, just having a hamburger with him."

"Jolie, I can't remember the last time Jake Strayhorn took anybody in Lockett to have a hamburger. I've thought he needed a steady woman in his life ever since I met him. When I first came back here, I even wished I might be that woman for a while, but I can see that he and I would never hit it off. He's too black-or-white, too right-or-wrong. But you know what? I can see *you* with him."

"Really?" Jolie asked, bewildered. "You see me as being that way?"

"That wasn't a negative comment. You strike me as being a patient person. What I see is you being able to put up with a man as hardheaded and iron-willed as Jake is. That's why he's still single, you know. There aren't many women who could live up to his standards."

"Oh," Jolie replied, unable to keep from smiling. Nothing would make her happier than "putting up" with Jake Strayhorn and "living up" to his standards. "I suppose I sort of am a patient person. I did live in a bad situation for longer than I should have."

Suzanne grinned. "Well, he's a sexy-looking devil and he's tougher than boot leather. Not a guy you'd ever want to cross. I'll tell you this much. If anyone ever asked me to describe a true man of the West, the first person who'd come to my mind is Jake Strayhorn."

"You won't say anything, will you? It probably wouldn't be good for him or me, either, if people were talking about us."

"Honey, you don't have to worry. I won't even say anything to Jude. After all, it's really nobody's business, right?"

"Right," Jolie replied, relieved, but still worried.

Suddenly Suzanne embraced her in a hug. "Go for it, Jolie. Grab him and hang on. I hope you land him."

Jolie blinked back a tear. "Thanks. Thank you for being my friend."

"You, too," Suzanne said, smiling. "We've got to get together sometime for some girl talk." Shrugging, she backed away. "Well, I gotta get back to work."

After Suzanne disappeared back into the grocery store, Jolie stood for a few minutes, taking stock of the conversation that had just occurred. She had never had a "friend" with whom she could "girl-talk," had never felt comfortable inviting women she knew to her home, had never had the time or the freedom to go out with girlfriends.

Then she remembered the time.

She found her keys, opened the pickup's driver's-side door and felt a presence. She jerked around, knowing who was behind her before he said a word.

"Hi, Jolie."

Jolie's heart almost stopped and a wave of nausea slammed into her stomach. "Billy!"

"Thought you got rid of me, didn't you?" he said.

Her mouth had gone dry and her pulse was racing so fast she was light-headed, but she managed to assess his appearance. He was filthy. And he was high. That much she could tell from his eyes. "What—what are you doing here?"

"Now, what would I be doing here?" he asked, sneering. "I wouldn't be trying to find my bitch of a wife who ran off with the goddamn car, now, would I?"

She scanned the street for his pickup, but didn't spot it. "How did you get here?"

"Hell, Jolie. A big-ass bird brought me here. Picked me up and dropped me right behind you."

"I want you to leave us alone, Billy," she said weakly. "I'm through with you."

"You're as full of shit as a Christmas turkey if you think you're through with *me*, baby. Now gimme those goddamn keys. I'm driving."

"No!" She slammed the door. Her shaking hands fumbled with the key fob for the lock button.

He seized her upper arm in a painful clench and wrenched the keys from her hand. "You dumb bitch." He dragged her around to the passenger side, ignoring that she stumbled on the curb, lost her shoe and skinned the top of her foot. "Get your ass in," he said.

For the first time she thanked God for the tall step into the pickup. Attempting to step up enabled her to jerk free from his grip. "No! Get away from me!"

She tried to duck around him. He grabbed her arm again, slamming her against the side of the pickup and knocking her breathless. She fell to her knees on the sidewalk. As she struggled to get to her feet again, he grabbed her arm again and jerked her up, bringing her up against him and shoving his face close to hers. "You're going back home," he said through clenched teeth, his breath foul and repulsive. "You and that useless kid both. And if you don't cut out the bull-shit and get your ass in that truck, I'll make goddamn sure she never sees you again."

"What do you mean?" she said breathlessly. "Where is Danni?"

"Wouldn't you like to know? Get in the goddamn truck!"

His words struck terror within Jolie, but before she could say more, Suzanne and Joyce, another grocery store employee, charged out of the store's front door carrying plastic grocery bags. With a two-handed grip, Suzanne whacked Billy in the middle of the back with the sack of something heavy.

Billy's back arched. He yelled in agony and turned on Suzanne, who was now defenseless. Her sack had broken and cans of food had scattered over the sidewalk.

Before Billy could reach Suzanne, Joyce swung her sack of something heavy and walloped him in the side. He howled and bent double.

Having no weapon, Jolie jumped astraddle his back and pummeled his head over and over with her fists.

Wildly flailing at the three of them, slugging with his fists and pulling handfuls of hair, Billy buckled to the ground.

Just then, they heard the blast of a siren and the squeal of tires. All at once, Jake waded into the fray, pulling each of them back and pushing them aside at the same time he latched on to Billy's clothing.

Billy staggered to his feet, his rage palpable. With a roar, he slammed his shoulder into Jake's midsection. In a matter of seconds, Jake had twisted his arm behind him, disabled him and had him in handcuffs. He marched him toward the backseat of his Willard County Sheriff SUV.

Jolie darted across the street behind Jake, still wearing only one shoe. A sob burst from her throat. "Jake, he's got Danni somewhere! He said he's got Danni."

Jake's jaw turned to stone; his eyes grew hot and fierce. He jerked the SUV's back door open, but before he could say a word, Billy looked back at him wide-eyed with terror. "No, no. I'm lying, I'm lying. I don't even know where the kid is."

"Where's she supposed to be?" Jake asked Jolie.

"At the ranch. I left her with Irene and Reuben."

Jake yanked his cell phone off his belt. "What's the number out there?"

Jolie said the number, her voice shaking. Jake keyed it in and handed the cell phone to Jolie. With shaking hands, she pressed the phone to her ear waiting for an answer. When Lola came on the line, Jolie schooled herself to sound casual. "Lola, is Danni in the kitchen?"

"I go see."

Soon Danni came on the phone.

Jolie cleared her throat and tried to force her voice not to wobble. "Just calling to let you know I'm running a little late."

"Okay," Danni replied. "I'm helping Irene. Will you bring me some candy?"

"I'll surprise you," Jolie said, fighting back tears of relief.

"You okay?" Jake asked when Jolie disconnected. She handed his phone back to him. Still feeling blood rushing through her veins, she nodded. "I feel so much better."

Across the street, Suzanne and Joyce huddled together jabbering and inspecting each other for injuries. Jolie walked back to where they stood with Jake behind her. Suzanne's ponytail had collapsed and hung to one side. Joyce, who wore barrettes in her hair, had lost her barrettes and a mouse was beginning to rise on one cheek. Apparently she had sustained a blow to the face. Jolie's knees burned like fire from where they had been scraped when she hit the sidewalk.

"You girls okay?" Jake asked. "How bad are you hurt?"

"We think we're okay," Suzanne said.

"Bastard!" Joyce said, scowling and wiping her face against her shirtsleeve.

"Asshole!" Suzanne said, breathing hard, her fists jammed against her hips.

Jake began picking up the cans of food from the sidewalk and looking at the labels. "Corn?" he asked.

"Six cans of corn in a sack makes a damn good weapon," Suzanne said smugly.

Jake chuckled and thumbed his hat back.

"Or green beans or pork and beans," Suzanne added.

"I don't doubt you," Jake said, still smiling.

Jolie turned to Joyce. "What was in that sack you hit him with?"

"A frozen chicken," Joyce answered, wiping her forehead with her palm.

"Frozen chicken?" Jake said.

"A three-pound roaster," Joyce said.

Everyone broke into laughter.

Jake looked each of them up and down. "You're sure you're not hurt? You don't need a doctor?"

All three women shook their heads.

Jake hauled his prisoner to jail. With Chuck and Amanda both out of town, he had to process Billy Jensen himself. He was unable to drop everything and take Jolie home, but being the trouper she was, she had assured him she could make it alone.

When Jake asked Jensen why he was in town and not on the job with AmDril Drilling, he learned Jensen had been fired and driven back to his truck after the foreman realized he was stoned. The last thing any drilling crew needed was a stoned roustabout. He also learned that Jensen didn't know where Jolie lived, but had just happened to see her walk out of the grocery store. As jaded as Jake had become, irony still had the power to amaze him.

Billy confessed to vandalizing the drilling company's trucks as well as to robbing the grocery store. Even if he got off for some reason for those crimes, the ones in Dallas County still awaited him.

Now that the Billy Jensen matter was settled, Jake felt free to pursue what he wanted, which was a relationship with Jolie. To make up for being unable to take her home after such a traumatic experience with Jensen, Jake called a florist in Abilene and ordered a dozen roses to be delivered to her at the Circle C Ranch.

His relationship with Jolie grew. It turned him into a kinder, gentler man. She was so giving, so open and honest, he couldn't bring himself to do something that would hurt her in even the tiniest way. At the same time, while she wasn't highly educated, she had so much common sense, he couldn't keep from admiring her ability to cut to the heart of any matter and express it in a way everybody around her understood.

On Memorial Day weekend, the Circle C held a picnic every year in the tiny park downtown, honoring Ben Strayhorn and other Willard County war dead of all ages. Locals played music, Buster Wardlow barbecued a steer and a pig, furnished by the Circle C. Everybody in the county would be present, including Jolie.

Jake was happy that he and Jolie were no longer a secret and no longer had to sneak around. They spent every moment she had free together. Chuck and Amanda both went out of their way to make sure the sheriff's office was covered when Jolie had time off so Jake and she could spend time together.

A week later, Jake was finishing up the paperwork related to a fender bender in front of the courthouse when he heard a voice he didn't quite recognize but instinctively knew he should. He dropped his glasses on his desktop and got to his feet, but before he could round the end of the desk, J. D. Strayhorn walked into his office.

Emergency! was Jake's first thought, and he felt an adrenaline spike.

His uncle stood there, his arms hanging loose at his sides as if he didn't quite know what to do with his hands. Finally, he placed them on his hips. "Jake," he said.

"What's up?" Jake asked, looking eye to eye with J.D. He hadn't seen the man except from a distance since boyhood, had never considered that he and J.D. were about the same height. He knew J.D. wore glasses, though he hadn't when Jake was fourteen.

J.D. calmly walked over and took a seat in front of Jake's desk, as if he had been invited to sit and as if he dropped in for regular visits. His attitude annoyed Jake at first, but he quelled it, accepting that J.D. was a man accustomed to power, a quality that had adapted him to sitting anywhere he wanted to without an invitation.

Though Jake now knew no emergency existed, his stomach still felt as if it had a butterfly in it. He returned to his own desk chair and sat down across from J.D. Behind the lenses of J.D.'s glasses were penetrating brown eyes that looked like Jude's.

"Are you planning on stealing our cook?" J.D. asked.

He was, of course, speaking of Jolie. She and Jake were spending most of her free time together and without a doubt the whole county was discussing their relationship. But Jake didn't believe for a minute Jolie was why J.D. had come to his office. "Not until you can find another. Jolie wouldn't leave you in a lurch like that."

"I appreciate that." He lifted off his hat. "Jude's still look-

ing for someone to replace her. Finding the right person isn't
that easy. We were lucky with Jolie."

"I agree. It'll be hard to replace her."

A few beats of silence passed. J.D. rubbed his jaw with
his palm. His discomfort was as glaring as neon. "I heard
you bought the old Petry place," he said finally.

Jake nodded.

"You and Jolie planning on setting up housekeeping out
there?"

"We haven't made plans like that."

"I thought I heard you're running for sheriff again."

"I am. One more term. Then I want to do something else."

"You're thinking of raising some cattle? Or horses? I
could—"

"Not my thing," Jake said, not letting him finish his offer.

This time, it was J.D. who nodded. "My daughter's been
talking to me." He leaned forward and braced his elbows
on his thighs, his hat dangling from his fingertips between
his knees. "She wants to have a wedding reception for her
friend out at the ranch. She thinks you and I are an obstacle
to that."

At last. J.D. was getting to the real reason he had come
here. Jake suppressed a groan. "I don't know why. I've told
Pat Garner he doesn't need me at a reception. For that matter, I've told him to feel free to ask somebody else to be his
best man. To tell the truth, I'm not quite sure why wedding
ceremonies and rituals are such a big deal."

J.D. chuckled. "We can agree on that, but the women
think it's important. Aren't you planning one of your own?"

"As I said, Jolie and I haven't made a plan."

J.D.'s gaze came at Jake with intensity. "The wedding
reception isn't the issue, Jake," he said softly.

"Then what is?"

"Family. That's the issue."

Shit, Jake thought. "J.D., let's—"

"I want you to know something." J.D. looked down, his
chin close to his chest. Now he was fooling with his hat brim.

"A few weeks ago, I visited your father's grave. It was the first time I've done that since he left us. As I stood there reading his stone, I thought of him as he was the last time I saw him. I thought of your mother. And the next person I thought of, Jake, was you."

At this late date, Jake didn't want to get into a discussion of "family" and all that it entailed, especially with a relative he scarcely knew.

Or did he?

He wasn't big on psychobabble. He believed he knew himself well, liked the man he saw in the mirror every morning. In spite of that, more than once he had wondered if reuniting with his blood kin was the real, if subconscious, reason he had returned to Willard County. "If you've been to his grave, J.D., you've done more than I have."

"A man's brother is his brother, Jake," his uncle said, his tone still subdued. "That's an unalterable fact no matter what went on in the past." J.D. paused and looked up pointedly. "And a man's father is his father."

Jake the Cynic didn't buy it. He had arrested men who had murdered their wives and children. "Fatherhood is more than a biological fact. I've run into lots of fathers who weren't worth the bullet it'd take to kill 'em," Jake replied.

J.D.'s head bobbed in a nod.

"My mother's buried in Dallas," Jake said.

"Until Dad died, I didn't know," J.D. replied, now looking at something behind Jake's shoulder. "I found that information in his records."

"I guess I oughtta say thanks to your grandmother for sending Mom money. Things were hard for Mom. The money made her life easier."

"Penny Ann cared about all the family. I'm sorry to say I didn't have her strength or compassion. I was too . . ." He heaved a great breath. "She's your grandmother, too, you know. Your great-grandmother, that is."

"I barely remember her."

J.D. looked up. "How about it, Jake? I'm extending a

personal invitation—no, it's more than an invitation. It's a plea for you to come to the ranch. You can use Suzanne's wedding reception as an excuse. . . . Or you don't have to wait for that. Come for supper some evening. I know you're still friends with Brady. And you know how Jude feels about you. The fact is, I'm going to have her on my back until you show up."

In his wildest imagination, Jake couldn't see himself driving between those limestone stanchions at the gate on the highway, or through that wrought-iron gate that was closer to the house. He couldn't imagine walking up to the front door of the Circle C ranch house. He shook his head. "I don't know, J.D.—"

"Just think about it. Promise me you'll think about it."

Knowing he would be a first-class asshole if he said no, Jake blew out a breath. "I'll try."

"Good," J.D. said, rising from his chair and smiling. "That's a first step. All we can expect."

The following morning before Jake had finished his first cup of coffee, Jude marched into his office and seated herself in front of his desk. "Daddy told me he came to see you yesterday."

"Good morning," Jake said. "Want some coffee?"

"Pregnant women shouldn't drink coffee and I know you don't have any apple juice. Daddy said you didn't accept his personal invitation."

Jake knew Jude's reputation for speaking her mind. He didn't reply, believing the best thing was to just let her vent.

"Do you know how hard that was for him?" she said. "What a big step it was for him to take?"

"Life's hard for everybody."

"But it doesn't need to be. None of us have ever knowingly harmed you, Jake, including Daddy."

"I know that."

"Then what's your problem? I've been wondering ever since you came back here."

Jake sat back in his chair. "Jude, I've got a lot to do today. I don't have time—"

She waggled a finger at him. "No, no. Don't you dare tell me you don't have time for this. I've wanted to get this off my chest for years. The whole family suffered a tragedy not of their making, Jake. The two responsible people have been gone since I was seven years old. It's time to put all of it in the grave with them. You're my cousin. You're my husband's friend. I want you to be a part of my child's life. I don't want to have to try to explain to her someday why we have this mysterious relative who doesn't associate with us."

Jake looked away, embarrassed, and feeling more than a little guilty. "Jude—"

"This is crazy," she said. "You're letting your stubborn pride rule your life and interfere with having a relationship with all of us."

"My stubborn pride is part of who I am, Jude. And that's that."

"Has it ever occurred to you that we might care about you?"

In fact, that hadn't occurred to him. Jake stared at her.

"Okay. Then tell me this. How long are you going to continue meeting Jolie away from where she lives as if you're involved in some kind of clandestine affair?"

Taken aback by her aggressiveness on something that was none of her business, Jake was speechless.

Jude got to her feet. "You are the most stubborn man I've ever met."

Jake stood, too. "Jude, let's just—"

"I'm here to plead with you to agree to come to a reception for Suzanne and Pat at the Circle C. With the wedding only three weeks away, it's almost too late to plan it."

Jake shook his head as ghosts from the past swirled around him. "I don't know, Jude. I just don't know."

His cousin made a growling sound and started for the door. "Men," she said. "I don't understand any of them."

As soon as she left, Jake picked his cell phone off his belt and keyed in Jolie's number. She answered right away. "Whatcha doing, sugar?"

"Just getting ready to put dinner on the table," she answered. He loved the sound of her voice, loved the happiness he heard every time they talked.

"I just got a major ass-chewing from Jude."

"About what?" Jake heard concern in her voice, as if she might be ready to defend him at all costs. She reminded him of a mother lion.

"About Pat and Suzanne's wedding reception. Jolie, do you want me to agree to come to it out at that ranch?"

"I think it would be nice. Oh, Jake, everyone wants you here so bad. It's all they talk about. Are you thinking about changing your mind?"

"I don't know. Maybe."

"There isn't much time left. It's only a few weeks away."

"I'm thinking about it."

Jake disconnected. Jolie was right. There wasn't much time left for a lot of things. He buzzed Amanda and asked her to get Pat Garner's phone number for him.

June turned out to be the most glorious month of Jolie's life. Jake had agreed to come to the reception and Jude buzzed around the house getting things ready. She seemed to be on the phone constantly. Jolie and Irene helped her as much as they could. At the same time, she played hostess to a huge wedding shower for Suzanne at the school's community room, for which Jolie baked dozens of cookies.

Danni was out of school, Brady's son, Andy, came for the summer. He and Danni became friends immediately.

Branding began. Mr. Strayhorn announced that they would brand approximately 3,486 calves, a number that made Jolie's jaw drop. For most of the month the house was empty of men. Mr. Strayhorn, Brady and his son were gone every day before daylight until after branding ended. Jolie and Danni accompanied Buster on the chuck wagon during branding now and then, but not every day. With so much activity surrounding Suzanne's wedding, Jude needed Jolie's help.

Off and on, Brady worked with Danni and Andy on horse care and horseback riding lessons.

Jolie couldn't imagine how life could get any better. Seeing Jake every Monday had become routine. The Monday before Suzanne's wedding, Jolie arrived at his apartment before lunch. He met her at the front door. He seemed uptight and nervous and instantly she began to worry.

"Come and sit here on the sofa." He urged her toward it. "I want to talk to you about something."

Oh, no. Something's happened. She almost broke into tears at the thought something bad was going to intrude on her happiness. Her eyes grew large and worried. "Okay." She sank to the edge of the sofa seat.

"Nothing's wrong," he said as if he read her thoughts. He dug into his jeans pocket and pulled out a tiny ring box. A flutter began inside her stomach. He sat down beside her and opened the box, revealing a ring with a beautiful diamond the size of a pencil eraser. Her breath caught and she couldn't speak.

"If you'll accept it, Jolie, this is for you." He picked up her left hand and slid it on her ring finger.

She stared down at the ring. Her heart was pounding so hard she thought she might faint. "Oh, my gosh," she whispered.

"Does it fit? Is it too big?"

She slid the ring back and forth on her finger, then broke into tears. "Oh, Jake." She threw her arms around him and hugged him fiercely.

He hugged her back. "Don't cry, sweetheart. I want you to be happy."

"I am happy," she said, sniffling. "Happier than I've ever been in my whole life."

They parted and she stared down at the ring again, moved

it back and forth on her finger again. "Does it fit?" he asked her again. "If it doesn't, we can get it sized."

"I think so," she answered in a tiny voice, then looked up at him with teary eyes. "Is it real?"

"Real? What do you mean? You're asking me if it's a real diamond?"

She nodded.

Jake chuckled. "God, I hope so. They told me it was."

"Oh, my gosh," she said again. "I've never had a ring. But I don't need a fancy ring, Jake."

"It isn't fancy. It's plain, but it's real pretty." He tilted her hand toward the sunlight. Tiny shards of blue and yellow light glinted off the stone. "See how pretty it is?"

"It's big, isn't it?"

"Kind of, I guess. But it's not *too* big." He took both her hands in his. "Jolie, this is just the beginning. I've got a plan for you and me and Danni."

She gazed at him expectantly. She didn't care what he planned as long as included her, Danni and him together as a unit.

"I want us to get married," he said. "I'm gonna run for sheriff again, but I'm gonna quit after the next term. While I'm keeping order in Willard County, I want us to fix up that house I bought. I want it to be our place to come home to."

"Are we going somewhere?"

"I'm gonna buy an RV. In the summer when Danni's not in school, I figure we can cover the country. Go see everything. It'll be a good education for Danni. And we'll have fun. Then after we finish doing that, I figure we could get a summer place in Colorado. Of course we'll always come back to Lockett so Danni can go to school here."

"Oh, my gosh. I've never been out of Texas." She went into his arms again. "Oh, Jake, I can't believe this. I never expected—"

"I never expected, either, Jolie. But here we are. So are you saying yes?"

"Yes," she said, laughing and crying at the same time. "I love you."

"I love you, too, Jolie. You're more than I ever expected to find."

They kissed a long time, leaning back against the sofa back. When they parted, they looked into each other's eyes. "You are, too, Jake. Until I met you, I didn't know someone like you could ever want me."

Epilogue

Suzanne and Pat were married on the afternoon of July 10, in the First Methodist Church as planned. Jolie watched, sitting beside Danni and Andy and Brady Fallon.

The church was packed. Sunlight streamed through the stained glass window behind the pulpit and cast an aura around Suzanne and Pat as they said their vows.

Suzanne looked beautiful with her long blond hair secured in a bun at her nape and her retro rodeo hat, a swath of turquoise blue chiffon tied around the band and trailing down her back. Pat, too, looked handsome in a Texas tux, Jolie thought, but he didn't compare to Jake Strayhorn.

She thought Jake was beautiful, also dressed in a Texas tux and standing beside Pat. She glanced down at the diamond ring on her left hand and thought of the day when she would marry Jake, though they hadn't yet determined a date. The Strayhorns hadn't yet found a new cook.

Billy was still in jail in Abilene, slated to be moved to Dallas, and Jolie had visited him. She was a mother figure to him and she knew that. She didn't mind. Billy had never had anyone to care about him in all of his life. He might be lost and misguided, but he wasn't worthless. No human being was worthless and he was, after all, the father of her daughter. When he wasn't on drugs, his propensity for crime diminished.

"Propensity" was a new word she had learned.

Jake came to her as soon as the ceremony ended to escort her to the reception at the Circle C Ranch. She could tell he was nervous. He fidgeted for the whole twenty-eight-mile drive from town to the ranch and kept tugging at his collar. Except for the day he proposed, she had never seen him nervous.

When he walked into the ranch house, Jude broke into tears and came and hugged him. Brady shook his hand and gave him one of those guy hugs. Even J.D. had to pull his handkerchief from his back pocket and dab his eyes. Jolie almost cried herself, blown away by the fact that all of these years these people had lived within driving distance of each other, but never associated with each other.

Jolie felt as if she were a part of something important. She felt so much happiness she thought her heart might burst. Three months ago, when she began the chaotic journey to change her life, she hadn't dreamed she would find so much of everything. She was a real-life Cinderella and she would soon marry a prince.

In case you missed it, read on for a peek
at Jude and Brady's story

Lone Star Woman

Available now from Signet Eclipse

The West Texas sun had peaked in a bright sky, and Judith Ann Strayhorn had already wasted more than half the day. Behind the wheel of her Dodge pickup truck, she raced along the highway on her way from Lockett to Abilene, a hundred miles away. Her mind was on Harley Beall, the state cop who had stopped her earlier for speeding. He hadn't been sympathetic when she told him she was on a mission. He had looked at her with cold eyes, his mouth set in a grim line. He must have been having a bad day because this time, he hadn't given her the usual warning. *This* time, he had given her a ticket. *Damn.* Now Daddy would try to badger her into going to driving school.

Since the first time she had been allowed to drive the twenty-eight miles from the Circle C ranch to the town of Lockett all alone, Jude had found adhering to the speed limit a burden. Today, after getting the ticket, she forced herself to drive slower while she considered whether to go to court and plead not guilty to driving eighty in a sixty. The judge would probably be accommodating, given that her grandfather and father allowed him hunting privileges on the family's rangeland. But in the county where Strayhorn wealth and influence overshadowed everything, Jude was cautious about throwing her family's weight around. She would never deliberately put Grandpa or Daddy in an awkward position.

Still debating the pros and cons of taking the matter to

court, she drew near the old 6-0 ranch, the thing that had her rushing toward Abilene. The ranch's cattle-guard entrance lay just ahead on the right, and at the end of the driveway, she saw a tan pickup truck. What was *that* about?

She lifted her foot from the accelerator, slowed and pulled partially off the highway onto the shoulder for a closer look. Not recognizing the tan pickup, she eased al the way off the pavement and stopped. She shoved the gearshift into park and sat a few seconds, studying the trespassing rig and pondering the best way to find out who owned it.

Her attention veered from the pickup to the old two-story house. Of Victorian style, rising from the middle of a sun-drenched Texas panhandle pasture, it couldn't have looked more out of place. It sat at the end of a quarter mile of caliche driveway, its fancy carved wood trim and much of its clapboard siding bare of paint and weathered to gray. The slatted shutters that had once framed two of the front windows in white had been missing for a while now.

Her eyes traveled to a two-story barn standing five hundred feet behind the house, canting to the east in sad shabbiness. In a coil the size of a car, rusted barbed wire leaned against the barn's east wall. Other outbuildings of both metal and wood in various stages of dilapidation baked in the brittle early-afternoon sun.

As far as Jude was concerned, the buildings were an inconsequential part of Marjorie Wallace's estate. The valuable part was the fifteen sections of land the buildings sat on— 9,600 acres of prime, rolling bluestem grassland that had been ungrazed for months. Enough land to run at least two hundred head of cows and calves. The very thought was enough to make her heart sing.

Jude wanted to own that 6-0 rangeland more than she had ever wanted to own anything. And she had the wherewithal to buy it. She hadn't yet made an offer, but without her father and grandfather knowing it, she had already started the wheels rolling to take the money from her trust fund. She had an appointment this afternoon to meet with the banker in Abilene to discuss it further and sign documents. No doubt when Daddy and Grandpa learned what she was up to, another family explosion would occur.

She could hear Daddy now: *Jude, why don't you spend your energy on finding a husband?*

And Grandpa: *Why, Judith Ann, that trust fund is for your future and the future of the children you should be concentrating on having.*

And the discussion wouldn't end there. Hadn't they already tried to marry her off twice?

But at the moment, she couldn't think about a hypothetical. The unfamiliar pickup had her curiosity jumping up and down. She shifted out of park, made a right turn and jostled and bumped up the neglected driveway until she came to a stop behind the newer-model Chevy Silverado. Its bed was filled with household furnishings: a mattress set, a cabinet-like thing that looked to be a dresser, some chairs and a table. Having been here several times, she knew the house and all the outbuildings had hasps and padlocks on the doors. Had the Silverado's owner broken in and taken that furniture from inside the house?

From where she sat, she couldn't see whether the lock on the front door had been removed. A sudden jolt of anxiety hit her stomach. She thought of her cell phone and her cousin Jake Strayhorn, who was the Willard County sheriff. She thought of her pistol, which she knew how to use and had a permit to carry. It was locked in Daddy's gun cabinet at home. *Damn.*

She pulled closer to the Silverado's back bumper and angled across the driveway's two tracks. The pickup could get out, but only with some skillful maneuvering. Without killing her engine, she continued to study the unfamiliar vehicle. It was clean and neatly kept. No dents, good tires. Not a rig she would associate with a burglar. The license plate holder said, COWTOWN CHEVROLET. The only city in Texas known as "Cowtown" was Fort Worth. Jude's ever-present curiosity began to outweigh her anxiety.

Jake would be able to find the pickup owner's name easily enough. His office could log in to computer networks that knew everything about everyone. She pulled a small spiral notebook from behind the sun visor and jotted down the plate number. As she returned the notebook to its place, she glanced around but saw no one. She switched off the motor and slid out, her boot heels cushioned by clumps of assorted weeds that had overtaken the driveway.

Silence engulfed her, so loud it roared in her ears. Rays of brilliant June sun pressed down hotly on her shoulders, and the vast blue sky made her feel small—a noteworthy accomplishment on the sky's part, since very little made her, the only daughter of the powerful J. D. Strayhorn, feel small.

A breeze gusted past and swirled her long hair around her face, pressing fine strands to her lips. She combed it back with her fingers, gathering it at her nape while she walked toward the house, still looking for the Silverado's owner.

Then she saw a man—a big man she didn't recognize. He came around the corner of the house. She could tell he had seen her. He paused for a second, then came directly toward her, long legs eating up the space between them. A squiggle of anxiety zoomed through her stomach again. He was at least as tall as Daddy, who was over six feet. He was wide shouldered but lean. He was clean and wearing a bright blue torso-hugging T-shirt that showed off muscles in his arms and shoulders. The shirt was neatly tucked in to starched and creased Wranglers. He had on cowboy boots, not worn-out, but well used. He looked like a cowboy, all right, but not a cowhand. Having spent her entire life around both, she knew the difference. Now she was sure he was no burglar.

But what was he? A shot of panic surged for a reason other than concern for her personal safety. Good Lord, could he be a buyer for this place? She summoned the boldness for which she was notorious. "Hey," she called to him.

His step didn't falter as he continued walking toward her. "Something I can do for you?" His voice was deep, but soft.

As he neared, she strained to see his eyes, but they were hidden in the shadow of a purple ball cap. It had the TCU logo, embroidered rather than stamped, so it was one of the better-quality caps. *TCU. Humph.* She no longer held so much as a shred of fear. TCU, Texas Christian University, was a sissy school in Fort Worth. Like her father, Jude Strayhorn was a proud graduate of the only college in Texas—or the whole United States, really—that mattered: Texas A&M. "This is private property," she said.

"I know," he replied almost absently, as he continued to look around.

"Then what are you doing here?" She had to raise her chin to look him in the eye. And those eyes, sitting above wide cheekbones and a lean jaw, were as blue as the Texas sky. He didn't answer her question, but she felt the intensity of his head-to-toe assessment, as if he were seeing through her clothes, all the way to her skin. She had been observed by men before, was used to not reacting. What she wasn't used to was the electricity in the air between them and the strange flutter agitating inside her midsection. She stood there sweating in the heat, waiting for him to explain himself.

His gaze moved to her pickup, parked across the driveway, blatantly displaying her intent. He looked back at her, his jaw and body taut. "What are *you* doing here?" His tone would have frozen water on a July day.

"I'm a neighbor from up the road."

"That doesn't tell me why you parked crossways and blocked my exit. Who the hell do you think you are?"

She flinched at his sharp tone, but didn't back down. "I stopped by, being neighborly. But I'll damn sure get out of your way. If you don't feel like telling *me* who you are, I guess you can tell the sheriff." She turned and willed herself to saunter toward her pickup as if she hadn't a concern in the world, but her heartbeat drummed in her ears. "He's my cousin," she added over her shoulder.

"Hold on," he called. She stopped, turned back and faced him.

He came to where she stood, the corners of his mouth tipping into a hint of a smile that fell somewhere between friendly and smirky. Whatever its meaning, it sent another odd reaction through her stomach. He stuck out his right hand. "Brady Fallon."

He said the name as if it should mean something to her, but she couldn't place it. She had a feeling she had seen him before, but she couldn't think where. Still, she gave him her hand. His big, rough hand engulfed hers in a strong, palm-touching grip. Startled by another odd little disturbance darting through her, she pulled her hand away and stuffed it into the back pocket of her jeans. "So, uh, I don't think I've seen you around here."

"Haven't been around here . . . lately."

Lately? Who *was* he? Was he kin to someone local? She thought she knew every living being in Willard County, all 1,653 of them.

She had to know what he was up to. Striving for nonchalance, she said, "The, um, owner of this place passed away recently. Are you looking to buy it?"

A faraway look came into his eyes and he glanced back over his shoulder toward the outbuildings. She wished she could read minds. His attention returned to her, his eyes intent on her face. "Nope," he said.

"You're leasing?" The question was no sooner out of her mouth than she thought she knew the answer. "No, you're a bird hunter." By the hundreds, game-bird hunters ventured from the Fort Worth/Dallas metroplex to shoot the abundant quail and dove on the West Texas high plains. Fewer came to Willard County than to the surrounding counties because Strayhorn Corp owned more than half of the rangeland and Daddy and Grandpa gave only a chosen few permission to hunt. Years back they had been more generous in allowing hunting, but after too many unfortunate incidents with livestock and fences, they substantially cut back hunting by outsiders.

The stranger chuckled, a deep, friendly sound. He flashed a boyish grin loaded with charm. "I never met a bird that deserved killing."

She couldn't keep from staring at his wide mouth and his even white teeth. "Actually, me neither. Personally, I don't like the taste of game birds. These dudes who come out here and use hunting as an excuse to get drunk and show off the shotgun they got for Christmas, it's a wonder they all don't shoot each other."

He shifted to a cock-kneed stance and propped his hands on his hips. "You didn't say your name."

"Jude Strayhorn. I live on the place that butts up to this one."

His chin lifted and his brow arched. "Ahh." His annoyance seemed to dissipate, as if he knew who she was.

But then, who in West Texas didn't know or hadn't heard—good or bad—of the Strayhorns? "So, what are you doing here?"

Those laser blue eyes fixed another steady look on her. Though the temperature had to be above ninety, she thought of icicles. Okay, so he didn't want to discuss it. Maybe she was being nosy. And maybe a little pushy.

A long pause. "This place belonged to my aunt Margie and uncle Harry." He looked down and appeared to study his boots. "Now I guess it belongs to me."

Jude barely halted a catch in her breath and willed her eyes not to bug. *Nooooo,* she wanted to scream, but she said, "What do you mean?"

He lifted his cap and reset it, revealing golden brown hair, bleached by the sun and darkened by sweat. "They never had any kids to leave it to. They sort of favored *me.*"

How could she not have heard about this? Jude wondered. She hadn't known Marjorie Wallace personally, but everyone in Willard County knew that a few weeks before her death, she had suddenly sold her cattle herd and taken up residence in the town of Lockett's only nursing home.

Only then did she reveal she had terminal cancer. Jude had assumed the 6-0 would be put on the market when its owner passed away.

Jude rarely found herself at a loss for words, but this unexpected news left her scrambling for what to say next. She gave the deceased woman's nephew a nervous titter. "Want to sell it?"

"I don't think so. I'm making this my home."

Now her heartbeat became a bass drum in her ears. She glanced at the furniture in the Silverado's bed, then the house, then him. "Margie Wallace didn't have any money to leave anybody, unless she kept some buried in the backyard. You rich?"

Frowning, he tucked back his chin. "That's no business of yours."

"Mister, I'm just saying, it's going to take a bunch of money to make this place even a little bit livable. I'd be surprised if the water well's even any good." She lifted her shoulders in a shrug and opened her palms in a show of feigned indifference. "But, hey. Like you say, it's none of my business."

She turned and started to her pickup again, drawing measured breaths to calm herself. She needed this land, had been planning to buy it for weeks. Owning her own place would give her a chance to try her ideas in cattle breeding without Daddy and Grandpa criticizing her every move and bellyaching about why she didn't just get married. And now the best chance she had run across lately to prove the points she constantly argued with her father had been snatched from her by some damn . . . *heir.*

The only thing that kept her from breaking down and bawling was that Jude Strayhorn didn't cry.